To *Seduce* an *Earl*

To *Seduce* *Earl*
an

LORI BRIGHTON

Montlake
Romance

Text copyright © 2011 Lori Brighton
Printed in the United States of America.

Published by Montlake Romance
P.O. Box 400818
Las Vegas, NV 89140

ISBN-13: 9781612187112
ISBN-10: 1612187110

For Sean. I never would have become an author without your support.

Chapter 1

He always received the virgins.

Really, it wasn't fair.

Alex sighed in disgust and sank into the wing back chair, the antique legs protesting with a creak. The decorative baroque style was more for show and offered only the façade of comfort. Much like his life.

Just once he'd like a woman who knew what she wanted, what she was capable of; a woman who would take charge and please *him*. But it wasn't about him. It never had been. It never would be.

His necktie felt suddenly too tight, the room too warm. With experienced fingers, he tugged the snowy white material loose. At Lady Lavender's Estate of Seduction, evening wear was a requirement.

Resisting the urge to fidget with his clothing, he tapped his fingers against the curved walnut arm of the chair, impatient to leave, impatient to begin the evening and get the entire ordeal over with. But like a lad at supper, he couldn't leave until *she* excused him.

"Bloody hell."

Ophelia glanced up sharply from behind her desk.

Shite, had he said that aloud?

Her amethyst eyes flashed eerily under the glow of the gas chandeliers she'd recently had installed throughout the first floor of the estate. When most of England was straining its eyes under candle and lamplight, Lady Lavender read in ease. "Watch your language."

It wasn't an elegant woman's desk made of delicate scrolls that she resided behind. It was a man's desk; massive, domineering. It was the only thing about her that wasn't feminine. She was proving a point with that desk. Although her business revolved around the pleasuring of women, it was still a business and she treated her business as a man would. No feelings. No attachments. No excuses.

Taking a page from her book, Alex refused to apologize for his use of profanity, but he did manage that charming smirk that had made him famous with his clients. Inside he seethed. He was bloody sick of apologizing.

His stubbornness gained him nothing but contempt. Her icy gaze continued to drill into him. She didn't back down. She wouldn't. Ophelia, or Lady Lavender as the world knew her, held the impression of a lady, but underneath she was as heartless as any male brothel owner. Twelve years ago her cold gaze would have had him shifting with unease. Hell, even four years ago. Now, he barely cared.

Ending their silent war, she sighed and stood. "Why must you be so difficult lately?"

He didn't bother to answer. What he had to say would merely get him into trouble…again. She strolled toward him. Those rounded hips swathed in the finest of imported silks, although

it was early spring and most women still wore wool. Her lavender gown, narrow at the waist, flared into a bell of frills and ribbons that ended at satin slippers. Completely inappropriate for the
chill English weather. Completely inappropriate for a woman who
must be at the very least forty, yet looked more of twenty.

Even in the privacy of her office she wore the highest of fashion, in imitation of Queen Victoria, she said. And Ophelia was a
queen, if only queen of her own sinful domain.

Even now, twelve years after the day she'd practically forced
him into prostitution, Ophelia was still beautiful. Not a speck of
gray in that white-blonde hair. Not a wrinkle around those amethyst eyes. Not a hint of time. When others aged, she didn't seem
to. A pact with the devil, Gideon always muttered. Perhaps he was
right.

She idly drew her hand down the blue velvet curtains, glancing casually out the windows. Did she truly see the beauty of the
setting sun, or was she ignorant of something so pure?

"Have I not given you shelter?" she asked, her voice holding
that slight accent he couldn't quite identify. "Have I not fed you?
Clothed you in the finest of suits?"

She glanced pointedly at his silk vest and black trousers with
thin gray stripes. The highest of fashion.

"Have I not kept your secrets, Alex?"

Unwanted memories swept through his mind. Memories he
tried to ignore. Annoyed, he didn't dare show his feelings on his
face. How dare she mention his family yet again. A veiled threat
that never went unnoticed. Damn, but he hated when she had the
audacity. How hard it had been those first years to pretend his
family didn't exist. All for their own good.

His hands tightened around the arms of his chair, fingernails
biting into hard wood. It had taken years for him to forget his
parents, and within an instant, she could bring back the painful
memories. Of course she did it on purpose…a reminder of what
she knew, the control she held over him. A verbal slap.

What was done was done. His parents would have given up their search and toasted Demitri as the new heir. Perhaps he should have tried to escape, in those early days, if he'd had the choice. But he'd been too damn afraid. When one was secluded in the country a good hour from London, with brutes watching your every move, escape had seemed impossible…at least to a boy of thirteen. Although her thinly veiled threats no longer intimidated him, now Alex stayed for an entirely different reason…he had no money and nowhere to go. He was pathetic.

God forbid she realized his true fear.

"Perhaps I no longer care about my secrets," he couldn't help but taunt in a soft voice. The war was over. Society no longer cared if you were from Russia; even he, secluded as he was, knew that must be true.

She paused behind him and casually placed her hands upon his shoulders. But he felt the stiffness in her touch. Anger and annoyance practically vibrated around her. She knew as well as he that she no longer held the power over him she once had. For one brief moment he couldn't help but gloat and savor the thrilling shiver of victory.

"Perhaps," she leaned down, her lips brushing the shell of his ear. Yet her touch offered no comfort, not even the stirrings of lust as it had when he was young. "But what will you do in the outside world, Alex? Return to the bosom of your family?"

Victory vanished. Suppressed ire flooded his neck in an unnatural heat that quickly moved higher to his cheeks. In one sentence she'd hit upon the problem. He had nowhere to go. Worthless. A useless whore.

Ophelia straightened away from him, but the cloying scent of lavender remained as a reminder of her presence. The scent hovered inside the estate and the fields around them. If he never saw a purple bloom, it would be too soon.

"Do you think they'll take you back? There is no place in the outside world for people like us. And think about what would happen if your family uncovered the truth...that you've been prostituting yourself for years." She paused in front of him, her eyes wide with feigned innocence. She rested her hand on her heart as if she cared. As if she had a heart. "Or worse, *society* uncovered the truth. Why, if your family has finally found a place within the *ton*, they'd be shunned within weeks." She shook her head and sighed as she moved toward the fireplace. "They'd certainly be forced back to Russia. And with the war over, the people starving, Russia is no place for loved ones."

His body had gone cold, numb. A threat that went too far, damn her. But he should have known she would use whatever she could to keep her claws deeply embedded in his soul.

"Alex, darling," she said. "You're charming. You know how to put a woman at ease. This new client *needs* you."

He resisted the urge to snort. Give, give, give, that's all he did. But he had a feeling that's how Lady Lavender wanted it. Punishment, but why punish him? What had he done to her? The eternal, unanswerable question that had plagued him for years.

He raked trembling hands through his hair, the wavy curls clinging to his fingers. Perhaps Gideon's paranoia was working its magic, but he didn't trust her any more than he had as a lad at thirteen, when she'd offered him the world and instead had given him hell.

She turned toward him in a swirl of skirts that showed off white petticoats. "Come, give me that charming grin the ladies so love."

Alex dampened down his ire and widened his smile, knowing the dimples flashed. At times he felt trapped in his own skin; a bear with a chain wrapped around his neck, as he'd once seen in the old country. And only she held the key to that lock.

Ophelia seemed to relax and floated toward the marble hearth, her footfalls quieted by the thick Persian carpet. The low fire, casting shadows across the papered walls, crackled and sputtered, hissing at her approach. "Take it easy on her for now. She's as scared as a doe at the end of a pistol. Her driver even insisted she be taken through the kitchens so as not to be seen."

Alex surged to his feet, eager to get away from Ophelia before he did something reckless, like throttle her. "As if anyone would see her. We're in the middle of a damn field, a good hour from London."

"Alex," she warned, throwing him a threatening glare.

He kept his smile in place. He was a machine; one of those factories that chugged away in the city, producing black smoke that hid the reality of dreary old London. Ophelia told him to smile, and he smiled. She said fuck, and he fucked. Why? Because he didn't care.

"Where is she?" he asked.

But she didn't answer immediately. Instead, she tilted her head to the side in a thoughtful manner, her eyes narrowing as if to study him. Alex grew uneasy.

"Your room. No intercourse. She merely wants to learn to kiss, touch."

Wonderful. Just bleedin' wonderful. "I'll see what I can do." But he had to wait for her dismissal and apparently she was in a hesitant mood this eve.

She floated forward, not pausing until she was a breath away. Slowly she tilted her head back and gazed directly into his eyes. For one brief moment she merely stared at him, as if trying to read his thoughts. Alex barely breathed, afraid she would. With their gazes locked, she slid her hand down his silk vest, lower to his waist. With a firm grip she cupped the front of his trousers, taking the bulge of his cock in hand. He didn't even flinch.

"Do not fail, Alex."

Her touch didn't do a damn thing to him. Neither did her threat. "Of course not."

She released her hold and gave him a dismissive wave. She'd moved on already to her next client, her next wad of cash. Alex gave a mocking bow to her back, then turned and made his way into the hall. How he hated her. How he despised everything about her.

Wavers, her guard dog, shifted from his position near her door. Watching them, always watching them through those beady black eyes. The bastard never spoke, but with a face like his, he didn't need to.

"Wavers." Alex brushed his fingers under his chin, a silent command to fuck off.

Ophelia's henchman didn't respond, but then none of them ever did. Her muscled statues had two purposes in life: protect their lady and, when her boys were behaving badly enough, beat them into submission. For that, she paid them handsomely, and like mutts, their loyalty was unwavering.

Feigning nonchalance, Alex started down the hall, whistling a tune under his breath. How impressed he'd been when he'd first arrived; a lad used to living in splendor, he expected nothing less and thought he'd found a second home. The estate was beautiful, having only the best. Marble floors, golden sconces highlighting the ornate scrolls hand painted on the walls. Above, gas chandeliers flickered and sputtered, adding warmth and modernity to the abode.

And there, on the outskirts, were objects meant to entice even the coldest of women. Statues of naked couples frolicking half-hidden around corners. Large tropical plants that added vitality. Warm scents meant to relax. Paintings of virile men hanging on the walls. It was a lush lifestyle meant to seduce and please, if one didn't mind selling one's soul.

Alex's fingers moved to the fine linen of his shirt, buttoning that top button. He smoothed down the silk embroidered vest. Outside appearances must be kept, even if inside he fumed. The cravat that hung loose around his neck was tied as quickly as his trembling fingers would allow. Thrumming through his mind, years of teaching prevailed. *Virgins tended to be skittish if you showed any skin.* Yes, he'd have to tiptoe around this one, as always.

At first, he'd loved holding the upper hand, making innocent women quiver under his touch. Knowing they not only wanted him, but underneath, feared him. A powerful aphrodisiac indeed. Now…hell, now he was damn tired of teaching them how to seduce their future husbands. Tired of their wide-eyed stares. Tired of their innocent blushes. Tired of the game.

"Another virgin?"

Startled from his thoughts, Alex paused, glancing toward the parlor. Gideon leaned against the doorframe, a scotch in hand. He'd changed in the past twelve years. Taller, broader. Those muscles, dark hair, and silver eyes made more than one woman tremble with fear and desire. But no matter how many beatings the man had endured as a youth, his stubbornness remained intact. The evidence was there…in the hardness of his face, the tenseness of his body. The idiot would get himself killed if he didn't at least pretend to play Ophelia's games.

Alex snatched the glass from the man's scarred fingers and drank the amber liquid. The alcohol burned a trail down his throat, making him wince.

"*Why do you have scars on your fingers, Gideon?*" he'd asked him once, when he, James, and Gideon had first arrived.

"*None of your damn business,*" Gideon had replied.

And so had been the start of a tumultuous relationship, an uneasy truce between three lads brought together. There were many things Alex didn't know about Gideon, but there were also things he'd deduced from years of companionship.

Alex had never been one to drink; he liked to have all his wits about him when facing the Angel of Hell, as he'd dubbed Ophelia. Gideon liked to deal with life by being in a habitual state of half drunkenness, although the man held his whiskey so well one could barely tell. James acted as if their lives were an honored position they should be proud of. And Alex, well, he pretended. He was good at pretending. He'd had years of practice with his parents. Pretending to be someone he wasn't, pretending to be happy, charming. And now, pretending he enjoyed pleasing women every day of the week.

"Yes, rotten luck, another virgin, unfortunately."

Gideon merely smiled, a rarity. "At least you won't have to worry about the pox."

"Hmm," Alex replied. *Small condolences.*

"You're too pretty." He said the words with disdain. "It's why she gives you virgins. Scar your face a bit. I'd be happy to hold the knife."

"Amusing." Alex brushed a piece of lint from his vest. "You're welcome to her."

"Oh no, she's all yours." Gideon set the glass on a small side table. His gaze slid down the hall where Wavers still stood silently watching. The atmosphere shifted, becoming thick with tension, and Alex knew what was to come.

"Did you think about it?" Gideon asked.

Alex swallowed hard and lowered his gaze to the hall runner. He felt like a coward; his thoughts jumbled when he knew he should have had a ready answer. Why? Why didn't he immediately agree? Why did his body grow cold and clammy with thoughts of escape?

"Yes, I've thought about it."

"And?"

His heart thumped madly in his chest, unease and desperation battling within. Once he agreed, he was placing his life in the hands of a man he barely trusted. Still, wasn't being dead better than being alive here? "Do you truly believe we'll be able to escape?"

"Yes. She's hoping our lack of fortune and lack of self-respect will bind us to her. And, of course, she's got her men. But her trust is building. Has she not decided to take you to the Rutherford Ball when you've never gone before?"

True. And there would be no better opportunity to escape than at a crowded ballroom.

"*And think about what would happen if they uncovered the truth...that you've been prostituting yourself for years.*"

Ophelia's warning whispered tauntingly through his head. The thought of his mother...his father...knowing that he was nothing more than a whore left him ill. He had no doubt, should he leave her establishment, Ophelia would post about his life in the dailies. But would the *ton* believe her word? "I'll have to think on it."

Gideon's jaw clenched, annoyance hardening his pewter gaze. "And James?" he asked.

Alex floundered for a response. James was tricky; he had always been a bit naïve. Did his loyalty to Lady Lavender supersede his loyalty to them? For some reason the idiot had the insane belief that Ophelia had saved them. "I don't know. He seems to believe he owes her."

Gideon snorted in disbelief. His feelings toward their savior were apparent in every glare he threw her way. Every murmured curse he whispered when she was near.

Two years ago Gideon had started dropping hints about escape. It was only in the last six months that they'd been seriously discussing the idea. Oddly, Alex didn't feel as excited by the prospect as he'd assumed he would. It was true; Ophelia was beginning to trust him. For the past year she'd taken him along when visiting gaming hells. And only recently she'd mentioned that he would attend the Rutherford Ball. Freedom tempted him. Although escaping gaming hells would be difficult with her henchmen nearby, at a ball surely there'd be plenty of opportunity.

He raked his hand through his hair, feeling discontent, unsure when he should have been thrilled. Even if they managed to escape this hell, what sort of life would they lead with pasts like theirs? Ophelia was right; he could never return home. Perhaps he'd known that all along, which was why he'd never tried to contact his family. He was too damn ashamed.

And what would happen when Ophelia told the world of his sinful ways? Dare he tell Gideon of Ophelia's latest threat? No.

Gideon wouldn't care, wouldn't understand why Alex would worry over his family's welfare. But then how could he understand? Gideon had no idea where Alex had come from, whom his family was related to.

Alex sighed. "I'll talk to James, see—"

"Ahem." Wavers cleared his throat, their warning to move on.

They'd talked longer than was deemed appropriate. Gideon narrowed those gray eyes, his bitter hatred palpable. Lady Lavender didn't like them to fraternize. But after being together for twelve bloody years, what did she expect?

"We're friends, we're all going to be great friends."

He could still remember the words she'd spoken those years ago when she'd tempted Alex to work for her. The words had been a lie, like everything else she'd said. Here, one didn't have friends. He barely trusted Gideon.

Still, there was no other alternative. Even though sweat broke out along his forehead, with renewed determination he gave Gideon a nod. "I'm in." And like that he'd jumped into a gray sea of churning waves threatening to take him under.

Gideon grinned.

As far as he knew, Lady Lavender had twenty men in her control. Yet he, James, and Gideon were the only three under constant watch. The only three who, as mere young boys, had been blackmailed. She hadn't started whoring them out right away. No, she'd waited until they were sixteen, tempting them with beautiful women, teasing them with seductive possibilities.

And how eager he'd been to relent. Gads, he could still remember that first time. He'd thought that having sex with women would be an ideal way to spend his evenings, and in return, Lady Lavender would keep the secrets of his family's ancestry buried. He hadn't realized he was selling his soul.

Gideon turned and disappeared into the parlor. Alex tipped an imaginary hat at Wavers and continued up the stairs. Taking in a deep breath, he contemplated the woman who would be waiting.

It didn't do to arrive wilted and uninterested. Yet it had been a long time since a woman had naturally aroused him. A sweet blonde with blue eyes? Dark and exotic?

In the first few years, his cock had flared to life merely at the thought of bedding a woman. Now…hell, now it took concentration to care.

One thing was certain: she'd be a trembling mess. But he'd make her quiver for an entirely different reason. If Alex was good at one thing, it was making the innocent relax. It was his looks, he knew, the dark curls, blue eyes, and dimples. He looked nothing like his domineering Russian father, but more like his English mother. He looked like a fucking angel, or so he'd been told on many occasions.

Yes, the mothers liked his looks and they'd send their innocent daughters to him. He supposed they were being kind. They'd rather their daughters lose their virginity to someone who would be gentle and intent on pleasing. Then, on their wedding night, daughters would not cry, there would be no pain, and pig's blood would be sprinkled upon the sheets. Husbands would leave their marriage bed happy in the knowledge that they had performed well indeed, with no idea that their wives had already lost their virginity to a whore.

He paused outside his door. Lady Lavender had done what she could to make the rooms void of sound, but noises seeped through…moans, whispers, groans of passion. Evening was a popular time. Vaguely he could remember waking to noises of the city—people calling out their wares, carriages over cobbled streets. Now, he woke to the sound of women being pleasured. At one time it was a magical, musical sound. Now it grated.

He gave a soft knock, just to warn his client, then wrapped his fingers around the cool porcelain knob. Without hesitation, he pushed the door wide.

She stood near the windows. The setting sun outlined her body with a heavenly glow. Heaven in this hell, how ironic. Not blonde. Not a brunette. Not raven haired. Almost…auburn? He stepped farther into the room. Yes, dark auburn, although a less astute man would have said brown. He smiled, surprised when he was rarely surprised anymore. He'd never had an auburn-haired woman. Thank God for small favors. Something different in his mundane life. Softly he shut the door, the latch giving a click.

She turned, spinning around in a flurry of brown skirts. "Oh."

Her voice was a gasp of surprise that hardly reached him. He could barely see her face, the setting sun too bright behind her. But he didn't need to see her features. Looks no longer mattered. She could have resembled old Bertie from the kitchen or a perfect goddess created by the heavens and it wouldn't have mattered.

He moved across the large room, his booted feet sinking into plush carpet, dulling any sound of footsteps. Only the best decorated Lady Lavender's estate. The walnut four-poster bed had cost a pretty pence. White curtains provided a seductive haven that cocooned lovers in a pure embrace, while the baby-blue walls reminded one of brilliant summer days in the country. It was luminous, beautiful, perfect for the innocent. He hated the room.

"A drink?" he asked, moving to the side table to lift the wick of the only lantern that was currently lit.

From the corner of his eye he could see her gloved hand flutter around her before settling on her chest like a nervous butterfly on a flower. "Um, yes, thank you. I'm sorry, I didn't get your name."

Her voice was husky, pretty really. He poured sherry into a glass and started toward her. The drink would help her relax, as would the fire crackling in the marble hearth. Expensive French chocolates sat on the table by the bed. Everything was in place, as it should be.

"Alex." His gaze shifted to her hazel eyes. A shock of awareness shot through his body, sucking the very air from his lungs. Rosy cheeks, pert nose slightly upturned, wide, innocent eyes not exactly blue, yet not green…Twenty-three, four? Almost on the shelf then. Yet there was something about her that called to him…

that stirred his interest. He cleared his throat and dropped his attention, scanning her form quickly, looking for something, anything to explain his sudden attraction. Brown cloak was perfectly cut, material fine, but it was serviceable. Nothing erotic.

"Alex," she repeated softly, her voice almost a caress. "Do you have a surname?"

He had, at one time. "No. Just Alex."

Remembering his purpose, he started toward her once more, stopping close…close enough that his heat tempted her, but not too close that she felt overwhelmed. He took in a deep breath and suddenly he was the one overwhelmed. Her scent invaded his senses; the freshness of spring and more…something homey… sweet…as if she'd been baking cookies.

Curious hazel eyes blinked up at him. She had a soft splattering of freckles across the bridge of her nose so light in color that one had to be close to notice them. Hell. Her innocence screamed at him. Yet…yet he couldn't seem to look away. As he studied those freckles he had the sudden urge to kiss her. Truly kiss her. No pretense, no practice, but the sudden rush of lust that could only be sated with an irrational kiss. She reminded him of innocence, of a life before he'd sold his soul. A time when he'd flirted with sweet milkmaids and farm girls. A life when anything had been possible.

She frowned, a crease forming between her brows. "It's hardly appropriate for me to call you by your first name."

He laughed at her jest. But as confusion swept over her oval face, his laughter faded. Was she serious?

"Drink." He softened his demand by smiling, his gifted, charmed smile complete with dimples. "And your name?"

She crossed her arms over her chest, refusing to take the glass and looking thoroughly disgruntled. "Since you've given me your first name, I now feel indebted to give you mine."

He parted his lips to respond when she held up her hand, cutting him off.

"I insist we be on equal footing."

He didn't know what the hell she was talking about, but he was intrigued enough to wait for her next statement.

"Grace," she said in a breath of air, as if admitting some great family secret. "Although it's hardly appropriate for you to use it."

His smile faltered. An odd virgin indeed. Damn, perhaps this wouldn't be easy after all. She was going to be difficult. "My dear, you're in my *bedchamber*; propriety doesn't matter much."

Her cheeks turned a charming shade of pink, and although she'd met his gaze directly only moments before, she now found sudden fascination with the carpet. "All the more reason to keep up morals."

Morals? Here? Was she mad?

Grace pulled her gloves from her fingers, one by one in a slow, unconcerned movement, as if she was in complete control. She looked rather unimpressed. And maybe she was. "Sir, as much as I adore small talk, I'd rather get on with it."

Holy hell. For not the first time that evening, Alex was shocked speechless.

Chapter 2

"I see," the incredibly handsome man murmured, staring at her intently.

He seemed confused. Why was he confused?

Grace stuffed the kid gloves into the pockets of her wool cloak and rubbed her aching temples. Blast, but she didn't have time for this nonsense. He either had the book or he didn't. But the man was watching her as if she were some odd specimen from the British Museum.

Perhaps her stepbrother hadn't mentioned she was female? Would be just like John to exclude something that society deemed important. And obviously this man, with his brilliant blue eyes and pretty face, thought a woman should be kept under lock and key as most men seemed to believe.

"See here, I understand this is a little untoward…" Managing to repress her ire, she gentled her voice to a calming murmur, "But I don't have time to dally; I have things to do, important things."

Something flashed deep within his gaze...amusement? Was he laughing at her? She stiffened, her anger flaring to life. Yes, of course, as a man he found it amusing when a woman spoke her mind. Damn it all to hell, she was tired of being laughed at. John was forever finding sport in the fact that she still hadn't married. And God forbid she attempt to submit a paper to the antiquities society. Yet if she lost her temper, she'd lose her chance at finding the book. And so she struggled to remain calm, collected.

"Shall we?" she urged with a tight smile.

He paused, looking unsure, weary. "You're positive?"

"Absolutely."

Slowly he set her glass upon a small side table and reached for his necktie. "Of course. If that's how you want it." With long, almost delicate fingers, he untied the material like an artist undressing his muse. Bizarre man. What *was* he doing now?

"Tell me about yourself," he urged.

Her gaze jumped to his face, and for one brief moment she swore her heart actually stopped. Angelic, really. And eyes so startling blue, they reminded her of the waters off the coast of Ireland. It was surprising that he would be studious. In her experience, studious men were usually old toads with narrow minds.

He was too attractive. Not that it mattered to her one way or another. Even if men found she had a pleasant face, once they realized she had a brain, they were already searching the ballroom for their next victim. And good riddance to them. Handsome men tended to make her nervous. One never knew quite what they were scheming. And they were *always* scheming.

"About myself?" She didn't know how to answer that question as no one had ever deemed it important to ask her. How should she respond?

Well, you see, I live with an obnoxious stepbrother who likes to torment and ridicule me for not being married. No, that was too personal for polite conversation. There was always the tried and true *my mother is on her deathbed*. That usually shut people up and rather quickly soured the mood. But she didn't want to sour this man's mood, at least until she got her book.

She supposed she could always fall back on the *my little sister likes to dress as a boy* tale she'd blurted out one time while she and Lord Rodrick had been left alone with nothing to discuss. Hmm. That might not be quite the thing either. Blast, but she was never good at making conversation.

"Well?" His eyes were smiling again, those crinkles at the corners mocking her.

"I…I…"

"Family?"

Flustered, she tucked a loose lock behind her ear. "Yes. Of course I have family." He was close. Too bloody close. She couldn't think with him this close. Couldn't breathe with him so near.

The cravat hung loosely around his neck, fluttering there like a sail on an ocean breeze. Slowly he pulled on one end until the snowy white material hung from his fingers, a sign of surrender. There, on the side of his bare neck, beat a pulse slow and steady. Fascinating, really. She'd always admired art, and this man was certainly a piece of art. That lean body, that square jaw, those broad shoulders and lips just made for…

Grace stepped back, her stomach tightening in an unfamiliar way that was neither upsetting nor exactly pleasant.

"Please, make yourself comfortable," she said, attempting to sound sarcastic, although her voice came out with a husky breathlessness that bespoke more interest than sarcasm.

Was it getting rather warm? She glanced toward the windows praying for a cool breeze, but they were tightly shut, forcing the spring wind at bay. Light was fading, night fast approaching. By merely coming here unescorted she'd risked her reputation. Every moment in this man's private bedchamber was placing her further onto the path of ruination. She needed to procure the book and leave.

"Pray, listen—"

"How about I make both of us comfortable?" He quirked a dark brow in a knowing manner.

Confused, Grace shook her head. She didn't want to be comfortable. She wanted the book, for God's sake. "I was told your specimen is amazing, perfectly preserved."

His lips lifted, ridiculously sweet dimples flashing in his cheeks. "Yes, I suppose some have called it perfect." His fingers rested at the top button of his vest. The movement sent his scent swirling toward her. A warm scent, a masculine scent that was quite intoxicating; the outdoors on a crisp winter eve. Not at all flamboyant and overwhelming as most men seemed to wear their cologne these days.

He stepped closer. She stumbled back. Her heart pattered against her ribs like a finch begging to be released from its bony cage. There was something about this man, something…animalistic almost. She looked behind her, for some odd reason thinking perhaps that heated gaze was pinned to someone else. But no, she was the only one in the room. He was actually stalking her. But…why?

"You have lovely green eyes."

"Rubbish," she whispered, backing up until her bottom hit the edge of a small table. Something fell over, rolling off the ledge and landing with a thud to the floor. She didn't dare turn to pick it up. "They're hazel."

"And lips that could make the angels cry." He paused then, only a breath away. So close she could see the gold that tipped his thick, dark lashes. Was he actually flirting with her? The thought made her feel oddly irate. It was impossible. No one flirted with her. Yet she couldn't deny the odd vibration that seemed to hum between them.

The room tipped. Waves of dizziness swept through her body, leaving her feeling off-balance and confused. Her corset felt too tight.

The man was being completely inappropriate. "Sir, I'd like to get on with business."

He paused, a quizzical look flashing in those heavenly blue eyes. "All right."

Thinking he'd relented, she almost relaxed. Stupid girl that she was. Before she could respond, he wrapped his muscled arm around her waist and jerked her forward. With a gasp, Grace fell into the man's hard chest. Fear and attraction swirled deep within her gut in a lethal combination.

He lowered his lips to her ear; his warm breath tiptoed temptingly down her neck. "You do surprise me."

He smelled so bloody good and he was warm, so warm. But this was wrong, so completely wrong. With a groan, she managed to cling to a tiny piece of reality and push back just far enough so she could move. Shoving her hand up between their bodies, Grace slapped him. Hard. He blinked, stunned.

Guilt fought with justification. Well, really, what did he expect? She curled her fingers against his chest, her palm still tingling from the contact of his cheek, rough with a day's growth of whiskers. "Y…you deserved that."

"I see," he murmured, his fingertips going to that red mark on his cheek. Those blue eyes were narrowed, but not in anger. No, he looked more…bemused. "Because…I was bad?"

Confused, Grace's nose wrinkled. Bad? What sort of question was that? "Yes, I suppose. Sir—"

"Alex."

She swatted at his arm, still wrapped firmly around her waist, but the blasted man refused to release his hold. "Alex, just because I've agreed to meet in your private quarters…" She wrapped her fingers around his forearm, pushing, "Doesn't mean…" She dared to glance up. He was watching her again, that odd look in his eyes, as if she was a puzzle he couldn't quite figure out. "I don't know what you think I'm here for—"

"I'm sorry, I assumed..." He shook his head, those dark curls shifting and shimmering under the light from the setting sun. "They said you were not knowledgeable in the fine art—"

"Unbelievable!" She shoved hard at his muscled chest, but the man didn't budge. "I can assure you, *Mr. Alex*, I am quite experienced. If you have what I want, give it to me now so I can leave. You will be paid handsomely."

He sighed, his face showing his exasperation. "I underestimated you. Usually Gideon gets the more experienced women. But if that's the way you like it, then I'm only happy to oblige."

Happy to oblige? Whatever did he mean? And who the hell was Gideon? This was becoming much, much too bizarre even for her ridiculous life. Lord, her breasts were crushed indecently to his chest; surely he could feel her heart's frantic beat.

"Listen," she started, thinking to soothe the beast until she could make her escape. "Just give me—"

A predatory look flared to life, replacing any humor that had lingered in his blue eyes. Grace sucked in a sharp breath, feeling the sudden desire to flee. Obviously there'd been a mistake. She parted her lips to tell him so when his arm tightened around her waist. Her gloves fell to the floor.

"Sir, please—"

Strong fingers bit into her waist, and with ease, he tossed her over his broad shoulder.

Grace yelped as her hair tumbled down. The tiny pins that had held the strands in place pattered across the carpet as if to make their escape. "Put me down! Put me down this instant!"

She should never have trusted her stepbrother. Damn John to hell! She slammed her fists against the man's back. He didn't even flinch. This Alex either thought to collect his pay with her body or John had sent her to the wrong place. Most likely it was her stepbrother's fault. John was a bloody idiot! She should have known Alex was too handsome to be a scholar.

"Not until I've had my way with you."

Grace rolled her eyes heavenward. He said the words as if he'd rehearsed them, as if they were in some god-awful play. Before she could protest, he tossed her on the bed and she sank into the feather tick. With a growl low in her throat, Grace pushed her hair from her face. He merely stood there, smirking down at her, a smile that didn't quite reach his eyes. For some reason he was annoyed, as if he didn't want to be doing this any more than she wanted him to. And for some unknown reason, she suddenly found the situation highly amusing.

A giggle worked its way up her throat, trembling past her lips. Grace floundered, swiping at her skirts in her attempt to sit upright. "Sir," she gasped between laughs. "I think there's been a mistake."

"Hmm, really. The lady doth protest too much." He tossed aside his embroidered vest.

Impressive really, yet slightly frightening as well, how quickly he could undress. And even as she wanted to deny her attraction, she found her gaze slipping down his body. Alex's muscles stretched the white fabric of his shirt in a magnificent display of masculinity.

"Dear God, it's like I'm trapped in a bloody gothic novel," she whispered.

"Gothic novel it is." He ripped open his shirt. Buttons popped and flew across the room, pattering like raindrops. A trail of dark hair covered his chest, valleys and hills of pure muscle. Like a sculpture. Grace had the insane urge to run her fingers over those dips and planes. But there, on the edges of insanity, lurked her rational mind.

Oh my, this was becoming rather serious indeed.

Grace shoved her booted feet into the tick, attempting to scramble upright. "You…you really shouldn't do that, you know. Buttons are an awful nuisance to sew."

Her gaze slid to the door. Could she make it in time? No, of course not. She could barely sit up as her boot heel seemed to be stuck in the hem of her gown. She would scream, she would...if she could stop giggling. Good heavens, she never giggled! What was wrong with her?

Alex leaned over her and Grace's giggles faded. Her gaze froze to his bare chest, that wide chest with dark hair that trailed down to the waistband of his trousers and farther...His hands were suddenly pressed into the bed on either side of her body. She had no place to go but back. A wavy lock had fallen across his forehead, his hair devilishly mussed. In his blue eyes was the promise of seduction...of pleasure. Grace sank back further into the mattress and swallowed hard, resisting the urge to give in to that temptation. He paused when he was only a breath away, the air between them mingling.

"Get off me." The words would have been more effective had her voice not quivered.

"Be still."

She didn't move. He shoved his knee between her thighs, parting her legs as much as her skirts would allow. Grace's fingers curled into the covers as he leaned closer, his mouth hovering over hers. She should scream. She should hit him. She should at least close her eyes...

He dipped his head and his warm, firm lips pressed to hers. His hard body relaxed, molding to her curves as if he fit there, perfectly. A missing puzzle piece. Stunned, Grace merely lay still as he kissed, nibbled, licked. It wasn't exactly...unpleasant.

A warm buzz vibrated through her body, as if a thousand bees had burrowed deep within her soul. Those strong hands cupped the sides of her face as he deepened the kiss. She gave in. With a moan, Grace's lashes fluttered down to her cheekbones. His essence surrounded her, tempting her senses. He tasted like mint and whiskey, erotic, addictive. She'd been kissed before; she was twenty-four, after all. Yet never had she been kissed like this, as if he was feasting upon her.

He groaned as his hands moved down her neck to her shoulders, his warm fingers tugging at her bodice. Her breasts grew heavy. For one brief, rational moment she thought to stop him, but then his rough tongue slipped across her lips. Shivers tiptoed down her back. She was gone. Utterly gone. Heat pooled low in her belly, producing an aching need that flared to life with his touch. Yes, oh yes, she wanted to tell him. He shifted, and something hard pressed against her thighs.

Grace's eyes popped open. Dear God. Something hard. *Hard!*

She might be a virgin, but she wasn't an idiot.

No! She turned her head, tearing her mouth from his. With all her strength, she shoved the palms of her hands into his hard chest. He pulled back, his breath heavy, her breath heavy. The bored look in his gaze had been replaced with pure lust. For one long moment they merely stared at each other, and she wasn't sure who looked more shocked.

"Get off me now!" she finally demanded.

He looked confused for a moment. "You're…you're serious?"

"Of course I'm bloody serious!"

He paused only a moment before finally sliding from the bed. She couldn't help but notice the way he trembled. Or was she trembling?

Standing in only his trousers, he watched her curiously as if she were an insect under a microscope. "I don't understand, did you or did you not come here of your own free will?"

She rolled from the bed, her booted feet hitting the carpet with a muffled thud. With the large piece of furniture separating them, she felt slightly more at ease. But the blasted room still spun and her corset was still too tight. She refused to faint in front of this man.

"Yes," she blurted out. "I did come here of my own free will."

Obviously frustrated, he raked both hands through his hair, tossing the wavy locks in a haphazard manner that made him look boyish. "Well then, am I not what you expected? Would you like someone else?"

She laughed a wry laugh as she smoothed down her bodice. If she ever decided to have anyone, he would do quite well indeed. But it would be a cold, cold day in hell before she'd admit her attraction. "No."

Those giggles were coming back. Damn it! She pressed her hands to her mouth, attempting to suppress her laughter.

"I'm sorry." He seemed annoyed now, as if she'd offended him. "Shall I ask Madam to send you another man?"

Confused, she shook her head. "I don't...I want to see whoever has what I came here for."

He placed his hands on his narrow hips. "Grace, I assure you I have what you need if you'll only give me a chance."

She sighed. Was she wrong? Did he have the book? She'd traveled all this way; she might as well see the novel. She crossed her arms over her chest. "Oh, bloody well, fine. Show me the book."

His hands went to his trousers. Before she could even blink, he dropped them. Grace's mouth fell open, shock, fear, and fascination fighting for control.

His cock stood straight at attention, large, intimidating... *amazing*. She'd seen a man's private parts before, but only in paintings and on statues. This...this was utterly *interesting!*

She pointed a trembling finger toward him. "That...that...is not, sir, what I need!"

At the same time he questioned, "The book?"

Heat shot straight to Grace's cheeks. Her desperate gaze jumped to his face. He didn't race to cover his nakedness. No, he stood there in all of his masculine finery merely staring at her as if she was the oddity. She spun around and rushed to the door. Anxiously she grabbed at the handle, but her slick palms couldn't seem to grasp the porcelain. Why wouldn't the bloody door open?

Two large hands slammed against the door on either side of her head. "My lady, I think there's been a mistake."

Obviously! She swallowed hard and turned. He was naked, his bare body pressed to hers, yet power radiated from his very being, and she was distinctly aware of the fact that he was larger, stronger. Grace's dress provided little barrier; she could feel his muscled arms through the sleeves of her bodice, his hard chest against hers, and his even harder anatomy pressing against her skirts. Crinoline was no match for his desire. Horrified, stunned, and slightly amused, she sank back against the door, refusing to look anywhere but his face.

"Tell me precisely what you want."

"I was told you have a rare book," her voice squeaked.

"A…a what?" He drew back as if she'd slapped him. As if *she'd* offended him.

"Sir," she asked, using all her strength to keep calm, "exactly what is this place?"

He smiled, a slow, heated smile that produced those blasted dimples. "You don't realize?"

She shook her head, her heart slamming madly in her chest, unsure if she wanted to know…but realizing she had to get the truth from his lips once and for all.

He leaned closer, his warm breath sending shivers over her skin. "My dear Grace, you're at Lady Lavender's."

She shrugged, her gaze focused on his mouth, vaguely aware of what he was saying yet finding more fascination with the way his lips moved. "And what is that exactly?"

He leaned closer, so close his lips brushed hers. Her heart skipped a beat. Would he kiss her again? She wanted him to kiss her…just one last time.

"Grace," he whispered. She stiffened as unwelcome heat spread across her skin. "You, my dear, are in a brothel for women."

Chapter 3

She was going to kill her stepbrother. Yes, she was going to murder him and she was going to enjoy every bloody moment. She'd start first with his fingers. Perhaps break a thumb. It would be awfully difficult to hold cards with a broken thumb. And if he couldn't hold cards, he couldn't squander his life.

Or maybe she'd tear out his hair, his prized possession, strand by brown strand. When many of his friends were starting to lose theirs, why shouldn't he join them? The preening peacock of a fool!

It was a lovely dream, a dream that kept her from cursing out loud and drawing stares from the evening crowd as she dodged the smash of carriages and rushed up the shallow steps of their London townhome. Grace threw open the front door, for once barely noting the peeling white paint. Marks, ever the faithful butler, sat napping in a chair.

"Where is he?" she demanded.

Startled from slumber, Marks jumped to his feet, stumbling back like a drunken sailor. "Ehh? What was that?"

"Marks! Calm yourself."

He narrowed his faded blue eyes and peered up at her under bushy gray brows as if he hadn't a clue who she was even though he'd worked for them a good ten years.

Grace sighed, rubbing her hands over her weary face. "My stepbrother. Where is he?"

He pointed a gloveless finger toward the hall. Grace frowned. The man had probably sold his gloves for whiskey. "The library," he muttered, his breath reeking of sour alcohol, confirming her suspicion. They should fire him, but they couldn't afford a decent butler, and blast it all, she still had a soft spot for the man who had been with them for so long.

Instead of letting him go, Grace merely ground her teeth. "Excellent. Thank you, Marks."

With a flurry of skirts, she started down the corridor. The butler skittered to the side. If she weren't so angry, she might have found the look of shock on the man's face amusing. He'd never seen her in a state of such distress. But as it was, she'd laughed enough for one day.

How dare John! How dare he make her think she was visiting an antiques dealer when he'd sent her to a…a *brothel*! What if someone had seen her? Had he not thought at all about her reputation? Her marriage prospects would be in complete tatters, and she knew quite well that her prospects of a match were already low.

She paused outside the door, cursing her body for trembling. She would attempt to glean at least a bit of control before she entered. John pounced on weakness like a cat on a mouse.

It just didn't make sense. He'd teased and tormented her before, and she'd always been able to ignore him, much to his annoyance. But this…this…was too much. She bit her lower lip, resisting the urge to give in to stinging tears. She would not cry in front of her stepbrother; he'd only use it to tease her later.

Dredging up her anger and clinging to the feeling, she shoved the door wide. The panel bounced against the wall, making the hanging pictures vibrate. John stood near the hearth, his back to her, the crackling fire making his brown hair shine. How she hated his shiny locks!

Any sense of control fled at the sight of him. "John, you bastard! How could you?"

The man turned, a look of utter shock upon his handsome face. But he wasn't John. Oh no. It was worse. Much, much worse. "Hello, Grace."

Heat shot to her cheeks. "Lord Rodrick." She dropped into a curtsy, frantically clawing through her mind for some rational explanation to justify her insanity. In the end she was left with a handful of muttered excuses that even a madman wouldn't believe. Straightening, she made an effort to smooth her face into a pleasant façade. It would not do at all for Rodrick to know their sordid family details.

He was smiling, his amber eyes laughing at her much like those brilliant blue eyes had laughed earlier. Was she forever to be at the tail end of some ridiculous jest she never quite understood? She bit back her sharp reply and instead forced her lips upward into a demure smile.

"I'm…I'm so sorry, I thought…" Oh hell, there was no way of getting out of this. "Siblings." She shrugged as if to say what can you do?

He leaned with elegant ease against the walnut mantel, his dark suit molding perfectly to his tall body. Slowly his gaze slid down her form and up again, looking at her in a completely thorough way, a way he'd never looked at her before.

"I understand." He lifted a drink to his lips, watching her… merely watching her when he'd barely paid her a glance in the past.

The heat inside her intensified. Rodrick was paying attention to her and all because she'd come barreling into the room like a cutthroat looking for a fight. Just bleedin' wonderful.

"Yes. They're quite dreadful at times." Suddenly aware of the exalted position of their guest, she studied the room from the corner of her eye. Mama's embroidered pillows with messages of love and hope were tossed haphazardly about the worn settee. Green curtains so old one could see the streetlamps through the fabric hung on the dingy windows.

And Patience, bless her younger sister, had left some sort of concoction in the middle of the floor. What was it? Metal pieces, wood, and…walnuts? Even though at sixteen Patience was much too old for play, she still made messes. And John, the idiot, had left his jacket and boots near their only fine wing back chair so that she'd have to clear the spot for Rodrick to sit, thereby drawing attention to the mess.

Gads, it was as if she lived with a houseful of children. And *what*, pray tell, was *that*? She inched closer to the chair. *Lord!* Was that a garter? Yes, most assuredly. She resisted the urge to groan. Miss Kitty had been playing with the laundry again. Grace pasted a stiff smile upon her face, attempting to draw Rodrick's gaze upward.

"Lovely evening," she muttered, using her foot to nudge the garter under the chair.

Rodrick set his glass upon the mantel and started toward her. His stroll was slow, unhurried, confident. And she could only stand there in her wrinkled gown, with her hair a rat's nest atop her head, not fit to polish his Wellingtons. A glance at that aristocratic face and one knew he was a man used to getting what he wanted. Her heart lurched and her fingers curled into her gown. Why couldn't he want her?

He paused a few feet away, his dark brows drawn together over pale brown eyes. "You look…is there something…"

She stiffened, sucking in a hopeful breath. "Yes?"

"Different. You look different." He smiled. A darling smile. He didn't have dimples, but then again no one was perfect. But he was close, so bloody close.

"Yes, it's your hair. Down about your shoulders."

Self-consciously she reached toward the locks. It hadn't been down, not until that...that...dear Lord, she couldn't even say the word...that infuriating man had pulled her hair loose in his mad fit of passion. But no, it hadn't been passion; he'd been acting. Whores were paid to act. Weren't they?

"Oh." She started to tuck her hair into the few remaining pins.

His hand rested on her forearm, an intimate touch that sent heat swirling low in the pit of her belly. He'd helped her into carriages before, in an indifferent manner, as if merely being polite. But this...this touch seemed new...as if they'd never touched before.

"No, leave your hair down."

And she did as he demanded because he was an earl, and one wouldn't dare ignore an earl. Slowly she lowered her arms. She'd never understood why a man like Rodrick would befriend her brother. Sympathy? Amusement? Not that John was a complete toad. She supposed some women found his gangly body and narrow face attractive, and he did have that silly little title of a baron. But her stepbrother wasn't known for his kindness and intelligence. While Rodrick...Rodrick was everything John wasn't. Tall, his body healthy, his suit never wrinkled, and those amber eyes... delicious and knowledgeable. Perhaps his beauty wouldn't make the angels cry, but she'd never fancied overly attractive men.

He stepped closer, the scent of sandalwood following him. An overwhelming scent that tickled her senses and made her want to sneeze. She wiggled her nose and focused on something more pleasant...his lips.

What would it be like if he kissed her? Would it feel as heated and consuming as Alex's kiss? The man's face flashed to mind... those sparkling blue eyes, those dimples. She pushed the image aside just as quickly as it had come and refocused on the earl.

"I'm sorry, that was forward of me." He turned and started toward the fireplace, leaving her trembling in his wake. "It's just that I often forget myself in front of you."

Her heart skipped a beat. They were perfect, meant to be together. Was he finally going to admit it?

"You being like a sister and all."

Her heart broke in two, crumbling into the pit of her hollow belly. *Sister?* She wanted to gag. To get sick all over the carpet like Miss Kitty coughing up a hairball.

"Grace. Rodrick."

The very sound of the familiar voice had her spinning around, anger flaring to life once more. John stood in the doorway, his weary gaze flickering back and forth between her and his friend. He was obviously wondering if she'd told the earl. The bastard was worried. He should be. Slowly her fingers curled as she imagined walking up to her brother and hitting him…hard.

"You're back already." He gave them a strained smile. His cravat was gone, his dark brown jacket and tanned breeches wrinkled, and his hair mussed, as if he'd been involved in fisticuffs.

"Yes." The word came out like a hiss, and even though she tried to keep her face blank of emotion, she knew her anger vibrated the very air around them.

His normally pale face flushed pink. "Well then, shall we go?" He glanced eagerly at Lord Rodrick, urging the man to move with frantic eyes.

Catching the hint, he started forward. "Yes, yes, by all means."

Unbelievable. How dare John try to sneak away just because they had company? "John, dear brother, I must speak with you in private."

Holding his hands up as if to ward her off, her stepbrother backtracked toward the door. "Really don't have time, you know. Very important events to attend."

"I must insist," she growled, resisting the urge to grab him by the collar and jerk him forward.

Rodrick had stilled in the middle of the room, his astute gaze moving between the two of them. He was obviously curious, but for once the man wasn't going to get the answers he wanted. His lips quivered, his amusement apparent. "I'll wait in the foyer."

The moment the door shut, John burst across the room, coattails flying. Instinctively Grace swung her fist, but the bloody bastard ducked behind the wing back chair.

"Come on!" he whined from his hiding place. "What did I do?"

"Oh, give over, you know exactly what you did!" Grace jumped onto the chair and swung her arm over the back, but her stepbrother managed to roll to the side, once more evading her swinging fist.

"Please!" John surged upright and retreated toward the door. "Just give me a moment to explain."

Forcing her feet to remain firmly planted, Grace took in a deep, trembling breath. She'd gone mad! Completely and utterly mad! She spun around and moved to the windows, needing distance to calm her nerves. Outside, the streets were dark, her own reflection the only thing staring back. Empty, just like John's soul. "How could you? Was it some sort of horrible jest?"

She could see his reflection as he moved to the sideboard and poured a drink. Leave it to her stepbrother; anytime things got complicated, he drank his problems into oblivion. "I don't know what you're referring to."

She turned. "Just because you like to visit whores doesn't mean I do!"

He gave her a sour glance. "Shhh!" Finally she'd gotten his attention. "I had to do it for your own good."

She laughed, finding amusement for the first time since she'd arrived home. John wasn't even going to try and deny it and was, no doubt, going to spin some ridiculous tale. "For my sake?" She crossed her arms over her chest, tucking her fisted hands close to her body. "Well, what a wonderful birthday present."

Her birthday had been two days ago. Twenty-four and most assuredly climbing that shelf. Not that John would know it was her birthday. Mother was too sick to remember. But at least dear Patience had attempted to make a cake—and had almost burned the kitchen down in the process. But had John noticed anything amiss? Of course not.

When her mother had married John's father, Grace had been thrilled. She'd always wanted a brother. Father had been too old to protect her from the harsh comments of village boys. And oh, how they'd loved to taunt her for having an Irish father. But an older brother would protect her...or so she'd thought. She'd come to the quick conclusion that the only person one could trust was oneself.

"You don't understand. You see..." John raked his hands through his hair. "Lord Rodrick..." He paused and heaved a long, melodramatic sigh.

Really, he should have been on the stage. "Yes?" she prompted.

He spun around and stomped toward her, his face holding a frantic edge that frightened her more than she wanted to admit. Grace held her ground, refusing to flinch.

"You're losing him!" he exclaimed.

She frowned, confused. "I've never had him."

John grasped her shoulders. Besides occasionally knocking her to the ground, it was the only time he'd ever touched her. It felt odd...wrong. "But you want him, don't you?"

She stiffened, wary over his sudden concern. "Perhaps." Any woman would. It was no secret. He was handsome, intelligent, rich, and, most important, always kind.

A gleam of success lit his dark eyes. "Exactly! And Lord Rodrick likes his women experienced. It's why he avoids virgins as if they have the plague. If you could learn a few tricks, he'd be clay in your hands."

Her mouth dropped open, her stomach falling to her toes. Was she imagining this conversation, because there was no possible way her stepbrother was telling her to seduce his best friend.

As if sensing her shock, he rushed on. "His mother was a cold prude, and he swore he'd never marry someone like her."

"So he wants a whore instead?"

He stepped back, frowning. "What's wrong with wanting a woman who is a little more experienced?" His lips lifted in a sneer. "You debutantes with your virginal sensibilities become rather annoying, you know."

She couldn't even find the words to respond to his ridiculous statement. "You want me to become a whore?"

He rolled his eyes heavenward, as if she was the one being ridiculous. "Not a whore, but at least someone who knows how to bloody kiss. Who doesn't flush with embarrassment when she's touched or, worse, flinch. The men at Lady Lavender's can teach you things, things you'd never be able to learn elsewhere, without ruining your reputation."

She must be dreaming, for this couldn't be real. "A whorehouse, John, you want me to go to a brothel to learn to kiss?"

He flushed and tugged at his collar as he'd done as a young man when he'd been caught doing something he shouldn't. "Not a whorehouse. A house of…pleasure, a place where women can learn to kiss…amongst…other things."

She wasn't sure if she should laugh or slap him. Instead, she merely stood there staring at him.

He stiffened, as if offended by her silence. "It's highly regarded, you know. I made sure they took you through the back entrance. Not a person saw you. The place is known for its discretion."

Grace finally found her voice. "You can't be serious. You're honestly going to say you're doing this for me? This is a jest, isn't it?"

He didn't respond, merely paced toward the windows, a man lost in some sort of odd delusion. John was twenty-seven; it was time for him to grow up. To stop teasing her, stop playing cruel pranks. And this most assuredly had to be a jest.

She'd had enough. "John, damn it, for once just leave me alone!" Grace started toward the door, forcing her legs to keep moving even though her muscles quivered and she wanted to do nothing but sink onto the settee.

"We need the money."

She froze. How she wished she'd misheard him, but she knew she hadn't. Slowly she turned. He wasn't looking at her but feigning interest in the carpet. Most likely attempting to deduce how much it would sell for.

Of course that was the problem. *Money*. She should have known. He was never home; she certainly knew that he wasn't at church praying. He was gambling, drinking, using what little money their fathers had left them. She'd been too busy to see the truth, even though it had been directly in front of her eyes.

Knees finally too weak, Grace sank into the chair. "How bad is it?"

"We're just hanging on by a thread. Three months from now..." He swallowed hard. "My creditors are insisting..." He let those dire words hang in the air, still refusing to meet her gaze. He looked tired. Exhausted. And for one brief moment she actually felt sorry for the man.

It was worse than she'd realized. She'd known this day would come, but not now. Not so soon. And with her mother ill, not at the worst possible time. Dear God, how much was he spending each day? It had to be a minor fortune. Her fingers curled around the curved arms of the chair. She shuddered to think about what else he didn't deem fit to mention. "I told you to let me handle the money."

His head jerked up, his face puckered into a mask of fury. "You're a woman." John rarely got angry, but when he did, he was as annoying as a toddler throwing a tantrum. "I will not be put on an allowance like some child! It's my inheritance, lest you forget!"

How could she forget when he reminded them weekly that they were there only because of his generosity. They were not blood related. He could have shoved them into a cottage in the wilds of England or sent them to their poor Irish relatives. But not all of the money was his. Mama had her small bit of savings,

savings she had planned to use as a dowry for Grace and Patience. But it was gone, apparently, with everything else.

"Or did you think to invest the money in your ridiculous treasure hunts?" His lips pulled back into a sneer. "Perhaps if you spent less time with your nose in a book and more in society, Rodrick wouldn't treat you like a bloody sister."

His words stung because they were true, but she'd sell her soul to the devil before she'd admit he'd hurt her. Grace looked away, afraid he'd read the truth in her eyes. "And my mother, does she know the details of our financial situation?"

"Of course not."

Thank the heavens for small miracles. Mama didn't need something else to worry about while she lay abed in pain. How stupid they'd been to let John handle their accounts, but what choice did they have? His house, his inheritance, as he'd said. The rotter. "And this...Lady Lavender." God, she could barely get the words out. "How did you pay her?"

He flushed, feigning interest in the carpet once more. "I borrowed the money."

Grace surged to her feet. "You didn't!"

"From Rodrick."

She sank into her chair. She was going to be sick. "Surely you didn't tell him what the money would be for?"

He frowned. "Of course not. I'm not a bloody idiot."

That was debatable.

He shifted, hesitating, then started forward. "I have things to do. I will not stand here and be questioned by a woman." He stormed across the room and jerked open the door.

Things to do. More money to spend. He left the room without another word, leaving her to pick up the pieces of his aftermath, as always.

She listened to the thump of her stepbrother's footfalls. The thud of the front door that followed his departure. Only when she heard the soft clomp of horses' hooves over cobbled stone did she feel strong enough to stand.

She'd known all along he was squandering money, but what could she have done to prevent it? As a woman, and not even a blood relation, not much. She'd hidden the few pieces of Mama's jewelry, but the money she would make selling them wouldn't last long.

Marks was no longer at his post, not surprisingly. He was most likely sleeping off his drink near the kitchen hearth. Grace made her way up the steps and paused outside her mother's door. Patience's soft murmur was a comforting melody. Smoothing her hair back from her face and pinching her cheeks, she prepared for Mama's astute gaze.

She pushed the door wide and slipped into the room. It would have been warm and cozy if it hadn't held the bitter and nauseating scent of medicines. A scent she knew well. First Father. Then her stepfather. Now Mama. One had to wonder if the family was cursed.

Patience looked up from her needlework, those green eyes flashing with barely concealed relief. "Good, you're finally back! Mama said I couldn't stop until you'd returned."

She tossed aside her needlework and rushed toward Grace. She was wearing trousers again. Grace bit her lip, refusing to reprimand her sister. Papa had so wanted a boy; it was his bloody fault. But Charlie had died at age two, and the only other child Mama had delivered was a golden girl. At sixteen, Patience should have been going to balls, wearing her blonde hair up, learning to flirt. Instead, she was stuck here with her spinster sister and dying mother.

"Did you find your book then? Can we start searching for the treasure?"

Grace laughed, sliding her arm around Patience's narrow shoulders. As a young girl, Grace had delved into the world of treasure hunting and unfortunately had pulled Patience in with her. Ridiculous, she knew, yet it was something to occupy her mind on lazy summer days. "No, my dear. I'm afraid the only treasures you'll find tonight are Martha's biscuits."

Patience grinned. "That will do. Sleep well, Mama." She threw their mother a kiss and disappeared into the hall.

Grace closed the door and moved softly to her mother's side. In the dim light of the lantern she looked even more fragile than normal. An angel too beautiful for this world. Patience had their mother's green eyes and golden hair, but Grace had received her father's Irish looks. She settled on the edge of the bed, careful not to jostle.

Although Mama had been stuck in her bed for a good month, she still managed to smile. "Is John home?"

Grace looked away, feigning interest in Patience's needle-work. A blob of red and yellow strings mixed together to form a… flower? Horse? Gads, her sister was hopeless, and it was her fault. She should have spent more time with Patience, teaching her to behave as a lady. "No. He only just left."

Her mother's thin hand settled atop hers, the skin pale, so translucent one could see the blue veins. "Hmm. And you're upset about this?"

Grace gave her mother a forced smile. "He spends too much time away, is all."

"I thought you'd be happy. You've never hidden your disdain for your stepbrother."

Grace bristled at the comment. "He's a bloody idiot, Mama, and he's been cruel to Patience and me since you married his father."

"Grace," her sharp voice belied her fragile condition. "He lost his mother at a young age. And only a few years ago, his father. He could have thrown us out, you know, when his father died."

Perhaps life would have been better if he had. But no, he'd kept them here, close by, where he could control her mother's small amount of money, control it and lose it. Her fingers curled into her skirt as she resisted the urge to blurt out the truth. She'd never thought much of John, but she was now growing to despise him. What would they do with no money? How would they care for Mama?

Grace wasn't stupid. She knew her mother was dying. How badly she wanted to make her last years comfortable. And what of Patience? What would become of her sister if they hadn't the money to find her a decent match? She would not allow Patience to follow her on the path toward loneliness.

Mama started coughing, sucking in sharp, wheezing breaths that tore at Grace's heart. She slid her arm under her mother's neck and lifted her, at the same time grabbing a glass of water from the bedside table.

Her mother pushed the glass away. "No. Just a moment." She closed her eyes, taking in deep, rattling breaths until finally her body settled into an uneasy stillness.

Those green eyes opened, watching Grace with an unsettling clarity. "'Tis amusing, you know, when you're dying and you need human touch more than any other time is when people are afraid to visit."

Grace's heart squeezed so painfully she could barely find breath. "Mama, I don't—"

"Shhh, my pet." She chuckled softly, closing her eyes. "All is well. But there are times when I actually wouldn't even mind a cat to cuddle."

A tear slipped from Grace's eye, trailing unheeded down her cheek. The guilt was almost unbearable. They tried to be with Mama as much as possible, but there were times when they couldn't. With the minimal number of servants in residence, it was up to Grace to keep house. "I'll bring you Miss Kitty, Mama. So when Patience and I aren't here, you can cuddle her."

She weakly patted Grace's hand. "'Tis all right; you're here now."

Grace rested her chin atop her mother's silky head and breathed in her scent, a scent she'd always adored as a child...roses...just barely noticeable over the bitter scent of illness.

"Don't be afraid, Mama. All will be well. You'll see." Grace's voice didn't even quiver at the lie. "We're here, Mama, and we'll always be here."

At least until the debt collectors threw them onto the street.

* * *

Alex pressed his fingers to his lips and slouched onto the settee. The flames in the marble hearth flickered and danced a seductive melody, but he barely noticed their warmth.

He swore he could still taste her. While most women tasted of sherry or wine, she had tasted of peppermint, as if she'd had a sweet before meeting with him. Her scent, her touch, even her taste had reeked of innocence. He reached into his pocket and pulled out her forgotten glove. The leather was worn smooth, soft as butter.

The look on her face when he'd told her where she was...Lord, he hadn't laughed so hard in...he didn't remember when. Unease settled like a boulder in his gut. She'd made him *feel*. First attraction when he hadn't felt lust in years and then amusement when there were so few things to laugh about. Something that felt oddly like anticipation hummed beneath his skin. Restless, his fingers stretched, then wrapped tightly around the glove.

He was intrigued despite himself. Why? Why this woman... this incorrigible, completely unattainable woman? He rubbed his lips once more, thinking of that heated kiss. She was lovely, surely, but it wasn't her looks. He'd been surrounded by beautiful women for most of his life. A veritable mystery, and he loved a good mystery. Not that it mattered, as she most likely wouldn't return. And that thought quickly soured his mood.

"That good, eh?"

He stuffed the glove back into his pocket and glanced over his shoulder. James stood near the door, dressed impeccably as ever in his pressed jacket and trousers. Not a blond hair out of place. He took his position seriously. Too seriously. He wasn't attending a meeting at the House of Lords, for God's sake.

"Good?" Alex chuckled wryly, studying the painted canaries that flew across the walls. "More…interesting."

He raised a brow. "Hmm. Well, I've finished my discussion with Lady Lavender. She said she'd be calling on you shortly."

Alex nodded and stretched, crossing his legs at the ankles as James moved to the sideboard for a drink. At the end of every night, in the wee hours of the morning, Ophelia called them one by one into her office in order to discuss the day's work. And she wanted details. It was insane, really, and at first he'd been horrifyingly embarrassed.

Those piercing lavender eyes watching him. *Do you think you did well, Alex?*

He'd shrug, heat traveling up his neck.

"Did she enjoy her experience? Did she reach ecstasy?"

He'd stutter out a response and she'd be pleased with him, or pleased with the fact that she'd embarrassed him thoroughly. Which, he wasn't sure. Now, hell, she could ask him pretty much anything and he wouldn't even flinch. Still, she insisted on seeing them. The problem was he wasn't sure what to say about this latest woman. Grace was her name. A pretty name. A name for an innocent. A lady. For some reason he didn't feel like discussing this woman with Ophelia.

"Good day," James said, making his way toward the door.

"James." Alex surged to his feet, pushing aside thoughts of a hazel-eyed innocent. He had a chance to talk to the man when he might not again for days.

James turned, a look of wariness flickering in those green eyes. "Yes?"

They didn't talk often. James didn't trust Alex or Gideon and had never hidden that fact. He couldn't understand why they weren't honored that Lady Lavender had chosen them. They couldn't understand why he couldn't see the truth, that Lady Lavender was nothing more than a demon in a beautiful woman's body.

"You're...content here?"

James shrugged. "What do you mean? I'm fed, clothed, and housed much better than I could have ever been." A clouded look crossed his features, a painful past memory. "Truth is if I'd continued on the way I was, I'd probably be dead by now. Either from a brawl or from starvation."

He painted a bleak picture, and Alex remembered the thin, underfed lad he'd been. A street rat. It gave Alex second thoughts about leaving. "I understand. I understand why you feel loyalty toward the woman, but James, think on it. You, Gideon, and I, brought here together by blackmail."

James bristled, his jaw working. "Not blackmail."

Alex released a harsh laugh. "She told you if you didn't do as she said, your family would starve to death."

James crossed his arms over his chest, a defensive position that told Alex he was wearing thin the man's patience. "And she was right, we would have. No one gets anything for free, Alex. She expected me to work." He smiled, a smile that didn't quite reach his eyes. "There are worse ways to make a living, you know."

"Indeed," Alex said softly, although he could think of a hundred different things he'd prefer. But he didn't have a choice. She and her henchmen made sure of that. He resided in a gilded prison, but a prison all the same.

"She's ready." Wavers appeared in the doorway, imposing, threatening in his silent way. Alex couldn't help but wonder if the man had overheard their conversation. If he had, Ophelia would find out soon enough and there'd be hell to pay.

"Wonderful." He swept by the man, feigning nonchalance. "Wavers, you're an arse." He gave the man a brilliant smile.

The huge bull didn't even flinch. No matter how Alex ridiculed him, the man pointedly ignored him. It drove Alex mad.

With a sigh, Alex moved down the hall, where the massive double door at the front of the entryway beckoned freedom. How he wished he could walk down those front steps. Walk away from this insanity. Thoughts of freedom sent his mind spinning, his gut clenching. The men standing on each side of the door weren't butlers. The moment he started toward those doors, they'd make sure he was promptly turned around. It didn't mean he couldn't find a way out…if he wanted. So why, in the twelve years he'd been here, had he never tried to escape? Because the thought of freedom, for some reason, made him scared as hell.

He paused at the second door on the right. A white-painted panel. Like every other door. There was a knick on the bottom left corner. A scratch at the top. He raised his hand and hesitated. A hard wood that rubbed against his knuckles in an irritating way. How many times had he stared at this door? He'd intentionally lost count. He let his fist fall, thumping softly once before pushing the door wide.

"Come in, Alex." Ophelia was sitting. She pushed aside some papers and waved him forward with a delicate hand. There behind her massive desk she looked like a fairy child pretending to be an adult. Insignificant. Yet for them—Gideon, James, and him—she was the woman who held their lives in her pale palms.

"Sit." She waved dismissively toward the chair across from her desk. "Do tell. I heard she left rather early."

Of course she'd heard, because she heard everything. "There was a…misunderstanding."

She frowned. "How so?"

"She was not informed she was in a house of ill repute. She thought she was here for a book."

"A book?" She shook her head and stood, her skirts rustling with the movement. "Ridiculous. Someone jesting with her then?"

At Alex's nod she skirted around the desk.

Alex slowly rubbed his jaw, watching her, attempting to uncover something, *anything* about the woman who'd destroyed his life. There had to be a reason why she'd picked him. "Her brother, I believe."

"Men are odd creatures." She moved to the fireplace and stared into the flames. For one long moment she seemed lost in thought, memories, actual emotion. But just as quickly as the flash of humanity had come, it disappeared, leaving him to wonder if he'd imagined the softening of her face. She turned, her lavender skirts flaring from her trim ankles.

"You've been requested for tomorrow evening. Mrs. Breur's daughter. Make sure she leaves happy."

It was a threat, a threat he didn't dare dismiss. He'd lost one client already; he couldn't lose another. Alex stood and bowed low. "Of course."

Chapter 4

She was an academic.

She studied culture, history, antiquities.

This was just like studying the ancient Egyptians...or...or the medieval castles of Europe...or David. Yes, the statue of David, in all his *naked* glory. Oh no...no, that wouldn't do at all. She blinked rapidly, forcing the picture from her mind.

Yes, she was a scholar, and she would treat this as she would any subject to be studied.

But then, she'd never studied in her bloomers while a man touched and stroked areas not meant to see the light of day.

That did pose a problem.

"Are you coming in or not?" The dark-haired god standing before her in his shirtsleeves and trousers quirked an impatient brow. His gaze reeked of annoyance, and the dark marks under his eyes told her he'd gotten little sleep, but there was also curiosity there, written on his handsome face.

Indecision held her captive. Her harsh breath sent the netting over her features close, then far, close, then far. Lord, she couldn't seem to calm her racing heart. She'd already sold the pearl ring Great-aunt Margaret had given to her on her seventeenth birthday. The appointment was paid for. She had no choice but to enter, as ridiculous as it now seemed.

From down the alley someone laughed.

Grace jerked her head toward the sound. Only a maid flirting with a footman. She didn't know why she was so worried about being seen. They were practically in the middle of nowhere and she'd gone to the back entrance. Besides that, a bonnet covered her hair and netting covered her features. Still…she shuddered to think of what would happen to her reputation should someone see through her flimsy disguise. Then again, surely no one she was acquainted with would visit a place like this.

She attempted to dredge up an image of Rodrick's smiling face, the very reason she'd risked her reputation. She'd been in love with the man since she was sixteen, and if she needed to learn how to kiss in order to seduce him, then so be it. But instead of Rodrick's fine features, Alex's face flashed to mind.

"Grace," he snapped impatiently.

"Shhh!" She leaned forward and slapped her hand over the man's mouth even as the realization that he'd remembered her name sent an odd, not unpleasant thrill through her body.

Shoving her free hand into his hard chest, she pushed him backward. They stumbled into the kitchen, Alex grasping her upper arms to hold her steady. Grace slid a glance left, then right. The maids had stopped cleaning the hearth, kneeling before the fireplace with stunned expressions upon their pale faces. The two women rolling out dough were frozen in action, their pins held in midair; another woman, with the bread door wide, stood with a peel in her hand; the lump of dough settled on the end of the paddle, waiting to be baked. Apparently clients didn't often burst in through the back door.

Heat shot to her cheeks. Had she so quickly made a muddle of things? Usually it was a good five minutes before people started staring. She shut the door behind her and leaned against the hard panel, taking pains to slow her thumping heart. Just as quickly as everything in the kitchen had stopped, the action resumed. Servants scurried back and forth across the brick floor snapping out orders.

The room smelled of scones, shepherd's pie, nutmeg, tea. She breathed deeply, taking comfort in the normalcy. It smelled like any other kitchen. Looked like any other kitchen. Her gaze traveled to the ceiling where water stains and smoke marred the plaster. But what went on in those rooms above was not like any other place she'd ever been.

Alex settled his hands on the door, on either side of her head. Grace started, realizing she had nowhere to look but at him. Blast, she didn't want to look at him. When she looked at him she couldn't think straight.

He leaned toward her, close, always too close. "Grace, you asked for me, dragged me from slumber. Please tell me it was not for nothing."

She peeked up at him through her lashes. Lord, he was as beautiful as she remembered. The dark circles under his eyes only made the blue more brilliant. And that scruff along his jaw added a manly appeal that most women would swoon over. "It's four in the afternoon. You were asleep?"

He smiled, a wicked, charming smile that produced those dimples. "My clientele prefers to be up in the evenings and at night."

Heat shot to her face, an embarrassed flush she couldn't seem to control. His clientele. And that's just what she would become if she went through with this nonsense. One of his women.

"Of course." She glanced around the room, so many people, so many eyes and ears. "Is there somewhere we can talk privately?"

He hesitated a brief moment, a small line of suspicion creasing that area between his brows. He looked leery, and she didn't realize until that moment that she worried he would refuse her.

"My room. You've got five minutes. I'm a busy man."

Busy indeed. She bit back her sarcastic reply. She was used to speaking her mind, even to John. It wasn't in her nature to be demure. But she'd try, if it would get her what she needed, if it got her Rodrick. "I did pay for thirty minutes."

He narrowed his eyes, as if he didn't believe her in the least. He'd met her only once; what did he know about her character? "You're lucky I wasn't with someone."

His words brought a wave of disgust roiling through her body, and something else…interest.

With a sigh, he raked his hand through his hair, the soft waves clinging to his fingers, and for one moment she remembered the feel of the strands…remembered those curls clinging to *her* fingers. So bloody beautiful. If he hadn't worked in a whorehouse, she would assume he was an archangel dropped on earth.

"Come along." He started toward the back stairs, a narrow set meant for servants to run up and down unseen…and for clients who didn't want to be noticed. Clients embarrassed and ashamed. Clients like…her.

Grace weaved around a butter churn and followed Alex up the steps. She pressed her gloved hands to the brick walls on either side, feeling suddenly dizzy. What the bloody hell was she doing? Insane! Her father was most likely rolling over in his grave. But Father was gone and John was an arse and someone had to save Patience and Mama. If this was the only way to make Rodrick notice her…

Undaunted, she moved onward. Still, each step up sent her heart pounding faster, blood soaring to her ears in a harsh roar. At the second floor Alex paused briefly. He glanced over his shoulder, as if to make sure she followed. Within an instant he'd turned again, but not quick enough that she didn't notice the bemusement in his gaze.

The look left her feeling odd, warm. Before she could decipher her reaction, he started down the dimly lit corridor. It was the same trail she'd followed when she'd arrived only two days ago thinking she was here to purchase a book. Right, left, then right until she was headed down the main hall. How impressed she'd been following that expensive carpet and those golden sconces.

When they'd led her to a room, she'd assumed it was a library of sorts. By the time her shock had worn off, they were gone, leaving her in a stranger's bedchamber. She'd tiptoed to the door, opening it and peeking out. No one had been there. As if the man who'd escorted her had disappeared. Only the soft lull of conversation and odd sounds of groans and moans had filtered down the hall. She'd thought perhaps someone was ill. How stupid she'd been. And then he'd appeared…Alex, a man too beautiful to be of this world, and she could barely think at all.

Yet even as she set foot into that carriage two days ago, at John's urging, she'd known she was risking her reputation, entering what she thought was some sort of hotel to visit with an unmarried man. But she was twenty-four, hardly in need of an escort. Besides, she'd always liked to think she was independent, bold, a risk taker. She'd had no idea how much of a risk she'd actually taken.

Hotel indeed. She could kill John. She should have been suspicious when the driver had dropped her off at the back door. And she sure as hell should have been suspicious at John's sudden interest in her. But no, naïve and trusting girl that she was. No wonder Lord Rodrick could think of her as nothing more than a sister.

But this man, this *Alex*, he didn't think of her as a sister. He'd made that quite clear just the other evening. Or was the passion of his kiss merely a pretense? How she wished she were experienced enough to know the difference. But then, if she were experienced, she wouldn't need to be here. She swallowed hard and peered at each closed door, wondering what lay beyond those rooms. Surely not every chamber held a couple in the throes of…

A soft moan whispered through a closed door. Ill people indeed. Grace sucked in a breath and her steps slowed. Gads, what was she doing? She couldn't…wouldn't…couldn't do what she'd planned.

"After you." At the end of the hall, he pushed a door wide.

When she hesitated, he didn't pressure her to enter, merely leaned against the doorjamb, his arms crossed, stretching his brilliant white shirt across his muscled chest. But it was his eyes that held her captive. They sparkled with mirth, as if he knew exactly what she felt, as if he could sense every nervous shiver that traveled over her skin. The war of propriety versus desperation raged in her mind. Lord save her, she didn't have many choices. At least that's what she told herself. But she knew…deep down… she knew that a part of her wanted to kiss his lips again, to know if the feelings she'd experienced under his touch had been real or something produced in her wild imagination.

She was four and twenty. She was worldly. If she wanted to kiss a man and experience the feelings of passion, who would stop her? With renewed determination, she swept into the room. It was as elegant as she remembered. She doubted the brothels men frequented were so clean.

The door shut with a soft thud, but it might as well have been a gunshot. Grace's courage sank with her stomach to the ground. He'd allowed her to leave last time, hadn't held her hostage. Would he be a gentleman now as well?

He paused in the middle of the room, watching her. "Well, what is it?"

She took in a deep, trembling breath. "I need you, Alex."

He grinned, a grin that sent those dimples to his cheeks. Her heart stuttered before bursting into a wild gallop. He was handsome. Merely handsome. Anyone would think so. Yet she'd seen men just as handsome before. Men who had flirted with her when her stepfather had been alive and they'd had money, so why did she react so to this man?

"I've heard that too often, Grace, to be shocked or pleased."

Her given name sounded odd and forbidden upon his lips. The lips of a stranger, really. Then again, how much of a stranger was he when she'd seen him naked? She and no doubt hundreds of other women.

He strolled across the carpet, his long and muscled legs tensing under tan trousers. "I'll need more detail."

He poured a glass of sherry and started toward her.

"I hate sherry," she blurted out.

He paused, looking at a loss for words, and that amused her when she should have been nervous. "Oh. Well, then. What's your choice?"

She lifted the netting of her bonnet. "Wine. Red."

He turned, making his way back to the sideboard. "Anything else?" His long fingers wrapped around a wine bottle. Like one addicted to opium, she realized with a start that she was addicted to him. Every tiny movement he made burst into focus, colors vivid, scents strong. She was completely and utterly aware of him.

She waved her hand dismissively. "No. Thank you."

Taking in a deep breath, she paced to the windows. The sun was making its descent. In the country they'd be settling to bed. In the city they'd be getting ready for a ball. Here, they were getting ready for...so much more. Heat spread uncomfortably through her body, taunting her already frayed nerves. Lord, she couldn't tell him what she wanted. She couldn't actually say the words.

She felt him move closer, pausing behind her so close she could feel his heat. Instead of feeling trapped, she had the odd urge to sink back into him. She spun around. Her harsh breath fanned across his neck. She couldn't tell him what she wanted, not while he was standing so close and looking down at her with those brilliant blue eyes, eyes that seemed to see into her very soul.

Biding time, she took the glass. Their fingers brushed, and fire shot up her arm. Startled, her gaze jumped to his. He didn't move, didn't say a word. Had he felt it? That heat, that intensity? Or perhaps he had some secret hold over women, knew what to do, to say, how to look at them so they felt wanted. She stepped back, needing distance, and turned toward the windows once more.

Before she lost her nerve, she blurted out, "I need an earl."

There was a short pause. "Sorry, can't help you there."

She turned to face him and, with one quick swig, downed her wine. Sweet, strong, bold, it gave her the courage she needed. "No, I…I need to marry one. For…money."

He quirked a brow. "Money?"

"No! I mean…" Gads, she was muddling this. "I love him."

"And you thought to come here?" He looked partly amused, partly incredulous.

She pressed her hand to her churning stomach and focused on the silver warming pan hanging next to the fireplace. She should have known better than to drink wine with an upset belly. It would be just the thing if she got sick all over him. He certainly wouldn't help her then.

"No, you don't understand. The man I wish to marry likes his women…experienced. If I want to attract his attention, I need to learn how."

He smirked as if amused with the upper crust's odd sensibilities. "Really?"

She nodded. "I want you to teach me how to seduce an earl."

* * *

The woman was insane. Bloody insane.

So why didn't he kindly escort her from his room?

Alex moved to the sideboard once more and poured himself a whiskey. Mostly to give himself time to think. She was turning him into a full-blown lush. Holy hell. One moment she was slapping him, the next she wanted him to teach her how to seduce. He downed the liquid, grimacing as it burned his throat.

What to do? If he turned down her offer, Lady Lavender would undoubtedly find out and hang him for losing business. Besides, he had a feeling Grace would merely find the next available man and that, for some odd reason, annoyed him. He poured another glass, ignoring the way his fingers trembled. Exhaustion. He hadn't gotten enough sleep. That was all.

He cleared his throat and turned toward her, the full glass still in hand. He had a feeling he'd need the fortitude in the coming moments. "What, exactly, do you want me to teach you?"

She looked confused. Her lips parted, then pressed tightly together. She shook her head, then folded her arms over her chest. That lovely pink tongue darted out to lick her top lip. "I…I…"

She hadn't a fucking clue. He rolled his eyes heavenward and downed the drink. The liquid burned a welcome path to his gut. His women were usually much more accommodating and much less confused.

"Kissing."

He coughed lightly, choking on the whiskey that remained on his tongue. "Kissing?"

She nodded so eagerly her straw bonnet tipped to the side, sitting at a haughty angle atop her head.

He set his glass deliberately on the table, staring at the top for one long moment, attempting to glean answers in the polished surface.

"Kissing." Anticipation hummed through his body. That long-forgotten sense of lust, of wondering what would come next, whispered through his mind. His life had fallen into a routine. A map planned out from where his lips would go to what murmured words of seduction he'd whisper. There were no surprises. But she surprised him.

Grace shifted closer, her sensible skirts swooshing over sensible black boots. "And…and touching."

His mind jumped to those skirts, those plain, green skirts that reminded him of early spring. He could almost hear the sound of rustling as he bunched the material up her smooth legs. And just the thought sent heat spiraling through his body. "Touching."

Dear God, he'd had only a hint of her lush form when he'd held her close. Full, soft breasts, narrow waist...what else lay beneath those thick skirts?

"But no...no actual..."

His gaze jerked to her face, interested in what she had to say when few things interested him lately.

She waved her hands about, like two nervous birds a'flight. "No intimacy."

He went cold. All the tease with no satisfaction. It figured. The one woman who for some ungodly reason he wanted didn't want him. Was it merely the chase? He slid a glance up and down her body. She was pretty, but it was a wholesome pretty...an innocence that called to him. There was something about her...layers upon layers of mystery...

She nodded, her face completely serious. "I need to know how to please a man. How to seduce a man. A...lord."

"I see." How to please a *man*.

A *man*. As if he wasn't one. As if he was nothing. And to most he probably was nothing. A vessel to be used. He tried to ignore those familiar feelings of worthlessness that swirled low in his gut, feelings he'd learned long ago to repress. He'd been important once. Now he was nothing.

"Kissing and touching," she added, those wide, innocent eyes belying the ridiculousness of her request.

Did she understand what she asked of him? Did she realize the repercussions of her actions? There could be nothing more than common attraction between them. If there was anything more, and he feared there would be, Lady Lavender would see him punished. Annoyed for some reason, he started intently toward her. "Kissing...touching."

He paused only a breath away, close, intimidating. Her shoulders lifted, as if she intended to shrink back, but then straightened, as if she was thinking better of it. Part of him wished she would leave, even if he had to deal with Lady Lavender's outrage. Another part of him...a small part he was trying to ignore... begged him to pull her close, to teach her whatever she wanted to know as long as she stayed...as long as she made him forget his life for one brief moment.

She trembled, but her gaze remained locked to his. Brave girl. She had something to do and no one would stand in her way. Reluctantly, he admired her for that. "It's not easy, you know." He reached out, boldly cupping the side of her face, the skin warm and smooth against his palm. She flinched.

He sighed. Dear God, he had a lot of work to do. "It will cost you."

She looked down, an enchanting flush flooding her high cheekbones. "Of course. I've already paid for this evening."

He frowned as guilt worked bitterly in his gut. Why, for the first time in years, did it bother him to speak of money and sex in the same breath? It was a business. She was willing to pay. He could do no less than charge her; hell, he was expected to charge her.

But he didn't want her to pay. He wanted...he wanted to be able to touch her, touch *someone*, just once, of his own free will.

"Touching first then?" she whispered, raising her hopeful gaze. Her breath was a warm caress against the inside of his wrist, a promise of what was to come.

"Yes," he said just as softly. "Touching."

They merely stared at each other for one long moment. And in her hazel eyes he tried to understand the truth. Why did he want her so? Why did his entire body ache with the need to kiss her? Make love to her? Perhaps because she had red hair. Or perhaps because she smelled of fresh air, warmth, and innocence. Or perhaps because she made him *feel*.

Slowly he trailed his fingers down her face, following the gentle slope of her jaw to the delicate curve of her neck. He played with the satiny green ribbons that tied her bonnet in place before pulling the bow free. He lifted the straw hat and settled it on the side table. In the light from the setting sun the red in her hair caught fire. He hesitated only a moment, then allowed his fingers to move over those silky strands, just barely touching her halo of hair.

"A simple touch can light the desire within until it's almost unbearable."

"Surely not," she said.

He smiled at her naïveté, at the vulnerability that tainted her words.

"Surely. For instance…" He took her hand in his and pulled the white glove from her fingertips, one by one. The glove dropped to the tabletop, leaving her hand bare. Pale, delicate. Fine lines crossed her palm, lines that could tell the future, according to some. How he wanted to know what those lines meant.

"My hand pressed to yours is intimate, perhaps." He watched her through his lashes, judging her reaction.

She didn't move. Barely looked as if she breathed.

He slipped his fingers through hers. She stared as if she'd never held hands with someone. Perhaps she hadn't. Perhaps they weren't so different after all. It was an intimate gesture between couples. A gesture done out of love and compassion. Something he hadn't experienced and probably never would.

He cleared his throat. "But for a man of experience, hand holding is something for milkmaids."

"I see."

But of course she didn't see. The woman was as innocent as they came. And by the tremble of her body, she was bloody nervous. Where had his charm gone? Usually by now he'd have a woman's dress undone and she'd be panting underneath him. But with Grace, for some reason he was in no rush. He wanted to savor the moment.

"If you take a man's hand," he started, "and gently stroke the palm…" Slowly he drew his finger over the hollow of her sensitive skin. Her pulse beat fast in her wrist, the blue veins under her skin delicate cobwebs that showed her aristocracy. "Or if you draw your fingers along the outside of his, as if you're a child tracing a hand on parchment…" He drew his finger over the tip of her thumb, down to that secret curve and slowly back up over her finger.

Her nostrils flared as she sucked in a slight breath, so slight that many might have missed it. But he hadn't. No, he couldn't seem to look away. He wanted to notice every detail, memorize the way her pupils flared, the way her lips parted, the way her lashes fluttered rapidly.

"Better yet…" Cradling the back of her hand in his palm, he brushed his thumb across her wrist, seeing how far he could push her. She jumped, the touch too intimate, the skin too sensitive. "The inside of the wrists…"

She pulled her arm away, holding her hand close to her chest as if she'd been injured…wounded. "Wonderful, thank you. I think I've learned enough." She snatched up her bonnet, preparing to flee. Hell, if a simple touch could make her so uneasy, she didn't stand a chance of winning her earl. Her footsteps were hurried as she started toward the door. Coward. He'd made her feel, and she wasn't used to such emotion.

"We're not done."

She looked back at him, helplessness shining in her eyes. She was going to run, and if she did, he doubted she'd ever return. He curled his fingers, the imprint of her hand still tingling unspoken upon his palm. *Let her go…Let her go…*

"You want to win your earl, don't you?" He didn't give her time to respond. "Now, even when at a ball, there are things you can do to encourage affection. For instance, you can place your hand on the back of a gentleman's body without notice." He stepped toward her and slid his arm around her waist. His heart beat frantically as he waited to see if she'd rebuff his advances or stay. He prayed she'd stay.

She stared up at him with wide, unblinking eyes, her mind twirling with thoughts that clouded her hazel gaze.

He rested his hand on her lower back, right where her vertebrae dipped deliciously into her bottom. She stiffened under his touch but didn't move. "And with your back to a wall, you could go lower…" His palm traveled the dip of her back slowly, over the bustle of her gown, the material crinkling with the movement.

She jumped away and suddenly he was alone once more. Blast it!

Without pause, she scurried toward the door. "Wonderful, I think I've had enough for now."

The thought of her leaving annoyed him, made him frantic almost. "Nonsense. Sit."

His voice came out harsher than he'd intended. She froze at the door. For a moment he thought she would refuse. For a moment he couldn't breathe.

Then slowly, God help her, she turned.

Chapter 5

She didn't say a word, merely stared at him. And although her face remained passive, void of smirk or frown, her eyes...her eyes spoke of everything. Weariness, nervousness, and something that made his gut clench...desire. She wanted him; she just didn't realize it yet.

Her fingers curled into her skirts, bunching the material. Even if they didn't make love, if she kept wrinkling her gown, others would think they had.

"You do not frighten me," she lied.

He didn't know whether to laugh or sigh in exasperation. Never had he met a woman so ridiculous, so brave, so stubborn. She hesitated only a moment, then thrust her shoulders back and, with renewed determination, made her way toward him. Those lush lips pressed into a firm line. She looked like a soldier marching to war instead of a woman about to be pleasured.

Elegantly, determinedly, she sank into the chair keeping her back perfectly straight. Instead of annoyed or even amused, Alex felt oddly relieved.

He'd spent the night dreaming of her, when he rarely dreamt. Having her here now was like opium to his craving body. He pulled a chair next to hers. If she meant to ignore him, she'd learn her lesson soon enough. Fate had thrown her in his path, had tormented him with thoughts of her lush body. He would not be tortured alone. No, she was in this with him whether she wanted to be or not.

He settled back in his chair, his thigh pressing intimately against her. A warm fire crackled in the hearth, highlighting the soft planes of her face and kissing her with a golden glow. She looked ethereal, almost untouchable, and he felt guilty for even thinking about seducing her.

He cleared his throat and his mind of lustful thoughts. "If you're at a dinner…"

She scooted as far away from him as her chair would allow. "Have you been to many?" she asked, as if trying to draw his attention away from the fact that she was inching toward escape.

He fought his smile as he rested his arm along the back of her chair, his fingers hovering close to her silky strands. He meant to tease her, but instead he merely tormented himself with her nearness. How desperately he wanted to stroke her hair. To pull those curls down from the confining pins and see those lustrous auburn waves cascade around her porcelain face. Lord, she had no idea what she was capable of.

"Alex?"

He blinked away his fantasy. "What?"

She tilted her head endearingly to the side and studied him through narrowed, suspicious eyes. "Dinners. Are you…invited to many?"

He smiled fleetingly and looked away. "You'd be surprised." Although James had always been able to escort Lady Lavender outside the walls of the estate, it was only recently that Alex had been chosen. The woman was finally starting to trust him, and he would use that to his advantage when the time was right.

"Oh," Grace whispered.

Did she realize her eyes showed her every thought? If she was truly in love with her earl, the man would be blind not to know. Her mind was spinning. She was wondering what sort of dinner parties he attended. With whom? Who would possibly allow a man like him to enter their home?

"She...she allows you to leave the place then?" A flush spread up her neck. "I noticed the men keeping watch."

Startled from the moment, he looked away, pulling back from her. It annoyed him that she realized he was in no more than a prison, helpless as an infant. "We mostly visit gaming hells." Where they were closely guarded. But he didn't want to talk about his lack of freedom. "Now, if you're at a dinner party with a tablecloth hiding all from view, it's amazing what one can accomplish."

Her lips pressed together, pursed in confusion. "Such as?"

"Such as..." Lord, he was going to find perverse pleasure in the next few moments. He boldly settled his hand on her knee. She jumped, sucking in a sharp breath as if she'd been hit by lightning. Truth was if he wanted he could have her on her back, panting underneath him. He certainly knew how to seduce a woman. Yet...yet it didn't feel right for some odd reason.

"A soft touch on the knee, or..." He drew his hand up her thigh and the warm tendrils of lust swirled through his body. The material underhand crinkled, bunching, lifting to reveal her trim ankles clad in...red stockings? He paused, surprised.

Her breath came out in sharp, short pants, drawing his attention back to her face. "I don't think that's appropriate..." She pushed his hand away and smoothed her skirts down, hiding those brilliant stockings from view.

Scarlet-red stockings. How very particular she was, and for some reason, he liked that about her. "Appropriate? My dear, nothing here is appropriate. Give me your foot."

Her eyes went wide. She looked as if he'd just asked for her virginity. "Pardon?"

"I'm not asking for your firstborn. Your foot." He held out his hand, waiting patiently, for he knew she'd be too curious to refuse.

"No thank you."

He almost started laughing. "No thank you?"

He was done being charming. Charming didn't work with Grace, thank God. No more pretense. He reached down and, before she could even guess his intentions, wrapped his fingers around her ankle. He pulled her foot upward and spun her around so she faced him. Grace tumbled back into the chair, her mouth falling open. "What are you doing?"

He settled her foot in his lap and started untying the boot laces. "Teaching you, of course. As you asked."

"I hardly see what feet have to do with seduction," she snapped, attempting to pull away.

He grasped her ankle firmly in his hand and chuckled. "Of course you don't. But you'll see soon enough." He pulled the boot from her foot and stared at that red stocking. It had little black flowers embroidered down the sides, curving over the swell of her calf. Wicked little flowers that taunted him. He wanted to make love to her while she was wearing those exotic stockings, and only the stockings.

"What are you staring at?" she demanded, sounding rather put out.

"Red. Like your hair." He smiled, amused for some reason. "It's rather bold of you."

"No one sees my stockings." She was frantically clawing at her skirts, attempting to hide the piece of finery, hide her true personality. "And my hair is far from red, thank you very much. It's brown. Plain brown."

He tilted his head, watching her for one long moment until she finally sensed his attention and paused in her mad dash to secure her modesty. "You, my dear, are an anarchist."

Her face flushed. "Am not!"

He drew his hand up her calf, his fingers dancing over the flowers. He didn't look at her, but he could hear her breath come out faster the closer to her knee he traveled. "You are. You pretend to be good, don't you? But you refuse to conform."

His fingers paused at her knee. There, just visible beneath the hem of her skirt, was a black garter and a brief flash of pale, smooth thigh. He'd seen hundreds of garters and hundreds of smooth thighs. Still, for one breathless moment Alex felt as if he'd been punched in the gut.

She slapped his hand away, jerking him from his thoughts. "They are merely red stockings. You presume too much, sir."

He settled back in his chair, she settled back in hers, two pugilists returning to their corners. They just stared at each other, her foot still resting in his lap. He was pushing her too far, too soon. Yet couldn't seem to stop.

"To pretend to know me is not only arrogant, it's…"

He pressed his thumbs into the arch of her foot, rubbing, kneading.

"It's…" She swallowed hard, her face relaxing into soft planes. "Oh my, that does feel good."

He fought his grin. She looked like a cat ready to curl up and purr. The outside world faded and there remained only the two of them. He could almost imagine a life this way, another life, another time, if he hadn't left his family. "You were saying?"

She looked up at him with drowsy eyes. "Hmm?"

"Something about my arrogance?"

He released his hold; she sat there glaring at him as if it was his fault she'd lost her thoughts. "You may place your foot on the floor now."

"What?" She glanced at his lap where her foot nestled intimately against his thighs. "Oh." Red slashed across her high cheekbones. She jumped away, placing both feet firmly to the floor, her toes curling into the carpet.

"If you wish to truly be bold, you might leave your bloomers at home." He couldn't quite help himself.

She looked away. "Don't be ridiculous."

He resisted the urge to grin. "Now, you wear slippers to dinner?"

She nodded. "Yes, of course."

"Easy to slip off and on."

She slid him a sidelong, suspicious glance. "I suppose I agree."

"No, you don't, but you will." He rested his hand on her knee. Startled, she gasped.

He moved her skirt higher and his fingertips grazed her thigh, there, where the stocking ended and pure skin began. Tiny bumps rose on the skin of her thigh, shivering from his touch. Her body was warm, but he was warmer. He had to resist the urge to shift, resist the urge to tug at the collar of his shirt. Damn, but he never should have kissed her. He never would have known how a kiss could be.

She took her plump lower lip between her teeth and stared at his hand. She didn't move, didn't seem to breathe. He was getting ahead of himself, losing control when he was always in control. He released her thigh, curling his hand and resting it at his side. His fingertips tingled.

"Lightly rest your foot atop of mine."

Her gaze flashed with bewilderment. "That's the oddest request I've ever had. Why?"

He chuckled, her honesty relieving some of the tension he felt. "Do you wish to learn to seduce or not?"

She clutched the edge of her seat, pausing a moment. Lord, she was stubborn. But oddly, he liked that about her. He'd gone too many years with women doing exactly as he asked in the bed-chamber. It was bloody nice to have someone not leap to his bidding. At the same time, he wanted her, wanted her to trust him, to touch him. And so he waited, his breath held. Finally she inched her foot toward his polished shoe. He barely felt the weight, yet the touch sent a whisper of heat swirling up his leg.

She sighed. "Fine. If it will land me my earl."

Her words were like a cold dagger slid between his ribs. Her earl. How Alex hated this earl. Hated the man for not having enough sense to know that Grace was a catch without having to do this. But mostly he hated the man because he knew that eventually he would realize how much Grace had to offer. And then…and then Grace would stop coming and he'd go numb again.

"Lovely," he said through gritted teeth. "Now draw it upward."

She frowned. "I don't understand."

"Your foot." He raked his fingers through his hair, his patience wearing thin. "Slowly slide your toes under the cuff of my trousers."

She laughed a throaty chuckle that burst from her full lips. "You can't be serious." She thought to laugh at him? His annoyance flared. So sure she knew everything, but the bedchamber was the one place she was clueless.

He leaned closer to her. "I'm very serious."

Her warm breath fanned across his mouth, tempting, taunting. For one insane moment he thought of pressing his lips to hers, of sweeping his tongue inside her mouth in a demanding kiss. She didn't flinch at his nearness, but keeping her gaze locked to his, she slowly slid her toes under his cuff.

"There." He smirked. "Was that so difficult?"

She looked bemused. "Truly, that excites a man?"

"Yes, it—"

With a daring quirk of her brow, she wiggled those toes, inching them up the muscle of his calf. Heat shot through his body, coiling tightly around his groin. His fingers bit into the arms of the chair.

The minx watched him intently, as if she were a scientist and he her experiment. "How's that?"

"Yes," he managed in a strangled whisper. Dear God, he needed to look away, focus on something else, but all he could focus on were her warm toes, sliding seductively down his leg.

"And this..." She rested her hand on his thigh, her eyes sparkling with mischief. His cock hardened, pressing painfully against his trousers. Alex jumped to his feet, turning his back to her. Somehow, at some point, he'd lost control. This wouldn't do. Wouldn't do at all.

"Yes. That's fine." His voice came out harsh.

"I'm sorry," she said, shoving her foot into her boot and standing. "Did I do something wrong?"

"No." He turned toward her with that charming smile, even though his chest was so tight he felt as if someone was squeezing his heart. "It's just that I have another appointment." It was a lie, but she didn't need to know that. He needed time alone. Time to regain control of his emotions. Regain control of his cock.

Her brows drew together, her eyes losing that sparkle of success, and damn if he didn't feel guilty for taking away her merriment. "Of course."

She picked up her bonnet, but paused, staring at the brim, waiting, as if she had something more to say. "I...I..."

For some reason he didn't want to know what words she sputtered to produce. He already thought too much of her. He didn't need her words of thanks or praise or, God forbid, rejection. He rushed forward, taking the bonnet from her hands. "Tuesday, five?"

She hesitated, then finally nodded.

He settled the bonnet atop her head, covering that brilliant hair. With deft fingers he tied the strings and pulled the netting over her face, obscuring her features, believing if he couldn't see her eyes clearly, he'd be able to think again.

"I...Thank you, Alex. That was quite informative."

He didn't respond, merely grasped her elbow and led her toward the door, his other hand resting on the small of her back. What the hell was he getting into? He couldn't seem to breathe, to think when she was near. Damn, but the woman made him forget, made him believe, made him hope, and if there was one thing he'd learned, it was never to let hope rule your life. He opened the door and there stood James, fist poised as if to knock.

"So sorry," he muttered, glancing at Grace. "I didn't realize you were with someone."

"I'm not." He gently pushed Grace into the hall, practically into James. The man skittered to the side as Grace spun around to face him. "James, you don't mind escorting her out back, do you? Thank you."

"Umm, no, of course not." James nodded reluctantly.

As Grace started to follow James, Alex felt as if she was slowly ripping the lungs from his chest. It was as if his very being was tethered to her. For some insane reason, he couldn't let her go without one last word, one last promise. He grasped her upper arm, drawing her back, close enough so that James could not overhear. She turned toward him, her eyes wide with surprise.

His lips brushed the shell of her ear, so close his breath made the fine net covering her face quiver. "Tuesday…kissing."

* * *

He shut the door in her face. Shut the door. In her face.

Unsure if she should be shocked more by his words or his actions, Grace merely stood there for one long moment. *Tuesday… kissing.*

The words whispered seductively through her mind. A delicious shiver ran the length of her body. Annoyed and confused, she lifted her fist, intending to knock, but like the coward she'd suddenly become, thought better of it. What if he rejected her? What if he pulled her inside and pressed his mouth to hers then and there? Of course that was the point of her visit, to learn to kiss…wasn't it?

How very odd he was! How very odd he made her feel. Warm. Achy. Confused. So many emotions spun around in her mind that she felt a headache forming. Yes, she was much better off with someone like Rodrick. Someone kind, someone dull...No! Not dull, but merely *dependable.*

"My dear?" Her escort had paused in the middle of the hall. His young face and large green eyes bespoke only sincerity and innocence, the complete opposite of Alex's charming smirk. How strange that he should work here.

And Alex...well, Alex was wicked underneath that angelic smile. There was no other explanation for the way he made her feel, the way he could make her entire being come to life. But this man, he seemed too boyish to belong at a brothel.

He smiled at her, a crooked smile that was more endearing than seductive. "I'm James."

She nodded; it was all she could manage at the moment. He was supposed to escort her outside. Yet she couldn't seem to move. Her legs had grown wooden. The world stood still, waiting for her next movement. Her time with Alex didn't seem over. She had too many questions...about him, about how he'd made her feel.

As if sensing her reluctance, James rested his hand on her elbow, a gentle touch, and started forward, leading her down the hall. But she was barely aware of his presence. She glanced back at Alex's door as if the wooden panel might provide answers.

A mere brush of his fingers on the pulse of her wrist and she'd practically melted like beeswax left in the sun. She wasn't sure how she felt. But one thing was certain...she *felt.* After hearing women praise that magical feeling of passion, she'd begun to think there was something wrong with her. Finally she understood. She understood lust. Sin. Desire. She was attracted to Rodrick, there was no doubt. And now, knowing how a simple kiss could feel so intense and amazing, she certainly wouldn't be nervous about touching the earl. In fact, she'd welcome his smiles, his gaze, his body. Yet why did she worry she'd think of Alex while Rodrick's lips were pressed to hers?

She paused, resting her hand to her beating heart. Why Alex? Why now? Why him, of all people? And why the hell had she ever agreed to this ridiculousness?

"My lady?" James was watching her, his green eyes filled with concern.

She pressed her fingers to her temples. "I'm sorry. I'm..."

Voices filtered from behind a closed door ahead. Murmured conversation coming closer. Grace jerked away from James. Was that feminine tone familiar? No. Certainly not. She was merely cautious. So why couldn't she prevent the bitter taste of panic from flooding her mouth? A door opened. The thought of being seen terrified her.

"I must hide!" Grace dove behind a tall statue of an embracing couple. James merely stood in the middle of the hall watching her as if she was playing some childish game he didn't understand.

Frantically she waved to him.

With a sigh, he sauntered to her side, kneeling behind her. "Is there a reason we're hiding?" he whispered, his breath tickling the back of her neck.

"I think I recognize that voice." Surely she was mistaken. No one she knew would be here. She stood on tiptoe and peeked between two marble arms. A couple twirled from a room, holding tightly to each other, twirling so fast and holding so tightly that she could barely tell man from woman.

"You do know what I like, don't you, darling?" the woman whispered seductively.

The man replied something too low to hear. He stopped and pressed the woman to the wall, her face finally visible.

Grace blanched. "Dear Lord," she whispered, unable to stop herself.

She knew the woman well. Lady Maxwell had had tea with her mother many times before Mama had grown too ill. Lady Maxwell, a woman praised for her high morals...a woman married for fifteen years now. And she was...*here*? The young man pressed his mouth to hers in a searing kiss that sent a blush to Grace's cheeks and made her think of Alex. While his hands, his hands were moving down her hips to her thighs. His fingers curled, bunching the blue material and lifting Lady Maxwell's skirts higher…higher…

Grace sucked in a breath and crouched lower, attempting to ignore the dull ache that burned in the pit of her belly. Embarrassment, shame, and what else?

"Come." James reached up behind him, wrapping slender fingers around the porcelain handle of some unmarked door.

She nodded frantically and took his offered hand.

Inside the safety of the room, she could finally breathe again.

"We can wait in here until they leave." Softly James shut the door. "No one will bother us."

Of course not, because they'd think they were involved in some torrid affair in a bedchamber made for that sort of thing. Grace glanced around the beautiful room where no expense was spared on comfort. It would seem like a typical chamber if not for the painting of a naked man and woman embracing above the fireplace. The man's hands covered the woman's breasts and her face…Grace tilted her head to the side, getting a better view. The woman's face radiated pure bliss. She jerked her attention away and focused on the papered walls, the only safe thing in the room.

Grace lifted the netting covering her face. James was watching her. She could feel the force of his gaze piercing her back. And why wouldn't he watch her? She was acting like a mad fool. Hiding behind statues like a child. Cowering in a bedchamber. She clasped her hands together, one bare, one covered with a glove. She realized with a sigh that she'd forgotten her other glove in Alex's room. Even though they were her best gloves, she didn't dare return for it.

How long would Lady Maxwell be in the hallway? Surely they wouldn't actually be intimate in the corridor where anyone could see. She turned her back to James and paced to the windows. The sun was a brilliant orange ball hovering on the horizon. The drive to her townhome took a good hour and Mama would worry.

"You're a client?" James asked.

Grace spun around to face him. "No!" Heat shot to her face. "I mean…maybe…no. I don't know." She covered her face with her hands and sank onto a wing back chair covered in a sinful red material.

"You're deciding if you're a client?"

She nodded, feeling miserably embarrassed. She was an academic. She was worldly. She was…a bloody idiot.

"And you're with Alex?"

She nodded again, settling her clasped hands in her lap and peeking up at him through her lashes. Why she cared about his opinion, she wasn't sure. But that blasted sincere and honest face begged to be trusted.

He watched her, merely watched, with no judgment upon his handsome features. "Do you desire someone new?"

"What?" The thought shocked her, repulsed her in some way.

"You don't seem happy with the situation. I'd be willing to talk to Lady Lavender. I'm sure we could find someone who would please you."

Please her? She truly could not be having this conversation. Oh, why wouldn't the floor open and swallow her whole?

"Lady Lavender?" she managed in a strangled whisper.

James nodded, frowning. "She is the woman who runs the brothel, and if there is a problem, she must know."

She surged to her feet, feeling suddenly annoyed. "No! Alex is…he…pleases me." Had she really just said those words? Blast, but she'd felt the sudden need to defend the man.

"I see," James said, but the way he said it made her bristle, as if he'd read the dishonesty in her words. Fortunately, he didn't argue. He merely paced to the windows, crossing his arms over his chest and looking outside.

"He does. He's…he's kind, charming." Now she was overdoing it a tad. Lord, she didn't know what Alex was, did she? She didn't even know the man's last name. She knew very little about the ridiculous situation she suddenly found herself in. "James, do you have a surname?"

"Just James."

Like "*just Alex*." As if they didn't deserve a surname. Or perhaps they didn't want one. James seemed suddenly melancholy, and for some reason she felt as if it was her fault. What was he thinking to produce such a morose look upon his face?

"How?" she whispered. "How did you fall into this position?" It was a personal question, too personal, yet he didn't seem offended. Then again, surely he'd been asked it before.

He turned, giving her that crooked smile. "Luck, perhaps."

She stiffened, confused by his answer. Had she misheard him? "Luck? I'd think you'd wish to be anywhere but here." She was being blunt, but this new world went against everything she understood.

He laughed, a wry chuckle that lacked humor. "My lady, my family was starving, my mother and sister near death. When Lady Lavender took me in, she also took in my family, in a way." He paused by the small window, the setting sun highlighting his handsome face. He looked so sure, so positive he was right in his beliefs that she didn't dare argue. "They would have died, my sister would have sold…"

Sold herself like a whore. She wanted to ask him why it was better that he sell himself, but knew she was getting dangerously close to asking too many intimate questions. "And Alex?" she continued, unable to stop herself.

He paused, his body went stiff, his face guarded. He seemed almost defensive. "What about him?" Did he not wish to discuss his friend's personal life, or did he not wish to discuss Alex at all?

"Why is he here?"

His smiled turned tight. "That's something you'll have to ask him."

They weren't friends then. That was obvious. Did Alex have any friends? The thought of him here, alone, made her suddenly melancholy. Yet he wasn't alone, was he? No, he had plenty of women to keep him company. "I'm sorry. I shouldn't have asked."

"No. It's fine. I'm merely…not quite sure." He paced across the small room, growing flustered and restless, his hands raking through his hair, then settling on his hips, only to cross over his chest as if he was trying to figure something out. She'd upset him, but why?

"We were brought here together, you know, me, Gideon, and Alex."

Of course she hadn't known. She barely knew anything about Alex. The only thing she knew about this Gideon was that he was the man who received the experienced women. Isn't that what Alex had said that first day when he'd nearly sent her to the man?

James cast her an intense glance. "You want to know about Alex?"

She paused for one long moment. Did she? Knowing about Alex would make him more…human. She'd care, damn it all. Yet she couldn't seem to stop herself from nodding.

"Alex is…is…charming."

She knew that. Of course Alex was charming. She only had to look at him to know. His smile, those lovely dimples, those sparkling blue eyes. That mouth…

"But…"

She stiffened, waiting.

"Just…" James's face softened, as if he was talking to a child. "Be careful. Alex isn't who you think he is."

A shiver of unease caressed her skin. A warning.

He smiled, as if to gentle his response. But it was too late; he'd already piqued her unease. "There are women…certain women…

who…are more innocent than others. Women who…might take these times and hold them close to their hearts."

Women? In other words, her? "What are you saying?"

He sighed. "Women who might take these times with their men and think they are more than merely a pleasurable experience." He paused for a long, dramatic moment. "Don't make the mistake of thinking Alex is in love with you."

An unnatural silence stretched before them. A long, pregnant silence that left her horrified and embarrassed. She realized as the words sank bitterly cold into her gut that he was waiting for her response. Love…with Alex? Of course she wouldn't…wasn't.

"I…I wouldn't." She released a shaky laugh. "I'm not in love with Alex. I barely know him!"

He smiled briefly. "Of course." He was finished with the conversation, yet she wasn't. No. The words still stung, still swirled through her head like an annoying gnat.

Don't make the mistake of thinking Alex is in love with you.

Alex didn't love, he merely pleasured…many.

James strolled unhurried to the door, leaving her frozen in the middle of the room. He paused, listening, then turned toward her. "They're gone now. Shall I escort you to your carriage?"

But odd thoughts and unfamiliar emotions kept her still. She would never fall in love with Alex and felt the need to defend herself. But would he think she protested too much?

In love…with a whore? Ridiculous!

Finally, slowly, she nodded and started toward the door, her legs stiff with reluctance. She didn't love Alex. She barely liked him. She was in a brothel, for God's sake, risking her reputation because she was in love with Rodrick.

So why in the world did going home suddenly feel so depressing?

Chapter 6

"Just think, Gracie, if we could find the treasure, we'd be rich."

Patience did a little skip on the footpath beside her. Completely inappropriate for her age. She garnered more than one passing stare. Grace bit her tongue to keep from reprimanding her sister. Patience needed to learn to rein in her excitement while in public. But at least the girl was wearing a dress. Patience was merely too lively for the London *ton*.

Grace worried about her. How would society react when her sister emerged? She didn't want Patience's feelings to be crushed because of the gossip and remarks of insensitive old biddies. But she feared that's what would happen when her sister made her debut. Then again, they might not have the money for a debut at all. Lord, at this rate they'd be forced to sell the carriage.

"Patience, please be…patient." She grinned at her own pun, finding amusement for the first time in two days. How could she be amused with James's dour warning ringing through her head?

Don't trust him. Why? Why couldn't she trust Alex? Sure, he could charm the habit from a nun, but he seemed harmless enough.

"Why not?" Patience asked, interrupting her thoughts. "You always say to think positive."

Treasure. Her sister was discussing buried treasure. "True." But the day was fine, too fine to worry about nonsensical treasures and their lack of money.

"Lady Maxwell called upon Mama yesterday when you were out."

"Really?" She hadn't seen the woman in months, and now, suddenly, she appears right after Grace had seen her at Lady Lavender's? Gads, perhaps James hadn't hidden her as well as she'd thought. Had the woman seen her? Grace rested her hands on her roiling belly. It was too risky, this business of learning to seduce. Perhaps it would be better if she didn't return.

Patience nodded thoughtfully. "Rather kind, considering most of Mama's acquaintances have abandoned her, afraid of catching her disease. And Lady Maxwell is so kind. The epitome of appropriateness, Mama calls her. I think she's praying the woman will rub off on me." Patience grinned up at Grace, but Grace was too lost in her own musings to respond with more than a vague nod.

Righteousness fought with guilt. How many horrible thoughts had she had about Lady Maxwell since seeing her at Lady Lavender's? A woman married but obviously engaging in an illicit affair. It was…wrong, immoral. But what Patience said was true; the woman was kind, always had been.

Grace frowned, her gaze sliding from passing couple to passing couple. Some familiar, some not, all finding their way down Regent Street. What did these people do in the privacy of their homes when no one was watching? What were their secrets?

Such exalted perfection—or so she'd thought. Now she couldn't help but wonder what they were hiding. If a woman like Lady Maxwell could be caught in such a nefarious position, what were others doing? The entire world seemed to be off-balance, as if she didn't truly know anything anymore. Up was suddenly down. Wrong suddenly right. Grace reached under her straw bonnet and rubbed her aching temples.

"Don't you agree?" Patience was looking up at her expectantly. Realizing Grace was lost in thought, she frowned. "You're not paying the least bit of attention to me, are you?"

"I'm sorry, my dear. You were saying something about treasure?"

Patience nodded eagerly. *Treasure.* Grace resisted the urge to scoff. Is this what she'd done, taught her sister that life would be well if only one could believe in ridiculous thoughts of fairy tales and buried treasures?

A few months ago, the idea of searching for treasure had been her passion. It had started when she was a child. The perfect shell. A rare rock or mineral to add to her collection. As she grew older, her interests went to artifacts from ancient cultures.

It was thrilling to know she'd found something no one else had. She'd brought to life something forgotten, ignored, buried for dead. Each piece was like a long lost friend, something that could never be taken away from her. Although her father had died, and although they'd had to move near London when Mama remarried, her collection had remained intact. A collection no one else had, which made her feel special, she supposed.

Now the idea of wasting time and money searching for treasure seemed ridiculous. She had more important things to worry about, like seeing her mother and sister fed. She'd already sold most of their valuables. How much dare she tell Patience about their finances? Her sister wasn't an idiot; surely she knew something was wrong. But what if she slipped and told Mama? Still, wasn't it better that Patience heard the news from Grace rather than John?

Grace paused there, amongst the crowds rushing up and down the footpath, stirring dust into the air, and rested her hand on Patience's forearm. "There's something…"

But Patience's gaze shifted to some point beyond Grace's shoulder. "Oh my."

Grace glanced back. "What is it?" She saw nothing out of the ordinary in the many people strolling the streets or the fancy carriages rolling down the lane.

"Lady Lavender!"

Grace's mouth fell open. "Where?" Realizing the importance of her little sister's words, she snapped her head toward Patience. "How do you know the woman?"

"Everyone knows about her. Don't tell me you don't!"

Grace latched on to her sister's hand and dragged her toward the front of a sweetshop, pressing her back between two dark beams of Tudor style. How many days had she spent wondering what this mysterious woman looked like? She'd only dealt with secretaries and servants. "Tell me everything, right now."

Patience shrugged, shifting uncomfortably. "Was merely something I'd heard. She's a woman...who owns a brothel. One meant only for women." Her brows lifted, her excitement almost palpable. "It's quite daring, don't you think? A place for women to find the passion they might be missing in the bedchamber?"

Grace resisted the urge to groan. Her sister was placing the woman on a pedestal and, even worse, discussing passion and bedchambers? "She is not daring! She's nothing more than a...a prison keeper."

Patience flushed, looking away, but Grace could tell her sister thought she was being the prude. "Where was she? Where did you see her?"

"It had to be her, I think." Patience turned her head, peering past the many storefronts. "It *must* have been her. She was wearing pale lavender; she always wears the color, you know. So no one else would dare, in fear of being associated with her."

"Yes, I know," Grace mumbled, even though she didn't. She didn't know anything of the woman. How dare her little sister know more about Lady Lavender than she. Flustered, Grace started down the footpath, dragging Patience along.

"She disappeared into the shop just ahead. And she has ice-blonde hair, a petite woman." She was panting, attempting to run along with Grace's fast pace. "And…" Deep breath. "And…" Another deep breath. "She is always escorted by men."

Grace froze. Patience ran into her back.

"Beautiful men," Patience mumbled into her shoulder.

Beautiful men? Grace spun around, her skirts flaring wide. "Did you see men with her just now?"

She nodded. Slowly Grace turned and peered into the shop. A familiar antiquities shop that she'd visited a few times before. Statues, art, artifacts, and jewelry crowded the shelves inside. Usually she'd have her face pressed to the dusty window looking for objects to add to her collection. Now she searched for an entirely new obsession. Was Alex with Lady Lavender? She could see a small group just beyond the shelves, but couldn't decipher one face from another. She stood on tiptoe, pressing her fingers to the cool glass and attempting to get a better look.

"A dark-haired man," she murmured. "Did you see a dark-haired man?"

Patience stepped closer to her, peering through the same window. "Not sure. Why?" And thank heaven, just as soon as she asked the question, she jumped to another. "Do you really think it's her?"

The group disappeared behind a shelf. *Blast!* Grace's fingers curled against the glass and she dropped to the flats of her boots. Her heart slammed erratically against her rib cage. Perhaps she'd had too much sunshine. Perhaps she should leave and they could continue on their way home. Yes, it would be best, yet her feet wouldn't seem to turn.

"I believe that's her carriage," Patience whispered.

Grace glanced over her shoulder. A fine carriage waited on the street. Two tall, broad-shouldered men stood silently by, watching them curiously. Obviously guards, but guarding what?

Grace took her lower lip between her teeth. She'd never met the infamous Lady Lavender. Had never even seen the woman. What did she look like? What hold did she have over these men?

Before she had time to regret her decision, Grace latched on to Patience's hand and pulled her toward that rounded wooden door.

"Where are we going?"

"I…I want to see if I can sell my brooch." True enough, she'd already sold her ring; why not the others? It was the least sentimental of her pieces, given to her by a wealthy friend long ago. A friend she'd lost contact with. She pressed her hand to her chest, feeling the weight of the pin.

"Why?"

Grace sighed, annoyed. Why must Patience question everything? "Because…because we'll need the money if we want to go treasure hunting, and we certainly can't ask John for coins, knowing how he'll scoff at our ideas." She wrapped her hand around the large iron bar and pulled open the door. A bell jingled their arrival, but no one swept forward to meet them. The front of the shop was wonderfully empty of people, if not objects. Shelves were lined with oddities, which usually would have had her panting, but now were barely given a glance.

"But you said Mr. Baskov never gave a fair price on objects," Patience whispered.

Blast, her sister would have to remember. "Yes," she muttered, ducking behind a shelf of Chinese vases, "but everyone deserves a second chance." Grace gently pushed two vases apart. A man with dark hair blocked her view. From the fine suit and lovely build, he must have been one of Lady Lavender's men.

"Grace?" Patience whispered next to her, stirring loose strands of her hair into her face and tickling her nose.

Grace sniffled. "Shhh!"

Patience sighed and wandered toward the clocks.

Irritation and impatience shot through Grace in a blur. *Move!* she wanted to demand of the man who was blocking her view just beyond those shelves.

"Lovely, Mr. Baskov," a woman murmured. "You do know what I like, don't you?"

The man shifted, *finally*, and a woman came into view. Grace drew back, stunned by her beauty. This was the person who was keeping Alex virtually imprisoned? She shoved the two vases together with a clank, wishing to see no more. Lady Lavender was not in the least what she'd expected. Petite with a heart-shaped face of pure perfection. The sort of woman men wanted and women envied.

Grace's heart gave a painful squeeze of what could only be jealousy. But no, she couldn't be jealous. Being jealous would mean she cared, and she didn't care. She only cared about Rodrick. She pressed her hand to her chest, as if that could stop the ache that had burrowed deep within her soul. Perhaps Alex was at Lady Lavender's because he wanted to be there.

"Can I help you?"

Grace spun around. Mr. Petrov, Mr. Baskov's apprentice, stood before her looking as intimidating and dour as ever. He was a tall ogre of a man with broad shoulders and the constant look of pure annoyance in his black eyes.

"Yes. Yes, of course." She reached under her fitted jacket for the cameo. "I've been meaning to sell this. Don't wear it anymore, you see." Her hands shook so badly she could barely get the piece unlatched. "I know Baskov," she lowered her voice, "is discreet."

If word got out that she was selling jewelry, their *friends* would certainly uncover the truth about their dire situation and word would get back to John. They'd be humiliated. And Grace and Patience could forget about ever making a decent match.

Petrov snatched the pin from her palm and with a critical eye studied it.

Grace took the moment to turn and peek through the vases. The group was gone, having disappeared into a back room where she knew the expensive pieces were kept.

"Five pounds."

Grace spun around, Lady Lavender forgotten for the moment. "You can't be serious! It's worth at least ten." She hadn't a clue what it was worth, but knowing Petrov, at least twice what he would offer. Blast, but she'd prayed for more! Patience, hearing their raised voices, turned and started toward Grace.

"Damaged," the man said in his thick Russian accent.

"Damaged? Indeed," she muttered, grabbing the piece from his monstrous palm. "Where?"

"Nick, there." He pointed to the top right corner.

The piece was as smooth as when she'd been given the gift three years ago. "I can't see it, and I have perfect eyesight."

"Is there a problem?" a familiar voice asked from behind her.

Everything inside Grace seemed to freeze, except her heart, which slammed madly against her rib cage, threatening to break free of her chest and hightail it from the shop. It couldn't be him... it wasn't possible. Yet she knew in her soul it was.

Slowly she turned. And there he was, taller, more handsome than she remembered. Alex was there. And damn it all, if she wasn't thrilled to see him.

* * *

She stared at him. Merely stared as if she couldn't quite place him, as if he was an insignificant dream she vaguely remembered. While he...he'd been obsessing about her for days now, praying she'd keep her appointment.

Wavy tendrils of hair had come loose and framed her pale face. Those luminous eyes shone with confusion, surprise, bemusement. He'd heard the arguing and thought his mind had finally gone mad. Nights of dreaming about Grace had finally taken their toll. For one brief moment he thought he'd imagined her, but then she'd started to argue with the man about the price of some piece, and he realized she was actually here, only too real. And he was an idiot to get involved with Lady Lavender so near.

Vaguely he was aware of a younger woman stepping close to Grace, as if to offer her moral support. She was a blonde, pretty thing, in a wholesome way, and her bold stare and that stubborn tilt of her chin told him she must be related.

"Alex, what are you doing here?" Grace whispered as if only he would hear her when it was obvious they were all shocked by the familiar use of his name on her lips.

He ignored the prying eyes of the other two and focused only on Grace. Seeing her was like a breath of fresh air when he'd been locked in a stale cell. He had the sudden urge to smile, to breathe deeply, to touch her. He stood firm his ground, curling his fingers into his thighs. "I do go out in public occasionally." Those visits were always heavily guarded, but she didn't need to know that.

She parted her lips as if to question him further, then thought better and pressed her mouth into a firm line. Good idea; he could only imagine what inappropriate question she'd ask.

Mr. Petrov shifted, impatient. "Five pounds, my lady."

Grace blushed and looked away, breaking their contact. "Fine."

She was selling her jewelry. Alex frowned. There was only one reason the *ton* sold their jewelry: they desperately needed the money. Alex held up his hand, stopping Petrov. "Your time, if you please, sir."

The man paused for one long moment, eyeing Alex suspiciously. "Very vell."

Alex gave Grace a quick bow then strolled toward the end of the aisle, knowing Petrov followed as his heavy footsteps vibrated the very floorboards underneath him. He turned when they were far enough away that Grace and her companion wouldn't overhear.

"*Moy droog*," he started in Russian.

Surprise crossed the other man's features, although he did quick work of covering his expression. He hadn't a clue Alex came from Russia, but then, only a few did know. "I am not your friend."

So that's how the man was going to be. Alex pressed his hand to his chest. "I'm heartbroken."

"I'm a busy man, *sir*." He sneered the last word, working Alex's already annoyed nerves.

"Of course." Alex smiled and rested his hand on the man's broad shoulder in a pretense of companionship. "You're fucking her over, *nyet*?"

The man stiffened. "*Nyet.* The piece is worth five pounds." His accent grew thicker the angrier he became. "Five pounds she get."

Alex slid Grace a glance. She waited at the end of the aisle nervously tucking her hair behind her ears. "She is a friend of mine. These English, they're so proper." He chuckled. "But in the old country, we understand loyalty. Don't we?"

The man's eyes narrowed.

Alex's smile fell. "You fuck with my friends, I fuck with you."

The man shifted, his gaze growing leery. A pulse beat quickly in the side of his thick neck. Alex wasn't an idiot; he knew the man was more worried about Lady Lavender than Alex's threat. She spent a lot of money in this shop. Whatever would work in Alex's favor, he'd take.

"Ten pounds then."

Alex smiled and slapped the man on the side of the face. "*Da.*"

The man gave a curt bow, a show of respect, although his eyes flashed dangerously with anger. "*Spasibo.*" Without another word, he turned back toward Grace. Alex merely stood there like an audience member watching a play, taking in the moment, every tiny detail, from the way her brows drew together, to the way her hair shone in the sunlight slicing through the windows…He had a feeling he could watch her forever.

Petrov bowed. "Ten pounds then."

Grace's gaze widened and jumped to Alex. He could tell even from where he stood that she was annoyed with his interference. It was that unmistakable spark in her hazel eyes.

"Wonderful," she muttered, then turned to the woman next to her. "Patience, can you please follow Mr. Petrov?"

The girl nodded, watching him with wide eyes that matched Grace's in shape if not color. Her sister then? For although their coloring was different, their features were the same. She left and they were alone. He knew he had only moments before someone would return. He could just see Wavers and Jensen outside standing watch at the carriage and knew two more men were stationed at the back door. They were there to keep him in line as much as they were there to protect Ophelia. Lady Lavender was a paranoid woman, and she should be. She'd received more than one death threat from men of the *ton*. It was fine if they partook in torrid events, but God forbid their women did.

Grace started forward in a flurry of skirts, her agitated movements matching her mood. "What did you say to him?"

"Nothing." He turned to leave. He couldn't be this close to her, smell her warm scent, not when they weren't alone and he wouldn't be able to touch her. Hell, he should have left the moment he heard her arguing with the Russian.

She latched on to his arm, her grip tight and strong for a woman. "You speak Russian?"

He bristled, pulling away. "I didn't say that."

"No, but you spoke a language other than English, I could tell, and since Petrov is Russian, I assumed."

He turned a corner and started down a row of Greek statues; women and men half-dressed, posed in an erotic marble embrace. Bad, bad aisle, for it brought to mind all sorts of nefarious ideas. "Perhaps you shouldn't assume."

She followed, but then he knew she would. Part of him wished she'd leave, but the other part, damn it all, the other part wanted to pull her close, breathe in her warm scent, do to her what those statues were doing.

"I know what I heard, Alex." A wall blocked the end of the aisle. Trapped. He was bloody trapped. He spun around, close to losing hold of that charm. He felt the panicked need to escape, as if she was stalking him, a tigress about to pounce. Didn't she understand? They couldn't talk like friends; they couldn't be seen together outside of the estate. He curled his fists and leaned against the brick wall. Grace stopped in front of him, her arms crossed over her chest, her face set in determined lines. So close he could feel the heat of her body.

"Who are you, Alex? James said…" She blanched as if realizing her mistake and looked away.

"What?" he demanded in a harsh whisper. "What did James say?"

She looked up at him, her eyes soft, yet behind that emotion was a leeriness that hadn't been there two days ago. She wasn't sure if she could trust him, and for some reason, that made him irate.

"He warned me about you," she whispered.

Anger simmered beneath his skin. He closed his eyes, attempting to regain control. James warned her? What exactly had he said? He could imagine. Damn, but he could kill the man. He opened his eyes, keeping his face blank. "I'm a whore. Nothing more than that."

She slowly shook her head, those curls shimmering with the movement. "I know that's not true."

He grabbed her upper arms and jerked her forward, crushing her soft breasts to his chest. Despite her look of surprise, anger, desire, and frustration pounded through his veins. "What do you know, Grace? What? Tell me. Tell me what you know."

Fear skittered across her features. He wanted to yell at her, tell her she should be afraid. She didn't know him. No one did. Instead, he released his hold and pushed her back. She stumbled and he had to resist the urge to catch her; catching her would show he cared. Regaining her balance she tilted her chin high and looked directly into his eyes.

"I know that charm is hiding your true pain," she whispered. "I know you don't want to be here, with *her*."

His heart did a queer little jump. He swallowed hard, his fingernails biting into the rough brick at his back.

She stepped closer, so close he could see the flecks of gold in her blue and green eyes. "Say it, Alex. Tell me you don't really want to work for Lady Lavender." There was a desperation in her voice, as if she was pleading for his agreement. "Tell me that the only reason you're doing what you're doing is because you have no choice."

Anguish clenched at his gut, tore at his soul. How desperately he wanted to tell her the truth…to finally tell someone the truth. But he couldn't. It wouldn't be fair to his family or her. She wanted him to be someone he wasn't. Even though he was under guard and constant watch, there was a part of him, a tiny part, that was afraid of leaving.

"Grace?" the girl named Patience called from down the aisle. She was watching them, clutching the money in her gloved hands and watching them with the innocence and naïveté only a young girl could. "Gracie, are you all right?"

"Yes, Patience." Grace stepped back, shaking her head. Disappointment hung heavily between them. "You know I'm right, Alex. You can pretend all you want, but I know you don't want to be here."

He didn't respond. She turned and walked slowly, deliberately toward her sister. Not pausing, she latched on to Patience's hand and pulled her toward the door. Only Patience looked back, her young face showing her confusion. And Alex wanted to go after Grace. And he wanted to explain. But he couldn't.

And then they were gone and he was left standing there… alone.

Chapter 7

Grace huddled under the warmth of her shawl attempting desperately to keep the spring chill from her bones and the memory of Alex's desperate gaze from her mind. She swore she could still feel his touch, smell the scent of his warm body. She hated that she had left feeling angry and abused in some way. She liked Alex, truly she did, and she had so few friends who accepted her the way she was. Blast it, why couldn't she put the man from her mind?

She couldn't get enough of his sinful touch. Thoughts of his lips on hers kept her up at night. Overwhelmed, she covered her face with her hands and sank into the wing back chair occupying the parlor. John was out doing only the good Lord knew what. Patience and Mama were abed. The house was quiet, but her thoughts were loud, tumbling around her head, clamoring for attention.

How stupid she'd been to enter that shop knowing he could be there. And her mind, her traitorous mind knew the truth: she had hoped he would. When she'd heard his voice, deep down she'd been thrilled. Deep down, she'd wanted to see him again. But he'd acted so odd. Angry, almost. Obviously he hadn't wished to see her and that hurt more than she wanted to admit.

Grace drew in a deep, shuddering breath.

The man was a mystery. A beautiful, seductive mystery. A buried treasure she desperately wanted to uncover. One moment he seemed to like her, the next to despise her. It made it very confusing to know her own thoughts.

She frowned, playing with the fringe on her shawl. Was he with a woman even as she obsessed over him? Her stomach clenched at the thought. How many had he pleasured? He certainly seemed comfortable enough with dropping his trousers and touching someone he barely knew. He seemed comfortable enough touching her. But was his desire merely a ruse?

Memories flashed through her mind...his hands on her breasts...her bottom...

She closed her eyes as heat seeped low in her belly. His broad chest sprinkled with dark hair that led a path directly to his... She fanned herself, suddenly warm. Only in statues and paintings had she seen a man's cock. Alex had been impressive indeed. A long shaft that thickened at the end, surely more impressive than any statue she'd seen. Part of her, the scientist, had been almost eager to study him. She released a wry laugh, her eyes opening. Yes, it would be just the thing to send to the science institute: *The Study of a Man's Cock.* But the woman in her...that sinful woman wanted to study him for an entirely different reason.

A soft knock sounded immediately before the door was pushed wide. Patience poked her golden head into the room. "Grace?"

Miss Kitty raced through the open door, her black coat shimmering under the lamplight. Grace stood, flushing as if Patience could read her thoughts, God forbid. "Yes, is Mama well?"

Patience swallowed hard, her face serious. Too serious for one so young. "I heard her coughing and I couldn't get back to sleep." She moved into the room, trousers hugging her long legs. Grace opened her mouth to reprimand, but thought better of it. Her sister was upset; what did clothing matter? The way they were headed, she wouldn't have a season or need for ball gowns anyway.

Patience paused in the middle of the room and bit on her thumbnail, the way she did when she was thinking or worried. Miss Kitty purred, rubbing against Grace's legs.

Grace reached down, smoothing her hand over the cat's spine, attempting to glean some sort of comfort from the soft animal. "What is it, dearest?"

Patience made her way to the fireplace and held out her hands, warming her fingers. Their home was old and drafty, and spring nights were still cold. "She isn't eating. I didn't want to tell you, but it's been two days since she's had anything other than water."

Grace's heart lurched, but she made quick work of smoothing her features into an unreadable mask. "Well then, we'll make her eat." She started toward the door.

Patience spun around. "No, not now. She's finally sleeping."

Against her better judgment Grace stopped but didn't dare turn to look at her sister. She couldn't, not knowing Patience would be able to read the despair in her eyes. She shouldn't have left the feeding to her sister, but Patience had wanted to prove her worth. Grace was the adult; her sister shouldn't have to deal with such things at her age. The helplessness she'd been desperately trying to keep at bay rushed through her in a wave of agony. Oh God, what would they do without Mama?

"It's not fair," Patience whispered.

Grace took in a deep, trembling breath, attempting to regain control of her emotions. She could imagine there were many things that weren't fair, but wondered what, in particular, her sister thought was unfair this evening.

"We have to sit here and do nothing at all but worry while John gets to do whatever he pleases. Even when his father was ill, it was you and Mama who took care of the old man."

Grace couldn't argue with her sister. Slowly she turned and made her way back to her chair. It was true. While men were able to leave when they wished, to gamble away the family savings, women had to wait and wonder. Still, it didn't make the guilt she felt lessen. Patience should be with friends, at balls, learning to flirt. At least Grace had experienced one brief season, until John's father had become ill. So long ago that the balls and pretty dresses seemed more like a faded dream.

Murmured voices from the hall interrupted the dreary silence.

"Is John home already?" Patience stiffened, her face going pale. Grace knew exactly why her sister was worried. Although Patience's heathen ways had always amused and exasperated Grace, John would ridicule her until she cried.

"Doesn't sound like him. But do go on, dear. Through the study."

"Thanks, Grace." Her sister gave her a fleeting smile and rushed into the next room, shutting the door behind her.

Grace hesitated a moment, just long enough to smooth down her skirts and pinch her cheeks. Who would come calling this late? Her heart skipped a beat, horror washing over her in a sickening churn. Gads, had someone uncovered her secret visits with Alex? She darted toward the hall, Miss Kitty following. As if she hadn't enough to worry about!

Marks stood in the entryway, blocking the visitor from view. For once he was doing his job. "My lord, as it's late and my lady is sleeping…"

My lord?

"Yes, of course, please, don't wake anyone. If I could merely borrow a few footmen—" The familiar voice was a welcome relief from the night's depressing thoughts.

Grace hurried forward, relieved yet embarrassed. Marks knew that a lord of Rodrick's position should not be kept waiting. "Lord Rodrick."

Miss Kitty hissed and raced down the hall toward the kitchens. She'd never cared for Rodrick for some odd reason.

"So sorry to bother you," the earl said.

Footmen. He was here for footmen. They no longer had footmen, thanks to John's spending, and soon Rodrick would know of their dire straits.

Marks stepped to the side, looking relieved. The man could barely stand, wavering about on his feet. Obviously he'd been drinking again. She prayed Rodrick hadn't noticed the inebriated servant. "Please, Marks, return to bed."

Not one to argue, or care, the old man immediately shuffled away. Grace turned back toward Rodrick. His hair was mussed, his cravat loose. She'd never seen him in such a relaxed state, and it felt odd to be here with him, only the two of them…almost intimate.

Yet she wasn't as excited as she should be. She ignored the uneasy feeling. "What is it?"

Rodrick raked his fingers through his hair, and for one brief moment she was reminded of Alex. She shook the thought aside as he began to speak. "Grace, I'm so sorry. I hadn't meant to disturb you…"

She raised her hand, stopping him. She had no time for such nonsense. If he had something important to say, he needed to say it. "No, please, what is it?" She'd never seen him like this, so unsure, so unkempt. Yet she kept her breathing even, refusing to panic. She had enough to deal with at the moment. There was no reason to give in to hysterics, although Rodrick watched closely as if he expected nothing less.

"Your brother."

Dread sank like a boulder into her stomach. "Oh God, what now?"

He hesitated, shifting. "It's not for a lady's ears…"

Grace dampened down her annoyance. Really, was this the same man who liked his women experienced and bold in the bedroom? "Please. He's my brother, my responsibility."

Rodrick sighed dramatically, almost…as if he was enjoying the moment. She pushed aside the disloyal thought as he began to explain.

"Fine, but I warn you, 'tis not pleasant. He's intoxicated, has been drinking himself into oblivion. Gambling, borrowing money from acquaintances only to lose it all."

Grace blanched. It was worse than she'd expected.

He paced across the foyer, his boots tapping with each step. "I've tried to escort him home, but he refuses to leave. Your town-house was closer, so I thought I could gather a couple footmen to assist me…"

She nodded. When John was drunk, he was a brute. Was that why Rodrick was so disheveled? Heated embarrassment rushed through her. What he must think of her family! There was no possible way he'd ever ask her to marry him now. John had made everything a million times worse, the bloody idiot. There was only one thing to do.

"I understand." She swept across the foyer, deeper into the house. At the stairs she glanced back. "I'll be just a moment. Did you take a hack?"

He frowned, confusion passing over his handsome face. "Yes, but—"

"Excellent, we'll not be identified." She rested her hand on the railing. For once she was glad of her sister's odd choice in clothing. With trousers and her hair under a hat, no one would know she was a woman.

Rodrick started after her, his footsteps quick and heavy over the floor planks. "Grace? What are you doing? I don't understand."

She paused, turning. "Going to change, of course. Will only take a moment."

He laughed, a forced sound that grated her nerves. "You can't be serious."

She fought her momentary irritation, telling herself he only cared about her welfare and reputation. "Of course I'm serious."

He paused in front of her. "He's in a brothel, for God's sake!"

Anger had her parting her lips, and for one brief, horrifying moment she almost blurted out that she'd been to a brothel before. Realizing her mistake, she clamped her mouth shut. How dare he tell her what she could and couldn't do? Is this what her life would become if she married him?

"*It's not fair,*" Patience's words whispered through her mind. "*We have to sit here and do nothing at all but worry.*"

"You'll ruin your reputation," he added feebly.

Grace sighed. It wasn't Rodrick's fault. The man had been raised to believe that a woman of privilege should always care about her reputation. "My brother's life is at stake." He certainly couldn't argue with that.

His lips pressed into a firm line. He wasn't going to agree, blast him.

"To hell with my reputation." She'd try another tactic. "I made my debut years ago, I'm hardly an innocent."

He lifted a brow, shocked by her blunt statement, yet there was something else there, a sparkling in his eyes…could it possibly be admiration? She took a step up so they were eye to eye and stared directly into his soft amber gaze.

"No one will recognize me. Besides, I'm the only person he'll listen to."

The corners of his lips quirked, as if he found her bluntness amusing. A delicious shiver raked her skin, her heart slamming erratically inside her chest. Anticipation? For one long moment they merely stared at each other. Rodrick as if he were seeing her for the first time.

She felt odd, bold, daring. That bit of rebellion had given her the confidence she needed. In that moment, she realized it was the perfect time to practice Alex's instructions. She took Rodrick's gloved hand in hers, feigning innocence and sincerity by blinking her eyes wide as she'd seen many a woman do.

His shoulders tensed, his lips parting in surprise.

Grace refused to blush, refused to drop her gaze. "Thank you, Rodrick. I haven't had the opportunity to thank you, and you've done so much for my brother, for *me*."

Then she waited. Her heart hammering, she waited for his response.

"Of course," he said softly, his gaze dropping to their clasped hands.

He didn't pull away.

It was her cue to be even bolder. "Really, I don't know what we'd do without you."

Time seemed to suspend. She lowered her gaze for one brief moment, and before she lost her nerve, she brushed her thumb across the inside of his wrist, right there, where his sleeve cuff didn't quite meet his glove, where his pale skin shone through. Such a simple touch, yet shockingly intimate.

She heard his sharp intake of breath and almost bolted up the steps in embarrassment. Instead, she forced herself to pull slowly away. She gave him a brilliant smile and said, "I'll be only a moment."

"Of...of course." He was stuttering, his cheeks flushed.

Grace turned and started up the steps, her legs trembling. She knew he watched her. She knew she'd affected him. She knew she'd won.

Her heart thumped madly, nerves fighting with relief. She'd done it. Dear God, help her. She'd taken the advice of a whore.

* * *

"Darling." Ophelia leaned toward Alex and rested her hand on his chest. "Sherry."

Alex's smile was brittle. "Yes. Of course." He stood from the settee they shared and smoothed down his vest and jacket. Not one man around the card table bothered to look his way. No, he was merely a pet of Lady Lavender's. Even though he was dressed better than most, he was not worth notice.

Rarely did Lady Lavender leave her estate for London, and even more rarely did she bring him along. When he did escort her, he was either being rewarded or punished. Tonight he was being punished. Her little lapdog. Humiliated in front of the other men. She did it on purpose. Of course she'd never admit that, but he knew the truth. He'd fucked up more than once with Grace.

And Ophelia insisted on happy customers. Thank God the woman didn't seem to know about the shop visit this morning.

Gideon swore Lady Lavender visited gaming hells and brothels to prove her power. Perhaps he was right. Alex wouldn't put it past her. Women weren't allowed in gaming hells, at least not decent women. Female companionship was provided only for sexual favors. But for some inexplicable reason Lady Lavender was allowed. He had a feeling, deep down, these men of the *ton* feared her; wanted to keep their enemy close and all that nonsense. Or perhaps she knew the owners' deepest, darkest secrets. Alex wouldn't have been surprised.

The few other women draped across men's laps were whores, people like him. Those women watched him openly, wondering, no doubt, how he had been driven into this sort of world and why. Some threw him lascivious winks, knowing smiles, smirks. Others seemed annoyed, as if he was stealing business from them, stepping into their territory. Still others, those women who had sold their souls long ago, barely noticed him at all but sat in a bewildered state of semiconsciousness, their movements puppet-like.

With that charming smirk in place, Alex sauntered down the hall. At the end of the corridor, just barely visible, two of Lady Ophelia's men stood guard. He knew without looking that two more would be out back. He tried to focus on the pleasantness of freedom, being able to roam the building without expectation to please. But the place was thick with smoke, the bitter scent of alcohol, and the overwhelming despair of gentlemen attempting to recoup their funds.

He was so unused to the sound of male companionship that on his first visit to a gaming hell with Ophelia, he'd been startled like a wild animal taken into the city. Some of the buildings, like this one, did their best to appear civilized: painted walls, carpeted floors, and fine furniture. But they couldn't hide what this place truly was…a hell.

Arguing, deep rumbling laughter, and amiable conversation rumbled from a variety of rooms. At Lavender House, silence was much appreciated. He paused at the opening of one room, peering inside at the group of men. Friends, from what he could gather. They laughed, patted each other on the back, sharing stories of women and drink. Not one noticed him.

A bitter gust of loneliness clenched his gut. If his family hadn't been ostracized…if Lady Lavender hadn't…if…

The soft scent of vanilla and spring wafted around him. A clean scent, a scent that didn't belong in this hell. An oddly familiar scent. Startled, he glanced over his shoulder just as two men swept by. The taller man was typical of these establishments. His dark suit perfectly cut, brown hair trimmed stylishly into place. But it was the smaller man who caught Alex's attention. A boy's cap covered his head. But his hips were too round, waist too narrow.

"We'll find him," the shorter man mumbled in a shockingly feminine voice. A familiar voice.

Hell, it couldn't be…she wouldn't…

"We aren't staying long. And for God's sake, keep your face down." The taller man settled his hand on the small of her back.

Recognition shocked Alex cold. Hell, she would. And why not? The woman frequented whorehouses, why not gaming hells as well? He supposed he shouldn't have been surprised, but he was. Surprised, annoyed, and…what was that? Yes, blast it all… thrilled to see her.

Alex frowned, hurrying to catch up to them. What was she doing here? Without thought, he followed the couple down the dank hall, further into the smoky pit of hell, brushing by stumbling guests too drunk to notice anything amiss. The odd couple turned into a room, disappearing from sight.

For one brief moment he panicked. Alex paused just inside the doorway, his frantic gaze searching the small room. There, near a table of men smoking and playing cards, she stood. Grace. There was no doubt now. Although the brim of her hat shadowed her face, he could still make out her features. A face so pure, that bearing so graceful, how the hell could they not all know she was female?

She leaned toward a dark-haired man who slouched in a chair, his build medium, his features plain, his demeanor despicable. Her stance was one of companionship, intimacy...as if she knew him well.

"Now, John," she whispered. "We're leaving now."

A few men lifted their blurry gazes to her, finding her sharp statement odd. The man named John glanced up and gave her a wavering smile that bespoke drunkenness. "Can't now. I'm just about to win back what I lost."

Her delicate, gloveless hands curled on her rounded hips. Alex knew that stubborn set of her jaw since he'd seen it before. In fact, he'd seen it only that morning in the shop. The woman was on a mission.

"I must insist we leave," the dandy man who'd come with her added his worthless two pence.

Alex frowned. She wouldn't take demands from him, but she would this bloody idiot? He was attractive, he supposed, and his obvious arrogance only added to his appeal. Who was he anyway? Certainly not her *earl*.

"I will not leave without John."

Alex smirked and leaned against the doorjamb, crossing his arms over his chest. If the man was her earl, she'd just shut him up quite nicely. And he was taking her snub to heart, if his flushed cheeks said anything.

"Really, I think we ought—"

She snapped her head toward her companion. "I will not leave…"

Those flashing hazel eyes met his and her voice trailed off. Damn if his heart didn't lurch. Feigning the arrogance he was so good at, he lifted a brow. Her companion glanced back at Alex, gave him a quick sweep, then stepped in front of her, blocking him from view. Another reason to hate the man.

"Your brother is in no condition—"

"Enough!" John roared, surging to his feet. "I will not leave until I win back my money!"

"You are ruining us!" Grace cried out in a voice so feminine that surely everyone else realized, yet no one seemed to notice, too drunk or stupid to care. They seemed more annoyed that their card game was being interrupted.

"See here," one man slurred. "Are you in or not?"

"I am saving us, you idiot!"

In a tantrum a toddler would envy, John tossed his cards into the air, the deck fluttering to the floor like ribbons on a maypole.

"Oi, why'd you do that?" someone grumbled, kneeling to pick up the cards.

Grace's face flushed, her eyes shimmering. "Oh, yes, saving us." She was close to tears, and Alex couldn't let her cry here, not now, in front of these men. She'd hate herself later. He could hear the mumbles behind him and realized they were attracting interest. Determined to save Grace from herself, Alex stepped farther into the room.

The soft, questioning mumbles grew as did the crowd at the door.

"What is it?"

"Who is that?" he heard more than one person whisper behind him.

"Get out!" Apparently having had enough, John stabbed his bony finger into her chest, sending Grace stumbling backward into the earl. Alex's ire flared. The earl fumbled to catch her, but, caught off-balance, he nearly took them both to the floor.

Leaping into the room, Alex grabbed Grace around the waist and pulled her back just in time. Her lush, warm body felt so bloody right in his arms that for a brief moment he merely savored the contact.

"Are you all right?" he asked softly against her silky hair.

"Yes," she whispered.

But he could feel the rapid beat of her heart against his chest. She wasn't all right, and hell, neither was he. While the others, finally annoyed enough, were attempting to pin good ole John's flailing arms to his side, Alex merely held Grace.

"Grace?" The earl stumbled upright and elbowed his way between them, giving Alex a discreet shove. He took Grace's hand in his, his boyish face puckered in concern. "Are you well?"

Grace's gaze jumped to Alex, then back to her earl. "Yes, yes, Rodrick, I'm fine."

Alex was about to shove the man aside and tell him to go to hell when someone called from the doorway.

"Excuse me, excuse me." A round man wobbled his way into the room, pausing only when he caught sight of Grace. The shock that flushed his face was almost laughable. "You cannot be here!"

Her ruse was up, finally, uncovered by the only sober man besides Alex. The remaining men froze, realizing something was wrong, something they'd missed. The crowd was thickening, men eager for a brawl piling into the doorway to get a peek.

"A woman," Alex heard someone whisper.

"An actual *lady*?" someone else asked, obviously horrified.

Alex snapped his head toward the earl, the idiot who'd brought her here. The moron was busy trying to tame John, leaving Grace to struggle on her own. Alex glanced back. Wavers was there, beyond the crowd, watching him. He knew Jensen would be standing watch at the front entrance.

Alex focused on the earl, disgusted with the dandy. "I suggest you escort her out of here, now."

"Of course," her companion replied, raking his hair back in frazzled and jerky movements that bespoke confusion and indecision. Alex doubted the earl had ever taken care of himself, let alone another human. He hadn't the slightest idea what to do.

Grace shook her head and spun away, out of reach. "Not without John."

"Grace, he refuses…" the earl whined.

But she didn't look at her earl; no, she looked at Alex, her direct gaze pleading with him to help. He felt her need like a knife through the heart. His gaze slid to the tabletop, the pile of coins obvious, glaring. She needed him, not for sex, but needed him to save what little family fortune her idiotic brother hadn't wasted. And for the first time in years, it was nice to be needed.

Alex strolled forward, lifted his fist, and hit the man in the jaw. Utter shock crossed John's face for one brief moment before his head snapped back, his knees buckled, and he crumpled to the floor. A few men laughed, a few gasped their outrage. But not Grace; no, instead she threw him a grateful smile, a smile that gripped his heart and squeezed.

"Now can you handle him?" Alex muttered.

Rodrick threw him an irritated glance. He paused only a moment, obviously not wanting to do the dirty work, before stomping toward Grace's brother. "Fine. Come along, someone help."

On impulse, Alex took the moment. "Let's go." Alex latched on to Grace's hand and pulled her toward the door, the crowd parting reluctantly. He noticed their suspicious glances. They were attempting to decipher if she was truly a woman and if they'd been duped. Wavers followed. Alex could feel the man's oppressive presence.

"Wh…what are you doing?" she whispered, her voice laced with outrage and confusion.

"Saving your sorry arse." He hadn't meant to escort her out of the fine establishment. If Ophelia noticed him giving attention to a woman…but he wouldn't worry about that now. The men who didn't move were shoved aside. Alex ignored their grumbles of annoyance, focused only on escorting Grace to safety, whether she wanted to or not.

"You can't just drag me out like you…like you *own* me."

Irritation gnawed at his gut. "Since your earl seems incapable, yes, I can." He was annoyed at her for putting herself in this situation. Annoyed at himself for being bound to Ophelia and unable to do more. But mostly he was annoyed at life in general. Every step closer to those front doors was like a noose tightening, pulling him back, warning him not to leave.

"What the hell were you thinking?" he snapped, taking his discomfort out on her.

She pressed her hand to her cap, holding it in place. "What do you mean?"

"What do I mean?" He looked down at her, exasperated. "Are you jesting?" He pulled her close as more than one man reached out to touch her as if to see if she was real. If they dared lay a finger on her, he'd have to kill them, and he didn't have time to murder hundreds of men.

"Of course not. I never jest."

He wrapped his arm around her waist, practically carrying her down the hall. "Why does that not surprise me?"

Behind them he could hear Rodrick wrestling John into the corridor. Dandy cock, couldn't control one man. Grace, hearing them, started to turn, but Alex held her firmly, dragging her forward toward those doors where Jensen watched them. "Your carriage is out front?"

"Yes, a hired hack."

"And you came with him? Lord Rodrick, the man you wish to seduce?"

She stiffened, throwing him a glare. "Shhh! Please, lower your voice!"

He gave her his cheeky grin, even though his stomach churned. That dandy? That bastard was the man she so badly wanted? She couldn't be attracted to him, could she? Please, Lord, let it only be for the money.

"Out the back if you please, sir." A butler appeared, nervously shooing them down a side hall.

Alex rolled his eyes heavenward. Amazing—they'd seen more vile things than Satan himself, yet one woman in the building threw the establishment into chaos. Alex jerked Grace left, down a narrow hall. He glanced back. Wavers was blocked by the earl and John. Taking an impossibly long time to stumble down the hall, four men each holding one of John's limbs. Bumbling buffoons, but he supposed he should be grateful since they were keeping Wavers at bay.

"Wait!" Grace pulled back, attempting to turn. "John and Lord Rodrick."

"They'll be along shortly, I'm sure."

Alex dampened down his amusement and pulled Grace closer, heading down the dimly lit corridor. At the end of the hall, the door stood unguarded. Perhaps Ophelia's men had left their post to uncover the cause of commotion. It didn't matter; all that mattered was the doors were unguarded.

"Alex," Grace breathed heavily beside him. "I want to apologize for the incident this morning."

Surprised, his steps slowed. No one had apologized to him in years. He wasn't sure how to feel. Heat shot to his cheeks, and at the same time his heart squeezed painfully.

"You don't have to…"

Two men turned the corner, heading directly toward them. "Keep your head down," Alex warned.

Grace dropped her gaze to the floor as the men stumbled toward them.

Off-balance, one bumped into Grace. Her cap fell backward, slipping from her head and revealing those lovely auburn locks. She gasped, reaching out, but it was too late. The garment lay upon the carpet like a dead cat.

"What's this?" one of the men exclaimed and gave a low whistle. "A beauty, she is. You're going to share, aren't you?" His friend laughed at the jest.

Growling low in his throat, Alex shoved Grace behind him. "No, I'm not."

One of the men shifted, stepping into the light of the wall sconce. Blue eyes, brown hair given to curl slightly. Familiar in some way...

The blond-haired man next to him waved his hand dismissively. "Oh, leave off, Demitri, she's taken."

Demitri. The walls faded. The room faded. The name sent Alex spinning backward in time.

A little boy raced after him. *"Alex, Alex, wait for me!"*

"Next time, Demitri, I promise."

Alex squeezed his eyes shut, emotion roiling through him, clenching at his gut in a sickening churn. He couldn't breathe, think, move. He wanted to die.

"Alex?" The plea in Grace's voice tore at him, awoke him from a dream.

He'd known it would happen one day. He thought he'd be prepared. He wasn't. Slowly Alex lifted his lashes and stared into the blue eyes of his brother.

Chapter 8

"Alex?" Grace knelt and snatched up her cap, pressing it firmly atop her head. Not that the hat mattered; word that she was a lady was spreading like cholera through the building. But that was the least of her worries.

Alex was acting strangely. All color had fled from his face, and his eyes glistened with an odd intensity that worried and frightened her. The pure happiness she'd experienced when first seeing him began to dissipate. She rested her hand on his forearm, his muscles tense under her touch. "Alex? Are you well?"

"Do I know you?" the man named Demitri asked at the same time.

But the man wasn't speaking to her. No, his gaze was focused on Alex. Alex, who was looking anything but pleased to have his attention. Grace glanced uneasily between the two. It was impossible to ignore the odd anxiety that pulsed between them. As much as Grace wanted to dismiss the idea, she could not deny there was something familiar about Demitri: the way he moved, that small line that creased the area between his brows, and the way he tilted his head to the side as if confused. Was it merely a trick of the dim light coming from the gas lamps above?

Alex shook his head. "No. You don't know me." He latched on to Grace's hand, his grip tight, too tight. "Come, we need to leave."

"Alex," Grace tripped beside him, trying to keep up with his fast pace. "What is it? What's wrong?"

"Nothing."

His face was blank, admitting nothing. But it was obvious something was wrong. She'd seen the bleakness hovering in his eyes. What had happened to upset him so? She glanced back. Demitri still stood there, still stared after them, although his friend was doing his best to gain his attention. Then they turned a corner and Demitri was gone.

Grace looked up at Alex. His gaze was focused determinedly ahead, as if he had something to accomplish and nothing would get in his way. She could admit the moment she'd seen him standing in the doorway, looking so arrogant, so charming, so handsome, the entire world seemed to cease. Her worries had almost vanished. And when he'd pulled her from the room, although she felt the need to protest, a surge of excitement washed over her. This was Alex, the man who made her feel alive, made her forget, for one brief moment, her dreary life. And now something was most definitely wrong.

He paused at the door as if something unseen was keeping him from leaving. Grace ran into his back, her palms flattening on his jacket. A fine jacket. His warmth tingled under her palms; his scent made her dizzy. One thing was certain: he didn't dress like a whore. There was no gaudy lace and satin. Only the finest material. She'd feared after this morning in the antiquities shop she'd never see him again. And now here they were, together once more. Was it fate or coincidence?

He pushed the door wide and they stumbled down the narrow steps into an alley. The door shut with a thud, closing out the noise and music of the gaming hell. In the narrow corridor they merely stood, gasping so heavily that Alex's breath formed cold clouds that hung suspended in the air. He wore no overcoat; neither did she. They'd both freeze if they stayed out here long.

Yet despite the cold, there was a fine sheen of sweat upon his brow. "Damn." He looked left, then right, desperately searching for what, she wasn't sure.

"Well, that was quite the adventure." At her words he jerked his head toward her, the surprise on his face evident. The surprise quickly gave way to a hardness that sent her a couple steps back.

He didn't look right. That charm was gone and in its place someone who seemed dark, desperate. He reminded her of a fox Patience had found years ago. They'd kept the poor beast for months, although he'd never been tamed. Finally they'd released him back into the forest, but instead of darting to freedom, he'd stayed frozen in place for one long moment, as if unsure what to do or how to proceed.

"I do thank you," she added. "But that was—"

"Idiotic?"

She stiffened in surprise. "I don't know what—"

"You were stupid to come here." His voice was heavy with disgust.

She dampened down her ire, refusing to fight with him yet again. She was not an idiot. John was the idiot. She was the intelligent one in the family. It was the one thing she possessed. "I was going to say quite the adventure."

She stepped back again, this time her foot landing on something soft. A squeak of protest rang out. Startled, Grace jumped. A small, dark shadow raced down the alleyway. A rat. Grace shuddered, reluctantly moving closer to Alex.

"I assume your fiancé has a coach waiting out front?" His voice still held that bitter edge, making her more than weary.

"He's not my fiancé...yet."

When he started down the alley, she tripped after him, skipping over refuse and garbage that she couldn't identify in the dark; things she didn't want to identify. The bitter, stale scent of alcohol and vomit hovered in a haze so thick she had to swim through it. She focused on breathing through her mouth while attempting to match Alex's long strides. "And yes, it's out front."

"Spare a coin?" a lump of material asked, a fist pushing a tin cup toward them.

Grace gasped as a man emerged from the pile of garbage. Alex reached into his pocket and tossed a coin into the cup. It spun around the bottom before settling down with a ting.

"Bless ye, sire."

Fascinated, Grace was still watching the man when Alex latched on to her elbow and led her to the street.

"I didn't realize your kind carried pocket change." Near their townhome they rarely saw the destitute. Lord, would this be she someday? Begging on the street?

He slid her an annoyed glance. "My kind? Whores, you mean?"

Heat shot to her cheeks even as she refused to be embarrassed. Flustered, she didn't respond, realizing how he'd taken her question. At times she feared she'd forever offend people. She seemed never to say the right thing.

"We're given a few coins here and there, just in case."

In case what? She was too afraid to ask. Grace frowned as they stepped out into the lane. The streetlamps cast a dull yellow glow that flickered and fought pathetically against the shadows. The thrill of excitement gave way to unease. Grace stepped closer to Alex. A woman in a gaudy red dress leaned against the building, her breasts practically popping from her low neckline.

"Like what ye see?" she said with a wink in Grace's direction. She fluffed her breasts, attempting to entice them.

Grace ignored the woman, focusing on Alex. "Then why not save your coins and leave? Perhaps find a real position."

"Yes, it's so incredibly easy to save my many coins and stroll away," he said wryly.

Why was he being so difficult? Of course it was easy; he was a man with no children, no wife…he had nothing to keep him there. Surely he could find a respectable position. Unless he didn't want to. He raked his hand through his hair, his palm pausing at his neck. He seemed unsure, flustered, out of his element.

"Do you want to stay?" Her voice came out high-pitched with outrage, but she was too upset to care. It was the same question she'd asked him at the shop, the same question he'd refused to answer. Her heart paused for one long moment as she waited for his response.

He narrowed his eyes, glaring down at her. "There are worse things than pleasuring women."

She stiffened in outrage and dug her heels into the dirt. His words shocked her. Bothered and annoyed her. Yet at the same time, she didn't believe a thing he said. She'd looked into the man's eyes, she'd seen something there…a hunger for more…a sadness that spoke of longing, a vulnerability. She'd seen the emotion, she was sure.

"Who was that man, Alex?"

He barely glanced her way as he latched on to her arm and jerked her forward. "What man?"

"The man inside. Demitri. You seemed to know him."

"Don't be ridiculous." When she refused to take another step, he gave in and rested his hands on his narrow hips. "What does your coach look like? I assume your earl took an unmarked vehicle."

"Why would you assume we took an unmarked vehicle?" she asked. She wasn't ready to leave. Not this way, not when she might not ever see him again.

His lips pulled up into a smirk. "Your earl is the worst kind, a young lord who doesn't want people to know what he does in secret. He would take an unmarked carriage so he wouldn't be identified and ruin his reputation. It's what most men like him do."

His words certainly disturbed her. "You're saying he's done this before?"

He laughed. "You're more naïve than I thought if you believe your earl doesn't frequent gaming hells and brothels like most men of his rank. Your fiancé has probably had as many female conquests as a...whore."

He was being intentionally cruel, although why, she wasn't sure. She pressed her hands to her lower belly. Her stomach churned at the thought of her future husband going to brothels. But then she'd done as much. Surely he wouldn't after they were married, would he? "It's common?"

"Very."

"But if...if these men sleep with so many women, how does it make them different from..." She flushed.

"Me? They pay. I get paid. That's the difference."

"Doesn't seem like much of a difference."

He paused there on the footpath and snapped his head toward her, as if she'd said something incredibly important. His gaze intense, he truly looked at her as if trying to uncover her deepest, darkest secret. She shifted, dropping her attention, uneasy under his scrutiny. Had she said something wrong again? The binding holding her breasts flat suddenly felt too tight.

"What?" She glanced up through her lashes and dared him to respond when she could take his bold stare no longer.

With a chuckle, he shook his head and look away. "Where are they? Where's the carriage?"

Reluctantly Grace pulled her attention away from Alex's handsome face and studied the street. Only two coaches rested across the lane, both privately owned. Panic flared in her gut. "It's not here. It's gone. The carriage, it's gone."

The night air and her nerves sent chills over her skin. She spun around, peering farther down the lane. Certainly they wouldn't leave her, yet the missing carriage indicated they had. What would she do? She didn't even have enough coins to make it home.

"What a gentleman you're fiancé is, a man who would abandon a woman in the slums."

She wanted to argue, but couldn't. What was Rodrick thinking? Damn the earl. And damn Alex! If he hadn't introduced her to a life of excitement and adventure, she wouldn't be in this position. She'd been having second thoughts about the earl lately, and now she knew why…all because of a dark-haired man with blue eyes. An impossible man, who confused her more than any other.

"Tonight can't get any worse," she muttered.

"Hello, mates," someone growled from behind them.

They spun around as one.

A man slipped from the shadows, the knife in his hand flashing under the dull lamplight.

Alex looked at her in exasperation. "You had to say it, didn't you?"

* * *

"You cannot seriously be thinking to blame me," Grace stated, sounding rather offended.

Alex sighed and pushed her behind his back. Lord, this evening was growing more bizarre with every moment. He curled his fingers, attempting to ease the tremble of his hand. But his heart… damn, his heart wouldn't stop its frantic beat. Too much surprise in one night.

"Alex?" Grace whispered.

Alex shook off his unease. "What can I do for you, kind sir?"

"Ye can give me yer money." The man's eyes flickered from Alex to his surroundings.

A street rat. Well, James had certainly taught him the tricks of a rat. But damn, he wished he'd left Grace with her Rodrick. Without a coach, they'd run into more than one cad looking for a coin. If Wavers didn't find him first. But where had her bastard of a fiancé gone? Some man. He sure as hell wouldn't let a stranger take his girl away, and he sure as hell wouldn't leave her to her own fate. Bastard. Pure and simple.

"I see," Alex replied, keeping his voice calm. "Well, sorry, mate, but I haven't got but a few coins, nothing worth your trouble."

The man shoved his knife forward in a jerky, unpracticed manner. "Even a pence is worth the trouble. And I don't believe ye. No wealthy gent at a gaming hell would have no coins."

"Your mistake is assuming that I'm a gentleman."

The whore leaning against the nearby wall chuckled at Alex's jest. At least someone found him amusing. The man looked anything but amused. He cleared his throat in a nervous way while looking Alex up and down carefully. Alex's fine clothing bespoke money, but the man had no idea that money wasn't his.

"He isn't a gentleman, I'll vouch for that," Grace said, peeking over his shoulder.

He threw her an exasperated glance. "Would you please refrain from interfering?"

She shrugged and dropped back down, hidden behind the protective barrier of his back.

"Now, where were we?"

"Ye were jist about tae give me yer money." But the man's tone had lost that hard edge. He was doubting whether he should continue. Alex was confident, and confidence was half the battle in a fight like this.

"No, I was just about to beat you to a bloody pulp." Alex shrugged his jacket from his shoulders and handed it to Grace. She took the garment reluctantly, watching him as if he'd gone mad. Obviously she didn't believe in his abilities as a man. He'd have to prove to her that he was indeed a man. Much more so than that dandy Rodrick.

The rat before him shifted in unease, watching him warily. Taking his time, Alex rolled his sleeves to his elbows. Feign confidence. Drag out the situation. He knew all of the tricks, and they were working. A dark form appeared at the end of the footpath. He didn't need to look directly to know it was Wavers, lurking in the shadows, watching, waiting. Annoyance fought with something he didn't want to identify…something that felt suspiciously like relief. At the end of the fight, Wavers would escort him back inside. Hopefully Ophelia would be in a forgiving mood. Grace would return home in her hack. Everything would be as it should.

"Come on, then," the man whined, shifting. "It's bloody cold out here."

His rags provided little warmth, and the cold made people desperate. Alex almost felt sorry for him…almost. "All in good time, my friend."

"Alex, what are you doing?" Grace whispered, obviously doubting his sanity.

"Trust me."

She lifted a brow. "Trust you? You want me to trust you?" She sounded quite incredulous, which amused him for some reason.

"Yes, we're quite good at loyalty, you know, we whores."

She flinched at the word. Apparently she could think of him as a whore, but he couldn't say the word? He shook his head and turned back to his opponent. "Well, shall we?"

"Uh…all right." The man shifted the knife from hand to hand. Slowly they circled each other, two animals after a bone…that bone being a few pence. How ridiculous.

They were matched in height. The man was thin, but Alex knew better than to underestimate him. He'd be a sinewy fellow, used to fighting for what he needed.

Grace sighed and took out a small watch from her pocket. "Will this take long?"

"Not if you cease your prattle."

That got another chuckle from the whore watching them with glee.

Grace gasped as if offended. "Well, really." She crossed her arms over her chest and tapped her foot impatiently.

Amused, he almost let the man get the first swipe. His arm lunged forward, the knife gleaming wickedly in the dim light. Alex jumped back. Grace gasped, scrambling out of the way. Finally the woman was taking their situation seriously. Was she worried about him? Or was she merely worried about her escort home?

The man thrust his arm forward again. Alex spun around, coming back to swing his fist wide. His knuckles connected with the man's jaw, sending him stumbling back. Alex had only a moment to catch his breath.

The rat had regained his balance. "Ye're good," he muttered, rubbing his jaw with his free hand. "But I'm better."

"That has yet to be seen, *mate*," Alex sneered.

The man growled low in his throat, his black eyes luminous pools of hatred. Alex silently cursed himself for taunting. He should have known better. Just as the man swung forward, Grace darted toward the alley. Alex spun away, turning to look for the blasted woman.

She was rummaging through the garbage. What was she doing? From the corner of his eye, a blur of movement sent his hackles rising. Too late. He jerked his head toward the rat. A sharp sting ripped across his forearm.

"Shite." Alex stumbled back, caught off guard. The cut wasn't deep. It stung too bloody much to be deep. If it was deep, it would be numb. "Now you've made me angry."

The rat chuckled, his yellow teeth gleaming. He was arrogantly sure he would win, and that would be his mistake. The whore pushed away from the wall, knowing the fight was getting good. She wasn't going to miss a thing. Or she was waiting for Alex to fall so she could rush forward and claim his valuables.

Alex's fingers curled, his gaze narrowing on the smirking rat.

"Come on," the man laughed wickedly.

Alex lowered, ready to launch himself, when Grace suddenly appeared behind the man. She was dragging what looked to be a long piece of wood across the footpath. Her hat was askew, her cheeks flushed, and her hair had come loose, hanging in long, feminine waves around her face. Sensing his attention, she looked up and gave him a brilliant smile.

Alex frowned. What the hell was she doing?

The rat lifted his hands, a come-hither expression on his face. "Come on then; haven't got all night."

Grace lifted the board and, with a grunt, swung. The man didn't see it coming. The whack vibrated through the night air. Grace stumbled back from the force of the blow, dropping the board to the ground. The whore cringed. The rat's eyes grew wide before rolling back in his head.

Slowly he slumped to the ground.

Chapter 9

Grace stumbled back as blood roared to her ears, drowning out any sound but the harsh beating of her heart. Had she truly just killed a man? "He's not…dead…is he?"

But Alex was merely staring at her with a stunned look on his handsome face. "Are you insane?"

The rush of fear was instantly replaced with annoyance. She huffed, resisting the urge to stomp her foot. "No, and I don't take kindly to you calling me mad! Now, I asked a simple question—is he dead?"

"Lawd," the whore whispered, dropping to her knees and quickly going through the man's clothing, looking for whatever she could find. Grace thought it rather disrespectful to steal from a dead man, but managed to keep her thoughts to herself.

"No," Alex snapped. "He's not dead."

Relief made her legs weak. She'd certainly never killed a man and didn't have any desire to start. She had already stained her soul by visiting not only a whorehouse, but a gaming hell. She wasn't sure God would forgive murder. "You're positive?"

A street urchin raced forward. Grace sucked in a surprised gasp and stumbled back into Alex's hard body. The boy grabbed the knife from the unconscious man, then darted back into the darkness, gone as quickly as he'd arrived. Who else lurked out there in the shadows? Alex picked up his jacket from where she'd dropped it and shook the material free of dust. His movements were slow, deliberate, as if he was attempting to regain control of his temper. Well, really, had he expected her to merely stand passively by?

"Alex," she started, intending to explain.

"Grace." Alex turned toward her, his jaw clenched. His features were fierce in the low light of the streetlamps, his cheekbones sharp, his eyes dark. Underneath that anger was the same look that Rodrick had worn when she'd insisted on escorting him to the gaming hell…disbelief.

Flirting had worked with Rodrick…She pasted an innocent smile upon her face and batted her lashes. "Yes?"

With a low growl, he stopped close, so close that over the scent of refuse and smoke, she could smell *him*, that wonderful manly scent of him. "You can't just—"

A shrill whistle pierced the air. Alex stiffened. Grace spun around, searching the darkness for the culprit. Shadows, human forms, darted across the street, disappearing into the night. Fear peppered the very air.

"The constable," she whispered. She jerked her gaze to him. "I can't be seen; I'll be ruined."

He didn't move, merely stared at her as indecision crossed his features. What was wrong with the man? Didn't he understand? She needed to leave…now! She released a frustrated sigh and latched tightly to his hand. "Alex, I understand if you can't escort me home, but I need to go."

Still he said nothing.

Despite the chill air, a fine sheen of sweat gathered between her shoulder blades. "I'm sorry." She could wait no longer. Reluctantly she released his hand and turned to leave.

"Wait!"

There was a desperation to that word that gave her pause. Grace glanced back. Alex was facing the prostitute in the gaudy dress, who was stumbling to her feet in her haste to escape.

"You, there. Where do you live?"

The whore froze, her brows snapping together, suspicion lacing her painted features. "What's it to ye?"

"Here." He tossed her a couple coins. She eagerly caught them in midair. "If you have a room, let us use it for a brief while. You take the night off, find a nice, warm pub, and have a bit to eat."

The whistle blew again, followed by footsteps thundering toward them. Shadows morphing from darkness. Grace trembled with unease. She could feel Alex's impatience like a nagging gnat. He darted a glance back. Grace followed his gaze. That tall, broad-shouldered man who always seemed to be lurking near Alex was heading toward them like a bull looking for a mate.

The whore grinned, showing empty spaces where her front teeth should have been. "No need to say more. Ye can do what ye will, none of my business." She glanced pointedly at Grace, then winked.

"Oh no," Grace started. "You don't understand—"

"Quiet," Alex demanded. "Hurry now."

"All right, calm the bloody hell down." The woman stuffed the coins in the valley between her breasts, hiked up her skirts, and bolted down a lane.

Alex gripped Grace's elbow and dove after the woman, Grace doing her best to match his long strides. The cap she wore tumbled from her head, her curls falling down around her shoulders.

"Alex!" she cried.

But he was relentless and refused to stop even long enough for her to complain. She hadn't a clue where they were headed and could only trust Alex, a man she barely knew. It seemed ridiculous now that she had been thrown into this situation, yet what choice did she have? They darted down a dark alley, leaping over crates and garbage. Alex's grip was tight and sure; he seemed to know where they were headed, but how could he when it was obvious he'd rarely left Lady Lavender's side?

"Just here," the whore panted, pointing toward a building that looked like it would tumble down under a small gust of wind. "'Ere ye are." She pushed open a door. "Top on the right."

Alex nodded. "Give us an hour."

She grinned. "However long ye need."

Grace glanced back. The alley was empty, indicating they'd actually lost their pursuers. They made their way up the rickety steps, Grace clinging to the railing in desperation. The place was exactly as she'd expected, dirty and in disrepair. Alex pushed open the door at the top and stood aside, waiting for her to enter.

She hesitated, peeking into the small garret. The air was stale, the ceiling low, suffocating.

"Merely for a brief while," he said, sensing her discomfort.

Grace nodded and stepped into the room. A bed that was no more than a mat lay in the far corner, while a chair sat near one of the two windows, covered with threadbare curtains that were no more than rags. Alex had to duck as he came inside and shut the door.

There was something incredibly depressing about the place. She moved across the room, the scarred floorboards creaking under her weight. From below, voices mumbled, people coughed, a couple was arguing. A deep, aching heaviness strangled the breath from her lungs. Is this what would become of her family? Forced into a small garret once their money was gone? She brushed aside a curtain and gazed out at the night sky.

Smoke billowed from chimneys, gray clouds upon black sky. A few stars managed to shine weakly through the fog, but their light was sad and pathetic. Too late for mongers selling their wares. The darkness almost hid the poverty—almost. But the lack of light couldn't cover the melancholy atmosphere.

"We'll wait here merely for a moment or two." His velvet voice was a shock to her body, a comfort to her soul. "Closer to dawn the streets will clear."

And then what? She had a home she could return to, at least until their money ran out. But where would Alex go? She turned to face him. The room was small, and Alex was large. She couldn't see him living in squalor, not dressed as richly as he was and certainly not with the air of superiority he had about him.

Alex pushed away from the wall and moved toward her, his hand cupping the back of his neck, rubbing the muscles. So beautiful, even in this squalor, but it was the way his hands trembled that she focused on. The very air around him stirred with unease.

What would he do now that he had left Lady Lavender? Or would he return? Her gaze raked his angelic features, to his wide shoulders, then lower, to the way his white shirt stretched across his broad chest. She froze, then jerked her gaze to his arm.

"What is that?" She met him in the middle of the room and latched on to his wrist, bringing his arm up for inspection. "You're injured!"

"I'm fine."

Ignoring his statement, she rolled his sleeve higher. A thin red gash marred his muscular forearm, blood drawing an angry red trail down his arm. "Oh, Alex," she whispered, her voice catching.

It was her fault. Damn it all. If she hadn't been trying to hide the fact that they had no footmen, if she hadn't set out to prove to Rodrick that she was no helpless female, this never would have happened. She dropped her hold and pulled her shirt loose from her waistband.

"'Tis nothing." He brushed by her, pausing at the window.

It might not have been deep, but it needed to be bandaged before it became infected. She slipped her finger into the tiny hole at the hem of her shirt and pulled. The material ripped easily, the sound a loud screech that raised the fine hairs on her body.

Alex glanced back. "There's no need to ruin your…is that *your* clothing?"

Grace flushed. "No. My sister's." She waved toward the chair. "Sit."

He sighed but moved toward the wing back that had certainly seen better days. It didn't matter that the chair was worn and tattered; he still looked like a king ruling over his domain. She bit back her smile and started toward him.

"Will just take a moment," she cooed, pausing before him. She'd taken care of many injuries, from her father, her step-father, and now her mother as they lay upon their sickbed. Merely another person to heal, yet Alex was not merely a person, but *Alex*. The man who heated her blood with a glance.

With her knee, she nudged his legs apart and stepped between them. He tilted his head back against the chair and watched her through those thick, dark lashes. More than ever, she was acutely aware that they were alone. Slowly she wrapped the bandage around his arm, forcing her fingers to remain steady, although her heart thumped madly in her chest. She could barely breathe, barely think with his gaze pinned to her.

"Thank you."

There was a sincerity to his voice and an intensity to his gaze that squeezed her heart and made her wonder if anyone had ever taken care of him. She smiled, tucking the loose ends under the bandage. "Of course." The obvious emotion in his heated gaze shouldn't have influenced her. She was in love with Rodrick, after all. But she couldn't deny that being this close to Alex sent her senses spinning.

"How shall I repay you?"

Startled, she stiffened. "There's no need. It was nothing."

"Perhaps to you." He stared at her for one long moment, his gaze so intense she felt as if he saw into her very soul. She started to step back. "We never had our next lesson."

Grace froze. *Kissing.*

His gaze darkened as that pulse in the side of his neck flickered to life. "You do remember, don't you?"

Of course she bloody remembered. Her entire body came awake with the memory. Places she had never known existed suddenly pulsed with life. "I have no money."

"Free of charge." His voice was a husky temptation. He slid his uninjured arm around her waist, bringing her close. She could feel his body trembling, but from anxiety or from passion she wasn't sure. He tilted his head and looked up at her. The erotic scent of spice and maleness swirled in the air, making her dizzy.

"Why?" she whispered, lifting her lashes to meet his gaze. "At times you barely seem to like me."

He smiled, a soft, emotional smile that tugged at her heart. "Oh, I like you, Grace. I like you an awful lot, and that, my dear, is the problem."

She parted her lips to question him further, but he placed his hands on her waist and all thoughts vanished. Slowly he pulled her toward his lap. She settled on his hard thighs, every muscle evident through the thin material of her trousers. His hand slid underneath her shirt, his long, elegant fingers moving over her smooth, bare back. Grace bit her lower lip. Reaching her binding, he paused.

"Whatever are you wearing?"

She swallowed hard. The warmth of his hands on her skin had her flustered. She felt odd, as if a fever was working its way through her body. "Binding, to—"

"I understand." He reached up and slid his fingers into her hair, dragging the locks down so they fell around her back and shoulders in a shimmering veil. Just when she thought he was done, he brought the strands forward, breathing in their scent. "Beautiful."

"Do you mean it?" she whispered, looking at him, frantic for the truth. "Or do you say that to all of your clients?"

He paused, his hands cupping the sides of her face. His eyes had grown serious, intense, yet she hadn't missed the flash of hurt that had briefly appeared. "Right now, in this moment, you're not a client."

His words were almost a warning. She was not a client; therefore, she was not in charge. They were merely a man and a woman indulging in an overwhelming attraction that would lead to nowhere. He tilted his head and pressed his mouth to her neck, his breath tickling her pulse. A tremor coursed through her body. Grace moaned, closing her eyes. Wrong, this was so wrong! Here, in this tiny room, they were alone, completely and utterly alone. Anything could happen.

"What color stockings are you wearing tonight?" he mumbled against her throat.

She racked her brain, trying to remember and at the same time wondering why it mattered. "Pink, I believe. With green leaves stitched along the sides."

He chuckled, although why he found it amusing she wasn't sure.

"Teach me," she whispered frantically, sliding her fingers into his hair. "Teach me to kiss."

The sparkle of amusement that shone in his eyes vanished. He deliberately lowered his gaze to her neck. "As you wish." With deft fingers, he flipped open the top button of her shirt and pressed his mouth to her collarbone, his soft curls tickling her cheek.

Grace sighed, relaxing and sinking into him. He was lovely, so incredibly lovely, and for this moment she could pretend he only wanted her. Pretend their forbidden relationship could exist. Pretend he hadn't done this with hundreds of other women. He flipped open two more buttons until her bound breasts were exposed.

"How terribly sad," he whispered. He pressed his mouth to the top of one soft mound while his hand moved to her bottom, cupping her and pulling her closer to his waist. The hard mound of his cock pressed to her thigh. Hot and cold chills tiptoed over her skin. Her breasts grew heavy, pressing against the binding, begging to be freed.

"Your neck is lovely, but shall I focus on your lips?" He lifted his head, those eyes midnight pools of seduction.

She could only nod. He cupped the back of her head and brought her closer. Grace's lashes fluttered down as she felt the warmth of his mouth on her lips. "Slow and passionate or bold and daring?"

She didn't understand a word he was muttering. She only wished he'd kiss her.

"Slow," he answered for her. "Make me forget, Grace."

A shimmer of heat wavered through her body. His lips molded to hers, softly, for one brief moment. Then he shifted his mouth, drawing her plump lower lip between his teeth. It wasn't the first time he'd kissed her, but it felt like it. Unable to stop herself, Grace slid her arms around his neck and pressed her breasts to his hard chest. It was all the coaxing he needed.

Alex's tongue slid like velvet between her lips. With a sigh she opened for him. He was unhurried, his movements languid as if he had all the time in the world. His hands traveled under her shirt, over the skin of her back, his fingers sensually kneading her muscles.

Grace tilted her head, deepening the kiss as his tongue swept into her mouth. His fingers found the binding and gently unwound the material flattening her breasts. She should stop him...It was wrong...so wrong...but it felt so bloody good!

Gently his tongue darted into her mouth, rubbing, tasting, tormenting her senses with long strokes that tightened her belly into a fiery knot of need. She wanted him, all of him. At this moment, in a whore's garret room, she would have given him everything. The material holding her breasts gave way. Grace's chest expanded, the air easing into her lungs. She tilted her head back as Alex pressed his mouth to her collarbone. His warm hands found her breasts, cupping the soft mounds.

"So lovely," he whispered right before his mouth covered a nipple.

Grace sucked in a sharp breath, her fingers sliding into his hair, tightening around the curls, intending to push him away. But then his tongue wrapped around her nipple, drawing the peak between his lips. Any thoughts of pushing him away disappeared, replaced with need so intense she thought she'd die.

With a whimper she squirmed against his lap, her bottom rubbing erotically against his hard cock.

"Dear God," he whispered, pulling back. "Grace, I can't take you here, not here." He turned his head away from her and squeezed his eyes tightly closed, his breathing ragged.

His cheek rested against the side of her left breast. She should have felt embarrassed; instead she felt disappointed. Acutely, horribly disappointed. Against her thigh she felt the hard proof of his arousal, pulsing, aching to be released.

It was her heart, his heart, beating against each other that tormented her soul. She closed her eyes, reveling in the feel of her body pressed to his. He wouldn't take her here…but would he ever take her? Grace leaned back and pulled her shirt together. She felt muddled, confused, and even a little angry. Angry at Alex, angry at the world, but mostly angry at herself.

"What will you do now, Alex?"

"The sun will be rising soon," he whispered. "I'll take you home."

He hadn't really answered her question, and she didn't want to go. She wanted to continue whatever it was they'd started, here, in this decrepit garret. But she wouldn't beg. No. And she knew, deep down, by stopping, Alex had saved her from a life of heartache.

* * *

There'd be hell to pay.

Alex let the curtain fall back into place over the dusty window and sank back into the corner of the hack. He recognized the carriage that followed. It was far enough behind that Grace wouldn't notice, but he had. Lady Lavender had located him already. But hadn't he known she would?

He pushed aside thoughts of escape, thoughts of freedom, and focused on Grace sitting so primly across from him. His mind spun, his senses still reeling from that kiss. How he'd wanted to stay in that dreary garret forever, and for a brief, insane moment he thought he could. He and Grace, live in a chamber and do nothing but make love. And they'd have babies. Babies with dirty faces and torn clothing. Babies that would cry because they were hungry. He tore his gaze away, unable to look her in the eyes. As if she'd ever have a man like him, a man with no money, no name, no soul.

Besides, if he managed to escape he had no doubt that within a day Lady Lavender would have hunted him down and forced him to return. She owned him. There was no use in trying to escape until he found a way to break free from her grasp forever.

Yes, he would pay for running off tonight. God, but it was worth it. For one brief moment he'd experienced freedom. He could still taste her lips, smell her vanilla scent upon his clothing. Those few brief moments with Grace had been worth whatever beating he'd endure.

"Thank you, Alex. It was an...adventure." Grace's soft voice whispered seductively from across the hired hack. An adventure. The kiss or the fight? Darkness hid her features from view, making it impossible to guess the way of her thoughts, and how desperately he wanted to know.

"You don't have to see me home, you know."

He flexed his fingers, his injured arm throbbing. "Any gentleman would."

She smiled, her white teeth flashing. "You said you were no gentleman."

He could no longer resist and shrugged, moving across the carriage to sit beside her. Her warm body pressed intimately to his. She didn't scoot away, but merely gazed up at him with eyes that shone with lingering passion. Eyes that reminded him of the intimacy they'd shared, eyes that remembered their kiss.

"I have my moments. Besides," he looked at her wryly, "you saved my life and all."

She grinned, a grin that made him want to kiss her all over again. "Yes, true." He slid his arm around her waist and drew her lush body closer, taking comfort in her presence.

"What are you doing?" she finally protested.

"It's bloody cold, and the first thing you learn in a brothel is that body heat is the best way to get warm." He was relieved when she didn't attempt to argue with his statement. "It was very stupid, you know, what you did."

"The board?" She tilted her head back and looked up at him.

"Yes."

She shrugged, not looking the least offended. "I thought to get on with it. You two were taking an awfully long time, dancing as you were."

He sighed, rubbing his tired eyelids. "We weren't dancing." He was more amused than annoyed. Perhaps they both knew their time together was limited. Why argue? He breathed deep the scent of her hair, attempting to memorize the smell. Underneath the stale scent of smoke and whiskey, he could smell that warmth. But there was something else there, a spicy scent…a masculine scent. Him, he realized with a start. She smelled like him. It was an oddly pleasant realization that warmed his heart. She unlatched her jacket and pulled it forward, tucking the edges around the two of them.

"Sometimes, many times, women must be the voice of reason."

He chuckled. "Really?"

"Yes. Men," she said, "tend—"

He took her hand under the jacket, his fingers slipping between hers. Neither of them wore gloves and their palms were intimately close; skin pressed to skin. Her breath came out in sharp little pants that stirred her loose tendrils and tickled his neck.

"Yes?" he prompted, secretly pleased that she'd lost her train of thought because of his touch. "You were saying?"

She shook her head. "That...that men tend to focus on silly pleasures, like gambling, horses, intimacy."

He rested the side of his face against her hair and soaked in her scent. "I assure you, my dear, there are as many women who are interested in sex as there are men."

He swore he could feel her face flush. The top of her head grew heated. The woman could walk, bold as you please, into a gaming hell dressed as a man, yet if he dared to say the word *sex*, she became a shy wallflower.

"Yes," she whispered. "Well, men don't realize how their actions affect their families."

He frowned, his humor fading. She was obviously speaking from experience. "And your lord Rodick—"

"Rodrick."

"Right, your lord Rodick. Is he different?"

She rested her free hand on his chest, playing with the collar of his shirt. Did she even realize her actions? "I don't know," she said. "I thought...no, I hoped...but..." She sighed, a long, pathetic sigh. "Do you think he gambles often?"

She looked up at him, trusting his answer. Damn it all. She would marry the earl for his money because of a wastrel brother. If not her dear lord Rodrick, it would be another man just as wretched. So why not just tell her the truth?

"No, I'm sure he only does upon occasion," he lied.

She smiled. "Thank you, Alex."

He nodded, a lump of some unidentifiable emotion forming in his throat. The carriage turned a corner and she sank farther into his side. They were moving closer to her home, the shacks giving way to townhomes. He wrapped his arm around her waist, the frantic need to keep her with him pounding through his veins. "Tell me something, anything about you that others don't know."

She frowned, a small crease hitching between her brows. "Well, on days when I'm feeling rather particularly melancholy, I like to go to the museum."

He smiled at her admission. No tawdry sexual affair as most women would have admitted to him. A secret pure and simple, yet something scandalous all the same. A woman who liked to *think*?

"And the book, the one you were searching for?"

"Oh, that." She spread her fingers over his, entwining them together more tightly. It was an action she did without thinking, yet it pleased him all the same. "Silly, really. It has to do with buried treasure."

He smiled, thinking back to his childhood. How many times had he and Dem searched for treasures? "Not so silly," he whispered.

She looked up at him. "Truly, you don't think so?"

He brushed his free hand down the side of her face, caressing her soft cheek. "Not at all."

For one long moment they merely stared at each other. There was a helplessness to her gaze that sent his heart thundering. An unspoken emotion that pulsed between them. The carriage slowed and the connection broke. Grace leaned forward, peeking out the window. "Home."

She didn't sound relieved. The carriage drew to a stop, but neither of them moved. He didn't want her to leave, didn't want the night to end. He didn't want to return to Lady Lavender's. Yes, the moment he'd stepped from that gaming hell the thought of freedom had terrified him. But now…knowing what freedom represented…now he felt the panicked need to hold it close, to hold Grace close.

"I should—"

"Yes," Alex replied in a husky voice, "you should."

So why did she continue to merely sit there as if she wanted something more from him? Alex's heart pounded, his body growing warm. She felt it...the inexplicable emotion coursing between them. How desperately he wanted to demand the driver take them to the closest train station. But no, he couldn't do that to her. She deserved more than he could give. She deserved her earl.

"Alex, I..." She dropped her gaze to his lips.

Tempting. So tempting. She wanted him to kiss her; he could feel it deep within. So why didn't he? Because he was afraid he wouldn't be able to stop.

From outside a door opened and shut, shattering the moment.

Alex glanced out the window. Rodrick stood on the front stoop of a stately brick home, like most of the other townhomes in the area. Nice. But little things...overgrown bushes, peeling paint...hinted that it was falling into disrepair. It certainly didn't compare to the mansions he'd lived in back on the continent. *Home.* He hadn't thought about home in years and he sure as hell wouldn't now.

"Grace," Rodrick called out, bounding down the steps.

Alex pulled back, handing Grace her jacket. "Where will you go?" she asked, obviously worried about him. He wasn't sure how to feel about her concern.

"Back to the estate."

"But why?" she demanded. "Alex, it's your chance to—"

"Thank the heavens," Rodrick exclaimed. "I was just about to send a constable after you. We couldn't locate your whereabouts, but John said you were in good hands." He jerked open the carriage door and glared at Alex as if he highly doubted John's statement. At least this Rodrick had more sense than Grace's brother.

Grace sighed an exasperated sigh. She didn't like being treated like a child. "I'm quite well, as you can see." She leaned forward, allowing Rodrick to help her from the carriage. But the moment her feet hit the ground, she turned toward Alex.

He knew she hadn't noticed the carriage following them and he didn't want her to know.

"Grace, you must come in before you catch a chill." Rodrick took her arm. For some reason the action irritated Alex. Damn it all, he wanted to say something…anything. But *thank you for a lovely evening* seemed rather ridiculous given the circumstances.

Grace hesitated, her soft eyes searching Alex's face; for what he wasn't sure.

"Go. I'm fine." Alex pulled the door shut and tapped the roof, urging the driver on. He had to leave now before he couldn't resist her. The image of snatching Grace from the street and taking off in the carriage would torment him the entire drive.

He had to let her go. She didn't belong with him. No, she belonged here, with men like Rodrick.

"Thank you," she called out as the carriage jerked to life.

He nodded, his fingers curling into his thighs. "It was nothing."

She stood in the middle of the street watching him until the carriage turned a corner and he could no longer see her. "It was nothing," he whispered to himself.

But the punishment he would receive when he returned would say otherwise.

Chapter 10

Alex had been injured. It was only natural that she should check on his health. After all, it was her fault he'd received the knife injury. So yes, it was perfectly natural to drive the hour to Lady Lavender's estate and inquire after his welfare.

So why then was she merely standing in the alley behind the estate house with the garbage?

Rodrick had been such a nuisance all morning, asking her questions about Alex. Of course she'd lied, inventing some story about how he was a distant cousin. But when he'd left, he'd still been frowning. He would most likely uncover the truth, but at the time she hadn't cared. She'd merely wanted him gone.

She'd tried to sleep, but had spent the rest of the night pacing her room until Patience had pleaded with her to stop; the creaking floorboards were driving her mad. By six in the morning, Grace had realized she would never rest until she knew if Alex was well. She wouldn't have the man die on her. The guilt would be too much.

So with Rodrick gone, John sleeping off his drink, and Patience watching Mama, she'd snuck out just as the sun had crested the horizon and used what little money she'd saved to hire a hack to drive her the hour outside London. The moment she'd smelled those lavender fields, her heart had leapt to life.

All that money spent, time gone…and here she stood, contemplating leaving. Grace adjusted her veil and stepped closer to the back door determined to get on with it. She was surprised by how easy it had been to walk through those gates. Surprised and confused. At times she thought Alex was here against his will; other times he almost seemed as if he enjoyed his position. Who was the true Alex? Only one way to find out.

Before she lost nerve, she let her knuckles fall, then quickly knocked twice more. Too late to leave now. With a shudder, she stepped back and waited. Moments later the door opened and a maid poked her freckled face outside.

"Yes, mum?"

"I need to speak with Alex."

"Who is it, Izzie?" someone called in a gruff voice.

An old woman pushed the girl aside. Her weathered face showed not the slightest bit of friendliness, and Grace had to resist the urge to shrink back.

"Alex, please," Grace demanded, as if she belonged there in that back alley.

The old woman slowly scanned her form, as if judging her worth. She shook her gray head, apparently finding her lacking. "If ye must see the men, ye have tae go through Lady Lavender. Enter through the front."

"I have the coins!"

The old woman started to close the door. Grace wedged her boot inside, preventing the action. "Please, I was here only the other day and was allowed to see him."

The woman snarled, showing gray gums. "Rules have changed."

She gave Grace's foot a swift kick.

"Owww!" Grace stumbled back, hopping up and down. The door slammed shut. "Well, I've never!"

Hopelessness welled as painfully as the ache in her foot. She'd have to make an appointment, which would mean more coins, coins she so desperately needed to save. Perhaps this Lady Lavender would allow her to make payments of some sort.

"Blast it." She merely wanted to make sure Alex was well. Slipping her fingers underneath her bonnet, she rubbed her aching temples and peered up at the windows. Did any lead into the hall? Perhaps she could just slip inside, unseen, quick and silent as a mouse. It was a ridiculous thought, yet her body seemed to have a mind of its own. Making sure no one was watching, she pushed a crate toward the wall, the wood scraping against the cobbles. Blast, but wearing pants was much easier. She was starting to have an entirely new appreciation for Patience.

"If you're trying to kill yourself, you'll have to climb higher than that."

Grace spun around.

A tall man stood in the shadows, leaning casually as you please against the wall. Handsome as a devil and dressed finely in a buff jacket and trousers, she assumed he was one of Lady Lavender's men. A cheroot hung between his fingers, a thin trail of smoke weaving its way into the air. Whereas Alex was all charm, this man was the opposite. Hair black as coal, gray, cold eyes, a face that seemed chiseled from stone. She supposed some might think of him as handsome, but she could only think about his size...very tall, very broad. A Scottish warrior of old.

She stepped back, her heart thundering in her chest. He was, without a doubt, *impressive*.

"I'm not trying to kill myself."

He placed his cheroot between his firm lips and released a puff of smoke. Slowly, meticulously, his gaze traveled down her form, then up again, leaving her feeling naked although she was wearing quite a dull green gown with a high neckline and long sleeves.

"Why do you wish to see Alex?" Was there the slightest accent to that voice? His intense gray eyes pierced hers, and for a moment she lost her train of thought. When she didn't respond quickly enough, he quirked a black brow. And for a moment, under the seductive intensity of his gaze, she could understand why women would find him attractive.

"Can you locate him?"

"Why do you wish to see him?" he repeated, crossing his arms over his chest.

"I just…that is…" Oh bother it! How did she explain without condemning the man? "He helped me last eve and I know he was injured. I wanted to make sure he's well. I sent a note, but he never responded."

The giant remained silent for one long moment, so long that she was preparing to turn and leave when he finally spoke again. "She won't allow for private correspondences."

"But…" Grace frowned. "But that…that's…is that even legal?"

He shrugged and dropped his cheroot to the ground. With a quick stomp, he crushed the butt, reducing the glow to cold ash. "Lady Lavender can do as she pleases."

"She sounds rather like a dictator." The moment the words were out she realized her mistake. This was his employer. He might not take kindly to someone speaking negatively toward her. "I do apologize."

Instead, he laughed, a deep, rumbling chuckle that, for some reason, surprised her. She had a feeling he didn't laugh often. "Come along."

Grace stiffened. "Where?"

He started toward her, his trousers stretching over thickly muscled thighs. Intimidating, to say the least. "If you wish to see Alex, I'll take you to him."

"Truly?" She watched him warily, unsure if she should trust the man.

He didn't seem to care whether she followed or not. With a shrug, he strolled toward the kitchen door. "Well? Are you coming?" He glanced back at her and those eyes, Lord, even though he was smiling, those eyes were cold.

Instinct told her to stay far away from this man. She glanced up at the building. There, within those many rooms, anything could happen to her.

"Well?" he demanded.

Grace swallowed hard. Her instincts had been off lately. Before she changed her mind, she scurried after the man. He pushed the door wide and stepped aside, allowing her entrance. The moment she moved into the kitchen, all work ceased. Grace jerked the netting over her face, hiding behind the thin veil.

With a smirk, the warrior took her hand in his. She started at his touch, his fingers so different from Alex's. This man's grip was tight, almost too tight. His large hand engulfed hers, his size overwhelming. While Alex's were more the hands of an artist, almost graceful, this man looked like he could kill with the strength of his fingers alone. He wasn't watching her, but looking straight ahead as if she didn't exist. Not a maid said a word as he made his way across the kitchen, but they watched them. Oh, how they watched! Grace had the childish desire to stick out her tongue toward the cook who had so rudely slammed the door in her face.

They traveled that narrow flight of steps, the same steps she had taken to Alex's room only days before. The closer they got, the more nervous she became. Would he be happy to see her? Or annoyed? Her heart slammed erratically inside her chest, begging her to flee. But at the second floor they didn't go to Alex's room, instead pausing halfway down the hallway.

"What—"

The warrior pushed the closest door wide and gently shoved her inside. Grace stumbled, attempting to regain her balance. She should have known better than to trust him! The door shut with a soft thud.

She spun around. "You...you said you'd take me to Alex."

He nodded, walking slowly toward her. "And I will."

But this obviously wasn't Alex's room. No, his room was calming, pretty almost, with its white curtains and soft bedspread. But this room...this room screamed brothel with its red velvet chairs and black silk bedspread. Grace shivered. "This isn't Alex's room."

He quirked a brow, amusement softening his hard features. "Indeed. You've been there before?"

She crossed her arms over her chest, hiding the trembling of her hands. She knew what it would imply if she answered his question. Yes, she'd been there. Yes, she was a client of his. "Perhaps."

He smiled, a wicked smile that she supposed did all sorts of warm things to women, but did nothing for her. "We'll go there soon. Calm your nerves. We need just a moment."

She lifted the netting of her bonnet. "A moment for what?"

He pressed his finger to his lips. Neither of them moved toward the door, merely continued to stand in the middle of the room. Waiting for what? His silence confused her, made her nervous.

"Sir, please. If you—"

"Here she comes." He glanced at the door.

Grace stiffened. "Who?"

He moved purposefully across the room, his strides long and sure as he drew closer, not bothering to respond to her question. Like an animal after a sure kill.

Grace moved back a step, pressing her hands to her churning belly. Really, it was quite annoying not knowing if she should be excited or nervous about said visitor. "What are you doing?"

He didn't pause in his stride, nor did he avert his gaze from her face. "I'm going to kiss you."

"What?" she demanded, her voice a high-pitched shriek.

But there was no amusement on his face. He was completely and utterly serious. "I'm going to kiss you and you're going to like it."

"That's debatable!" Grace stumbled backward, her thighs hitting the bed.

He paused in front of her, so close she could feel the warmth of his large body. "Trust me."

She started to laugh at his absurd request when he wrapped a muscled arm around her waist and jerked her close. Her breasts smashed to his hard chest, too close, too intimate. When he leaned over her, she felt as if she would be crushed. It all happened so very quickly that she wasn't prepared. His firm lips pressed to hers, and for one odd moment, Grace merely stood there, once again allowing a complete stranger to kiss her.

He cupped the back of her head and with his other hand used his thumb to press her chin downward. Before she could guess his intentions, his tongue slipped into her mouth, bold as you please, like warm velvet and not exactly unpleasant. Yet...odd. So very odd. She wasn't sure if she liked it or not. Although she couldn't deny that he knew how to kiss, his touch left her feeling off...like when she'd just gotten over a cold. Pleasant, yet no spark of sudden desire.

Then Alex's face came to mind and a slight, unwelcome tingle warmed her insides.

Vaguely she was aware of the door opening. "Gideon." A woman's sharp voice cracked across the room like a slap to her senses. "Please come into the hall."

He pulled back and gave her a wink. "Stay here."

Gideon. This was the Gideon who received the more experienced women? Bemused, Grace slumped back against the bed. She could only sit there, blinking weakly as he made his way into the hall. When he shut the door, she pressed her fingers to her tingling lips. "How very odd."

It wasn't the first time she'd been kissed. No, the first *true* and utterly *thorough* kiss she'd received had been from Alex. As she sat there, she couldn't help but compare the warrior's kiss to Alex's. Compare his touch to Alex. Compare his scent…his voice…his taste…And she found this warrior…*lacking* for some reason that she couldn't quite explain.

"A client," she heard the man named Gideon mutter, the words whispering through the closed door and bringing her back into the moment.

She stood, testing her legs. Finding she could stand without collapsing, she moved across the room and pressed her ear to the door. This man, Gideon, was pretending she was here for him. But why? Was this Lady Lavender so truly horrible that she wouldn't allow Grace a quick, completely innocent visit with Alex?

"You're not signed up for anyone," she replied in a refined voice that spoke more of drawing rooms than brothels. Grace's interest was piqued. Who was this woman?

"Yes, I know. She was recommended and wasn't sure she wanted to go through with the visit. I was making her sure." Gideon's voice was so strong, demanding, that even Grace almost believed him.

"Marie said she asked for Alex." Apparently Lady Lavender had her doubts and her spies. Did the woman notice everything?

"Marie was mistaken."

"Lady Lavender," someone called from down the hall.

There was a frustrated sigh. "Yes, what is it?"

"A problem with payment."

There was a short pause. Grace held her breath, waiting, hoping, praying. "Very well. I'll speak with you later."

Giddy with relief, Grace stumbled back just as the door opened. Gideon swept inside, that gray gaze intense once more. "You have a short while before she'll return."

Any giddiness fled. His words sounded rather dire. Confused, she let him grab her hand and jerk her into the hall. "I don't understand." Which wasn't an oddity. She hadn't understood much in the past fortnight.

In three long steps they were at the end of the hall. Gideon pushed open Alex's door and shoved her into the dark room. Regaining her balance, Grace spun around to face him.

"If you hear anyone, hide," he said. "If you get caught, I'm not responsible."

"But—"

He shut the door, trapping her in total darkness. Grace turned, her heart hammering in her chest. She could only stand there, waiting for her eyes to adjust. A fire crackled in the hearth, the red light more sinister than comforting.

"Alex?" she whispered, her voice quivering.

A soft moan came from the vicinity of the bed. Grace froze. Her heart plummeted to her feet. She was going to be sick. Oh dear God, he was…entertaining.

She stumbled back until she hit the hard, unforgiving door. "I'm so sorry. I…"

A dark shadow shifted on the bed. There was a soft swoosh and a flare of brilliant light as a lamp was lit. "Grace, is that you?"

"Alex?"

His voice sounded odd, strained, but the light was too fast; her eyes hadn't had time to adjust and she couldn't see his face.

"Yes, but I'll leave. I'll…" There was no other movement, no other dark shadows. Was he alone?

Grace shaded her eyes and stepped hesitantly forward, closer to the bed, closer to Alex. She could barely see his features.

"Alex, what—"

A bitter scent hovered in the air. She paused. Grace knew the scent well. The scent of medicines. The scent of sickness. Her heart stopped. For one brief moment she swore her heart actually stopped. "Dear God, Alex, what happened to you?"

* * *

She was *not* here.

Yet even as he wanted to deny it, even as he wanted to pretend he was dreaming, he knew she was real. He could smell her. That clean, warm scent that momentarily disrupted the bitter odor of the salve that had been rubbed onto his wounds. Alex groaned and sank back into the bed. The movement sent dizzying pain rippling through his torso. He didn't know whether to be horrified by her presence or thrilled.

"Go away before you get us both killed."

"Nonsense," she whispered, but he noticed the way her voice quavered. She wasn't as strong as she pretended. She pulled on the ribbon holding her bonnet in place. "No one will murder me; my stepfather was titled."

He rolled his eyes and pressed his face into his pillow. Lady Lavender didn't care about connections; she had too many of her own. If Grace only knew about his background and how little his title had protected him. Would she be impressed by his family? No, not Grace. "A title means nothing in my life, sweet."

"Is that…"

He noticed her glove lying there pristine white near his pillow at the same time she did. Embarrassed heat washed over him. Lord, as if he needed anything else to add to his unease.

"You forgot it," he said gruffly, tossing it toward her.

She caught it close to her chest. "I…see."

And she did see, he could tell by the tone of her voice. *Shite.* She was wondering if he cared…if he could possibly have feelings for her.

"What's that scent?" She sniffed delicately as she moved around the bed and set her bonnet on the table. How the hell had she made it to his room unseen? Lady Lavender wouldn't have allowed it. Had she snuck in? Yes, he supposed women could come and go easily through the gates; men much less so. Hell, he didn't care. She had to leave before Ophelia found them. She already knew that Alex had escorted Grace home, thanks to Wavers. Surely she suspected that Alex cared more for Grace than he should.

"Wonderful, now you're saying I smell. Go away, Grace."

"Medicine, that's what it is." She rushed the last few steps, her skirts rustling with the movement. "You're ill!" She said the words as if they were an accusation.

Despair washed over him. He didn't want her comfort; he couldn't handle compassion at the moment. He must be hard, unemotional, because it was the only way he would ever survive this hell. His hands fisted in the sheets until feathers poked through to his palms. "Bloody hell, will you please just go away?"

"No! Not until I know you're well."

"Why?" he asked, his voice almost pleading, and he hated himself for it. "Why do you care?" He hadn't meant to ask her, yet once the words were out, he couldn't deny that he eagerly awaited her response.

She paused for one long, breathless moment. "Because...I owe you."

He released a harsh laugh and closed his eyes. She owed him. The worst possible word she could have said. *Owed*. He'd heard the word too much in his lifetime. Hadn't he thought he'd owed it to his family to prove he could protect them? And look where that had gotten him.

"I know the scent of sickness well," she said softly.

He reluctantly opened his eyes, his interest piqued. Why did she know it well? Damn, he hurt too much to ask. She settled on the edge of his bed. The slight movement sent his bones jarring, and pain shot through his body once more. He gritted his teeth, grimacing.

"You're hurt." Her voice was a soft caress.

He didn't respond. He was in too much pain to talk. It didn't matter that she knew. Nothing mattered at the moment. Every bone in his torso felt cracked, every muscle pulled with sharp pain at the slightest movement. The two bulls who had beaten him had fists like bricks.

She raised the wick of the lantern. The flame flared to life, sending blinding light over his face. How long had he been lying in the dark? Hours? A day? He vaguely remembered a maid applying the salve to his back. Lady Lavender had sent her; his employer wasn't a complete monster after all. No, she wanted him well again so that when his clients came calling, he'd be ready.

"Where does it hurt?"

He managed to hide his face under his arm, afraid she'd read the pain in his eyes. It was too much, too humiliating, and he despised Ophelia more than he ever had before. "Everywhere."

Those cool fingers wrapped around his wrist. Slowly, carefully, she moved his injured arm. The knife wound he'd received after visiting the gaming hell was the least of his worries. She pressed her palm to his forehead, a gentle touch, a caring touch. "No fever."

She started to pull away, but in a desperate need to keep her close, he reached out, grasping her wrist, keeping her palm to his head. A touch, a soft touch, a touch for no reason other than the fact that she was concerned for his well-being. At least he could pretend she was concerned. He closed his eyes, focusing on the feel of her soft skin. How long had it been since someone had comforted him? An unidentifiable emotion clawed its way into his throat, taking permanent residence in the form of a lump.

"Don't move," he begged, hating himself for his weakness.

"All right."

She slid closer to him, her hip pressed to his shoulder. But it wasn't enough. No, she wrapped her arm around him, and with her free hand she brushed her fingers through his curls. His jaw clenched, the feeling bittersweet. How long had it been since someone had cared? His hands curled into the sheets as he resisted the urge to wrap his arms around her, to hold her tightly to his body, to breathe in her scent. But he feared if he touched her he'd never let her go.

"Tell me, what is it?"

"Nothing," he lied. "Merely an aching head."

"Hmm, and the medicine I smell?"

"For the pain."

"What is it?" she demanded. Before he could respond, she tore his covers away. "Oh, Alex." The way she said his name...he wasn't sure if he should be annoyed or thrilled. He didn't want her to care, couldn't depend on her emotions. Yet he'd gone so many years without someone caring that, like a starved mongrel, he hungered for her.

"It's nothing." Slowly he rolled to his side, his back to her.

"What happened? Was it after I left you on that street? Were you attacked?" She pulled the blanket down farther, revealing his bare backside. Realizing he was naked, she paused. He could imagine her face flushing and smiled over it.

"Yes," he said. "Attacked."

"Nonsense, you're lying."

He rolled to his back, even though the movement sent more pain through his body, and glared up at her. "How do you bloody know?" He grabbed the blanket and jerked it back up to his chest.

"Because," she said, lifting an impertinent brow. "They didn't hit your face."

She rested her hand on the side of his cheek, her heat seeping through his skin. He closed his eyes. Damn woman was too smart for her own good.

"She did this to you? Lady Lavender?"

"No, not her." Which was true enough. Her hands had never touched him.

"But she ordered it done."

"Yes," he snapped, hating Ophelia and especially hating the fact that now Grace realized just how little control he had over his life.

"Is that what you want to hear?" He dared to sit up, his ribs pulling, aching with the movement. With his back to her, he settled his bare feet on the carpet. "She has henchmen. Big, burly men too damn ugly to be whores. Men she uses as guards, and when we disobey…"

"Oh God, Alex." Her voice was tight, high. "I'm so sorry."

He gave a wry chuckle. "What do you expect; we're a brothel. You think because we're men it's any different?"

She didn't respond, which meant yes, she had thought it different.

"We might dress better," he said bitterly. "Our rooms may look better, but that's merely to present a façade for the women who come here. We're still whores and we're still treated no better than animals."

"You have to leave Alex. You must at least try to escape."

The fire crackling in the hearth was the only sound. He didn't dare move, barely breathed for fear she would say something more, for fear she would realize the truth. He was going to leave. He'd decided the moment Wavers's fist had connected with his gut. He would take this no longer, but if he told Grace, she would want to be involved, and he would not endanger her any more than he had already.

"It was because of me, wasn't it?"

"Of course not," he whispered.

"Because you left the gaming hell with me? I saw that man, watching on the corner. Was he the one who beat you?"

He closed his eyes, pressing his lips tightly together. He would say no more. Already he'd said too much. If Ophelia would do this to him, what would she do to an outsider like Grace? It was best she know as little as possible.

But Grace stood and moved around the bed. "Why, Alex? Why are you here?" She stopped only feet from him and wrapped her arm around the bedpost. She wore a green dress today, a dress that made him think of country fields in spring.

"You think I had a choice?" He looked up at her, looked into her clean, pure face, and part of him hated her. A woman too good for him. A woman he could never have. Bitterness washed through him, tearing at his insides. He surged to his feet, welcoming the pain the movement brought. What to tell her? That part of him had always been afraid to leave? Not only because of the horrible beating he knew would follow when he was found, but because he had nowhere to go, nowhere he belonged but here, a whorehouse?

"I like it. That's why I'm here. Now leave before we're caught and you make things worse."

She stared up at him, those eyes wide and luminous. "I'm so sorry, Alex."

Sorry for what? For coming here? Or for making him dream impossible things? He chuckled, a harsh, unnatural sound. "Why? I obey her, I get to fuck a variety of women. What's there to complain about? Every man's dream."

She didn't even flinch at his harsh words. And the fact that she didn't flinch panicked him. She knew. Dear God, she knew he didn't want to be here. He could see the sympathy in her eyes. A softness that made him sick.

"You don't mean that," she said. "I can see it on your face. How old were you when you were taken?"

He didn't want to answer, didn't want to continue this line of conversation, yet his mind and body no longer seemed connected, he no longer held control. "Twelve or thirteen, I barely remember." He lied. He remembered every moment of that day.

Tears swam in her eyes. "So young." She moved closer, her warm scent reaching out to him. "Had you even been kissed?"

He swallowed hard. "Of course."

She paused in front of him, her warm breath whispering across his neck. "And since? Have you been kissed, Alex?"

He forced himself to laugh. "Of course I've been kissed."

Lamplight played across her face, kissing her features with a golden glow. "No, have you ever been kissed because you wanted to kiss someone, because you were caught in the moment and all you wanted to do was see how their lips would feel against yours. See how they tasted. How warm their breath was."

The words tore at his heart, made him feel pain he didn't want to feel. Yes. Damn her. She knew the answer. When they'd kissed in that garret. Utterly alone.

She moved closer. So temptingly close. That dull, constant ache that kept him up at night when he thought about her flared to life.

"Don't," he whispered. "I won't have you kiss me out of pity or sympathy."

She stood on tiptoe, making sure not to touch him, but leaning close…so close he could feel her all the same. "Then how about because I want to?"

Before he could respond, she pressed her lips to his. A soft, gentle kiss. Alex shivered, his body sinking into hers. He wanted to crush her to him, take her, have her, make her his. His hands trembling, he cupped the sides of her face and slid his fingers into her silky hair. Timidly her tongue swept across his lips. The touch was his undoing.

With a groan, he opened his mouth and deepened the kiss. He needed this, needed her. His hands clasped her upper arms, bringing her closer. He wanted her. Wanted her as he'd never wanted anyone.

Vaguely he was aware of the door opening. "Alex," Gideon's harsh voice snapped through the room. "Ophelia. She's headed this way."

Alex tore his mouth from Grace but didn't pull away. He needed to keep touching her, needed her strength. He couldn't seem to let go. Gideon stood in the hall looking as grim as always.

"What is it?" Grace asked, blinking in confusion, not even aware Gideon was behind them.

"Go." He gently pushed her toward the door.

She stumbled, only to be caught in Gideon's capable hands. Alex dampened down his irritation. Dampened down the need to reach out and pull her back to his side. "Get her out of here, now."

Gideon tugged her into the hall, but she fought him, twisting in his grasp only to turn toward Alex. "When will I see you again?" she asked.

The question surprised him, made him pause. It wasn't the words, but the need laced under the question. She wanted him. The words were out, the desire left hanging there between them.

As if sensing the importance of her statement, she flushed. "For an appointment, I mean."

"I'll be at the Rutherfords' masked ball," he blurted out.

"But the Rutherford ball is for…"

She didn't finish; she didn't need to. The Rutherford ball wasn't for innocents like her. For one long moment they merely stared at each other. With that simple question, she'd changed everything. Even Gideon showed his shock when he rarely showed any emotion. The man frowned, and Alex knew exactly what he was thinking: Alex and Grace had crossed a line. But Gideon didn't realize that at the ball Alex would make his escape. He merely needed to see Grace one last time.

"Go, now," Alex demanded.

He reached forward, pulling the door shut and blocking her from view. But it was too late. It was too damn late. Her words had pierced his heart. He knew in that moment she'd done the unthinkable and fallen for a whore. God help him, he was pleased.

Chapter 11

There was one time, and one time only, when Lady Lavender allowed her boys to leave their gilded prison and enter the normal world.

Masked balls.

Not that people didn't know who Lady Lavender was merely because she had a mask of brilliant violet and green peacock feathers surrounding those icy eyes. No, she was as noticeable with a mask as she was without one. That flaxen hair, the petite yet curvy body, and her violet dress with a neckline so low it was almost unlawful. They knew exactly who she was, but during a masked ball they could pretend to be ignorant. The next day they'd feign horror, all the while secretly thrilled that Ophelia had brought attention to their ball.

But tonight, only tonight, as Lady Lavender swirled around the ballroom, all eyes were drawn to her. There was no pretense that she didn't exist. The men watched her warily, wondering if the rumors were true, while at the same time the desire was evident in their lusty gazes. The women, on the other hand, either ignored her or threw her tiny smirks that bespoke feminine secrets. She was watched. She was feared. She was adored by all, the men who wanted her, yet feared her, and the women who needed her.

But she didn't arrive alone. Lady Lavender always attended masked balls with at least two of her pretty boys at hand. James, her favorite, had attended so many that he was almost at ease amongst the *ton*. Ironic, considering James had been born a street rat.

While Alex had been born to privilege, he felt anything but relaxed. He scanned the thickening crowd, dampening down the panicked need for air. Afraid he'd see someone he knew or that someone would recognize him from a former life. Fear of being out in the open with normal society. Fear of seeing his family. But mostly he despised the fact that he was treated exactly as he feared he would be...like a *thing*.

Yes, he and James were perfect specimens. Two men dressed impeccably in black suits, his jacket embroidered with golden thread that surely cost a small fortune, their handsome faces obscured only by a small black mask. Their demeanor as brooding and mysterious as a hero in any gothic novel. It was a time for Lady Lavender to parade her wares, to tempt the women of the *ton* to her side. He'd been pinched, leered at, and groped by a variety of women and a few men. And still Alex had kept that charming, mysterious smile in place. Sure, his teeth were gritted so hard he was surprised they hadn't cracked in his skull, but a feat indeed. They stayed near the walls, out of the way of the crowd, their backs protected. They stayed on the outskirts of revelry, never belonging. Like statues placed along the perimeter for adoration. They were watched closely by everyone. Even now he could feel their gazes like insects crawling over his skin.

They wondered who he was, how he'd be in bed, and, most important, what he could do for them. Alex swallowed hard, his hands trembling. But none of that mattered tonight. None of that mattered because Grace had not attended.

He'd searched every female form, every masked face, hoping, praying to see her, but it was obvious she had decided not to attend. And perhaps that was for the best. A relationship would only complicate things. Why then, did his chest feel so tight? Why did he feel as if the world around him no longer mattered?

Taking in a deep breath, Alex set his flute of champagne upon a small side table. "James, you don't tire of this?"

James glanced at him through the small mask he wore. "What do you mean?"

"Being nothing more than a toy."

James shrugged, glancing quickly around to make sure they were not being overheard. Between the loud conversations, laughter, and music, Alex knew they had as much privacy as they would in their bedchambers, but still the lad worried their conversation would travel back to Ophelia. And they mustn't upset her.

"It's a position. A job I do well. There could be worse things in life than pleasuring beautiful women."

Alex patted him on the back, attempting to ignore the ire he felt at James's statement. "That's where you're wrong, my boy. It's not a job; it's a hell in which we have no choice but to reside."

James shrugged and started to walk away to make his rounds—or flee Alex's intense statements more like. "It could be worse."

Alex frowned, biting back a reply. James refused to understand; refused to open his eyes. He insisted Lady Lavender had saved them. He couldn't see that they were no better than prisoners, forced to sell their bodies. Of course it had taken Alex sometime to understand the truth of his situation. It was Gideon who had started putting ideas into his head.

"*Why us?*"

It was the first question Gideon had whispered to Alex and it was enough. With that question, something had shifted, a tiny flare of life had grown when he'd been so numb before. Why had Lady Lavender focused on them?

"Alex, darling, is that you?" someone whispered.

The rich scent of sherry and lilies swirled around him, a familiar scent, although one he couldn't quite place. He turned. Brilliant golden hair, dark eyes behind a mask of red feathers. He searched his memory until a name popped to mind. He'd been her first, although certainly not her last. "My lady Sweetin."

Her painted red lips pulled into a grin. "You remember me?"

She was bold to approach him when she knew people would notice. But then she liked attention. She wore her bodices low and paint on her face when it was frowned upon. She had found him on purpose, no doubt, knowing people would whisper. Perhaps she was attempting to make her husband jealous.

He took her gloved hand, bowing over the pristine white fingers, the only thing pristine about her. "I could never forget you. Although shame on you; I haven't seen you in ages." He fell back into his regular routine. Reel them in. Make a profit. "I've missed you."

She giggled, sidling closer to him. Her perfume was cloying, as was her personality. He resisted the urge to cough. She was gaudy, much like the ballroom. Gold and marble, velvet curtains.

"You look delicious," she whispered, her hand sliding to his backside and squeezing. He didn't even flinch. Oddly, he wasn't numb to her touch. Ire swarmed low in his belly like a swarm of bees. The anger was so sudden, so unexpected, that it shocked him into silence. Confused, he shifted his fingers through his hair. He was tired. Merely tired of them all, whether groping women or quivering virgins. But not Grace. A breath of fresh air.

No. He wouldn't think of her. He wouldn't think of Grace and her sweet eyes and her even sweeter mouth. He wouldn't think about the fact that she made him dream of impossible things. Or the fact that she'd been completely ready to nurse him back to health when all others had forgotten him. He wouldn't think of her because he'd told her he'd be at this ball, yet she hadn't come.

Lady Sweetin drew her hand down his injured arm, the skin tingling in protest. "Meet me in the gardens." It wasn't a question but a demand, and as Lady Sweetin was one of their highest-paying clients, he didn't dare refuse. Besides, meeting with a client could provide him with the perfect opportunity to escape.

Alex inclined his head. "Of course."

She flittered away, those round hips swooshing back and forth and commanding more than one man's attention. Always work to be done. Lord, he didn't want to play right now, but he had no choice. Never any choice. It had been days since he'd had a woman, and Ophelia would be eager for him to get back into the chase.

He scanned the crowd, looking for the one woman whose permission he needed. Even thinking about leaving without Ophelia's approval caused his body to ache all over again. He placed his hand on his ribs, rubbing a sore spot that refused to heal. Four days later and there was still some pain. Had her minions finally cracked a rib? They were supposedly trained to inflict pain, but not permanent damage.

He caught a flash of violet from the corner of his eye and turned, spotting Ophelia next to James. Just the sight of the woman made him sick. As if sensing him, she turned. No doubt she was making sure her boy was where he was supposed to be. He gave her a slight nod. A silent message that told her he was working on a client and might be gone for a while.

She frowned but nodded back. She'd check on him, he knew that. Most likely send James to the garden in a few minutes. And James, the bastard, would no doubt run back to tell her all. Slowly he edged along the perimeter of the ball, following the wall. So many colorful dresses, surrounded by black suits. Men and women flirting, moving amongst each other in a rhythm of give and take. Couples coming together because they were attracted to each other, not because they had to flirt.

Disgust ate at his gut. He looked away. A flash of auburn hair had him jerking his head upright. Had he imagined it? Was he so bloody mad that he was finally seeing things? Someone shifted, there it was again. Shimmering auburn locks, curls cascading over creamy bare shoulders and a back covered with a light blue gown that pinched a tiny waist and flared to the floor in a wave of shimmering folds. He froze. She was here. Grace had come. Damn her.

His heart slammed in his chest, his blood thrumming under his skin. His soul sensed her. His fingers curled as he resisted the urge to go to her…and say what? No, he'd ruin her reputation by singling her out.

As if sensing his attention, she turned. Like everyone else she wore a mask, her upper face covered, unrecognizable behind its simple blue covering. But those lush lips were free. He didn't need to see her face completely to know it was Grace. He sensed her. Felt her deep within his being.

Her gaze scanned the crowd as if looking for something or someone. Looking for him? His heart stopped, fear and eagerness fighting for attention. Before she noticed him he slipped behind a column. He leaned back against the cool marble and took in a deep, trembling breath.

Although beautiful, she looked so out of place here amongst the cruel and callous *ton*. An angel in hell. She glowed with purity when they all faded with dullness.

Alex pushed away from the column. *And if she did have feelings?* his mind taunted. Well then, it had happened before. Clients falling for their men. Lady Lavender always made quick work of putting an end to any affection they might share. But it didn't matter because he was leaving. He wasn't a complete arse. He'd send her a note and explain to her that he'd had to escape, that they could never see each other again. Perhaps she'd be upset at first, but she'd move on…most likely finding comfort in the arms of her earl.

No, she wasn't enamored. Women often thought they had feelings for their men after they'd been intimate, but the most he and Grace had done was kiss. No, she wasn't enamored; she merely felt indebted to him. With renewed determination, he started toward the doors that led into the garden. He would ignore her. He would not search her out. He would not think about her.

The cool air fluttered the tails of his coat, cooled his fevered skin. But on the inside he still simmered. His feet hit the marble patio, tap, tap, tap. Keep going. Do not look back. But his body had a mind of its own. He froze. He would not look…

He turned, searching through the windows for Grace. She was coming straight at him, her face set in determination.

"Shite." He stepped back, hiding halfway behind an open door.

He felt her appearance like a caress. So close that he swore he could feel her body's warmth. She paused on the patio, those delicate shoulders rising and falling with each sharp breath. Was she looking for him? Damn, had she seen him? Lifting the hem of her gown, she darted down the steps and between two yews, gone within a moment. What was she doing? Surely she wasn't meeting someone for a rendezvous? If she was, she might as well label herself ruined for all of London.

He moved quickly, purposefully down those steps, following her footprints in the damp grass. He knew what could happen to an unescorted lady. Apparently she didn't. Where was her brother or that dandy prat Rodrick? He pushed between the two yews and froze. She'd disappeared. Nowhere to be seen. He was just about to turn, thinking perhaps he'd missed her, when he heard the beautiful sound of her voice.

"Hell," she whispered from somewhere above.

Alex tilted his head back. Blue skirts and white petticoats ruffled seductively above. She hovered over him, hidden in the branches, and he could see directly up her skirts, those long legs clad in wicked black stockings. Dear Lord, he'd never seen a more beautiful view.

* * *

Grace had never seen a more tantalizing or shocking view.

She had never actually witnessed a couple making love, but feared that this was exactly what she was seeing. In some unidentifiable room above the ball, where a couple had hidden away, not realizing they were visible for all in the garden to see, or perhaps not caring. Thank God, she seemed to be the only one who was far enough in the garden to notice.

Blast, but this was ridiculous. She should be hiking up her skirts and climbing over the wall, the only unseen way out of this hell, as John had refused to escort her home or loan her the carriage. The ballroom had been a crush of odd people who had immediately made her uneasy. She'd heard the rumors…that the Rutherford Ball was not for the innocent, and she should have listened. Almost from the moment she'd stepped inside, she'd wanted to leave, but John had insisted it would be rude to bow out when just arriving. John could go to hell.

She'd snuck outside for a breath of fresh air and had the sudden and ridiculous urge to escape and all because of Alex, blast him. She'd found the man quickly enough. Aye, she'd found him all right and the many, many women flirting with him, circling him like wolves after a tasty meal. Watching them had made her ill.

Here and now, thoughts of Alex and his friendly flirts disappeared. She found sudden fascination with the way the man in the window was kissing that woman's neck. The way she tilted her head. The way she parted her lips and grasped the strands of his hair in such a tight grip that surely it hurt.

Grace brushed aside a branch to get a better view. And in her mind she saw Alex, doing those things to her. She saw Alex pressing his firm lips to her throat. Alex sliding her sleeves down her shoulders to kiss her collarbone…farther to the tops of her breasts.

"We do offer such amusements for a small fee, you know."

The deep, velvet voice shocked Grace cold. Instinctively she released her grip on the branches above, then tried to snatch at them again. Too late. Caught completely off-balance, she threw her arms wide, her fingers desperately searching for a sure hold. She found nothing. Gravity did its job well and pulled her toward the ground. She was falling and she knew she'd land on her arse in front of Alex. Grace squeezed her eyes shut, preparing to hit the ground.

But she didn't slam unceremoniously into the grass. Instead, she hit strong arms, which pulled her to a hard chest. At the impact, a gasp escaped her lips. Her lashes lifted and she stared into two brilliant blue eyes. A mask covered half his face, but still, she knew his scent over the sweetness of roses climbing the wall; musk and warm spring. She knew his voice, husky and deep. She knew those lips, just made for pleasure…

"What are you doing here?" she asked, attempting to smooth her face into unreadable lines. Silly, really. She'd been caught red-handed spying on a couple making love and was playing the innocent. Yet instead of being embarrassed, the only feeling that swept through her was pure euphoria at seeing Alex.

"What are *you* doing here?" he repeated her same words.

"I…I was…" And for one brief moment she almost blurted out the truth. But if she admitted the truth, he'd think she cared. And she knew as well as anyone that she couldn't care, not about Alex, a man about as attainable as the prince.

She swallowed hard and pressed her lips into a firm line, staring directly into his hooded gaze. She didn't need to defend herself. When she didn't respond, he loosened his hold and she slid down his hard body, every muscle evident through the fine material of their clothing. Her feet hit the damp grass while her heart dropped to her toes.

He looked annoyed. His jaw clenched, his body stiff. She'd never seen him this way. Why was he annoyed? Were his injuries still paining him? Four days, it had been four days since she'd seen him, but it felt a year. She wanted to grab him and hug him. She wanted to kiss him. She wanted to tell him every tiny detail that had happened in her life since she'd seen him last.

"I didn't realize you were interested in that sort of thing," he murmured.

She stepped back, farther away from him, even though the fall had made her dizzy and she had the urge to use his strength as support. "What sort of thing?"

"Watching."

Confused, wary, she shook her head. "I don't understand."

He settled his bare hands on her shoulders. He wore no gloves. Indecent, really, but then she shouldn't be surprised. Slowly he turned her so her back pressed to his chest. He reached his arm around her, his forearm pressing to her breasts, his finger under her chin. Slowly, carefully, he tilted her head back until her gaze locked to that window. Heat shot to Grace's face. Oh God, Alex thought...he thought she was...thought she liked...

"No, I—"

"You can watch, you know." He leaned his head down so his breath whispered seductively across the side of her face. "Not many women ask for it, but it is possible. Of course there's a fee. Always a fee."

There was a cruel taunt to his voice, a tone she didn't like. She shook her head, unable to say anything more, for how could she defend herself? He drew her back, closer, her bottom fitting to his hard thighs. Too intimate.

"No," she whispered breathlessly. "I wasn't—"

"Do you like to watch?" His warm breath tickled her ear. "Or were you merely remembering how it feels to have someone's lips pressed to your neck?"

"No, I—" His mouth skimmed the sensitive skin directly below her ear. "Oh my, that does feel rather lovely." Her knees gave out as she sank back into him.

"Or the way his hand moves to her breast." His fingers moved down her neck and boldly cupped a breast, his palm warm through her gown. Her nipples instantly hardened, her breasts growing heavy with desire. She'd seen him naked, yet he'd never touched her like this, never so boldly. Damn her, but she liked it; she didn't want him to stop.

"Or the way his hand moves down her lower belly." With his left hand still cupping her breast, his right hand moved across her satin bodice. Lower, his warm fingers slid to that area between her legs. A heavy ache seeped low in her gut. Grace sucked in a sharp breath. He paused, torturing her. She resisted the urge to move, to bring him closer and, at the same time, push him away.

Slowly he bunched up the material of her gown. She knew she should stop him, but couldn't seem to get the words past her trembling lips. Higher the material traveled until her legs were exposed to the cool night air.

"Alex," she said, her voice tight.

"Shhh, let me touch you." His breath was warm against her ear, warm and seductive, and she let him pull her skirts higher, even knowing his actions were wrong. She felt his palm flatten to her lower belly, and the ache between her legs twisted, burning with a need she didn't understand. Grace whimpered, shifting. His fingers slipped under the waistband of her bloomers.

"Let me touch you," he repeated, then licked the shell of her ear.

Before she could respond one way or another, he slipped his fingers through the soft curls at the junction of her thighs. Grace bit her lower lip, staring at the few stars that managed to peek from the clouds. She couldn't seem to breathe, couldn't speak, could barely stand. The only thing she could focus on was his finger currently slipping between her sleek folds.

She wanted to tell him to cease, but instead "Please," slipped from her mouth.

Alex slid his finger lower, between the wet folds. Grace groaned, her head lolling back against his shoulders.

"You feel so good," he whispered. "So wet, so ready for me."

Yes. She wanted to be ready for him. She wanted Alex, had wanted him for days. His thumb brushed the sensitive bud that nestled between her folds. Grace gasped, arching her back as sensation after brilliant sensation burst through her body. It was as if he'd taken the stars from the sky and thrown them into her soul. It was too much, almost too much, yet she wanted more.

"Hold tight, my love. I'll show you a pleasure you could only dream of." His finger slid into her tight sheath. Foreign, yet so very welcome. "So ready for me," he murmured, pressing his lips to her neck.

Yes, yes she was ready for him.

"Tonight only, we're allowed to let women sample our wares, you know."

His words entered her muddled mind and pierced her heart with a cold chill. Her eyes opened. She stiffened in his hold. He felt cold and hard behind her. The couple in the room upstairs had turned off the lantern, the window went dark.

"Say the word, Gracie, if you want me to show you pleasure."

Need fought with common sense. She pushed his hand away, her skirts falling down around her ankles. Gasping for air, she spun around and with the heels of her palms pushed him. He stumbled back a step, hitting the stone wall. The surprised look upon his handsome face was worth it.

"You arse! I was sneaking out because watching you flirt with everyone in a skirt made me ill, and John refused to take me home. I wasn't here to watch some couple make love in the windows."

Sudden tears stung her eyes. She turned around and stomped toward the yews. She'd gotten only a couple feet away when strong fingers bit into her waist. She was spun around and found herself face-to-face with Alex.

For one long moment they merely stared at each other. Emotion…shock, bemusement, need…flickering between them. How she wished she could tear off his mask, see his face entirely.

"I'm sorry," he whispered, pulling her close.

Her hands flattened to his hard chest as he lowered his head. It was a soft kiss, a yielding kiss. One of passion and apologies. And she, damn it all, forgave him immediately.

Grace slid her arms around his neck, standing on tiptoe to press her body to his. No one had ever apologized to her, not John for being an ass, not her mama for allowing their stepfather to be cruel. But Alex had, and he didn't need to.

His teeth nibbled on her full bottom lip until she sighed. Making quick work of deepening the kiss, his tongue slid into her mouth, rubbing, licking, tasting. Grace groaned, arching into him as her fingers slipped into those silky curls tossed about his head. He tasted of mint and champagne, he tasted lovely, and she feared she'd become addicted.

His mouth moved to her jawline, lower…following the curve of her neck, he placed soft, delicate kisses. "You're so beautiful, *dushenka*."

Vaguely she was aware that he'd spoken another language, but for some reason it didn't seem to matter much at the moment. His tongue darted out, tracing a hot path to her ear. Grace's knees grew weak. At her lower belly she could feel his hard arousal pulsing against her skirts, begging to be touched. She would oblige. She would give him all. She knew in that moment, she would give him all of her.

"Well, well, what is this?" A woman's voice pierced her foggy reality. Alex froze, his body stiffening. "You found us a plaything, how wonderful, Alex."

Grace looked into Alex's face, but he was staring at someone beyond her shoulder. Oh dear God! Grace fumbled with her mask, making sure it was in place before she turned. A woman stood before them, a feathered mask obscuring her features from view, but Grace recognized the voice and had probably been introduced to the woman.

"Three is better than two, isn't it, my dear?" The woman moved forward, her hips swaying seductively with each step.

Grace felt as if she'd been punched in the gut. Alex wasn't here for her; Alex had come into the garden to meet with this woman. To touch this woman. To kiss this woman.

"No," Grace whispered. Anger and hurt mixed in a sickening combination. Her frantic gaze found his. Alex merely stood there, his jaw clenched, those hands, which had only moments ago touched her so gently, fisted at his sides. He didn't deny it. Didn't say a word. He merely stood there.

Grace stumbled back a step, the frantic need to escape overwhelming.

Dear God, she was falling for the man and he was here for another woman. Tears burned her eyes. She was an idiot. She blinked rapidly, refusing to cry in front of them.

"Gracie," he finally whispered, the word so soft that perhaps it was merely the breeze and she only imagined he'd said her name.

"No," she said again, shaking her head. "He's yours." She turned and ran, bursting blindly through the yews, leaving behind the bloodied pieces of her broken heart.

Chapter 12

"Well, that was…*interesting.*" Lady Sweetin started toward Alex, the swoosh of her skirts unnaturally loud.

He jerked his gaze toward her, his breathing harsh, his body tense. An animal hunted. The urge to go after Grace overwhelmed any good sense. He couldn't. He wouldn't. He curled his fingers so tight, his nails bit into his palms. He swore he could still smell her scent over Lady Sweetin's strong perfume.

"Some women just aren't adventurous." Lady Sweetin rested her hand on his chest, her touch chill, repulsive.

He wanted to shove her away. To erase the woman from his mind. All women but Grace. With Lady Sweetin so near, he no longer felt free. Caged. Imprisoned by her hold.

She trailed her fingers up his chest and slipped her arm around his neck. Alex merely stood there, stiff in her embrace. Undaunted, she stood on tiptoe, hovering near his mouth, her breath smelling of sherry.

"*I hate sherry*," Grace had said.

Suddenly he did too.

Leaning forward, Lady Sweetin flattened her breasts to his chest and kissed him. "Mmm," she whispered against his mouth.

Numb, Alex didn't move. It was as if he'd left his body entirely. What little soul he contained had escaped with Grace. Lady Sweetin's tongue darted out, sliding against his lips like a wet eel. The touch sent his stomach churning. He couldn't do this.

His heart slammed erratically inside his chest. Blast it, he wanted to push her away. He wanted to tell her to go fuck herself.

He couldn't.

"What is it?" she whispered, sensing his reluctance.

He didn't respond, afraid the truth would slip from his lips. Clamping his mouth shut, he remained stubbornly silent and stared at that dark window where only moments ago Grace had watched the couple inside. What could he say? That Lady Sweetin repulsed him. That he hated her smell. That he hated the feel of her hands on him. That she made him *sick*.

Her fingers slid down his chest to his trousers. "A quick one? That will make you feel better." She was smiling, amused that he should have feelings. He'd seen the look before on their faces, women who thought of him as nothing more than a cock. Women who held the mistaken belief that he enjoyed fucking strangers. No attachments, merely sex. Any man's dream.

"One so handsome shouldn't pout."

He clenched his jaw. She was treating him like a child. And like a child, he couldn't seem to regain control of his emotions. Heated anger pulsed through his very blood, boiling below his skin, preparing to erupt in rage. Grace had never treated him as anything but a man. A normal man.

Lady Sweetin's hand slipped inside his trousers. Alex closed his eyes, gritting his teeth. Allowing Grace to leave had been the one honorable thing he'd done in years. She didn't deserve this life; she didn't deserve a whore. And that's what he was, a whore. How ridiculous he'd been to think of escaping.

He would stay in this garden and pretend to enjoy Lady Sweetin. Yet his cock didn't even stir as she wrapped her fingers around his shaft. No desire heated his veins. There wasn't the slightest tingling of lust. Frantic, his heart slammed against his chest. He couldn't lose it…the ability to react. He'd be as good as dead.

Grace. *Think of Grace.* Think of Grace's hand on his cock. Her soft breasts pressed to his chest. Her warm, clean breath on his neck. *Think of Grace.* His cock stirred, blood roaring through his body. *Think of Grace.*

Alex gripped Lady Sweetin's narrow shoulders and pulled her closer, lowering his head to meet her lips. They were thin, cold. Not Grace's lush mouth. Not the taste of warmth and happiness. He paused, Grace's face slipping from his mind.

"Yes," Lady Sweetin whispered in a husky voice.

No.

No, no, no.

It was wrong, so wrong. His stomach churned. Bile rose to his throat. His skin felt tight, dirty. He couldn't stop thinking about Grace. He couldn't stop imagining her touch…her scent.

"Damn it, Alex. What is it?" Lady Sweetin pulled back, her face flushed with anger, her eyes flashing with irritation. "Is it that little whore?"

"Of course not." Sweat broke out between his shoulder blades. The silence stretched uncomfortably around them. The only sound was the soft murmur of music drifting through the open windows.

"Dear God, have you fallen for her?"

Surprise gave way to fear. Ophelia could not uncover how much Grace meant to him. There'd be hell to pay and Grace could be in danger.

Her lips pulled back into a smirk. "How silly you are."

He stepped away from her unexpectedly, watching with satisfaction as the smirk fell from her lips and she stumbled to regain her footing.

"What do you want from me?" he demanded, his voice harsh, leaving no room for politeness.

"Your cock," she snapped, glaring up at him.

She was angry, angry that he didn't want her. God forbid that he had one evening when he didn't want to perform. Her selfishness sent him over the edge where only darkness remained.

"Fine, you want me?" He gripped her upper arms and spun around, slamming her up against the brick wall that surrounded the garden.

He'd show her what he was truly capable of. Alex crushed his mouth to hers, shoving his tongue between her lips. Instead of pushing him away, Lady Sweetin's hands gripped his arse, pulling him close.

"Yes, more," she said against his mouth.

Disgust tasted bitter. She was titillated, not afraid. She didn't give a shite about him and what he wanted. With a growl, he shoved her away and stumbled back. He swiped the back of his hand across his lips to erase the taste of her. Lady Sweetin's heated gaze turned to outrage.

"What are you doing?" she gasped, her flat chest heaving.

"What I should have done the moment you entered the garden." Alex turned and stalked away knowing she would tell Ophelia. Knowing he would be punished. Knowing everything would change. He didn't care, because for some reason he felt he had already been punished enough.

Grace was gone. Nothing else mattered.

"How dare you!" Lady Sweetin cried, her voice echoing shrilly through the garden.

He didn't respond.

"Alex! Come back!"

He pushed through the yews, his heart hammering so frantically he feared it might explode. He must leave. His lungs were shrinking, the world before him fading. He couldn't seem to breathe. Forefront in his mind was the need to escape.

"Alex?" James appeared before him, his face hidden by his mask. A dark, soulless monster stepping from the shadows into the torchlight.

Alex stumbled to a stop. Hell, he felt almost…faint.

"Alex?" James's voice sounded muffled. His blond brows snapped together as he reached out to him. "What is it?"

"Get out of my way." Alex didn't know where he was going. He didn't care. He shoved the heel of his hand into James's chest and pushed him aside.

"Where are you going?"

"I don't know, I don't care." He focused on those French doors, his salvation. If he could make it through the crush of the ball and out the front doors…If no one stopped him…Ophelia wouldn't want to make a scene. "Away from all of this."

"Damn it, Alex, stop!" James latched on to his arm, his grip strong. "You can't leave. Where will you go? How will you survive?"

Alex jerked his arm away. Stumbling off-balance, he fell against the rough bark of an apple tree. He felt almost drunk, the sky above spinning. "I don't care."

"Just stop, calm your nerves." James, always so bloody rational.

"You were spying on me, weren't you?" Alex growled and shoved James hard. The thinner man stumbled back. Alex was looking for a fight, anything to relieve the tension.

James's patient look gave way to irritation. He straightened, righting his mask. "I was merely checking on your welfare."

"Liar!" Alex stepped closer, seething. "I don't need someone to check on my welfare. You were spying. Damn you, whose side are you on?"

James smoothed down his jacket, his movements slow and determined. "I'm on the side of the woman who gives money to my family to stay fed and warm."

Alex laughed, a manic sound. "You're a fucking idiot if you trust her. That sister you're supposedly feeding is probably prostituting herself at this very moment. Spreading her legs for a coin, just like you."

James went pale. For the first time since they'd met, Alex could see the desperate, uncultured person James had been. Alex didn't have time to duck. James threw his fist wide and his knuckles connected with Alex's jaw. Alex's head jerked back, and for one blessed moment splintering pain pierced the numbness that had settled in his body. Then he stumbled back, the garden spinning. He'd forgotten that James's sinewy appearance belied a well-muscled body.

Slowly the garden stopped turning and James came back into focus. Anger pulsed from the man's very being. That perfectly combed hair was ruffled, his eyes ablaze. "You deserved that and more, you arse."

Alex rubbed his jaw, feeling the slightest twinge of guilt. "I know."

"What have you done?" Lady Lavender's voice snapped through the garden.

Alex turned. Behind her, a few women stood watching with a mixture of shock and amusement. They were thrilled by the sight of two men fighting, and Alex wouldn't have been surprised if they were hoping he and James were fighting over one of them.

"James? What happened?" Ophelia demanded, of course asking him. She knew James wouldn't lie to her.

Surprisingly, James merely shook his head. "Nothing of importance. Nothing at all." He lifted his lips, pasting a pleasant smile upon his face, and turned toward the women. "So sorry. Where are our manners?" And just like that, unflappable James was back.

Ophelia's icy gaze settled on Alex, clearly waiting for him to smooth things over, regain control of that façade. Apologize.

But Alex's mouth wouldn't lift into a dimpled smile. His eyes refused to crinkle at the corners. He felt that cage closing in once more. He would not be an animal who had briefly tasted freedom.

There was no returning to what life had been. Everything had changed and all because of a woman with red stockings.

* * *

"Grace?" Rodrick was suddenly in front of her, exactly when she needed him.

She looked up at the man who could save her from utter humiliation. The man who could save her family. Was he a rake who frequented gaming hells or the caring, titled gent she'd always assumed him to be? His face half-covered by a black mask, she saw only kindness and worry in his gaze. What had she been thinking to trust Alex over Rodrick?

"I want to go home." She hadn't meant to say the words, and in such a pathetic whimper, but she couldn't quite help herself. Her heart felt as if it was breaking, crumbling to her feet piece by piece. And that was ridiculous because that would mean she actually cared for Alex and she couldn't care. She *wouldn't*.

Rodrick boldly cupped her elbow, even though many around them were starting to whisper. "What do you mean?"

He looked confused, and she didn't blame him. She knew she must look a mess—her face pale, her body trembling. Even now her eyes were filling with tears and she feared they would fall here, in front of a crowd so eager to see a spectacle.

"Please, can you find John?"

"Tell me, what is it?"

Unnatural heat flooded her body. The music was suddenly too loud. The candlelight and dresses were suddenly too bright. And this world…this world was too dark. A world of prostitution, of sexual favors and addictions, a world with no hope. She never should have attended the party. She'd known it wasn't a ball for the innocent and that most people here reveled in the sinful side of life, but she'd been desperate to see Alex.

"Please," she whispered once more.

"Come, I'll escort you home." He grasped her upper arm and turned her toward the stairs.

Grace tried to pull back, acutely aware of guests who were staring. They were wondering, no doubt, why a titled gentleman like Rodrick would escort a woman like her. She could imagine rumors of an engagement already taking form. Why didn't the thought thrill her like it should?

"No, please, you don't have to."

"Of course I do." He tucked her arm through his, close to his body. "Your well-being is my top priority."

A week ago those words would have made her heart soar. They warmed her indeed. After all, he was admitting he cared. At least *someone* cared. But they didn't touch her as they should have, and she was afraid it was because the words weren't coming from Alex, damn him to hell! He'd ruined everything. The mere thought of Alex with Lady Sweetin made her ill. That woman…that horrible, horrible woman.

Sweat dotted the area between her shoulder blades and a wave of nausea nearly brought her to her knees. "Please…can we go?"

"Of course." He rested his hand on her lower back, his fingers strong, comforting, and warm.

Grace was determined to feel the way she'd felt about Rodrick before. She would forget Alex, the man who'd given her a first real kiss. The man who had touched her in ways she'd never been touched before. She would merely continue with her life as planned…marry Rodrick and be the best wife he could want.

She *would* forget Alex.

They started up the wide, shallow steps, her pulse pounding so furiously she felt dizzy.

She *would* forget Alex.

"Pardon," Rodrick repeated over and over until a path cleared and the doors were visible ahead.

She *must* forget Alex.

A few moments. Only a few more moments and she could escape into the cool evening air. Escape the pressure of prying eyes. Grace was completely aware of the crush of the crowd as they moved closer, attempting to overhear the murmured words of comfort Rodrick was whispering into her ear.

The gossip would be severe and her reputation would be shattered unless Rodrick offered for her. Still, they all shifted out of the way, making room for Rodrick and giving him the respect he deserved. When they married, *if* they married, Grace would be given their respect as well, and tonight would be a distant memory. Only a few more steps up the stairs...

A couple shifted, and a tall man came into view, his elegance and demeanor begging for attention.

Alex. His name whispered through her mind as if called down from heaven.

Grace's eyes locked with his. She was sure, if only she could look down, that she would see her heart flip-flopping across the marble floor. And Alex just stood there in the corner, half-hidden where no one would notice him. His face was pale, his eyes wide, almost...frantic. An animal on the brink of wildness. She hadn't expected him to look so haunted. Grace took a half step toward him before she realized what she was doing.

"Are you well?" Rodrick asked.

Still she was unable to look away even though people were starting to notice. She waited...waited for even the slightest hint of an apology. Lady Lavender swept up behind him, the rich material of her lavender silk gown glimmering under the lamplight. Alex hadn't come to apologize to her. He was merely going about his business. Lady Lavender leaned forward, pressing her ample bosom to Alex's back. Her lips were near his ear as she whispered something. Alex averted his gaze, breaking contact with Grace. She almost closed her eyes then and there, almost crumpled to the floor, the pain in her chest so severe.

In that moment she felt as if they were an ocean apart.

"Yes, I'm well. Please," her voice came out as a bare whisper, "take me home." She followed Rodrick through the wide, open doors, forcing her feet to move…one in front of the other. The cool night air eased her fevered skin but did little to calm her racing heart.

Rodrick cupped her elbow, leading her down the steps toward the waiting carriage. The farther away she walked, the more her heart pulled, aching to return as if connected to Alex.

"Grace," she thought she heard her name whispered, or perhaps it was merely the wind.

Frantic, she glanced over her shoulder. No one was there. The shrubs lining the stairs were dark. The path empty. The pain in her chest almost unbearable.

"Are you ready?" Rodrick asked, his voice filled with concern.

She reached out, blindly grasping his gloved hand, taking comfort in his strength. "Yes, please," she whispered.

"Of course." His dark brows were drawn together over worried amber eyes. "Come along. The carriage is here."

Boldly he wrapped his arm around her waist and helped her into his splendid vehicle. Grace settled stiffly onto the soft leather seat, hiding in the shadows where the lanterns did not reach. Leaving John behind, the carriage took off, wheels rattling over cobbled stone and drowning out the sounds of merriment. Only once they turned the corner could she finally breathe with some normalcy.

Grace tore off her mask and closed her eyes, sinking into the soft leather seat. Rodrick's spicy scent permeated the air, a comfortable scent, a scent she knew well, for the spice was worn by many of the male *ton*.

She belonged here with Rodrick in his splendid carriage. With Rodrick she would have a stable, well-bred man who wouldn't ruin her reputation. A man who could support Mama and Patience.

"Tell me what happened." Rodrick leaned forward and rested his hand on her knee. She should have been shocked by his bold touch, but little surprised her any longer. Besides, his handsome features showed only compassion. "Please, Grace, tell me now so I can call the man out."

She certainly couldn't tell Rodrick about Alex. The thought of him uncovering their relationship, whatever the relationship happened to be, was unthinkable. And so she lied. "No, please, it was nothing."

He tore the mask from his face. "Was it him?" His gaze grew hard, that square jaw set in determination. "The man who brought you home the night of the gaming hell?"

She swallowed hard and forced herself to smile. "It was nothing, I promise you. A simple misunderstanding." She'd misunderstood all right; she'd thought Alex actually cared for her.

Rodrick moved across the carriage, sitting intimately next to her. "Grace." He took her hand, his grip warm even through the layers of their gloves.

He was close, and he was so kind that she should have reveled in his attention. Yet Grace felt the overwhelming need to pull back. No, she couldn't cringe from his touch. She wouldn't pull away from the warmth of his body. She'd wanted this. She'd prayed for this.

"Kiss me," she whispered desperately.

He blinked, obviously taken aback. Obviously horrified.

Heat shot to her cheeks. Lord, what had she said? She looked away, tears of sorrow turning into tears of humiliation. "I'm sorry, I didn't mean…"

His fingers lightly touched her chin, turning her head toward him. A soft caress, a whispered promise. She knew what would happen and was determined to force Alex from her mind. Brazenly she met Rodrick's gaze. The lust in his eyes sent nerves fluttering in her belly. Still, when he lowered his head, she didn't protest, merely closed her eyes and waited.

His lips brushed hers, softly at first. Not a kiss of passion. Disappointed and frantic for something more, she wrapped her arms around his neck, urging him to try once more. He needed no further encouragement. Rodrick moaned and deepened the kiss.

For years she'd dreamt of this moment, for years she'd wanted Rodrick to see her as anything other than a friend. Now that it was happening, Grace felt completely and utterly…underwhelmed.

His lips were soft, kind, pleasant. When she felt his wet tongue press to her mouth, she parted for him, allowing him access, hoping the intimate touch would stir longing deep within her soul. His hands cupped the back of her head as his tongue stroked the inside of her mouth. And it was…nice. Wet. Odd. She'd felt more when Gideon had kissed her.

There was no spark. There was no intense heat. There was no ache low in her gut. Only his lips on hers. It felt…*wrong*. So very *wrong*.

Bile churned in her belly. Fearing she'd be ill, Grace pressed her hands into Rodrick's chest and pushed back. He was breathing harshly, his gaze hooded and dark with lust. She was old enough to know the look well. He wanted her, but would he still respect her?

"I'm sorry," she whispered, wondering if she'd ruined her chances.

"No." He rested his hand on her thigh; she resisted the urge to flinch at his bold contact. "Don't be. I enjoyed that very much."

She forced her lips to turn upward. It was all she could manage. What would she say to the man? The kiss had been…*nice*? And it had been, well…nice. But certainly there hadn't been fire. Certainly it hadn't been like kissing…Alex.

No! Damn him! She wouldn't think about Alex. Finally things were moving forward with Rodrick. She would not destroy her chances at a decent match.

Rodrick leaned back, his face hidden in the shadows. "There could be…more, if you like."

Startled, she almost wished she could pretend not to have heard him. "What do you mean?"

"More kissing. More…" He let the word drift away, a promise of what would come if she married him. "I like you, Grace. I like you very, very much."

He hadn't said he loved her. He hadn't said he wanted to marry her, but he might as well have said the words. She couldn't breathe. Grace pressed her gloved hand to her racing heart. It was the very moment she had been waiting for, and all she could think about was Alex and his blue eyes.

"Do you care for me, Grace?"

"Of course," she blurted out a little too quickly.

He glanced away, then up through those thick lashes. "Are you attracted to me?"

It was a bold question. Something he would have never asked a debutante, but she was no naïve innocent. She was practically on the shelf, and this was her opportunity, her dream come true, to finally have the honorable, safe family she'd always wanted.

His finger skimmed softly down the line of her jaw, startling her although it was a gentle touch. "Grace?"

"Yes, I'm attracted to you," she blurted out.

It wasn't a complete lie. She had been attracted to him only weeks ago. She was still attracted to him. She simply couldn't feel the longing over the confusing emotions Alex had stirred within. A few days from now, with Alex a distant memory, she would once again be interested in Rodrick.

He smiled, a truly delighted smile. And she tried to feel that same happiness that sparkled within his eyes. She tried to grasp the realization that Rodrick finally wanted her! Yet there was something missing…something cold and bitter that encased her heart and prevented any joy from seeping inside.

Oh, why wouldn't Alex go away?

"Wonderful." Rodrick cupped the back of her head and brought her forward. Before she could even guess his intentions, his lips found hers. A quick and possessive kiss that left her baffled. The kind of kiss that said she belonged to him already.

Belonged. The thought panicked her for some reason.

Trembling, Grace pulled back, ignoring the gleam of success that lit Rodrick's eyes.

Why did she feel as if she'd just sold her soul to the devil?

Chapter 13

She'd left with Rodrick.

How Alex hated the man.

How he wanted to hunt him down and slam his fist into his aristocratic face.

Alex paced his large hotel room…back and forth…back and forth, like an animal caged.

The idea of Grace and Rodrick together had kept him awake all night until he thought he'd go mad. The idea of any other man touching her sickened him.

Rodrick had taken her home, but had he left her there alone or had the man dared to stay overnight? Alex brushed aside the thick velvet curtains and glanced out the windows onto London.

The soft morning breeze whispered through the open window, the scent of lavender seeping inside. A vendor selling the blooms below. Dear God, even in the city he couldn't escape the scent. Alex pushed away from the windows and moved to the cold, empty hearth, sinking into a chair. Grace had probably arrived at the ball with the dandy as well. But for some reason, the fact that she'd left with Rodrick made Alex see red.

He wasn't tired, even though they'd returned to the hotel a good four hours ago when the sun had peeked above the horizon. And even though his body ached with the need for rest, he couldn't even close his eyes without seeing Rodrick and Grace together. He knew it wasn't rational. He knew she didn't belong to him, nor ever could, but it didn't matter. What little soul he had left cried out for her.

A soft knock rang through the room. Alex didn't respond. Didn't bother to turn in his chair to glance at the door. It opened anyway, as he knew it would. They had no privacy.

"Alex." James's footsteps were quick and sure as he moved across the carpet. "Good, you're up early. We need to talk."

Still Alex didn't stir.

James paused by his chair and sighed. For one moment neither spoke, the tick of the clock on the mantel the only sound.

"If you want out, then ask to be released," James finally said. "Ophelia will allow you to leave. She's not the monster you think."

He laughed, finding amusement for the first time in days.

His wry laugh didn't stop James from continuing. "Just speak with her. Tell her you wish to be released from your contract."

He finally looked at the man he'd known for years. A man always kind, always loyal, always so damn honorable. That boyish face was completely serious. How could anyone who was so smart on the streets be so damn stupid now? "That easy, huh?"

James raked his hand through his hair, mussing his usually tidy locks. "Yes, if you've fallen for this woman…"

Alex surged to his feet and brushed by James, sending him stumbling back. He didn't want to talk about Grace, and he certainly didn't want to discuss James's ridiculous ideas about the fair and the great Lady Lavender. "You're a bloody idiot, James."

"Why?" he demanded. "You tell me why, when I'm merely trying to help your sorry arse, I'm the bloody idiot?"

Alex paused and pinched the bridge of his nose. It was like trying to teach mathematics to a dunce. His patience was growing incredibly thin. For all his street smarts, James was completely naïve toward the real world. "If Lady Lavender allows me to leave—"

"She will."

Alex turned to glare James into silence. "*If* she lets me go, do you honestly think Grace will have me? I'm nothing more than a whore."

James was quiet for a moment, his blond brows drawn together in confusion. The man just couldn't understand, as if he'd never thought on the fact that they were no longer acceptable society. Or perhaps he'd never been acceptable, so the idea was something completely foreign.

"If she loves you, that won't matter."

Alex stared at James in disbelief. Was the man really waxing poetical about true love?

"What?" James bristled, his shoulders visibly stiffening. "You don't believe in love?"

"No more than any whore does."

"Nonsense," James snapped, his face flushing. "If there was no such thing as love, why would I be here saving my family? If there was no love, why are we all here? My mother and sister would be starving, even dead without the money I've made."

"What are you saying? You hope to one day settle into matrimonial bliss? To find a woman who will overlook the fact that you've sold your body?"

James didn't respond. He didn't need to; his emotions were clearly written across his face. Lord be, the street rat had dreams. How utterly ridiculous. As if sensing Alex's disgust, James spun around and started toward the door.

Even as he wanted to dismiss James's emotional words, Alex couldn't help but admit he was right, in some way. Wasn't he here for similar reasons? To keep his family's secrets because…he loved them. Or had at one time. Now…now he didn't know them. He didn't know the brother he'd seen at that club…a man who had been a mere boy when Alex had left home.

"Alex." James paused at the door. So he had one last piece of advice, did he? "If you truly want to leave, then talk to Lady Lavender. What harm will it do?"

With those words, he left.

Talk to Lady Lavender. Perhaps James wasn't as stupid as he seemed.

He'd never truly had a heartfelt conversation with Ophelia. Never even tried. But then he hadn't thought she'd possessed a heart. Besides, there had always been the threat, hinted at and unspoken, hovering around them. Instinct told him not to trust her in the least.

Still, what other choice did he have?

Alex glanced at the door that led into Ophelia's adjoining bedchamber. They'd stayed at a hotel in London so she could see the sights for the next few days. More likely so she could hear the gossip she'd created at the ball last night. He made his way across the room, booted feet sinking into thick carpet and muffling the sound. What did he have to lose?

Everything. Everything he held dear…hope for a future. Hope for a new life. At the door he didn't pause but let his fist fall against the wooden panel that separated them. The door creaked open and Wavers stood there, black eyes void of soul.

"I need to speak with Lady Lavender."

He merely stared at Alex for one long, unpleasant moment as if he knew exactly why Alex was there. He thought Wavers might refuse. Part of him hoped he would. Slowly the guard held up his hand, a silent command for Alex to wait. Wavers disappeared inside the darkness, leaving Alex on the threshold. He could hear the soft mumble of conversation. The pause ate at his nerves, screamed at him to turn and leave. But before Alex could relent, Wavers was back.

"Enter."

Determined, Alex swept into the front parlor, moving steadily across the room toward the bedchamber. The place was just as richly decorated as Lady Lavender's home. Fans hung from the ceiling where servants would pull the string hour after hour, making sure their guests did not sweat. Today the burgundy-colored sitting room was empty.

At the doorway into the bedchamber, Alex paused, allowing his eyes to adjust to the lack of light. She lay upon a large four-poster bed, a small, dainty shadow of a woman. In a white night-dress of silk and with a plate of chocolates at her side, she looked every bit the seducer. Lady Lavender had been the first woman he'd slept with. Reeling him in when he was a young lad of sixteen, only to push him aside for others when she was finished. She'd used him and left him dangling. He still couldn't think of that night without feeling the rush of heated humiliation.

"You're up rather early."

"I never went to bed."

"I see." She picked up a small square of chocolate and popped it into her mouth. Sweets were her one vice. "What is bothering you, Alex? To make such a scene at the ball. So unlike you." She sat up, reclining upon her satin pillows.

"I want out." The words burst from his throat. He felt no relief, only anxiety at the admission.

She frowned, her full lips pouting, but she didn't look surprised. "I'm sorry to hear that." She patted the bed. "Come, sit, let us discuss this turn of events."

He didn't want to sit. He wanted to hear her response. But he knew who held the true power here. Still, Alex waited for a moment, merely to show her he wouldn't jump to do her bidding. Of course, as always, he relented and settled beside her.

"I want to leave," he said again, more forcefully this time.

She lifted a perfectly plucked brow. "And do what?"

"Have a life."

She smiled then, a smug smile. "What sort of life can you have, Alex?" She moved closer and rested her hand on his arm. The neckline of her silk gown dipped low, showing her pale breasts. She'd tempt him, sell herself to keep him near. He looked toward the marble hearth where a fire crackled and leered, laughing at him. She didn't realize that her beauty did not influence him any longer.

"Who would have you Alex, if your secret escaped? If they knew what you'd been doing for the last twelve years and more? What would your dear mother think of your past?"

She was right. Even as Alex's ire flared and he had to resist the urge to strangle the woman, he knew she was right. She pressed her full chest to his back and ran her hands over his shoulders. Her fingers felt like spiders crawling over his body. Her breath, warm on the side of his face, smelled of chocolate. He felt sick.

"My family has no friends; they won't care," he insisted.

"Don't they?" He could practically feel her smiling. "Word is they've established themselves quite well. Your brother is even thought of as quite the rake, wanted by many a young lady. He's sure to make a good match."

He wasn't sure which shocked him more, that Lady Lavender had been keeping watch over his family or that his family had gone on living without him. Alex didn't move, barely even breathed as the words sank in, heavy and heart wrenching.

"But here…here, Alex, is where you belong."

Anger flared through him. Alex spun around and shoved Ophelia back into the bedding. Any restraint fled, replaced with an anger that had been simmering for over a decade. Panting, like a deranged madman, he hovered over her, his hard body pressing her into the soft comforter. "And if I no longer wish to be here?"

She didn't look afraid in the least. Boldly she reached up and cupped the back of his head. Gripping his hair tight between her fingers, she jerked him closer, his face a breath away from hers. As if she owned him, she pressed her mouth to his, her warm tongue sliding over his lips. There was no shiver of anticipation or lust. Only disgust wavered through him.

"You didn't complain when you first started working for me and beautiful women were throwing themselves at you," she whispered against his lips. "Admit it, Alex. You didn't complain when I showed you what pleasure there could be between a man and woman. There's a connection between you and me. You belong here."

The words struck him hard. What if she was right? What if this was where he belonged now? What if she had ruined him?

Nothing better than a whore.

Alex squeezed his eyes shut. No, he wouldn't let her play these mind games with him. His hands moved up her arms, over her shoulders, his fingers pausing at the sensitive skin on her throat. How he hated her. Hated her for destroying his life. Hated her even more for making him doubt himself. Alex wrapped his fingers around the pale column of her throat, his thumbs pressing that shallow spot. He could kill her so easily. As much control as she had, her physical strength was no match for his.

As he pressed his thumbs into her neck, she merely grinned, lifting her hips and pressing her pelvis to his. "You want to kill me, Alex?" Her voice came out raspy through the narrowed pipe. "The woman who saved you? Who saved your family?"

Yes. He did. For one brief moment, he wanted to push his thumbs down, to squeeze until she stopped breathing. Stopped moving. Stopped ruining lives.

She rested her cold fingers at his wrists. "But you don't really want to kill me, do you? Not truly, because deep down you feel some odd connection to me. Killing me would be like killing a part of yourself." Her fingers trailed over the straining muscles in his forearms. "I own you."

Her words chilled his very soul. She was right. Deep down, he knew she was right. She owned him. Perhaps it wasn't on paper, but she held his soul in her chilled hands all the same.

"Then again," she said softly, "if you left, I suppose I could always recruit your brother. What do you think; would he do?"

She was trying to frighten him. It worked. Alex released his grip and stumbled back from the bed. Sweat slid between his shoulder blades. She merely lay there, her golden hair spread out across the white pillows, her body small and frail, like a damned angel.

Dear God, he had wanted to kill her. She had made him insane.

"Stand down, Wavers. Alex won't harm me." She lifted a brow. "Will you?"

Alex turned and shoved Wavers to the side. He couldn't seem to breathe. Couldn't feel his body. Panic tortured his very soul. He was trapped. Trapped in this hell.

On wooden legs, Alex moved to the door.

"Alex," she called out.

Without thought he paused in the doorway, trained to do her bidding and hating himself for his immediate reaction.

"Bathe and dress. We're going to the museum today. I expect you to behave."

His trembling fingers curled around the door handle. He knew why she was forcing him to attend…to test his loyalty. But also to humiliate him. She would show him that no matter where they were, he belonged to her.

And he would attend and he would behave. He would do whatever she said, because she was right. He was nothing. She owned him.

* * *

Alex didn't say a word.

As he entered Ophelia's gaudy carriage. As she settled across from him, ever watchful. As they made their way through London, the streets so crowded he could practically feel the people pressing in on the edges of the coach. Alex didn't say a word. What was there to say?

Nothing. He was not paid to think. Thinking was dangerous. Thinking gave one hope, silly ideas, and dreams. He was a whore, merely a whore. There was no reason to think any longer. There was no reason to feel. To speak. He was numb.

"You will be charming, won't you, Alex?" Lady Lavender finally broke their silence, her voice barely audible over the wheels rattling over cobbled streets and the mongers calling out their wares.

Slowly Alex pulled his gaze from the corner of the carriage where he'd been staring at nothing for the past hour or so. He couldn't read her features, for a veil of light lavender hung from a feather-covered bonnet and hid her face.

She was relaxed as she leaned back against the cushioned seat. She was curious, but not nervous. No, she held too much power over him to be worried. Still, he wondered idly how much she actually knew about his family. Was she truly keeping watch over them, or was she exaggerating her influence?

"And if my family is there?" he asked in a calm, steady voice, refusing to show any emotion. She'd never taken him out in public before, at least not where anyone respectable would be caught. He didn't expect to see his family, and he doubted they'd recognize him if they happened upon each other, but he was curious about Lady Lavender's sudden desire to keep him close at hand.

She smoothed down her muslin lavender gown with the tiny white flowers embroidered along the hem and waist. "They won't be."

So sure, he almost believed her. "How do you know?"

The carriage slowed and she picked up her small lavender bag, the dangling pearls swaying back and forth. "I know." She smiled then, a practiced, seductive smile. "I have…connections."

She was watching his family? Most likely had been all along. The thought should have shocked and unnerved him. Instead, he was merely curious. Why? Why the intense interest in his lineage? There was something he was missing…a reason why he was here and not another man. The longer he twisted and turned the question around in his mind, the more the numbness faded, leaving him exasperated.

His fingers curled against his thighs, his body trembling with the need to demand answers. She'd wanted a reaction; she'd gotten one. "How are they?"

She quirked a brow, amused that he should care, or amused because he had broken his silence. She'd won once again. "Your family?"

He paused, fighting the urge, then nodded, hating the fact that he had to ask her, beg her, really.

"They're quite well." The carriage drew to a stop. She glanced toward the window where the break in the curtains allowed a brief peek onto the streets of London. "Ah, here we are."

Quite well? What the bloody hell did that mean? But the door opened and he knew their conversation was over. She would give him just enough information to bother him. He wouldn't beg.

How he hated her.

Alex took hold of the beaver hat settled beside him on the seat and moved from the carriage. Wavers and Jensen had stepped from their perch at the back of the vehicle and surrounded Ophelia. The rush of the crowds was overwhelming, the scent of factories and the Thames nauseating. All he could think about was that Grace was somewhere out there in that crush. Shopping perhaps, strolling through the park. Mayhap she was doing embroidery in the parlor of their crumbling townhome, hoping and praying Rodrick would make an offer.

"Flowers for milady?" a woman called out, rushing forward with a basket in hand.

Wavers was quick to step in front of Lady Lavender, guarding her from the onslaught of city dwellers. As they started up the wide, shallow steps, Alex trailed behind like a good little lapdog.

The crowd was thick. It would be easy…so easy to slip into the fray unseen. To get lost in the hum of the city. Become part of the madness.

"Ridiculous," Ophelia muttered, sounding rather put out. "A free gallery, as if the poor could possibly appreciate art."

The comment gave Alex pause. Another piece to the puzzle that was Lady Lavender. She'd made snide comments before about the less fortunate. A peek into her character. Could she have possibly been born to a wealthy family? She had received money from someone to start her business. Or was she so incredibly arrogant that she had forgotten a former life of destitution?

His questions were pushed aside as they neared the arched doorway. Alex took in a deep breath, air tainted by the quickly breeding factories, but air all the same. He flicked a glance at the sky. Not even the weather could cooperate and match his mood with gray clouds and fat raindrops. No, for once London was all blue skies and fluffy clouds that floated by the Grecian-style museum. How he remembered those skies in Russia. Playing with his brother in the fields while the farmers attempted to grow crops in the hard earth. Days of freedom, days of joy, days of innocence.

He shook aside the thought. He was not here to enjoy the fine day. He was not here to enjoy the art and artifacts stolen from some foreign land. And he certainly wasn't here to enjoy socializing. He pulled the beaver hat he wore lower, shading his eyes as he made his way up the shallow steps behind Ophelia, always trailing. Never in front or beside her.

He didn't worry about seeing some long ago childhood friend. He'd had few friends in England and he'd changed enough in appearance that no one would recognize him. They certainly would never suspect him of becoming one of Lady Lavender's men. Yet he did wonder if he ran into his mother or father, would they know him? Just the thought sent the bitter taste of panic to his mouth.

Wavers and Jensen hovered around him, formidable walls blocking his exit should he wish to flee. But Alex wouldn't run. No, he'd tilt his chin high and accept the fact that people turned away from him and refused to meet his gaze.

Wavers led the way toward the entrance, making sure no one would dare get close to Ophelia. Crowds parted, perhaps sensing her power, or perhaps wanting to get away from the lady of sin. They wanted no association with her, at least not in public.

The clamor of carriage wheels gave way to the echo of murmured conversation from the museum crowd. He focused on the inside of the building, resisting the urge to lean against the strength of those domineering walls. He would escort her through the exhibits. Like Wavers, he would keep his stare straight ahead. The whispered words and giggles would not bother him this afternoon. The glares and looks of disgust from the men would not either. Today he would be those statues they stared at. He would have no emotion, no feelings. And they would not see the way his hands trembled.

Inside the marbled walls, the building was cool, yet the crowds and attention brought a heated rush to his body. They slowed as they entered the long, main hall, and Ophelia took in the paintings. A woman bumped him from the side. He didn't stumble, didn't even respond to her apology.

"Excuse me." A beautiful blonde woman raced by him. "Jules!" she cried out, waving toward her friend. She didn't seem to notice the crush, but thrived in it. And why not? She had nothing to be ashamed of. A young girl in the prime of innocence, filled with hope. Perhaps he would have married someone like her had he not been seduced by Lady Lavender. He might not have given Grace a second glance should they have been introduced. Grace. Quiet and reserved on the surface, she would have escaped his notice. And he would have been the worse man for it. Yes, if anything good had come out of his life, it was meeting Grace.

"Good day."

Alex started, realizing the soft, feminine voice was directed at him. He lowered his gaze to the young woman standing at his side. A familiar golden-haired chit on the verge of becoming a woman. Grace's sister. His heart jumped in his chest, partly with fear, partly with hope. He darted a glance at Ophelia, making sure the woman was still studying the pastoral landscape painting. Just as quickly, he was searching for that familiar auburn hair.

"Where's your sister?" His voice came out raspy.

He hadn't meant to sound so harsh, and when she blinked her eyes wide, he realized he might have frightened her. He managed that dimpled smile and attempted to soften his voice.

"Surely you're not alone." He dared to glance at Ophelia, making sure she was unaware of his conversation. She was, but not Wavers. No, the man was watching him intently.

The young woman's lips trembled upward, daring to smile. "No, not alone. Grace is here…" She glanced over her shoulder. "Somewhere."

She was such a sweet-looking child, her face and eyes full of adventure and mischief. An innocent who still believed that anything was possible. Beautiful, with her blonde hair and green eyes. More than one man was glancing her way and, damn it all, if she wasn't chatting with him as if they were the best of friends. Grace should know better than to leave her younger sister unattended. Hell, she'd ruin her reputation before she'd even gotten a chance to debut.

"Alex," Ophelia called out, drawing even more attention to them.

He resisted the urge to curse. Ophelia's curious lavender gaze studied Patience. She would not be rude to the young woman. Ophelia was never rude to another woman, for they were always potential clients. "Who do we have here?" Her skirts swooshed, whispering over marble floors as she started toward them.

"The sister of a client," he decided to tell the truth for once.

She would not ask for names. They never spoke names in public, although with Patience standing next to them her reputation was slowly being destroyed anyway. Ophelia smiled then, looking her up and down like a lion after a lamb. He knew what she was thinking: was the child old enough to start learning about the pleasures of sex? Of course she was. Girls were married at her age. Hell, even younger.

The thought made him sick. He wanted to usher her away before that innocent gaze was ruined forever. He would not let Ophelia touch her. He knew his desire to protect Grace's sister wasn't natural, but he felt it all the same.

"Might I take the girl for a stroll?" he asked, doing his damnedest to remain calm.

Ophelia studied him, searching his features for only God knew what. He kept his face passive; he'd had years to learn to control his emotions, at least on the outside. Inside, his body was in turmoil, emotions he'd rarely experienced fighting for control. Foremost was the need to see Grace once more.

She gave Patience a practiced smile. "Yes, of course."

Alex nodded. He knew one of her men would follow at a discreet pace, watching for anything suspicious. Guarding her property. But he'd won this small battle.

He latched on to Patience's elbow and steered her down the main hall in the opposite direction from where Ophelia stood. "Keep a few paces away from me." He released his hold.

"But why?" She blinked up at him with wide, trusting eyes.

He resisted the urge to sigh. "Because your reputation is being destroyed even now as we speak."

She frowned, slowing her pace, thank God, so that she was a little behind him. "I don't care about my reputation," he heard just above the roar of the crowd. "It doesn't bother me in the least what others think."

Lord, had he ever been that naïve? "If you don't now, someday you will. By then it will be too late." He wanted to shake her, to make her realize she'd ruin her life with pride.

"I don't care," she insisted, so incredibly stubborn, just like her sister.

He slid her a glance from the corner of his eye. "You will. And you'll be surprised by how quickly your reputation can be shattered, never to be repaired. If you don't care about yourself, think of your sister."

She shook her head; blonde tendrils that had been tucked underneath her straw bonnet came loose. "Grace? She has nothing to do with me."

He laughed, steering her toward an alcove where they were half-hidden by a velvet curtain. "Don't be daft. Every one of your actions influences your sister's reputation." He spun around to face her, annoyed with the chit. "You think she wants to be an old maid? You think she wants to take care of you, your mother, and stepbrother for the rest of her life?"

Patience's frown deepened.

"She wants a life, she *deserves* a life, and you'll ruin it with your carelessness."

"Enough," Grace's sharp voice cracked through the alcove.

His heart slammed madly against his chest, his lungs tightening so he could barely breathe air. Anticipation was sweet and cruel. He'd gotten what he wanted, to see Grace once more. And it was pure torture.

Slowly he turned. Grace stood before him wearing a soft brown dress that nipped in at the waist and flared to her scuffed black boots. Her cheeks were flushed with anger, her eyes flashing. She'd never looked more beautiful.

"Grace—"

"How dare you," she whispered, her hands fisting at her sides.

He stepped closer, unable to stop himself as if pulled by a string. "I apologize, but your sister needs to understand—"

"I am not an old maid!"

Fortunately the crowd was too thick and loud to overhear. She spun around and started down the hall. For one moment he merely stood there, too shocked to move. Grace had caught Patience talking to a whore in the middle of London for all to see. But instead of worrying about her sister's reputation, she was upset because he'd called her an old maid? Could it possibly mean she cared what he thought about her?

"Go on then," Patience whispered. "You've done it now. Best apologize before she gets away."

Alex didn't need to be told twice.

Chapter 14

How dare he call her an old maid. Alex had gone too far. Last night he'd crushed her soul in that garden, meeting with Lady Sweetin. Now this? Damn him, why'd he have to be here? Why'd he have to look at her with such emotion in his blue eyes that it almost brought her to her knees? And why, damn him to hell, why did her body seem to come awake the instant she'd seen him standing there with Patience? He was ruining everything!

Last night Rodrick had dropped her off at the townhome, pressing his mouth to hers in a gentle yet possessive kiss. True, the touch of his lips had produced no spark, but it had been pleasant enough. As she'd slipped between the cold sheets on her cold bed, she had told herself that she could live with pleasant. She and Rodrick would be happy.

And now Alex had ruined everything by simply appearing when she'd wanted to do nothing more than get lost in the crush of London.

Desperate for peace, Grace slipped into another alcove half-hidden by a velvet curtain and pressed her gloved fingers to her throbbing temples, realizing she'd left her bonnet somewhere. Blast, but she'd have to head back down the hall to find it. She'd already lost her gloves to Alex; she would not lose a bonnet as well. But not now. Not yet. No, she needed a moment before seeing him again.

How dare he ruin her life! How dare he make her think that kissing and touching should be more than merely pleasant. How dare he make her hope for more than a simple marriage!

"Grace," Alex said softly.

Grace bit back her groan of frustration. For the briefest of moments she closed her eyes and prayed he'd leave her be. She couldn't see him now. Not when her soul cried out for her to touch him. Not when her heart slammed wildly in her chest as if attempting to break free merely to be closer to him.

"Grace, we must talk."

Angry, she spun around to face him, but he wasn't looking directly at her; no, he was staring at an Italian painting, most likely attempting to protect her reputation by not making eye contact.

She had the sudden and spiteful desire to slap him—or kiss him. To do something ridiculous to draw attention to them, society be damned.

"I meant no offense," he whispered, his voice catching in some odd, emotional way that gave her pause, made her almost annoyed. How could she be angry with him?

She glanced up and down the corridor. No one was looking their way. No, the guests were interested in either the art or the latest gossip. Over the many top hats and bonnets, Grace could see Patience speaking with Lady Maxwell. Lady Maxwell, a woman who understood the need to visit Lady Lavender's.

Would Lady Maxwell acknowledge Lady Lavender should they happen upon each other? Doubtful. So much secrecy, so many lies. She didn't understand this world any longer.

"Surely you must realize…" His voice broke, the emotion startling her so that she looked directly at him, not caring who noticed their communication.

His jaw was clenched tight, his gaze focused unrelentingly on that painting of Mary and Child. She knew, in that moment, whatever he had to say would change everything. Grace shifted, unsure if she should step away from him or step closer.

"What?" she whispered desperately.

He turned his head ever so slightly, a mere tilt so he could meet her gaze. "Surely you must know how I think about you."

She tore her gaze from him, worried the emotion she felt welling within might be visible in her eyes. "How do I know you're not using your charm on me even now? Lady Lavender wouldn't want to offend and lose a client, would she?"

She didn't miss the way his hand lifted slightly, then fell back to his side, his fingers curling against his trousers as if he resisted the urge to touch her. "You know you are no client to me, Gracie. You are more, so much more."

Her chest felt tight as her heart and soul warred with each other. He would break her heart, but her soul didn't care…her soul craved the man. A sob of desperation clogged her throat.

Lord, she couldn't do this. She couldn't be friends with Alex, not knowing he was kissing…touching…sleeping with other women. She couldn't do it, knowing she'd never have him for her own. Yet how could she possibly be without him? When he was near the world changed. The sun was brighter, the day warmer, life seemed full of possibilities.

"Walk with me?" The words burst from her lips before she could take them back.

He closed his eyes, knowing what she offered with that simple demand. "We can't. Your reputation will be destroyed."

"I don't care." She was being reckless, but need consumed any rationality.

He lifted his thick lashes, determination glinting in those blue orbs. "I care."

At an impasse, they were silent for one long moment, but she wasn't one to give in easily. Even if it was for the briefest of moments, she had to be with him, to know if his feelings were true. "Come, follow me."

She started forward, weaving her way around guests, knowing he followed for she could feel his very presence. Desperately she searched for her sister. Patience still stood next to Lady Maxwell. As if sensing her attention, the older woman looked up. Her gaze went to Alex, then Grace, and an unspoken acknowledgment moved between them. She would look after Patience. There was no damnation, no judgment. Still Grace looked away, flushing.

She'd talked to the curators often enough to know which rooms were open to the public. Over the thundering of her heart, she heard the tap of Alex's footsteps, quick and steady. Her pulse swelled with every step closer he got. She turned down a dark hall, the crowds gone. The silence was overwhelming. Only the soft tap of her footsteps…his…the swoosh of her skirts, the pant of her breath bouncing off the walls and echoing down the corridor. They could be caught. Her reputation ruined. Rodrick would never marry her…

Yet she didn't stop. Didn't turn back. She knew Alex followed, could sense his presence. The wooden door was there, at the end of the hall…coming closer…closer. She reached out. Even through her glove, the porcelain knob was cold. For one brief moment she paused. Alex's broad chest pressed to her back as he leaned forward, enveloping her in his spicy scent. She savored the feel of his warm breath whispering against her temple. He settled his hand atop hers and twisted the handle. The door swung open easily.

The room had recently been added and was in a state of dishevelment with unpainted walls and dusty floors, although no workers were here now. The curtains of two large windows were thrown wide, allowing the brilliant light of day to enter. Although they faced the back of the property, anyone could walk by and see them. She didn't pause until she made it to the middle of the large room. She was highly aware of the door closing softly behind her. Highly aware that she was alone with Alex and this time it was different. This time Lady Lavender had not given her approval. This time she had not paid for his attentions.

Alone. They were alone…again. Somehow they always managed to find each other. Alex's footsteps were slow and unhurried as they tapped against the wooden floorboards. Grace felt his nearness like a caress, as if he touched her even now, pulling her closer…closer. She shouldn't be here. She shouldn't. Yet she was, and all because…blast it, he cared. But were his feelings merely a ruse?

She could stand it no longer. The desperate need to hear the truth overwhelmed her good sense. Grace spun around. "Alex, I…"

But he wasn't looking at her. No, he was focused on something behind her. Confused, Grace turned. There was a settee and three oriental paintings against the far wall. And there…in the middle of the white space was a narrow case holding a variety of artifacts. Alex moved slowly, as if in a trance, toward that tall case. His back was taut through the fitted length of his dark brown overcoat. His hands fisted around the rim of his beaver hat.

"Alex," she said softly, stepping closer.

He paused at that case and lifted his hand, his fingers pressed to the glass. Mesmerized, he merely stared at the case as if he hadn't heard her, didn't even know she was there. Bemused, Grace paused next to him. A sword, a tiara of some sort, and other objects that looked decidedly Old World. Pretty things, although not necessarily worth much. The large lock on the case would deter desperate thieves.

"What is it, Alex?"

"Russian," he whispered.

She glanced toward the case again. Royal artifacts, most likely. She stepped closer, focusing on the card in the case. "The czar's," she read.

He turned away, the spell broken. "The sword was his uncle's, not the czar's."

Startled, her gaze jumped to him. She didn't question how Alex knew. No, she remembered him speaking Russian at the antiquities shop. "You know about antiquities then?"

He released a harsh laugh. "No. No, I don't."

No other explanation. He moved toward the settee and settled down, his elbows on his knees, his head in his hands. He looked so desolate, so unlike himself that her heart lurched and all her harsh thoughts toward the man were momentarily forgotten. She had the insane desire to comfort him, to save him, but she didn't know how.

Grace hesitated, then went to him, kneeling and resting her hand on his thigh. "Alex?"

He didn't stir. She tugged her gloves from her fingers and dropped them to the ground, then reached out and rested her hand gently against the side of his face, those dark curls at his temple clinging to her fingers. Dear, lost Alex. She smoothed the locks back, a motherly touch, a caring touch. He was not the man who had taught her seduction. Not the man she wanted in her bed. But the man she ached for.

He lifted his head, turning his face into her touch. The bristle on his cheek rubbed erotically against her sensitive palm. "What is it?"

"You can't possibly understand," his lips whispered against the inside of her wrist, sending shivers over her skin.

She swallowed her retort. Perhaps she didn't understand. Everyone had their own, unique problems in life. But she could try to understand, if only he'd let her in. If only he'd trust her enough. Whatever his demons were, they were draining him. He could no longer continue the charming pretense, the social façade of normalcy.

"I apologize." He stood, his body trembling slightly.

She stumbled to her feet, stepping back from him. His words were curt, that wall slammed back into place around his heart. His face was hard, blank, the emotions hidden deep within. Grace felt his withdrawal as if he'd physically moved away.

He looked everywhere but at her. "We should return before we're missed."

He started forward. Grace reached out, boldly grasping his arm. "No."

He froze, as if the touch of her hand was poison.

"Please," she whispered.

Finally he lifted his gaze. Those beautiful eyes held hers for one long, breathless moment. There was something there in the blue depths that haunted her, that tore through her very being… a pleading look as if he was searching for answers and she was his salvation. He needed something…something…but she didn't know what he needed, nor did she know if she was capable of saving him. Yet she couldn't let him go, not now, perhaps not ever.

"Alex…I…" Giving into temptation, she stepped close, pressing her body to his and wrapping her arms around his neck. She rested the side of her face against his shoulder and squeezed him tightly. She held him, not expecting anything in return, just held him as she'd hug a family member or a friend. He was stiff for a moment, but ever so slowly his body relaxed into hers as his hands inched up her back, pulling her closer. Alex pressed his face into her hair, breathing softly.

Their hearts pounded together, slowly, steady. One.

Grace closed her eyes, her hands fisting against the lapels of his overcoat, the material warm from his body. She didn't want to let go and had no bloody idea why. Somehow Alex had burrowed into her heart, her soul.

She breathed deep his scent…man, leather, and spice. A scent that stirred her longing like no other. She had a feeling she'd never tire of Alex. She lifted her head, pressing the side of her face to his, her breath stirring the dark strands of hair that curled close to his ear.

"I want you, Alex," she whispered. She knew the words were bold, but they had slipped from her lips before she could stop them. Not words meant to encourage his amorous desires, but more a plea…a cry for help.

Her hands whispered up his muscled arms, over his broad shoulders, lingering at the sides of his face. She played with those strands of hair at his temples, entwining the locks around her fingers, savoring the feel of the smooth texture.

Alex's breath grew harsh against her cheek, a warm caress that seeped through her body, down into her very being. A feeling she had never had with Rodrick. A feeling she worried she'd never have with him. But no, she wouldn't think of Rodrick now. Her time with Alex was precious. Grace stood on tiptoe and pressed her lips to the shell of his ear. She wanted to forget her problems, needed to think of nothing other than the warm, aching sensations that swirled deep within her gut whenever she thought of Alex.

He didn't move, merely stood still, his arms wrapped stiffly around her, as if he feared any movement. Emboldened, Grace turned her head, pressing kisses along his jawline…unassuming, gentle kisses. Kisses that bespoke affection. Of care. Of hope.

When she'd left that garden last night, she hadn't expected to see him again. She'd felt his absence like a death. Now he was here and she was alive once more. She worked her way up, pressing her mouth to the corner of his lips. Still he didn't move, barely breathed. Did he wish her to stop? His eyes were closed, his body stiff under her touch. She could read nothing in his features. But it didn't matter what his feelings were, the need within her was too great to resist. How she couldn't get enough of him!

Grace tilted her head and pressed her mouth fully to his. Alex groaned. Reputation be damned! Her tongue darted out, drawing a soft line against his lips. Alex sighed, opening his mouth to her. What was it about this man that made her forget her reputation?

Alex tightened his hold, his hands cupping her bottom and drawing her closer. Even through the layers of skirts and petticoats she could feel his erection, thick and hard. His tongue stroked hers, quick, passionate strokes that sent shivers down her spine. As he kissed her, the world fell away. The universe revolved around them. Nothing mattered but him.

"How I want you," he whispered against her mouth.

One moment she was pressed to his body, the next she was in his arms, cradled against his hard chest. Grace's skirts crinkled and bunched under his touch, trailing behind him as he swept toward the settee. Against the side of her breast, she could feel his heart slamming erratically. His gaze was hard, his jaw set stubbornly.

When he lowered her to the settee she didn't argue, didn't even care that they might be caught in a more-than-compromising situation. Alex followed her down, his hard form pressing into her body.

"You are so lovely," he whispered, resting his face against the side of her neck, his lips finding the sensitive skin. Grace shivered.

He cupped the sides of her face. "So incredibly lovely."

As wonderful as his words were, she noted the desperation in his voice, and she had the oddest feeling that he needed her to believe him. His hands traveled down her body, his movements almost frantic, so unpracticed, so unlike him. She turned her head and pressed her lips to his temple, offering him comfort in the only way she could.

"God, Gracie, you make me feel."

He pressed his lips to hers, a soft kiss. A gentle kiss. A kiss he'd never given her before. A kiss that seemed to reach down to her very soul. A kiss that swept through her body and made her want more. How she wished to be closer to him, wanted all of him.

Grace pressed her own lips to his, her tongue tracing his mouth. He groaned, slipped his knee between her legs, and spread her thighs as much as her skirts would allow. His hard, lean body settled atop hers, molding perfectly to her form as if they were meant to be together. But no, she wouldn't think such ridiculous, romantic thoughts. She would only think about the now, this moment, and the wonderful feelings he stirred within.

Alex pulled his lips from hers. "I can't stop thinking about you."

She couldn't stop thinking about him.

"I want you all the time."

And how she wanted him!

His lips found the hollow of her throat while his fingers worked the buttons of her bodice. The world faded and they floated in oblivion, alone, untouchable. Her bodice parted, exposing the edge of her white corset. Her breasts rose sharply with every harsh intake of air.

"So beautiful." His fingers brushed across the soft mounds, sending shivers over her skin.

He pressed his mouth there, between the valley of her breasts. Agony. Need. Hope. All rippled through her body on a heated wave. His breath was warm, his tongue rough and damp as he licked her skin. Grace groaned, sliding her fingers into his hair.

"You taste amazing," he whispered.

His fingers went to the strings of her corset, loosening the bindings so she could finally breathe again. Grace tried to help, wiggling beneath him until the straps of her shift lowered. It was a wild, frantic struggle to be as close to him as possible.

"I can't eat," he said, his hands brushing hers aside so he could pull her shift lower. Her right breast came free, the nipple a hard, pink bud. His eyes darkened as he cupped the breast, his palm so warm she felt it deep within her soul. "I can't sleep since tasting you."

Through her muddled and hazy state, she allowed him to lift her skirts. His hands moved to her legs, sliding over her silk stockings, pulling her skirts higher…higher. She felt his warm breath on her breast right before he lowered, taking her nipple between his lips. A bolt of pleasure struck her core.

Grace arched her back. "Please, Alex."

She was begging and should have felt the heat of shame. Instead, she felt only desire. He stroked her upper thigh, his fingers resting at her bloomers. "How I've wanted to have you completely."

His hand slid into her undergarments, through the soft curls shielding her femininity. Grace sucked in a sharp breath as the aching need turned into pleasure.

"How I want you, Gracie."

The hard length of his erection pressed to her thigh. How she wanted to touch him there! To wrap her fingers around the length of him. To show him the pleasure he showed her.

Alex's fingers slipped between her damp folds. Fevered heat raced through her body. Grace moaned, turning her flushed face into the settee cushion. No one had ever touched her so, and she knew it was wrong, knew she should stop him, but she didn't care.

"How wet you are," he said, then took the lobe of her ear between his teeth.

Grace bit her lip, lifting her hips, taking his fingers farther inside her.

"Come for me, Gracie," he whispered into her ear.

His finger slid into her tight sheath as his thumb found that sensitive nub hidden in her curls. Lightning branched through her body. Grace cried out. The sensations were too strong, too much even for her aching body. She should have been horrified by her wanton behavior, yet found her hips lifting, rocking against his hand.

"Grace, look at me." He lifted himself higher, his warm breath brushing her cheek. She heard the slight plea in his voice and turned her head, meeting his gaze. The air between them mingled. His eyes were fierce and emotional, and in that moment she knew he truly cared. Something deep within her shifted, time seemed to stand still, and nothing existed but them.

"Alex," she whispered, bemused by the flood of emotion that swept through her body.

Dear God, she *loved* him.

She cried out, arching her back. The ache seeped lower, spreading through her body and tightening in that tender spot between her legs. Her very soul seemed to tremble deep within. Grace shifted, feeling feverish. And Alex, lovely Alex, slipped a second finger inside her.

"Please," she whispered, her nails biting into his back through the smooth texture of his jacket.

She no longer felt alone in this world, but part of Alex and he a part of her. Unable to stand the ache any longer, Grace rocked against his hand.

"Come for me, Grace," he said.

His words were like magic. The aching knot in her womb unwound. Grace cried out as her entire body trembled, her soul exploding into a million white stars. Heaven. For one long moment, she swore she was floating in heaven.

Vaguely she was aware of Alex pressing kisses to her lips, his mouth anchoring her in reality. A reality she no longer feared, but desired.

"You're so sweet," he whispered against her mouth.

Releasing a harsh, shaky breath, she wrapped her arms around his shoulders and held him close. Her heart slammed against his, begging for reprieve, her soul begging for more. He shifted and she was acutely reminded of his steel erection pressing to her thighs. The hum of satisfaction still vibrated within her, but she wanted more. She wanted all of him.

"Alex, please." She cuddled the bulge of his erection between her thighs. "I want all of you."

"Grace, my love," he sighed, resting his forehead to hers. "You don't know how badly I want to comply, but not here, not now."

Was he forever to say those words? She opened her mouth to protest when the squeak of the door stunned her into silence. Frantic, Grace hid her face against Alex's shoulder.

"Time to leave," a deep voice demanded. There was no surprise in the tone, only insistence.

A tremble raked Alex's frame, a shiver of regret? Need? Unfulfilled desire? She wasn't sure. She peeked over Alex's shoulder. A giant of a man stood in the doorway, a man she'd seen before at the brothel. One of Lady Lavender's guards. He didn't look shocked, he didn't seem to care, yet there was no denying that his presence commanded obedience.

Alex pressed his hands into the settee and stood, smoothing down Grace's skirts. She felt the loss of his warm body as if he'd ripped out her heart. She curled her fingers, resisting the urge to reach out to him. Slowly Grace settled her feet upon the floorboards, her body spent and quivering. She felt almost faint with emotion, feelings she couldn't identify and now wouldn't have time to explore. She wanted to scream, to cry out in frustration. It wasn't fair!

She surged to her feet, ignoring the guard in the doorway. "Don't go," she whispered.

Alex didn't respond, but she noticed the flash of emotion that crossed his hooded eyes. Staring intently at the floor, he grasped her upper arms and pulled her closer. He didn't kiss her, didn't agree to stay, but simply buttoned her bodice. His touch was stiff, his mouth pressed into a firm, uncompromising line. A man she didn't know.

"Alex," she whispered, trapping his hands against her chest. "You don't have to go with him. You are not a prisoner."

His gaze met hers. There was a sadness there that made her ache for him. "Yes, I am."

"No!" she said a little more harshly this time.

"We leave now," the big man snapped from the doorway.

Grace threw him a glare. How she hated him! How she hated Lady Lavender!

Alex cupped the sides of her face, forcing her attention back to him. "Oh, Grace, what the bloody hell am I going to do without you?"

His words pierced her very heart. Shocked her into silence.

Without another word, without a kiss or touch, he turned and left her there.

Chapter 15

There was no hope left.

It was better that he acknowledge his bleak reality. He knew Grace cared about him in some way. Of course he cared about her, more than he'd cared about anyone in a long, long while. But what could possibly happen between a whore and a lady? Nothing.

Life would be much simpler if he accepted his fate.

Alex pushed away from the wing back chair where he'd been resting. The same wing back chair he'd sat in every day since starting work at Lady Lavender's. The same wing back chair where he'd sat with Grace and realized there was more to the woman than he'd first thought.

He picked up his jacket and slipped his arms through the sleeves. His motions were rehearsed, almost unconscious. There was no feeling attached to them. Elegantly dressed, he stared at himself in the gilded mirror hanging on the wall near his bed.

No longer in London, he felt a world away from Grace.

He felt sick. His stomach roiled, and for the first time in years he felt as if he'd lose his breakfast. He swiped at the back of his forehead, sweat dampening his hand.

He wished it were influenza.

Hell, he wished it were some wasting disease in which death was sure to come.

But no. He wasn't so lucky. He knew what made him ill.

Grace.

The woman who had kept him from sleep for three days now. The woman who had tortured his nights with dreams of her lush body. The woman he couldn't seem to cease thinking about.

Grace.

How could he continue without her? How could he touch another woman when the mere thought left him cold and ill? Alex paced to the windows and stared out on those lavender fields that surrounded the estate. Even in the spring when the plants were mere seedlings, he could still smell their scent.

Completely landlocked. Those fields traveled on forever. He missed his grandfather's cottage on the coast they used to visit when he was a child. A place of warm summers and innocence. A place where anything was possible. He owned that cottage. It had been left to him years ago when he was still a lad. Dare he reclaim his rightful possession? He turned and paced to the hearth where a fire burned that was supposed to be cheerful and bright, but instead seemed spiteful.

No doubt the cottage had fallen into disrepair. Or perhaps his family used it even still when on holiday. Or mayhap they had sold it in order to survive. It would have been easy enough for them to forge his signature. He pushed aside thoughts of the small estate. He didn't dare think about the client who was to arrive at any moment. He would perform his duty, pretend, as he was so good at pretending. He would not think about Grace.

Grace. He closed his eyes and rested his fisted hands on the mantel. Grace, who questioned his rationale, who made him think, who made him believe in a better life. Grace, who made him feel like a human, like a man.

Oh God, he couldn't do this. He couldn't make love to another woman while thinking about Grace. While picturing her sweet lips, while remembering her taste. The door opened. Alex blanched and spun around to face his demise.

Wavers stood in the doorway, his silence condemning.

Breath held, Alex waited for his client to appear. Wavers stepped aside and a woman wearing a brilliant blue dress swept into the room as if she'd been here before. A regular then? Yes, for even though her face was covered by black netting, there was something familiar in the way she moved. Alex weaved on his feet, feeling lightheaded, panicked. He couldn't pretend with a regular; she would know.

"Good…" He'd meant to say "good evening," but she turned toward him and in that moment he recognized the flare of those hips, the dip of that waist, that regal bearing. "Good God."

Gracie. Grace was his client? Euphoria swept through him, but he didn't dare show his excitement until Wavers left them alone. His hands fisted on his thighs as he resisted the urge to rush toward her. She paused in the middle of the room, and even though he couldn't see her face, he knew she looked at him, could feel the excitement roll off her body like a cool, refreshing breeze. She too was holding back.

The moment Wavers shut the door Grace's shoulders relaxed. She lifted her netting, those familiar features flushed with emotion.

"How?" he asked, stepping toward her.

"I sold a necklace of no importance." She waved her hand through the air, dismissing the comment. But couldn't she understand how important her actions were? She'd sold her jewelry just so she could be with him. The realization warmed his very being. Made him realize that perhaps people were good, that life wasn't a terrible jest.

"Grace—"

"I need help with these letters."

She shoved forward a packet of envelopes tied with a red ribbon that he'd been too excited to notice before. The package hit his chest with a thump.

His euphoria wavered. Confused, he grasped the bundle and looked blankly at the cream-colored papers. "Wh...what?"

"Letters," she said in a breathless whisper, her excitement almost tangible. "I need you to translate them."

Realization sank heavily into his gut. She was a treasure hunter; it's what she lived for. Apparently the one thing that thrilled her like nothing else. He would never have met her otherwise. "You're not here for...a lesson?"

She laughed. Actually laughed, and the knowledge that she didn't ache for him as he did her turned his blood cold.

"Don't be silly. This is better, so much better!" She started pacing in front of him, a dizzying whirl of excitement. "Alex, these letters hold the clues to a treasure supposedly lost during the war, but they're in Russian. I purchased them from a collector five years ago. If we—"

"Get out."

Grace froze, jerking her head toward him. "Wh...what?"

He tossed the letters to her and she fumbled to catch them. "The appointment is for women who want to be pleasured. If you're not here to fuck, leave."

She swallowed hard, her eyes going wide with shock, and for a moment he actually believed he'd hurt her feelings. "You don't mean that."

As if she cared what he said to her. "I do. Now go." He forced himself to turn his back to her and made his way to the fireplace. His entire body trembled, his mind warring with his soul. She didn't want him.

"Alex—"

"Leave!" His voice came out harsher than he'd intended, but he couldn't take it back. Not now. Everything Lady Lavender had said was right. No one would want him. He belonged here.

His harsh tone did not frighten her. In fact, he could hear the rustle of her skirts as she came closer. Damn her! Why wouldn't she leave him in peace? "But, Alex, I—"

He spun around so quickly, his face so furious, she actually took a step back. Her fear gave him perverse pleasure. "I want you gone now, and don't ever return."

He brushed by her and made his way to the door, his steps hurried. She needed to leave, now, before he said too much. "I'm fucking tired of these games. Do you understand? Tired of them."

"Alex." She started toward him, taking off her bonnet and tossing it in a chair as if she meant to stay. "You don't understand."

He turned, forcing himself to look at her, truly look at her. His gaze was hard, his emotions cold. "I understand completely. Perhaps I am forced to allow Lady Lavender to use me, but I will not allow you to do the same."

"But Alex." She reached out, resting her delicate hand on his forearm. Her touch burned all the way to his soul. He started to shrug her off when she continued, "It's for us."

He froze, staring down into her hazel eyes, trying to understand.

She blushed and released her hold. "That is…for you and me."

He didn't understand her words. He knew something had changed, that perhaps he had been wrong, yet he couldn't quite understand how.

"If you…if *we* find this treasure, I'll be free of my stepbrother." She pressed the letters to her bosom with one hand and the other she rested on his chest, directly over his heart. "I know it's unlikely we will, but if we do…Alex, you'll be free. We'll both be free and we can—"

"Free?"

She nodded, her sable brows drawing together. "I just…I assumed…you do this for the money, but if you had the money you wouldn't…"

Her voice became an odd buzz that murmured through his brain. He was barely aware of what she said. Possibility surged within him, a warmth that flooded his soul. She wanted him to help her find a ridiculous treasure so they could both be free, but free to do what?

"And after?" he demanded, interrupting her ramble.

"After?" She shook her head, obviously confused.

Deep down he feared her answer, but he had to know the truth. "Will you still speak with me, Grace?" He stepped closer, needing to be near. "Can we still…see each other?"

Pink flooded her high cheekbones. She understood his hidden question. "I don't see why not," she whispered, looking up at him with such trusting eyes that his heart melted.

Alex swallowed hard. "You won't worry…being attached to someone like me?"

The left corner of her mouth quirked into a completely adorable, completely wry smile. "I've never cared much what others thought."

A surge of emotion swept through his body; emotions he didn't understand, had never felt before…compassion, honor, adoration…so much more, so many feelings he couldn't identify.

She frowned, a tiny crease forming between her brows. "There are things we do that perhaps we shouldn't, but, blast it all, Alex, I like you and…"

He gripped her upper arms.

Grace let out a startled gasp. Before she could protest he jerked her forward and crushed his lips to hers. She didn't fight, but sank into him as if she belonged there, in his arms. Nothing had ever felt so natural, so right, so wonderful.

He wouldn't think about how inevitably their relationship would end. He wouldn't think about tomorrow. He would only think of the here and now. It was a quick kiss, a possessive kiss, and all too soon he was pulling back.

"Tell me you care about me," he whispered.

She cupped the sides of his face, her eyes sparkling with unshed tears. "I wouldn't be here if I didn't."

It was all he needed to hear. He scooped her up into his arms, cradling her against his chest. She didn't protest, merely snuggled closer to him. They had this moment together, however brief it might be, and he would show her how much her words meant.

He was at the bed in two steps. Gently he placed her on the mattress, his body following. "You're so lovely, Grace. Do you realize that?"

She didn't respond; she was too busy working the buttons of his jacket. Her fingers were fumbling, her hands trembling. She was determined, and she wanted him. But she didn't merely want him, she *liked* him.

He smiled down at her, his gaze memorizing every detail of her face as his fingers moved to her bodice. He wanted to see her, all of her. Even as he fought the urge to tear the clothing from her, he knew going further would change things between them. They would both end up heartbroken. The selfish being in him didn't care.

He was quicker at undressing, and her bodice fell away, revealing the lovely swell of her breasts, spilling over her corset and shift.

"So very beautiful," he whispered, pressing a kiss to her neck.

Grace shivered and slipped the jacket from his shoulders, tossing the garment aside. "You're ridiculous, you know that?"

His hands moved to her corset, his heavy breath stirring the loose tendrils around her face. "Why is that?"

"Because I'm quite on the shelf. You're the only man who has told me I'm beautiful."

"Most men are idiots." The corset fell open. "Believe me, Grace, a man would have to be blind not to see your beauty. Most men are just intimidated by a woman with a brain."

She grinned, unbuttoning his shirt. "And you're not intimidated by anything?"

His fingers paused at the laces of her shift as her words struck him like a punch to the gut. He couldn't respond; what to say? True, when you had nothing to live for, very few things intimidated a man. But now...now that he had Gracie everything worried him, for he had so much to lose. Alex swallowed hard and focused on her face, the pert nose with the ever-so-light splattering of freckles. The bow shape of her pink lips. The sparkle of her eyes.

"I find everything about you adorable," he said, not answering her question.

Still smiling, she pushed the shirt off his shoulders and moved her hands down his chest, her fingers splaying through the crisp line of hair that trailed to his trousers. The smile on her face wavered, her look turning pensive. "You do like me, truly. It's not a ruse?"

Alex groaned, cupping the sides of her face and lowering his head until he was only a breath away from her mouth. "You have no idea how much I like you."

He kissed her again, a soft, lingering kiss as his hands moved down her waist, bunching her skirts to her hips. Through the thick layers of crinoline and petticoats, over the smooth, silk stockings, to...touch...

Holy hell! Alex jerked his head upright. "Grace?"

She flushed, lowering her hands to his waistband and her gaze to his chest. "Someone told me that bloomers merely got in the way. So I decided to test his theory and forgo my undergarments for the day."

Alex laughed, truly amused and more than thrilled. "Do you know I've laughed more with you than I have laughed in the past fifteen years?"

"With me or at me?" she muttered, frowning.

"With you," he whispered, lowering his lips to the bridge of her nose. "Always with you." His right hand slid up her silky leg, teasing the curls at the junction of her thighs.

"Please, Alex, let me touch you as well."

He paused, surprised. Usually women were more interested in being touched than touching him, and for years he'd liked that he had had the upper hand; he was in control…in the bedroom at least.

"Please," she whispered. When her hands went to his waistband, blood rushed to his cock, urging him to agree. He wanted her too badly to protest. Wanted to feel her hands on his throbbing erection. To know she wanted him as much as he wanted her.

She pushed his trousers down his hips. His cock sprang forward, hard, heavy, pressing eagerly into her warm hands. Grace's eyes widened, a sharp intake of breath showing her surprise. For a moment, she merely held him. Hell, just when he thought he'd die of anticipation, she tentatively moved her hands down his shaft.

Alex groaned as pain and pleasure combined. He fell to his back. The ache that settled in his groin was almost unbearable. He didn't dare move for fear of frightening her away, but hell, there was only so much a man could take. Grace pushed her skirts high and straddled his thighs.

Her warm hands gripped his cock once more. "I want to give you pleasure, Alex."

Such a declaration from such sweet lips. How could he resist? Alex stared into her face, attempted to memorize every detail. From the gold-tipped lashes, so long they produced shadows on her upper cheeks, to the way her lips quirked at the corners as if she knew some humorous secret.

And she was giving him pleasure merely by being here. If he could respond, he would tell her so. She moved her fingers up to the head of his cock, cupping the bulb. Fire burned a path through his body ending straight at his groin. As she played with his erection, Alex gripped her smooth thighs, wanting desperately to pleasure her as much as she was pleasuring him.

"You don't know what you do to me," he said.

Embolden by his words, she ran her hand down his cock, tentatively cupping him. Alex didn't want to experience the raw emotions she stirred within him. Emotions that made him feel vulnerable and helpless. But controlling his emotions around Grace was like trying to control the weather: impossible.

He found the inside of her thighs and brushed his knuckles against those soft curls shielding her folds. Grace gasped, jerking at the touch. Her face was flushed, her eyes half-closed. When he slipped his finger into her wet sheath, wanting desperately to pleasure her as much as she was pleasuring him, she trembled almost violently.

Anticipation whispered over his skin. How he wanted their clothing gone; how he wanted to touch her skin to skin, to feel her sleek body sliding up his. Alex found that nub hidden in her curls and gently rubbed his thumb over the sensitive spot.

Grace practically purred, arching her back and tightening her hold. Her warm scent covered him in a gentle kiss, vanilla and spring. He breathed deep that scent as he slid two fingers into her sheath.

She wiggled above him, taking his fingers deeper into her body. She was so very tight, so very hot, so very wet. He knew no other man had caressed her like this. She was his. Branded by his touch. By his kiss. By his affection.

Her face was flushed, her hair coming loose, falling in auburn waves down around her shoulders. She was a woman who knew the ultimate pleasure.

"How I dream about you at night," he whispered.

Grace moaned, a purely sexual sound that sent a shock of need through his body.

"How I dream about tasting you. Having you completely."

She was panting as she cupped the head of his shaft with both hands, holding it like a treasured possession. Alex lifted his hips. He felt mad with need, with want of this woman. While she caressed his cock, he slipped his fingers into her tight sheath, in and out.

"Oh, Alex," she whispered.

Her entire body tightened around him. As she came on a wave of pleasure that softened her features and made her positively glow, he could no longer hold back. Grace cried out with pleasure, releasing her hold on his erection at the same time Alex came upon the sheets with a throbbing intensity that momentarily blinded him.

Although he wanted desperately to lose himself deep within her, he knew it was better this way. Even if it left him feeling empty. His fingers curled in the sheets. How desperately he wanted to be inside her. Deep within her.

"Alex." Grace rolled over to her side, nestling next to him and resting her hand on his sweaty chest. Her body was warm, lovely, her breath a soft pant on the side of his neck. "I want...I want..."

"No, don't say it." He brushed away her hand and turned, planting his feet on the carpet.

"Alex."

He stood, although his body still trembled, and jerked his trousers up, fumbling in his haste. If she said the words, he had a feeling he'd immediately relent. If he took Grace completely, he knew he'd lose whatever little soul he had left.

"But—"

"Don't, Grace." He turned and wrapped his fingers around her waist, helping her stand before him. While she wavered on her feet, he tightened her corset and fixed her bodice.

She swatted his touch away, as if he was an annoying gnat. "I don't understand," she said, smoothing down her skirts.

Alex spun around, pacing to the windows. He pushed open the pane, allowing a cool spring breeze to waft inside.

"Alex?"

Steeling himself, he faced her. Grace's hair was lopsided, her cheeks flushed, her lips swollen from his kisses. God, how could he look at her and not want her all over again? The woman had burrowed deep within his soul. She'd become a part of him, the only decent piece holding him together.

He started toward her. "Grace, we can't do this. I won't do this to you, not now, not here in this place."

"Why?" Her lower lip quivered. "Am I not good enough? Am I not the kind of woman who…who inspires such passion you can't help yourself?" There was a defiant look in her eyes. She was daring him to reject her.

Anger and fear swirled within him. Alex grabbed her hand and pressed it to his cock. "Even now I'm hardening for you." He dropped her hand, gaining no pleasure from her shocked expression. "Blast it, don't you understand? I'm not good enough for you." He raked his hands through his hair. "We can never have a relationship. It's ridiculous to dream."

She slammed her fists into his chest, sending him stumbling backward. "That's nonsense! I've told you that I don't care!"

He grabbed her wrists, holding her immobile. "But you will, someday."

She jerked away from him, stepping back. Anger pulsed from her body, her feelings evident in the flush of her face and tremble of her being. "You're ridiculous, Alex!" She scooped up the letters that lay forgotten on the floor. "I'm offering you a life, but you're too damn afraid to take it. Don't you dare use me as an excuse."

She grabbed her bonnet, and without another glance back, she stormed across the room and tore open the door.

How he wanted to deny her accusations. How he wanted to escape with her.

But Alex merely closed his eyes and let her go because she was right; he *was* afraid.

Chapter 16

"Alex." Gideon strolled boldly into the parlor, heading straight for the sideboard. "You know I care as little about your feelings as Ophelia does, but you've been brooding for two days, and frankly it's become tiresome." He poured himself a brandy and turned to watch him. "What the hell is wrong with you?"

A variety of things, although he'd die a slow, painful death before he'd admit that much. Alex frowned, pulled from his miserable thoughts. "I'm sorry, what do you mean?"

"I heard Ophelia mention you were ill and not seeing clients. You look hearty enough to me."

What could he say? That he couldn't even think of touching another woman? Gideon would know he lied and Ophelia would only buy his excuses for so long.

"You look even more pathetic than normal." Gideon's eyes narrowed. "Did someone hurt your fragile feelings?"

"Sod off," Alex muttered.

Smirking, Gideon leaned casually against the mantel. "Something's different about you."

"Of course not." Alex leaned forward, resting his elbows on his knees and his face in his palms. He rubbed his hands over his eyes, but nothing would erase the image of Grace's face from his mind. The surprised look that had quickly turned to sadness as she stormed from his room. He didn't blame her. She'd been right. He was a fool and he was afraid. But what would she have him do? He was trying to keep her safe, damn it all.

"I'm merely tired."

He heard Gideon shift, knew he came closer, and cursed the man for not having the good sense to leave. "No, that's not it."

Hell, why couldn't they let well enough be? Everyone wanted something from him. Alex surged to his feet and paced to the fireplace. The dancing flames were warm, but he barely felt their comforting caress. "What do you want from me? A life story? I had no idea you were so concerned with feelings."

"Fine. To hell with your feelings. We have more important things to discuss anyway." Gideon stepped closer, his steel gaze fierce. "I want a damn agreement. Look at you, man. You want out as badly as I do."

"Agreement?" Alex seethed. He was tired of people constantly wanting something from him, always something. "Written in blood? Would that do?"

Gideon quirked an arrogant brow, his lips lifting. "Perhaps."

They were silent as Alex glared and Gideon smirked, knowing he'd hit a sensitive spot. In the end, Alex relented, realizing Gideon had him. With or without Grace, he could not live here any longer.

Alex released a frustrated sigh and stalked toward the sideboard, ignoring the flash of success in Gideon's eyes. As much as Alex was loath to admit it, they both knew he would agree to Gideon's ridiculous plans.

"When?" Alex asked, pouring himself a brandy. Did Gideon notice the way his hands trembled? If he had, he didn't mention it. Thank God for small favors.

"Two weeks…"

James strolled inside, putting an end to their conversation for the moment. "Oh, hello. Didn't realize you'd both be here." He looked confused, a little nervous and leery as he paused in the middle of the parlor. "Gid, did you still wish to speak with me?"

"Yes, but Alex can hear. We both wish to talk with you."

Hell, Gideon was truly going to let the cat out of the bag. Alex still wasn't sure if they could trust James. How did they know the man wouldn't rush to Lady Lavender the moment they admitted their plan?

"What's this about?" James asked, eyeing them warily.

Gideon glanced at Alex, as if he should explain. Bloody hell, he'd have to. Alex raked back his hair, stepping forward to do Gideon's work. He would try to be calm and rational before Gideon blasted the man with truths James wasn't quite ready to accept.

"James, you know as well as I that what she has done to us isn't right."

James knew immediately who they were discussing. How could he not? Anger crossed his boyish features, making his green eyes blaze.

"Think on it, James," Alex said calmly, strolling casually toward the door and blocking the man's exit should he wish to flee. "We three were brought here at approximately the same time. There must be a link, but until we tell each other the truth, we can't possibly understand."

"I know why I'm here," James snapped. "Ophelia offered me a position, a way to save my family, and I grabbed the opportunity."

Alex slid Gideon a glance and knew the man was thinking the same thing as he: there had to be more to it all, secrets James wasn't telling them. Alex had admitted to Gideon that he'd come from a titled family; Gideon had admitted he had as well. But James...James was the odd man out. The riffraff.

James's lips lifted into a sneer. "So tell me, Alex, what are your secrets? You're so eager for me to share mine; why don't you start."

"Why did you need it?" Gideon snapped out, saving Alex from having to answer. "Why did you need the money?"

"Why do you think?" James's youthful faced flushed red. "Me father died when I was young; we hadn't a pence. We were starving, so ye'll have to excuse me if I don't think yer plan is so keen."

His voice was slipping back into the voice of the street rat he was, his emotions evident in the panicked flush of his face. The sheen of genteelness that Ophelia had taught him was gone.

"Tell me about your father," Gideon demanded.

James threw his arms wide. "What's there to know? He was a coachman for a well-ta-do family. A driver for a titled gent who left 'im with not a pence to his name. He died ashamed and poor."

Alex parted his lips, intending to end the argument before it escalated into fisticuffs and Ophelia found out. Having James irate wouldn't help anyone. The man obviously didn't trust them, and he obviously didn't want to talk.

"Who did he work for?" Gideon demanded.

James narrowed his eyes. "I don't remember."

"Liar."

"Fuck you."

"Who, James?" Gideon demanded, stepping closer, doing his best to intimidate the man. Gideon outweighed and outmuscled James, but the smaller man didn't cower.

"Lord Collins," James finally hissed between clenched teeth.

An unfamiliar name, but Alex wasn't surprised. He'd known few titled Englishmen when they'd arrived those years ago. Gideon didn't flinch either, but Alex knew the man well, for they'd been living in the same abode for years. He saw the slight flaring of Gideon's eyes, the tightening of his jaw. The name bothered him for some inexplicable reason.

"If that is all, I'm leaving." James spun around and stomped from the room.

For one long moment neither Alex nor Gideon said a word. The only sound was the crackle of the fire and the rush of blood to Alex's ears. He wanted to demand answers, but knew better. One never demanded anything of Gideon. He would tell Alex when the time was right, if ever.

"That didn't go well," Alex muttered.

Gideon downed the rest of his brandy, then set the tumbler on a table. "No, it went well enough. We needed to plant doubt in his stubborn mind, and we did. He'll notice things now, things that will make him question her as he should."

Alex wasn't so confident. He had the sinking feeling that Gideon's plan was going to blow up in their faces before they'd even started. "How do you know he won't admit all to her?"

"Because he went right toward his bedchamber, not left toward her office." Gideon started toward the door. "Besides, the idiot is as loyal as they come. He might not like us, but he feels loyal to us."

Alex wasn't so sure. Not that James was a terrible sort, but the man had put Ophelia onto a pedestal. Surely his loyalty to her superseded his loyalty, if he held any, to them.

"As for you," Gideon said, pausing near the door, his back to Alex. "I'm not so sure."

Alex bristled. What the hell did that mean? He'd had too little sleep and too many confusing emotions swirling through his head to be toyed with now.

Gideon turned, grinning. "Calm down. I meant no offense, but it's obvious there's something going on between you and that Irish lass."

Irish lass? Grace? He hadn't thought of her as Irish, but obviously he wasn't the only one to notice the red in her hair. His bewilderment turned to annoyance. *Shite*, what else had Gideon noticed?

"Go then," Gideon nodded. "Find out what your feelings are before you commit to what we have planned."

Frustrated, Alex leaned against the mantel. "What do you mean? You imply that I not only have feelings for a client, but that I will be unable to concentrate on our task because of these feelings?" Alex wasn't sure whether to laugh or hit Gideon square in the face.

Gideon nodded. "That's exactly what I'm implying. You won't be able to concentrate until you sort out your feelings toward her."

Alex's fingers curled, his anger flaring. How dare Gideon speak of feelings? How dare he even think of Grace? "And how do you suggest I *sort out* my feelings, since you're apparently an expert?"

Gideon stepped into the hall. "Go to her."

The thought was so ridiculous Alex almost laughed. "You know as well as I that escape is practically impossible. Ophelia would never allow it."

Gideon shrugged, completely unconcerned. "There's always a way. I'll create a diversion while you escape."

Hope and determination swelled within. Gideon couldn't be serious. The man wouldn't truly help him, would he? "How?"

Gideon grinned an evil grin. "Fire works wonders. Just give me ten minutes…"

It was all he needed to hear. Alex was out the door, brushing by Gideon before the man had finished his sentence.

* * *

Hot one moment, cold the next.

That was how Grace thought of Alex.

He seemed to be attracted to her yet was constantly pushing her away. Was he purposefully attempting to drive her mad? She closed her bedroom door and leaned against the hard, unforgiving panel. The hearth was cold, but coal was expensive and Mama and Patience needed it more than she.

Her rock and mineral collections sat upon the mantel, the crystal pieces sparkling under the low lamplight. A piece of clear quartz she'd found with Papa while on a walk. A palm-sized specimen of dolomite she'd found with her father while on their only visit to Ireland. A fossilized shell Mama had picked up while walking along the beach. A useless collection worth but a pittance, but pieces worth so much more than money.

Only a small lantern glowed softly upon the bedside table, not daring to reach the shadows in the corners. She frowned. Had she forgotten to extinguish the light? She hadn't remembered lighting a lantern.

Exhausted, she moved across the worn floorboards, floor bare and cold, for the carpet had been sold long ago. Soon they'd run out of objects to trade, and then what? At the windows, she nudged aside the curtains and looked out upon the streets of London. Raindrops trailed down the glass. The lanes were empty, the damp cobbles glistening under gas lamps. The weather had kept most at home. Warm, in their beds, or perhaps having lazy family meals, laughing and chatting over supper. She remembered a past with happy chatter and family adoration. A time before Papa had died.

What would Papa think of Alex? He would like the man. She was sure he would. His tendency to laugh and smile. The way he jested. They'd be friends, if not...well, if not for the fact that Alex worked for Lady Lavender. Would Papa understand the reason for the man's actions? Would he forgive his transgressions? Perhaps not. Even Papa had had his limits. So why then did she find it so easy to forget what Alex did?

She closed her eyes and leaned her forehead against the cool glass. Because...because she loved Alex. She could admit that, at least to herself. When a woman is in love, Mama said, she can overlook many, many things.

How embarrassed she'd been during their first meetings. Ashamed that she could be attracted to such a man. And then... then he had smiled at her and the entire world seemed brighter, life seemed worthwhile. Perhaps she should be ashamed of her feelings, but she wasn't.

She was attracted to Alex. Desperately. She dreamed of him. She wanted him. Perhaps she would even sell her soul to be with him. She rested her fingertips on the cold glass.

Where was he this eve? Was he with another woman? Just the thought sent a sharp pang of jealousy rippling through her chest…squeezing her heart painfully.

Tears of frustration burned her eyes. Grace bit her lower lip to keep from crying. She wanted Alex for her own. But would he ever want her in the same manner? Would his feelings for her ever supersede his fears of life?

Graced fisted her hands against the glass window. "Damn you, Alex!"

"Such harsh words from such a gentle lady."

The familiar voice had her gasping in surprise. Grace spun around, her heart hammering with hope. "Alex?"

She searched the room, frantic to find him, praying she wasn't so desperate that she'd imagined his voice.

A shadow separated from the far corner, a human shape emerging from the darkness. "Please, you must explain why you're cursing my name."

He was here! He was truly in her bedchamber! She didn't care about the how or why, she only cared that he was here now. "Alex, is it truly you?"

She didn't wait for his response but rushed forward and threw her arms around his neck. His hard body was proof enough that she was not imagining things. His clothing was damp, his skin cold, and he smelled of rain and fresh air. She didn't care that it was completely shocking and inappropriate that he was in her chamber. She didn't care that he was soaking wet. She didn't care that she was showing her emotions for a man who might not feel the same.

"I had to see you," he whispered against her neck, his breath so warm it sent shivers over her skin.

The words melted her insides. She sank into him, closing her eyes and savoring the moment.

"There are so many things I need to tell you," he continued, his voice almost desperate. But damn it all, she didn't want to discuss why they couldn't be together or why he couldn't leave Lady Lavender. She merely wanted to feel. Feel him.

"It can wait."

She didn't know how he had gotten here, or why. She didn't care. Grace stood on tiptoe and pressed her mouth to his. Alex groaned, sliding his arms around her waist and drawing her even closer. For one long moment they merely kissed. When she parted her lips, his velvety tongue delved into her mouth. A kiss of desperation. A kiss of passion. A kiss of love. She felt that kiss all the way through her body, to her toes and into her soul.

When his hands moved downward to cup her bottom and pull her up against his hard erection, Grace gasped, tearing her mouth from his. How she adored the man! How he made her forget the world. She reached for the buttons on his jacket. She would have him this time, all of him. Blast it, her fingers were too cold and her body trembling too badly to work properly.

"So many things…" he gasped. "I must…need to…"

She finally got the buttons undone and shoved the jacket from his broad shoulders. Eagerly she pressed her lips to the side of his neck where his pulse beat erratically. He tasted of spicy male, of night air and rain. Her trembling fingers crawled down the buttons of his linen shirt, eager, so bloody eager.

"Grace, please."

"What things?" she asked in a breathless whisper. His shirt parted. Grace spread the material wide and slipped her hands up his chest, her fingers tracing the carved muscle, spreading through the crisp, dark hair sprinkled across his torso. So bloody warm under her touch. She'd never get enough of the man.

"Things…such as…Good Lord, stop." He grabbed her wrists, his grip so tight she paused in surprise. "I can't think when you're touching me and I need to think."

Did he not wish to be intimate? The thought chilled her blood, confused her. Before she could question him further, he took her hand and pulled her toward the chair near the empty fireplace. "Sit." He gently pushed her down, then grabbed a shawl and tossed it over her shoulders.

Grace tightened her fingers on the fringe of her wrap and resisted the urge to stand again and demand answers. His face was so serious that he was almost frightening. He did want her, didn't he? He had come to make amends, hadn't he?

He raked his hands through his hair in the way he did when he was flustered. "There's so much I haven't told you, that I haven't told anyone."

"What is it?" Surely nothing he could say would be more shocking than what she already knew about him. Still, Grace couldn't deny that her nerves were tingling in warning.

"I'm from Russia," he blurted out.

She nodded. "Yes, I assumed." Was that why he was so nervous? "Your nationality does not concern me." Although she had certainly wondered how he had gotten here. But it was his story to tell and she'd always been patient.

He started pacing in front of her, the floorboards squeaking in protest. "I wasn't always…a whore."

She nodded again, glancing at the door, worried John would arrive home soon and notice Alex's heavy footsteps. "Please, Alex, what is it? You're driving me mad with suspense."

He stopped and faced her. How she wished she could read his features, but the darkness made it nearly impossible. Still, she didn't need to read his face to know he was upset. The air practically vibrated with unease.

"My family was related to the Russian royals."

Grace waited for his laughter.

It never came.

"Dear Lord, you're serious."

He moved to the cold hearth, resting his hands on the mantel, his back to her. "My mother was English, my father Russian. We fled to England during the Crimean war when I was but a boy. We knew very few. My mother's family was not part of the *ton* but wealthy farmers who kept to the countryside. We hid here, in London, fearing retribution because we were Russian."

He paused then and the silence stretched between them. Alex was related to royalty. Why did that not surprise her as much as it should? Instead of shock, Grace felt oddly numb.

"I…I see," she whispered, knowing she must say something. "But…how are you here, in this situation?"

He swallowed hard, his unease almost tangible, like a wave in the air that trembled and quaked. "Lady Lavender threatened to destroy my family if I didn't work for her. She would tell the world who we really were. At the time, the English didn't particularly care for Russians. Now that I'm older, I realize we could have hidden in the countryside, but as a young lad, I was… frightened." He paced in front of her. "I was not allowed contact with my parents, not allowed to explain my sudden disappearance. After years I'd had enough. I knew the war was over and assumed we would be safe. That's when she swore to tell the world what I had been. When she threatened to go after my brother, I knew she had me. And then…then I saw my brother that day at the gaming hell."

Demitri. She remembered the situation so vividly, for it was one of the first times Alex had shown true emotion. The man had been his brother? So many thoughts tumbled through Grace's mind she wasn't sure which to latch on to. How she hated Lady Lavender. How she wanted to go to her gaudy estate and wrap her very fingers around the woman's neck.

"And then I met you." Startled, Grace turned her attention to him once more. Alex knelt before her, his eyes pleading. "Please,

Grace. You must believe me. We were in dire circumstances, running out of money…"

She threw her arms around his neck. "Oh, Alex. I'm so sorry." His entire body seemed to sink into her, as if breathing a huge sigh of relief. He wrapped his arms around her waist, pulling her tightly to him.

"You forgive me?" he whispered into her hair.

His heart beat so rapid, so frantic against her chest. "There is nothing to forgive. When I met you, I couldn't resist your charm. I knew there was something there, underneath it all, and I was right. You're an honorable man."

He pulled back and cupped the sides of her face. A desperation shone in his eyes that tore at her gut, squeezed at her heart. "You don't know how much your words mean to me, even if I don't deserve them."

"You do!" She pressed a quick kiss to his cold lips. "And your family will think the same."

He stiffened. Grace resisted the urge to cringe. Had she overstepped? "You do…you do plan to tell them?"

Slowly he pulled away from her and stood. He suddenly seemed a county away. Without a word, he turned and paced toward the fireplace.

"Alex?"

He paused, his back to her, his shoulders stiff. What was he thinking? Had she ruined everything?

"The war is over, Alex." She went to him slowly, fearful of frightening him away. She rested her palms on his damp jacket, soaking in the heat radiating from his body. "You need to find your family. You need to tell them the truth. They deserve it. You deserve it."

He was silent for one long, horrible moment. Grace bit her lower lip, stepping back and giving him space to think. Was she wrong in coaxing him? She could see the little lost boy in his eyes. Alex needed his family, as she needed hers. But would he trust her enough to listen to her beliefs? Or would he push her away as he'd done before?

He glanced over his shoulder, a shy look of hesitation that tugged at her heart. "And if I do…can you…do you think you could possibly go with me?"

Euphoria and relief mixed in a dizzying combination. Alex wanted her. Alex needed her. Alex respected her opinion. He might not love her, but at the moment it didn't matter.

The tears she'd been trying to keep at bay slipped one by one down her cheeks. "Alex, whether you go to your family or not, I will always be here for you."

Chapter 17

How the hell had he ended up here?

Alex's grip tightened on Grace's chilled hand. The woman was half his size, yet he drew comfort from her steady presence all the same. She squeezed his fingers, a silent show of support, obviously sensing his reluctance. Of course the fact that he'd been standing on the front stoop for a good ten minutes might have given her a clue.

She hadn't needed to escort him to his parents' home. But he'd asked her and she hadn't hesitated to agree. And now they stood in front of a townhouse in a reputable part of London. The paint on the door was not peeling, nor were the hedges overgrown as at Grace's townhome. There wasn't even a feeling of sadness or loss. It was well kept.

Even a child would surmise the family who lived here was unconcerned with money. Probably titled. They were not living in poverty. They were not starving. They were not pining for him.

Alex had a feeling this was a horrible, terrible idea.

"You found their address so easily," he said, more to evade the inevitable than to make conversation.

Grace shrugged, feigning nonchalance, but he knew what she was thinking: the same thing as he. Perhaps he wouldn't be well received after all. "I knew if they had even stepped foot in society, Lady Maxwell would have heard of them. I promise you, she will be discreet."

And his parents had been out in society. Apparently his mother was known and respected among the *ton*. And Dem... Dem was a local rake and favorite among the ladies, a title Alex most likely would have claimed if his life hadn't been stolen at such a young age. Yet he held no bitterness. No, because the thought of being married off to some spoiled, titled woman sickened him. He'd gone through years of hell, but perhaps, in the end, if Grace stayed by his side, the pain would be worth it.

He glanced down at Grace, her face half-hidden under the rim of her straw bonnet. She was so serene, so lovely as the wind tugged at the loose tendrils framing her features and the glow from the lamps on either side of the door kissed her skin. She would stand by his side, and perhaps, once he confronted his past, they could have a life. That thought, and only that thought, spurred him forward.

Alex lifted his hand and let his fist fall. The sound thundered through the evening air, disrupting the thump of carriage wheels over cobbled lanes. His nerves were on edge. He felt like a damn debutante at her first ball. It could go smashingly—or wretchedly.

They didn't have to wait long. Moments later Alex heard footsteps from inside the house. He stiffened, his heart slamming wildly in his chest, but he managed to stand his ground. He could feel the frantic pulse at Grace's wrist and knew she was as nervous as he. The realization calmed him for some reason, knowing that she cared, that she would not abandon him to his fate...

The door opened and a graying butler stood before them, his long face dour, his expression leery. "Yes?"

"Is the family in residence?" Alex asked, knowing quite well they were.

The man quirked an arrogant brow and Alex had the sudden urge to slam his fist into his face. He should expect such arrogance. He should get used to such shows of disrespect. Once the world uncovered what he truly was, no one would look him in the eyes again.

"My lady is not taking callers." He started to shut the door. Alex shoved his foot inside. In any other instance, he would have found the shocked look on the man's face amusing.

"I will see my mother."

"Mother?" The butler paled slightly, yet suspicion also clouded his pale-blue eyes. "Sir, I think you have the wrong address."

Oh, how he wished. How he wished he could pretend he had no family. How he wished he could simply leave with Grace, never to return. But Grace deserved more, and if he could offer her a royal lineage, perhaps he wouldn't feel so wanting.

"Henry, what is it?" Even years later, the soft, feminine voice was as familiar as his own, and suddenly Alex was a child once more. Time seemed to actually stand still for one brief moment.

The butler stepped aside and his mother came into view. The same petite woman, but shockingly older. Her upswept hair, which had once been blonde, was now peppered with gray. Wrinkles that had never been there before lined the areas around her blue eyes. Alex swept his gaze down the rich velvet of her dress, back up to her face, looking for signs that she hadn't changed.

She was thinner. Perhaps life had taken its toll, but she had recovered, for she was dressed for a ball. He couldn't help but notice with some shock the large blue sapphires that hung from her ears and neck. Love and anger combined. How he'd missed her, yet at the same time the bitter part of him lifted its ugly head. She'd obviously gotten over his disappearance.

"Can we help…" The confusion cleared as did the color in her face. She went pale, her blue eyes growing wide. "Alex?"

He swallowed hard, his throat suddenly dry. He hadn't cried in over a decade, yet felt the sudden urge to do so now. "Mother."

Her head lolled back and she started to sink to the ground. Alex reached her before she hit the floor. Lord, she was light, so frail. It wasn't exactly the reaction he'd expected. He cradled her thin body to him, marveling over the difference. He'd been as tall as her when he'd left. Now...now he towered over his mother.

"Where is the sitting room?" Grace demanded of the butler.

"Th...there," Henry stammered out, pointing down the hall. Alex carried his mother's still body toward the room, watching her face, praying she recovered. He could hear Grace snapping out orders for smelling salts, a wet washing cloth, and warm tea, and he thanked God she had escorted him.

What a lovely way of reentering his family's life. He'd practically killed her. Killed his own mother with his sudden appearance. Or perhaps she had fainted from horror.

He placed her gently upon a richly upholstered settee. Still she didn't move. Seeing her so quiet, so pale, so *old*, Alex's reserve wavered. Graced rushed into the room, smelling salts in hand. She knelt beside Alex and reached toward his mother. Her experienced hands did not tremble; Grace had done this before.

"No." His mother swatted Grace's hand away. "I'm well enough."

Startled, Grace pulled back and glanced worriedly at Alex. He barely breathed as he waited for his mother to open her eyes. Her thin lashes lifted, those blue eyes focusing on him, peering deep within his soul, searching for the truth.

"My God, Alex, is it truly you?"

He nodded, unable to say more.

Her gaze traveled his face as if attempting to find something, *anything* familiar. "You look...so very different, so grown up. But your eyes...your eyes are the same." She reached out a thin hand and placed it against the side of his face. Her cold fingers trembled, her eyes filling with tears. "I thought you gone forever. Where have you been?"

Alex resisted the urge to reach out to her, to draw comfort from her presence. "First, tell me that everyone is well." His voice was gruff with emotion. This was his mother, the woman who had kissed his bruises. The woman who would sneak food into his room when Father said no dinner for some mishap. The woman who gave him life, for God's sake. So why did he feel as if she was a stranger?

She pushed herself upright, smoothing her skirts down her lap. "Yes, your father, Dem, all of us. We are well." Tears trembled on her eyelashes before trailing down her pale cheeks.

Her tears confused him, made him uneasy. Had they suffered from his absence after all? Or was she merely crying because he'd given her a start?

A maid rushed into the room, the tea service on her tray clattering in her haste. Alex was vaguely aware of Grace pouring, heard her murmured thanks, but he couldn't look away from his mother. From the wrinkles on her face, the graying of her hair. Perhaps, for some odd reason, he thought time would stand still while he was gone. But life had continued on; his family had loved and lived while he had rotted away.

"A year after you disappeared..." His mother paused and glanced at Grace, as if judging her worth and trustworthiness.

"Whatever you have to say you can say in front of Grace."

The woman hesitated, then reluctantly nodded. They'd always been a private family, keeping their secrets close. "Very well. The year after you left, your father worked out a deal with the British government. He provided information, and in return we were able to stay here, unharmed. We've done...quite well."

The words hit him like a punch to the gut. It was for nothing. Everything he had done was for nothing. Years of hell. Destroying his reputation.

His hands curled into his thighs, the room becoming a faded reality. If he had held tight for only another year, he wouldn't have had to sell his body and soul. He wouldn't have ruined his life.

"So you see, we worried for nothing." His mother gave him a weak smile, then leaned forward, grasping on to his hands and jerking him back into reality. "Oh, Alex, please tell me where you have been. Why did you leave? I thought you dead!"

The truth. Alex stumbled to his feet, stepping back and pulling away from her. How could he tell her the truth now? His mother was watching him, expecting answers. Grace was watching him, expecting the truth. But how could he tell his mother what had happened? How could he watch the spark of hope fade from her eyes?

He closed his eyes for the briefest of moments. No, he wouldn't regret his past. He had done what he had to do for his family, and because of that, he had met Grace...the very reason he stood here now. The reason he would humiliate himself and tell his family the truth. The very reason he now wanted a life.

And it would sort itself out and everything would be well, as Grace always seemed to think. Everything could be well now that he was here. Yet even as he thought the words, he knew nothing could ever be normal again. Even if they forgave him, they would never look at him the same.

"Alex?" His mother's smile faded.

"My dear," a gruff male voice boomed through the room.

Alex jerked around, facing the door.

"Henry said..." His father paused just over the threshold, his voice trailing off as confusion washed over his features. The man had gained weight in his midsection, his dark hair had thinned and turned gray, but he was still the dour-looking brute Alex had known and feared as a child. Instead of the overwhelming emotions he'd felt when seeing his mother, at his father's appearance Alex felt oddly numb.

"Hello, Father."

His father took a few stumbling steps forward for the briefest of moments, his emotions unschooled. "My God, Alex, is that you?"

Alex nodded, his only response. For one long moment not one person said a word. The only sounds were the click of the porcelain clock on the mantel and the crackle of the fire in the hearth. The very world seemed to pause, but life went on quickly enough.

His father's face went from stunned to flushed, his anger almost palpable. "Where the hell have you been?"

This was the father he'd known. His sire had not changed in all these years. For some reason, this realization made him feel somewhat relieved. "You should sit," Alex said patiently. He'd known all along his father would be his toughest opponent. Things would not go as easy as they had with his mother.

His father stomped toward him, a big bull of a man dressed in black ballroom attire. They had aged, their positions had bettered, but in reality nothing had changed. His father still couldn't control his anger and his mother still cowered before the man.

His father's footsteps vibrated the floorboards. "Do you know how many times your mother cried herself to sleep at night? Do you know how many months and months we searched for you? Our only consolation was that we thought you to be dead and that was why you had left without a word. And now you show up here, healthy and hale?"

Alex didn't even flinch, although he noticed Grace's eyes flash toward him. The outrage and sympathy he witnessed in her gaze should have made him feel better, but it didn't. She was witnessing his father's ire, witnessing the life he'd led, the people he'd disappointed. Was there nothing decent he could offer her?

"I did what I had to do," he said, his voice catching.

His father paused a good five feet from him, his lips lifting into a sneer. "And what was that?" That condescending tone. The same voice he'd used when punishing them as children. That same look of disgust. Only this time Alex did not fear the man. The smirk the old man had on his face would soon be gone. He now had the power to hurt them all beyond measure.

"When I was thirteen a woman approached me. She knew who I was. She knew who you were. She knew everything about our family, including our connection to the royals." He looked at Grace. It was easier to speak to her as if his parents weren't in attendance. As much as he wanted to abandon this ridiculous need to speak the truth, he knew there was no turning back now. "She told me she would keep our secrets safe."

"In exchange for vhat?" his father demanded, his accent growing thick.

Alex looked the man directly into his eyes. "In exchange, I would sell my body. I would become a whore."

His mother gasped. His father grew pale.

"You're jesting," his father insisted.

"It's not true!" His mother surged to her feet, only to waver as if she would faint again. This time Alex didn't dare go to her side. "No!" She shook her head, tears once more welling in her faded blue eyes, eyes that had once looked at him with love and kindness and now only held horror. "Please tell me it's not true."

"Dear God." His father pressed his hand to his chest. "*No.*"

Guilt and shame should have been foremost in his heart. Instead, Alex only felt that odd numbing buzz, as if he were merely witnessing a play that had nothing to do with his life's story. "I'm sorry, but I did what I thought I had to."

"You should 'ave trusted me!" his father roared. "You should 'ave told me da truth!"

Numbness gave way to anger. Alex surged forward, his hands fisted. Suddenly he was a part of his family again, thrust back into the role of the stubborn elder son. "Trust you? You had done nothing for us!" He shoved his finger into his father's chest. "We were starving, practically destitute, and you had done nothing to change that!"

His father's face grew flushed, his nostrils flaring as he struggled for breath. "You are related to royalty and you have tainted their blood! God willing, you should have died that day." He turned his back to Alex. "You never should 'ave returned home. We were better off not knowing."

The words didn't pierce his soul. No, Alex had been expecting this. For Grace's sake he'd hoped for more, but deep down he'd known all along this would be the outcome.

"No," his mother whimpered, reaching out to him, her pathetic attempt at reconciliation. But she would not protect him. She might have snuck him dinner when he was sent to his room as a child, but she would never contradict his father.

"You vill ruin vhat little reputation I 'ave worked so hard to regain," his father added, as if attempting to offer Alex some lame excuse, the most he would do. He didn't face his son. No, instead he moved to the fireplace as if disgusted.

But Alex needed no excuses and expected nothing more. He swallowed hard, focusing on the roar of blood to his ears. "No, I won't ruin your reputation. I will leave, I won't return. I promise you'll never see me again." He turned, and that's when he noticed Grace standing there so still, her face so pale, a marble statue.

Grace. Beautiful, untainted Grace. He reached out, and she took his hand, not hesitating. There was no shame on her face, nothing but caring compassion. The frantic need to escape clawed its way through his being.

"Alex, please, don't run off," Grace whispered. "Your mother will help him see reason."

But Alex knew the truth.

Without explanation, he led Grace through the door and into the hall. He couldn't feel her fingers. He couldn't feel his feet hitting the marble floor. The lights were an odd blur as if the entire world had grown hazy. Henry, ever the faithful butler, pulled open the front door, no doubt eager to see them gone. For some reason he found that amusing and would have laughed if he could feel his face. It all seemed to happen within the blink of an eye. They were in the house, attempting a reconciliation, the next minute it was over.

"Alex, please!" Grace tugged on his arm as they stepped out onto the front stoop, forcing him to pause there, in the rain.

"Grace, you know nothing about my family," he finally managed.

The door shut, the lock clicking in place. The sound was like a gunshot through the quiet evening air. The scene had ended.

"You must make them understand—"

Alex started down the steps. There was nothing left for him here. He was oddly resigned to the fact that his life with his family was forever over.

Grace scampered after him. "They will understand, Alex."

He paused there on the footpath, the gas lamps casting a heavenly glow through the fog drifting over the cobbled streets. He stopped there and let the cool rain patter against his face, but it would not wash away his sorrow, his pain, his past.

"Why? Why should I try to explain? Why should I try, when he's right?"

Grace latched on to the lapels of his jacket, her grip almost desperate. "No, Alex. He isn't right. Don't you dare give up! I don't care if society accepts us. I only want you!"

He cupped the side of her face, his heart crumbling, breaking piece by piece because he knew this would be the last time he would see her. "Think of your family and marry your earl."

Her eyes flashed with anger. "I won't."

He lifted his hand, hailing a passing hack. "You will, Grace. Because I don't love you. I never will. Whores like me are incapable of love."

Her face went pale, her lower lip trembling. "You don't mean that."

Her pain was like a knife to his heart. He didn't defend his statement; he didn't try to reason with her. Instead, without looking back, he turned and walked away from Grace and his only chance at life.

Chapter 18

Grace moved numbly into the townhome, closing and bolting the door behind her. The rain had thickened, soaking her clothing and leaving her body as numb as her heart.

He had left her. Perhaps she'd never see him again. She wasn't shocked by his reaction. She knew how his heart ached. Who wouldn't after such rejection by one's family? Alex had been devastated by his father's harsh words. She'd seen the look in his eyes…that odd blankness that had taken away any life.

How she despised his father! How she despised Lady Lavender! How she even despised Alex's mother for not confronting her husband.

Grace moved toward the parlor, her footsteps slow and unhurried. There was no reason to rush. There was no one waiting for her, but she knew the red coals in the parlor hearth might as least still provide some warmth. The butler and one maid they'd managed to retain were abed, the house silent. John, no doubt, was out gambling what little money they had left.

She'd always craved a moment of silence or two, grasping it whenever she could. Now…now it was merely upsetting. The loneliness too heavy.

The parlor door stood open, a yawning rectangle of darkness. Like red demon's eyes, the coal in the hearth leered at her from across the room. Grace tossed her sodden cloak to the settee and moved toward the fireplace. She had a feeling she would never be warm again. Morose, she sniffed and kicked off her slippers. Where was Alex now? Had he returned to Lady Lavender's or had he run off, never to be heard of again like some ancient myth? A memory she would cling to on lonely nights?

Grace hiked up her skirts and pulled off her damp stockings, placing them upon the screen to dry. She would ignore the tears burning her eyes. She had cried enough in the carriage, she would not shed more.

If he had returned to Lady Lavender's, at least she could hunt him down, but would Alex accept her if she came to call? It was selfish of her to wish him there when he hated it so. She reached for her bodice, her fingers cold and trembling. It was impossible to believe that only hours ago he had been in her bedchamber. Her arms fell to her sides as hopelessness washed over her. No, he couldn't be gone!

"Please, don't stop on my account."

The familiar male voice sent her heart racing, but not for the reason she would have liked. Grace spun around. Rodrick reclined in their wing back chair looking for all the world like a man at ease. She pressed her hand to her racing heart, stunned and confused.

"Rodrick, I wasn't expecting you."

He smiled, his teeth flashing white in the darkness, much too much like a wolf after a sheep. What was he doing here? Truly, she had no desire to deal with anyone at the moment, especially a spoiled gent. And as much as she liked him, she couldn't deny that he was spoiled. Rodrick didn't know struggle or pain. He didn't understand the constant thoughts of worry that kept a person up at night.

"Yes, well," he stood, unfolding his tall body. "I wanted to talk to you."

She glanced around the room, looking for John. Surely he hadn't come here merely to speak with her. Or was John up to his old tricks and Rodrick needed her help once more?

"Me? How long have you been waiting?"

He shrugged, not pausing until he was close to her…too close. His jacket was gone, hung over the wing back chair. He wasn't wet; his body and scent were warm. He had been waiting a good while, but that was no reason for the man to be so comfortable. How very odd he was acting tonight.

Grace crossed her arms over her chest, feeling ill at ease. "What's happened?"

"Nothing to be alarmed about." He grasped her shoulders and turned her away from him. "In fact, this is something to celebrate."

She was stiff, confused by his brazen hold. "Truly?"

"Truly." His warm fingers were at the back of her neck. With deft movements she suddenly felt her hair come loose, trailing down her back in heavy, damp waves.

Grace gasped, her hands going to her head. "What are you doing?" She spun around to face him, stunned, outraged.

"I thought you'd be more comfortable." He moved to the fireplace, completely unconcerned. Who did he think he was, coming into her home and touching her so? Had he gone mad? "Grace, we have things to discuss."

She felt suddenly vulnerable, enclosed in this small place with a man she'd known for years yet didn't really understand.

"The other night in the carriage…"

Grace flushed, remembering the kiss. It all made sense… his comfortableness with her home, his ease with touching her in such a familiar way. Lord, he wasn't truly going to ask her to marry him now of all times? She couldn't stomach it!

"We understand each other, Grace."

He was.

She felt sick. Grace stumbled back, collapsing onto the settee. Everything she had always wanted, everything she needed was being offered on a silver platter. She was getting exactly what she had always wanted, except now…she didn't want any of it.

He turned to face her, but she couldn't read his expression. "We do well together, Grace, which is why—"

"No!" Grace surged to her feet. She would find some way to save Mama and Patience, but she couldn't, wouldn't marry Rodrick. "I don't…I'm not in love with you."

He paused, startled. Lord, she'd done it now. Would he make a scene? Or would he flush with embarrassment and leave immediately? She glanced nervously at the door, realizing just how alone they were.

Then he laughed. A hard, loud laugh that surprised her. "What does love matter?" He started toward her, his gait easy and unhurried. She knew many in the *ton* didn't marry for love, but still, coming from him, it seemed strange.

"I assumed…that is…if you don't love me, why would you want to marry me?" She laughed nervously. "We both know that it can't be my dowry."

He paused, his face showing his confusion.

Perhaps he saw marriage as a friendship. Not romantic, but they did get along well enough. Could she marry without love? Could she never see Alex again? The thought swirled deep within her chest and squeezed her heart painfully.

She shook her head, knowing quite well she was ruining everything by denying him. "No, I'm sorry, Rodrick, I can't marry you."

He quirked an arrogant brow. "My dear, I never wanted marriage." He shrugged. "I suppose someday I shall marry, but it won't be soon. I have no desire to settle into matrimony hell as my parents did."

"But then...what..." Reality slapped her sharply across the face.

He leaned forward and grinned as if he was talking with a silly child who believed in fairy tales. "I don't want marriage, Grace, but I do want you."

Shock fled and anger took its place. "You can't be serious."

Any mirth faded from his amber eyes. He straightened and stepped back, almost as if offended. "Please, do not try and feign the virginal innocence with me. Who do you think paid for your visits to Lady Lavender?"

Grace went cold. "John—"

"John hasn't a pence to his name." He smoothed down the cuffs of his shirt. "The idiot has gambled everything away."

Grace pressed her hands to her stomach, feeling ill. Rodrick knew about her visits with Alex. The room grew blurry, her mind numb. Rodrick didn't want her, never had respected her. And John...how much did John know? She wouldn't be surprised if he knew everything. He'd probably given the man his blessing. "Why? Why do you want me?"

He shrugged, clasping his hands behind his back. "I like you, Grace. You have a fire inside you that is quite attractive. I think we'd do well in bed together, and it's obvious you fancy me."

"Fancy you?" She shook her head, disgusted.

"You're attracted to me, Grace; you always have been. When John offered your services three months ago, I admit I wasn't sure if you would work well."

Anger rushed through her being, too much emotion at once. The light seemed to dim, her entire world had come down to one moment. John had sold her. Grace felt dizzy, the room spinning. "I...I can't."

Rodrick's face flushed, his anger palpable. Surely he wouldn't harm her here, in her own home with her mother upstairs? "John assured me, and I assumed because you had no trouble kissing me in the carriage, that—"

"Marriage!" Grace cried out. "I assumed you wanted marriage!"

He scoffed, an irritating laugh that made him look almost ugly. "No offense, but you should feel quite lucky to become my mistress."

Was he quite serious? "No offense, but you should be lucky I haven't hit you by now."

He narrowed his eyes. Any affection toward her was gone, his gaze hard, unrelenting. "So that's how it will be?"

She didn't respond. How could she? There was nothing left to say. She'd lost not only Alex, the man she loved, but she'd also lost Rodrick, a man who was supposed to be her friend.

He strolled toward the chair and picked up his jacket. "You realize I own this home?" he stated quite casually.

She shouldn't have been surprised, yet she was.

Facing her, he smiled a cold smile that didn't quite reach his eyes. "Yes, you see John owes me quite a bit of money."

This couldn't be good. Grace had a horrible, sinking feeling.

"In fact, he sold me the house just two weeks ago, assuming you'd work off the debt."

Grace had never been so furious. "Get out." Her entire body trembled, sweat beading between her shoulder blades as she resisted the urge to slap him. Who was this man she'd supposedly known for years? He was gone, and in his place was the truth…a monster.

He quirked a brow. "Are you sure you wish for me to leave?"

A soft click broke through the tension-filled room. Grace spun around. Patience stood in the doorway, a pistol in her hand, a pistol pointed directly at Rodrick.

Grace blanched, resisting the urge to rush forward. "No, Patience!" If her sister shot the man, she'd end up in Newgate.

Rodrick laughed, completely unconcerned. "Fine then. I'll leave, but I will be back to stake my claim, and very soon indeed."

He started toward the door, his stroll unhurried, unconcerned. Pistol still pointed at the man, Patience scurried out of his way. When he disappeared into the hall, Grace could finally breathe again.

Neither of them spoke until they heard the front door close.

Patience lowered the pistol, her body visibly shaking.

"Patience." Grace ran to her sister and threw her arms around her waist, drawing her thin body close. "Oh, Patience, what were you thinking?"

"I couldn't let him ruin you." Her voice was muffled against Grace's shoulder.

Grace pulled back, looking down into her sister's upturned face. A pretty face on the verge of becoming beautiful. "He won't. No one will be ruined. We will find a way out of this situation."

Patience nodded, giving Grace a wavering smile, but it was obvious even to Grace that her sister didn't believe the lie.

* * *

Alex slouched over the scarred wooden table, staring into the amber ale inside his mug. Two hours later his clothes were still damp from the rain, but he had made no move to stand by the fireplace in the pub. It didn't matter that it was the only clothing he owned or that he had just spent his last pence on his third cup of ale. Nothing mattered.

He had nowhere to go. He had no money. He had nothing.

He deserved nothing. A common whore. Dirty. Without soul. How he wished he could tear the skin from his own body. Be free of his sin. Be free of this life.

He could return to Lady Lavender. Perhaps he would. Yet he couldn't seem to stand and leave. Only three other men sat in the place, all slouched, all staring at nothing in particular. All lost.

And he was lost without Grace.

Grace.

How he wanted to go to her. How he wanted her for his own, to make him smile, to make him laugh, to make him believe once more.

Grace.

His hands curled against that worn table. Hardening his heart, he pushed back and stood. He could not ruin her. He wouldn't. She deserved more than what he could offer, and he could offer nothing. He'd been ridiculous to think he'd return to his old life and all would be forgiven.

Alex turned to leave. The fist came out of nowhere. Hard knuckles connected with his chin and propelled him backward. He hit the table, the edge digging painfully into his back. Before he could regain his bearings, hands gripped his shirt and jerked him forward. Two men grabbed his arms, holding him immobile, while another man stood before Alex, wavering in and out of focus like a vague dream. Alex shook his head, fuzzy with an ale-induced haze.

"You'll pay, you scum."

The familiar voice sent hatred pulsing through his blood.

Rodrick.

Alex growled low in his throat and focused on the dandy he despised. Anger like he'd never known poured through him, simmering, bubbling in his veins. He might not be able to punish Ophelia or his parents, but he sure as hell could do some damage to this arse. Alex jerked forward, freeing his right arm. With a quick jab he slammed his fist into Rodrick's gut.

The man stumbled back, gasping for breath.

"He's a fighter," John said, stepping into view. The bastard had been hiding behind Rodrick. "You stay away from my sister," John said, but in his eyes, Alex saw the truth. The man was scared. Alex shoved his hand into the man's chest, sending him flying back into the table. John cried out, stumbling to the ground in a tangle of arms and legs.

Alex didn't have time to gloat. Firm fingers bit into his biceps, jerking his arms behind his back. Alex growled, struggling to regain his freedom. None of the few patrons offered any help. Most didn't even look up from their mugs. The owner was worse, glancing away when Alex met his gaze.

"I'll kill you," Alex growled, meaning every word.

A burlap bag was thrown over his head, musty and dirty from use. Rough rope was twisted around his wrists, pulling his arms painfully behind his back.

"Outside with ye," the pub owner finally growled.

Rodrick's men jerked him forward. Alex stumbled and would have fallen to his knees if they hadn't been holding him upright. Shuffling, he forced his instincts to become alert. How many were there?

"We'll be seen," John grumbled from somewhere ahead.

"Don't be an idiot. No one will interfere," Rodrick snapped back.

Rodrick, John, and the two dragging him forward. Cold air hit his exposed hands and he could hear the muffled sound of carriages on cobbled stone. They were outside, but no one in this part of town would assist him. They would not get involved, especially since Rodrick was obviously a lord.

From somewhere nearby a horse snorted. Hands shoved him forward. Alex was tossed into what he assumed was a carriage. He fell to the floor with a muffled grunt. Someone climbed in beside him. Rodrick, for he could smell his sandalwood cologne. Alex's legs were shoved inside; the door closed with a thump. It all happened within moments. Before he could react, the carriage jerked forward.

For a heartbeat, he merely lay there, his breathing harsh and warm against the rough bag. Suddenly hands gripped his upper arms and jerked him up onto a soft seat. Alex sat stiffly, waiting. He knew there were others in the carriage with him, for he could hear their breathing, but wasn't sure how many.

"We have something to discuss," Rodrick said from across the carriage.

Alex's lips lifted into a snarl. How he wanted to kill the man.

"You were hired to do a job," the dandy continued. "And that was to prepare Grace...for me. Somewhere along the way, you seemed to think you could actually have her as your own. I don't know if you're toying with her or if you're serious, but it will end now."

Had Rodrick sent Grace to Lady Lavender's? Someone grunted beside him. Someone smelling of stale beer and regret.

John, Grace's stepbrother, most likely.

"And what if I tell you to fuck off?" Alex hissed. His voice was muffled, but he knew they heard him all the same.

There was a soft rustle as someone moved. Fingers gripped the burlap sack and jerked it from his head, pulling his hair in the process. Alex glared at Rodrick, aware that John sat cowering in the corner next to him.

Rodrick dropped the sack to the floor. "Do you think anyone will notice if you disappear?"

Alex didn't respond. He knew where Rodrick was headed with his statement and he wouldn't take the bait.

"Perhaps your Lady Ophelia might take up the search for a day or two, but your disappearance would not alarm Scotland Yard."

Rodrick leaned forward, a smirk marring his face. Alex couldn't quite help himself. With a growl, he jerked his head forward, slamming his forehead against the man's nose.

"Shite!" Rodrick cried out, falling back.

"Lord," John muttered, tapping on the roof of the carriage with frantic movements.

The vehicle slowed, but Alex was barely aware. He was taking too much glee in the sight of blood running down Rodrick's lips and chin. The carriage stopped and the door was ripped open.

John was the first to leave, stumbling outside as if his coattails were on fire. Rodrick, who had managed to find a handkerchief and was holding it to his injured nose, followed. Left without assistance, Alex hopped outside, grinning for the first time that night.

John lifted his arm, a pistol clenched in his hands. Alex kept his grin in place, not daring to show weakness. The idiot was trembling so hard Alex wouldn't be surprised if he shot him by accident.

"You will leave Grace alone," Rodrick demanded, his voice muffled behind the handkerchief.

"Why, will you marry her?" Alex jeered. "Live happily ever after?"

John shifted, glancing at the ground. Certainly a suspicious movement. What were they up to?

Rodrick snarled. "Don't be ridiculous."

Alex jerked his gaze from John to Rodrick. Something was wrong, horribly wrong. His gaze went to John once more. "He is going to marry your sister, isn't he?"

"Rodrick doesn't wish to marry," John mumbled.

But by the way the man was avoiding his gaze, Alex knew there was more to the tale. "What does he wish to do then?"

Rodrick grabbed the lapels of Alex's jacket and jerked him forward. The man's pretty face was smeared with blood. "Grace will become my mistress. I'll use her, and she'll enjoy it, and I can thank you for preparing her."

Alex saw red. He lifted his knee, hitting Rodrick between the legs. Rodrick gasped and stumbled back into a rock wall. Frantic, Alex turned toward John.

"You'll do this? Allow your sister to be used?"

"Fuck off," John muttered.

Alex gritted his teeth. He'd kill them. He'd kill them both.

Surely Grace hadn't agreed to this. Yet...yet he knew Grace would do anything for her mother and sister. No, he wouldn't allow her to sell herself as he had. He'd kill her brother and Rodrick first, even if it meant he'd hang in prison.

"You will stay away from my mistress." Rodrick shoved his fist into Alex's gut. Pain rippled through his body, adding coal to his anger. Alex stumbled back. John grabbed his arms, holding him immobile as Alex gasped for air.

Finding courage now that Alex was immobile, Rodrick stepped closer, smirking. "Shall we mess up those pretty-boy features of yours?"

Alex hadn't time to prepare. The man hit him in the face, the knuckles connecting with the area under his eye so hard Alex heard the skin split. His head jerked back, hitting John in the chin. The sting gave way to wet warmth as blood dripped down his cheek.

"Now for the nose."

"You'll stop now or you'll regret it, *my lord*." James's familiar voice was surprising and welcome. John's hold loosened.

Rodrick narrowed his eyes, studying his opponent as James strolled from the shadows and into the light of the streetlamp. He was dressed just as richly as Rodrick, and Alex knew the man was trying to decipher James's identity. Perhaps Rodrick wouldn't fear James, but he would fear Ophelia's men who stood behind him.

"Well, well." Rodrick quirked a brow. "You have friends. How sweet."

"Friends who know how to fight, friends who own pistols," James said.

As grateful as Alex was, he knew James wasn't there to help, merely to protect Lady Lavender's property. John dropped his hold completely and stepped away. The coward knew when to flee. He didn't even look back as he jumped into the carriage.

Rodrick glared at Alex, weighing his choices. "Stay away from her."

"Sod off," Alex muttered.

Rodrick hesitated as if he wanted to say more, but instead he strolled to the carriage with an easy gait that belied the fear Alex had seen in his eyes.

"She sent you to find her property," Alex said, watching the carriage as it jerked to life and disappeared around the corner. With Rodrick's absence, he had to focus his anger somewhere, and James made a lovely target.

James reached forward, using a knife to cut Alex's bindings. "She was worried."

Alex released a harsh laugh and slumped back against the brick wall of a building. How had his life become so utterly ridiculous? If he returned to Lady Lavender, he would die a slow, torturous death, his soul crumbling from the inside. Yet why leave when he had nothing? Was nothing? He slid down the wall until his arse hit the dirt. He felt numb, cold, alone.

He could start over as a coal miner, a fisherman. *Anything.* He drew his knees up and rested his forehead in his hands. Truth was, he didn't know if he could leave Grace. Could he let her become Rodrick's mistress and make the same mistakes he had made? Perhaps she would reject Rodrick's offer, and then what? She'd starve?

"Alex," James said. "What are you doing? What is this about?"

Alex leaned his head back against the hard wall and stared up into the starless night, the sky hazy with smoke from the London factories. A hysterical bubble of laughter clogged his throat. "I don't know. I don't bloody know."

James sighed. "It's the girl, right? The one who visited a time or two?"

"Grace," he whispered her name.

James reached down and grabbed the lapels of his jacket. His face only inches from Alex. "Then go to her," he whispered low enough so Wavers and the other man wouldn't hear. "Tell her the truth." He hauled Alex to his feet and shoved a small leather pouch into his hands. "From Gideon and me."

Alex gripped the pouch, the clank of coins a merry greeting in the dark night. He shoved the pouch toward James, but he refused to take it. "I can't ruin her."

"Hell, Alex. She has a brother ready to sell her to the highest bidder and a man who wants to make her his mistress. I don't really see how you're a worse choice!"

God help him, but James's argument was starting to sound reasonable. Alex glanced behind James at Ophelia's two henchmen who stood guard as silently as ever. They would not argue with James, Ophelia's prized pupil. "Lady Lavender will—"

"She'll understand," James whispered.

She wouldn't, but he didn't care to argue with James. No, because for the first time that night he felt the slightest stirrings of hope.

The offer was tempting...so tempting.

Chapter 19

"You told me three pounds just last week!"

The woman before Grace shrugged her thin, French shoulders. "Times have changed. I can only give you *deux* now."

"Oh stuff and nonsense!" Grace grabbed the velvet dress and shoved it back into her carpet bag. Perhaps she was letting her pride get in the way, but blast it all, she was tired of people taking advantage of her dire state. "I will sell it for three pounds and nothing less."

The woman shrugged again, looking completely unconcerned. She wasn't going to budge. She knew how badly Grace needed the coins. But this seamstress, with her velvet curtains, chandeliers, and ideal shop on Bond Street, was thriving. She had no need for the dress.

Fuming, Grace ignored the stunned expressions of the two women working with Madame Nicolette and shoved the door wide, the bell overhead tinkling. She left the fancy shop that smelled of French perfume and stepped into the brilliant spring morning. But the warmth and promise of summer did not lighten her mood.

Yes, she refused to sell even though they'd only had potatoes and chicken broth for dinner last night. Even though the maid had left this morning, fearing if she kept working for them her next payment would never come. And even though Grace wanted to see Alex so badly it actually hurt. Lord, she was a silly twit.

Overwhelmed, Grace paused there in the middle of the footpath, heedless to the people pushing past her, making her stumble off-balance. Although she should be worried about her future and her mother and sister's welfare, the person forefront in her mind was *him*.

Damn Alex to hell!

She'd paced her room last night, attempting to understand her infatuation. He was a whore. He pleasured women. That fact alone made her ill, so how could she possibly want to be with him? Because...because she'd seen into his soul. His lovely, broken soul.

Ahead, Patience waved from the window of the hired hack. But Grace felt frozen with indecision, want, and need. Dare she send a note to Lavender Hills, praying the missive would make it to Alex's hands? Would he even respond if she did?

Blast it! She wanted to curse Alex for abandoning her. Curse him for making her care. But mostly, she wanted to curse Madame Nicolette for making her take two pounds.

With a sigh of resignation, Grace forced Alex from her mind and turned back toward the dress shop. She had taken only two steps when a muscled arm wrapped around her waist. She didn't have time to cry out. There was not a moment to think, nor time to search for a weapon. A hand clamped over her lips, and suddenly she was jerked into an alley, pulled behind a stack of crates.

"Shhh, 'tis I."

Fear faded, leaving her trembling with relief. The familiar voice swept away the cold chill of unease. She must be dreaming.

Perhaps she had gone mad. She couldn't dare hope it was truly him.

"Alex!" She wasn't sure if she wanted to kiss him or hit him.

Instead, she turned and threw her arms around his neck. He stumbled back, hitting the brick wall of the building behind. The darkness of the alley hid them from prying eyes, but she knew they could easily be caught. She didn't care. Didn't bloody care. Only cared that she was with Alex, finally.

"I thought I'd never see you again," she said, her voice catching on a horrifying sob.

"Please tell me you haven't accepted Rodrick's offer," he whispered.

She closed her eyes, refusing to cry. Instead, she focused on the scent of morning and spring flowers that clung to his jacket. Which offer he was referring to she wasn't sure. Did Alex think Rodrick had proposed, or did he somehow know of his sinful proposition? "No, of course not," she said. "Never."

He pressed a kiss to her forehead. "Thank God."

"Alex, where have…"

She finally managed to pull back, and that's when she noticed the dark bruise marring the area under his eye. Outraged, she cupped the sides of his face. "What happened to you?"

He still wore the clothing he'd worn when they'd visited his family only yesterday, although the material was quite wrinkled. His hair was mussed, shadows marked the area under his eyes as if he hadn't slept. Her worry burst anew.

"It doesn't matter what happened," he said, taking her hands in his. His blue eyes were serious, so bloody serious. "What matters is that we have little time before they come searching for us." His words sent a shiver of unease through her body. Alex turned, pressing her against the hard brick wall. His face was intense, so intense that it made her nervous. "Listen to me. I'm leaving. I can't stay here any longer; there is nothing for me."

She flinched over his harsh words. Nothing? Not even she could keep him?

"Grace." He cupped the sides of her face and stepped closer, his body pressed to hers. "I have no life without you."

Her heart swelled with hope and possibilities.

"Will you?" he whispered.

She didn't dare breathe for fear that this was all a dream and breathing would wake her. She didn't dare move, not wanting to disrupt the image of his intense gaze. Vaguely she was aware of warm tears slipping down her cheeks. He gave her a quivering, hesitant smile as he brushed them away with his thumbs. He hadn't forgotten her after all.

"What are you saying?" she finally managed to ask.

"Come with me and—"

"Yes," she blurted out.

She'd stunned him. That was obvious by the surprise that crossed his features. Grace laughed, giddy as the anxiety of the last few days faded. "Shall I be demure? Feign indecision? I can't, Alex. I can't hide what I truly feel when you are near."

He brushed his hands over her shoulders, down her arms. Although her sleeves were long, she felt his touch through the material as if he'd branded her. "Never feel you have to hide your emotions from me."

His knuckles brushed her cheek, his gaze taking on that soft look she loved so well. When he lowered his head and pressed his mouth to hers, Grace lifted on tiptoes. She closed her eyes, sinking into his hard body, molding her lips to his. How she wanted to breathe in his very essence, to memorize every detail of the moment.

All too soon, he pulled away. "Lady Lavender will look for me, most likely already is, but we can escape."

She dared to believe him. She had no other choice.

"Grace?" Patience called from the street.

Startled, Grace turned. Her sister stood hesitantly in the open alleyway. Grace's happiness wavered. Patience. So sweet. So young. So innocent.

Realization dawned with sickening reality. She couldn't leave her family. What had she been thinking? Her tears of happiness turned to tears of sorrow. Angrily she stepped away from Alex and swiped at her damp cheeks.

"My mother, my sister—"

Alex nodded. "I understand. Once we find the treasure, we'll send for them."

"Treasure?" She frowned, wondering if she'd misheard him. Surely she wasn't getting embroiled in another ridiculous treasure hunt. Had everyone gone mad? "I don't understand."

His face grew serious, completely and utterly serious. "My grandfather's cottage in Devon." He released a sigh and raked his hands through his hair, as if finally realizing how ridiculous he sounded. "As a child my mother spoke of a treasure there. It was a great jest amongst us, but I have a feeling there just might be some truth to the story. The cottage is in my name, given to me years ago when I was a lad. We will find that treasure, Grace. We must."

Did he truly wish her to believe in treasures and legend now of all times? Alex, for his part, looked quite serious indeed. Why was it that the moment she'd given up on fanciful dreams they came rushing back? A few months ago she would have been thrilled by the thought of a treasure hunt. Now she felt merely confused and bewildered.

"Grace?" The excitement in Alex's gaze faded.

He had made an effort to see her. She would not have him regret his actions. Although doubt remained firmly planted in her rational mind, she forced a smile and nodded, all the while wondering how in the world they'd make it to Devon.

Alex's shoulders visibly relaxed. "I know it sounds ridiculous, but it's all we have." He took a couple steps back and glanced briefly at Patience, who had come closer, watching them curiously. "Go home now. Pack a small bag and meet me at the railroad station."

He was actually going to leave her here, in an alley? "But… Alex."

"Please, Grace. Say your good-byes, pack what you can."

He didn't wait for her response, but turned and raced down the alley, his footsteps echoing between the brick walls and matching the wild thump of her heart. She wanted to call out to him, worried she would never see him again if he left her now.

Instead, she merely watched him until he disappeared around a corner, listening until she could no longer hear his footsteps and the clomping of horses' hooves from the street out front invaded.

Hang her hopes on a silly dream? Leave her mother, her sister? Leave everything she knew? Dare she?

"Grace?" Patience suddenly stood next to her.

Grace slumped against the wall and slid a glance toward her sister. How much had she overheard? Overwhelmed, Grace covered her eyes with her hands. She couldn't face her sister right now. What to do?

Patience rested a hand on Grace's shoulder. "Return home and pack. Then go to him."

Had her sister read her mind? Grace jerked her head upright. "What?"

"You heard me." She took Grace's hands. "You will go with him."

Grace sighed. To Patience, who lived her life based on her emotions, every problem was easy to solve. "My dear, this treasure may not exist. I find it hard to abandon you and Mama for fairy tales."

Patience led Grace down the alley and toward the street where their hack waited. "But the treasure might be real. You must try, Grace, you must. For all of us, but mostly for *you*. This is your chance at happiness."

Perhaps her last chance. Instead of comforting her, the words only made Grace nervous. How dire Patience sounded. They stepped onto the street, merging into the crowds. "But Mama—"

Patience sighed, stopping there in the middle of the footpath so that others were forced to travel around them. "I know you think I'm too young to do much good, but I am old enough to take care of Mama."

Her sister's face was so determined that Grace didn't dare argue the point. Would Mama be well for a few days? A soft glimmer of what could only be excitement wavered low in her belly. The same blasted feeling she got when she'd gone on a treasure hunt as a child. The feeling of hope. Of better things to come. "If I go…if we don't find the treasure, it will be for nothing."

"No," Patience said, smiling. "Not nothing. It will be for everything. It will be for love."

* * *

She hadn't arrived.

Haunted, Alex watched the passengers board the train with a sickening feeling of numbness. Perhaps Rodrick or John had prevented her. Perhaps she had lost her way.

Or perhaps…perhaps she had realized what a foolish idea he'd had.

Alex sank onto a bench as a father and child walked hand in hand down the platform. The child was chatting amiably as the father nodded, smiling in the sort of approving way only a doting parent could. He felt no jealousy at the image, not even sadness. He felt…nothing.

"Ye coming?" the guard asked, strolling briskly by Alex. He had things to do, people to send off, interesting places to go.

Alex could merely shake his head as he sat alone on that bench, the tickets gripped tightly in his hands. Had he been delusional to think she would give up her life for him? Delusional to think she could possibly care? Sadly, he didn't blame her. No, he didn't blame her in the least. But it didn't stop his heart from crumbling, from breaking piece by wretched piece.

She hadn't come.

The crowds grew thick as people boarded the trains. The roar of conversation was almost overwhelming. The weary faces of men trudging home after a day's work. Wealthy families headed to the countryside for fresh air. And he could identify those country folk who had moved to the city hoping for a better life and work. The haggard faces and soulless eyes, finding the city had little to offer but sinful ways for the poor, returning to their homes after a battle well fought, but lost all the same.

"'Tis so very exciting!" a little girl cried out, skipping beside her mother as they raced toward the train.

And then there were the children. The children who still believed that wonderful things could happen. Who only saw the good.

"Mustn't be late," the mother replied, one hand in her child's, the other holding her feathered bonnet to her head. The child's dark red hair was plaited in a braid that swung eagerly across her back. Her flushed face full of hope and innocence reminded him of what Grace might have looked like at that age.

Alex's heart squeezed painfully. How he had wished for the normalcy of a family, even daring to go so far as to believe it wasn't an impossible dream. For over an hour he'd stood on that platform, ignoring the crush of strangers and waiting for Grace, dreaming of a cottage full of children, as if their innocence could erase his sins.

But the dreams were fading now, leaving him cold and alone. He was a statue. Some image of a man who once was. No longer part of life. Grace had been his one hope for a brighter future. This morn, with the possibility of Grace by his side, the world had seemed new. Anything had seemed attainable. Now…now…He'd thought if only he went to her, told her the truth, he could mend things between them. It hadn't worked.

Grace.

He felt utterly alone. Utterly...lost, floating in a city of strangers. Where would he go?

He barely cared.

Grace hadn't come. He leaned forward, resting his head in his hands. Nothing mattered because she hadn't arrived.

A shrill whistle pierced the evening air. The sound of shuffling feet and passengers racing to the cars interrupted the roar of farewells. Still, he didn't bother to lift his head, drowning in hopelessness.

"Alex?"

The soft voice was like a call from heaven. Blood roared to his ears, his body stirring to life. He didn't dare turn, fearing that if he did and she wasn't there, he would be forced to face his own insanity.

"Alex..." Her voice was stronger this time, closer.

His heart flip-flopped, slamming wildly against his rib cage. Dare he hope?

A warm hand rested on his shoulder, the touch from a goddess, an angel. Alex surged to his feet, the rush of emotion making him almost dizzy. Too much hope, too soon. He spun around. The bench stood between them, a hateful barrier, but he felt her nearness as if she was a very part of him.

Lovingly he soaked in the sight of his saving Grace. His gaze went from that green dress that had reminded him of innocence to the straw bonnet that framed her flushed face, only to jump to the carpetbag gripped in her gloveless hand. She was spring and everything good in the world. In her smile he saw the promise of renewal. Of hope. For one long moment he merely stared at her, worried that if he blinked, she'd disappear. Worried that in his crazed mind he was seeing things.

"Grace?" his voice came out gruff with emotion.

She nodded, smiling a brilliant smile that he felt all the way to his toes. "I'm here, Alex. I'm sorry I'm late," she continued. "But it was rather difficult to escape..."

He surged forward and cupped the sides of her face, leaning into the bench. "You're here."

He lowered his mouth to hers. The kiss was gentle, lovely, and there were plenty to witness their sin. He wanted to memorize every detail of the moment. To breathe in her scent. To taste her forever. In that soft kiss he poured his soul, telling her how much she meant to him. How much he cared.

Overcome by the awkward bench between them, he was finally forced to step back, but he still felt the pressure of their kiss upon his tingling lips. She had arrived. But the fear was still there, lingering and taunting in the deep recesses of his heart. As much as he wanted to pull her onto the train and escape the hells of London, he had to make sure she wanted this completely.

"All aboard!" a guard called.

Grace started for the train, but Alex stepped in front of her, halting her progress. "What if the treasure is a lie? Some silly fairy tale?"

She shook her head, the stray strands of hair that had come loose wavering on the soft evening breeze. Her excitement was obvious by the flush of her face, but did she truly understand what she was doing? "It won't be. I can feel it, deep down. I'm never wrong about these things, you know."

She was so ready to believe in treasures, in fairy tales…in him. Dare he believe as well? "Your family—"

She skirted around the bench, taking his hand in hers, those fingers tight and warm. "Patience will look after Mama. They both gave me their blessing." She tugged on his hand, impatient. "Hurry, Alex, we'll miss the train."

She was grinning, her eyes sparkling with a happiness he always wished to see upon her lovely face. Any hesitation and worry fled. He shoved the tickets into the guard's hand and followed the sway of her skirts up the steps. The second-class carriage was crowded with fathers returning home from work and families traveling to the countryside. Women brushed aside their wide skirts, making room for them to move down the aisle. The air held the stench of soaps, colognes, and a few unwashed bodies. The quarters were crowded; there was no privacy. And how he wished for privacy.

His excitement wavered as they took their seats, nothing more than two wooden benches placed side by side. Settled next to the dusty window, Grace faced him, that excitement still there, the sparkle remaining firmly in her gaze no matter what the situation.

"I've never been on a train before. We're up so high! I've seen them rush by, you know, and marveled over their speed."

She was endearing, always seeing hope and beauty when most would see none. Unable to resist, he cupped the side of her flushed face, sliding his fingers under the stiff straw bonnet and into the silky strands of hair at her temple. Slowly he leaned forward, his chest pressing into her shoulder, and molded his mouth to hers, heedless of the curious stares of their traveling companions.

"You must be newlywed," the old woman seated across from them chuckled.

Alex pulled back, grinning over Grace's bemused look. "Indeed," he replied to the woman. It wasn't exactly a lie; if he had his way, they would be very soon. Grace merely blinked at the woman, bewildered by his kiss or his response. Perhaps both.

"Next time we'll be in a first-class carriage," he whispered near her ear.

She shook her head, looking completely serious. "I haven't the slightest desire to return to London."

His heart swelled. He wasn't sure if she didn't care for the city or if she was thinking of him by not returning to a place where anyone might identify him. It was all too good to be true. The survivor in him warned not to get too comfortable. Something horrible was sure to happen and ruin his hopeful plans.

It would take at least a couple days to make it to their destination. Two long days in which she could come to her senses and change her mind. But for once he took Grace's position in life and believed that anything was possible.

A shrill whistle sounded one last time and the train jerked to life. Sucking in a breath of excitement, Grace squeezed his hand, her palm warm and smooth against his.

"Grace, I can't promise you anything," he warned.

She looked at him, her eyes sparkling underneath the rim of her bonnet, and in her gaze he saw her heart, her soul. "I only want you."

It was all he needed to hear.

Chapter 20

Alex in the fancy clothing Lady Lavender forced him to wear was enticing indeed. But Alex in workman's garb, simple and well fitted, was even better. There was something incredibly erotic about the way his plain white shirt hugged his chest, the color contrasting with his dark hair. The way his rough brown trousers encased his long, muscled legs. Grace couldn't look away as he strolled toward her, his gait easy and relaxed. He was a different man. And wearing simple clothing, there was nothing to compete with the beauty of his features.

Tonight they would be alone without a chance of interference. Their first night alone. A shiver of awareness caressed her skin, desire and nervousness simmering deep within her core. Alex would not force her to do anything she did not wish to do, but there were so very many, many things she *wanted* to do.

She didn't miss the way other women, even those in a hurry, slid him an appreciative glance. And she certainly didn't miss the fact that Alex didn't even notice their attention. No, his sweet grin was focused on her. Only her. She shifted on the edge of the rock wall where she sat, enjoying the warmth of the afternoon while waiting for him. The day lovely, the sun bright, and the world full of possibilities.

Any cares she'd had vanished the moment they stepped into town, their town now. The village closest to their cottage. She studied the scenery under the rim of her bonnet. Perhaps the woman walking by with the kind smile and brilliant blonde hair would one day be her friend, someone she might chat with when coming to town for supplies. They would talk about their children or trade recipes. Perhaps the men standing where two footpaths met would one day welcome Alex into their fold as they discussed the weather or the best spots for fishing.

Grace breathed deeply the scent of saltwater. Yes, she could see a life here. A life of happiness and friendships and love. A life where Alex could forget his past and move toward a lovely future…with her.

Alex darted between two carriages and appeared beside Grace, his hair ruffled by the sea breeze. "Well, I was able to procure this fine outfit and two blankets." He flashed her a grin, quite proud of himself.

Grace jumped from her perch and grinned back, resisting the urge to kiss him there in front of everyone. Resisting the urge to run her hands over his broad shoulders and that lovely, muscled back. "Fine indeed. Well done."

She slipped her arm through his as they made their way down the road, away from the small town. It was a simple village of whitewashed cottages where one could find only the necessities. But they needed nothing more. In fact, she quite craved the simple things in life. What more did she need if she had Alex?

The carriage they'd taken from the train station had dropped them off in the center of the small town early that morn. Although she couldn't spot the ocean just yet, Grace swore she could smell the sea the moment she had stepped from the coach. The very air seemed cleaner…fresh, alive with possibility! The shrill cries of the gulls above were like music to her ears. There was no need to speak, for their dreams and their future were proclaimed on the beautiful wings of the butterflies that floated on the wildflowers, on the wind that swayed the grasses.

They left the town and followed the lane. On either side, birch trees waved their hellos, shiny green leaves unfurling with summer's approach.

"With your two blankets and the bread, cheese, and apples we were able to purchase with the coins, we'll do quite well," she said.

Alex gave her a tight smile, and she knew he was worried about the days *after* their food was gone. But the sun was bright, the sky blue, and the day much too wonderful for melancholy thoughts. Alex took the burlap bag she carried, stuffed the blankets inside, and tossed the sack over his shoulder.

"Devon is lovely," she said. "I do believe I could be quite happy here." Truly happy. The moment she'd stepped from the carriage and her foot hit the soil, she felt as if a great weight had lifted. Still Alex didn't speak.

She glanced up at him, wondering if he felt the same. There was something about his demeanor that had changed when they'd arrived. She could sense his ease, see it in the relaxed lines of his face and gait of his walk. "Do you like it? Is it everything you remember it to be?"

He grinned, the sort of excited grin she'd never seen on his face before. The grin of true happiness. "It is."

And with his grin, all was well in her world.

Hand in hand they followed a path that weaved through tall grass and wildflowers of purple and blue. They were like two children on a treasure hunt. Instead of jewels or gold coins, their treasure was a new life.

Eagerly she matched his stride. After two days on a train, she was ready to be completely alone with him. Gulls cried out overhead, hovering on the wind over a backdrop of fluffy white clouds. In the distance she could hear the soft roar of the waves, a magical sound that rang true to her ears.

"And," he said as they followed the footpath up a hill, "could you imagine, perhaps, living here forever?"

She froze there at the crest, her heart hammering erratically with disbelief, with hope. Was Alex asking…She looked up into his brilliant blue eyes, studied the way his lips tightened slightly as if he was anxious. Her fallen angel. She knew he was asking her to stay with him…but was he asking marriage? She'd already misinterpreted Rodrick's offer, she wouldn't make the same mistake. The question was if Alex never offered marriage, could she live with him in sin? The answer came almost immediately, a whispered declaration.

"Yes," she breathed. "Yes, I could live here forever."

His chest seemed to grow broader as he took in a deep breath, his face relaxing as if a load of weight had been taken off his body. Although he seemed relieved, the words she so desperately wished to hear never came.

Will you marry me?

He started forward, and because she couldn't bloody well merely stand there, she followed, determined not to let his lack of devotion sting. She knew exactly what she was strolling into, knew what could happen to her reputation by escorting Alex to the south. She had chosen her path and she would not regret her actions.

"According to the vicar, who, by the way, assumes we are married, the cottage is just around the bend."

His words stung. A sharp twist of irony that pierced her soul. *According to the vicar, who, by the way, assumes we are married…*

She gritted her teeth and smiled. Eventually Alex would ask her to marry him, wouldn't he? Perhaps he wasn't the kind to marry. Perhaps he was perfectly fine living in sin, for hadn't he been all this time?

Confused over her own beliefs and feelings, she lapsed into silence. Lost in his own musings, Alex didn't seem to notice. Daisies brushed against her skirts in welcome as they moved into a patch of white birch trees. She would not focus on the future; she would stay grounded in today. She would take comfort in the flowers and the birds fluttering from the tall grasses. The sky so very blue it took her breath away.

"There it is," Alex whispered, pausing as they crested a hill.

She followed his line of vision. For one moment the sun was too brilliant for her to see much of anything. Soon enough she realized those sparkles of light, those rainbows of color, were actually waves tumbling and turning toward the sandy beach.

"Ohhhh," Grace breathed because she could say no more.

She'd been to the shore only a few times as a child. She swore she would one day dwell by the ocean. The mystery of it all was just as magical as when she'd been a child. Alex hadn't asked her to marry him, but it didn't matter. She knew without a doubt she had come home.

"'Tis exactly as I remember it. The beauty, the magical pull…" He rested his hand on a birch tree, his fingers caressing the curling bark, and she wondered if he'd done the same as a child to this very tree. "I loved the cottage, the many days spent running through the fields, swimming in the sea. I was only a lad when my mother's father died and left the cottage to me. I haven't been here in years."

She could hear the pride in his voice and smiled over it. "And now it's yours."

Alex claimed they had nothing. He worried he couldn't give her everything she needed. But he was wrong. They had a lovely cottage and, most important, they had each other. They would settle into the cottage by the sea and she would send for Mama and Patience. They would be happy here.

He glanced down at her and smiled. "Ours. 'Tis ours."

It was all she needed to hear. The happiness she felt only flared brighter, sweeping through her body in a flush of excitement. Alex took her hand and they started down the path where the birch trees thinned. Grace saw their future there, in those windswept hills and crashing waves. In the mornings, when the sun was shining and birds chirping, they would take a dip in the sea. In the afternoons, perhaps have a picnic on the hill, gathering wildflowers to decorate the cottage. She'd take their children to the shore to search for shells and…

"That can't be it." Alex's horrified voice broke into her musings.

Grace jerked her head upright, following his line of vision. A whitewashed cottage sat nestled at the bottom of a hill near the shore. A lovely picture, if it weren't for the broken windows and holes in the thatched roof.

Grace's happiness wavered. *This* was Alex's cottage? She wasn't one to wallow, and instinctively she opened her mouth to say something cheerful, yet the words wouldn't come. They might as well sleep outside. Worry burst anew, but not for herself. No. One look at Alex's pale face and she worried over his welfare. He'd so desperately wanted to impress her.

"It's wretched," he muttered.

"No," she lied. "It's…it only needs a little work. Nothing we can't overcome."

He dropped his hold and pulled away from her, swiping his hands over his face, weary and tense when only moments ago he'd been thrilled and relaxed. She felt his distance as if they'd been parted by the very ocean. He was rebuilding that wall around his heart, brick by wretched brick.

"I knew it would need work, but…" He paused near what had once been a stone wall around the front garden but was now merely a crumbling ruin, and shook his head in disgust.

Overgrown red roses burst in bloom. Rather pretty, really. She reached out, drawing a velvety petal between her fingers. The gardens would be easy enough to improve. With a little pruning, the flowers would be as good as new. Grace took off her bonnet and set it upon the top of the rock wall.

"I hadn't expected—"

"Nonsense, 'tis lovely, Alex. You're not seeing the possibilities." Taking in a deep breath of fortitude, she strolled across the garden. Although the tall grass was doing everything in its power to keep her from the front door, she surged forward, ignoring the burrs that stuck to her skirts.

"Look at the variety of beautiful flowers." She swept her arms wide. "Your grandfather must have been quite the gardener!" She paused in the open doorway of the cottage, relieved to have made it through the jungle, and peered into the darkness. It was empty and dank, smelling of mildew. She shivered to think of what might be living in their cottage. "And the woodwork!" She rested her hands on either side of the door. "The foundation seems quite sound."

"'Tis a mess. You're just trying to make me feel better."

She glanced at him over her shoulder and grinned. "Not at all. It's lovely and it's yours; you should feel proud."

But he didn't look any happier. Merely folded his arms across his chest and frowned up at the building like a father unhappy with a child.

"'Tis true." She stepped into the foyer, stirring dust into the air.

Although the empty rooms were in disrepair, instead of focusing on the dishevelment, she thought of Alex. She thought of a dark-haired little boy rushing through the rooms while playing games with his brother. A happier time. A time of innocence and family love.

Abandoned, but she swore she could still feel the memories of that happier time clinging to the walls and floorboards, waiting to be revealed. This was their chance to add their own happy memories.

She turned, full of renewed hope. "Alex, look at the potential! There's no better view in England. The house merely needs a little work."

"Little," he scoffed, strolling toward her. Although she'd had trouble making it through the jungle of a front garden, the very weeds seemed to part for him, as if sensing he was king of the manor. How could he not see that he belonged here? How could he not feel the very heartbeat of this cottage, waiting for him to bring it back from deep slumber?

At the door, Alex paused. "Twenty years ago this place was thriving." His handsome face was remote, cold, bitterness tightening the edges of his eyes and mouth. "What happened to it? To my family name? We were respected, respectable, once."

She saw the look in his eyes, that light fading. How she wanted him smiling and happy! Couldn't he see that they were better off now than yesterday? Couldn't he see that bright future she dreamt of? He moved into the room, his footsteps heavy. "We'll find the treasure, Alex, and all will be well."

"What have I done to you?" she thought she heard him whisper.

Her heart squeezed, aching. Lady Lavender had done so much more to Alex than merely selling his body. She'd destroyed his soul, made him believe he was unworthy of life and love.

Grace briefly closed her eyes, praying for help. "Don't. Please."

She felt him look at her, felt his confusion. He didn't even understand the ways of his depressing thoughts, could no more control them than he could control the ocean waves. For Alex it was completely natural to believe that life was a horrible, dark, and empty place. Perhaps she had seen glimpses of that darkness, but she refused to even dip her toes into that churning sea of emptiness. She had to believe in the good of the world, she *must*. Otherwise, what was the point?

"Don't what?" he finally asked.

She opened her eyes. "Do not give up on us."

His entire body seemed to soften. "Gracie," he whispered.

She refused to give in to his emotional gaze. "I feel rather dusty and hot." She reached for the buttons on her bodice and made her way to the door, wondering if he watched. She had thought to wait until tonight to seduce him. Damn it all, she wanted him smiling again; she wanted to feel the warmth of his touch, the caress of his fingers. When he held her, she believed in heaven, she believed in life and love.

"I'll need to repair the roof first," he muttered. She could practically see him adding up the coins in his head and resisted the urge to sigh.

She'd take his mind off of his worries. Her heart hammered madly in her chest. She'd never much been the temptress before and worried she would make a complete muddle of things.

But desperate times called for desperate measures. Hopefully he wouldn't laugh at her antics. She pulled the bodice from her arms, letting it fall to the floor with a soft swoosh.

She wouldn't regret her actions. She'd wanted this for so long now, always waylaid by some excuse or another. She'd hoped for nighttime and the soft, forgiving glow of the moon. But the late afternoon light would do just as well. Swallowing hard, Grace paused on the threshold and turned toward Alex.

He was looking around the parlor, barely aware of her existence. Instead finding fault with every floorboard, every crack of the plastered walls. "The floors seem sound, down here anyway. Upstairs, who knows." He raked his hair back from his face. "Lord, Grace, how can I expect you to live here?"

She dropped her skirt as he turned toward her. In the doorway, with the sunlight brilliant against her back, she stood in her shift and corset knowing he could see every line of her body. She wouldn't be nervous; she wanted this. Lord, she was practically upon the shelf, so why did she feel like a virgin on her wedding night?

The look upon his face shifted from one of worry to one of pure shock.

"Might you help me with the rest, Alex? The bindings are a bloody nuisance, they are." She was proud of the fact that her voice didn't quiver. "The sea looks ever so cool. Shall we wash away the grime of travel?"

The look of shock upon his face turned into a look of need so heated she felt it all the way to her toes. A look that pierced her very body and warmed her soul.

His footsteps were soft as he made his way toward her. She had no doubt that he wanted her. She could see his desire in the hardness of his body, the softness of his eyes, the way his hands curled, the way that pulse beat frantically in the side of his neck. "Ah, Gracie, what are you trying to do to me?"

This time no one would interrupt them. This time they were alone. Utterly alone. "Merely reminding you of what you have to be grateful for."

He paused in front of her, and she had to resist the urge to sink into his strong body. That warm, tantalizing scent of spice and male swirled around her, peppering the very air.

"You?" he whispered. His hands were trembling as he reached forward, his knuckle brushing the tops of her breasts as he undid the strings of her corset. Her nipples grew hard, her breasts felt heavy, aching with a need to be touched. "Do I have you?"

"Of course you do." The corset slid from her torso, landing with a thud to the floor.

Air...pure, wonderful air whispered seductively down her throat and into her lungs. She could finally breathe without the confinement of her London garb! She found herself laughing, and it had been so long since she'd laughed. Spinning around, Grace darted through the door and toward the path that led to the sea, wearing only her shift, stockings, and boots.

"Gracie," Alex called out.

She ignored him, not daring to turn. "The day is much too lovely for depressing contemplation!"

The warm air caressed her skin, played with the locks that fell from the chignon at the back of her neck. They had no money, little shelter, yet for the first time in her life she felt free.

The path dipped toward the water and she paused…there on the crest of the small hill, right were the grass gave way to sand, she paused. Their very own oasis. The brilliant blue water sparkled and shone under the setting sun. The waves rolled toward the shore, licking the sand and leaving behind shells and rocks, treasures from the bottom of the ocean. Stunning, lovely, magical.

"Perfect," she whispered.

She heard Alex come to a stop beside her, smelled his musky scent, and sensed his very being as if they were connected by some unknown force. Grace turned toward him. "Alex, it's perfect!"

A smile wavered upon his lips as if he felt that magical pull but wasn't quite sure if he could trust the feeling or not. "We swam here as children. Before the war, before we lost everything."

And perhaps someday their children would as well, although she didn't dare speak her hopes and dreams aloud. "Come along then!"

She didn't wait for him but grabbed the sack from his hands and sank into the sand. Still he merely stood there, a tall shadow that blocked the sun. So be it. She would get his attention.

Grace pulled out a blanket and spread it upon the shore, hoping he didn't notice the way her hands trembled. He would think her nerves odd and grow suspicious. If she was going to seduce him, she must catch him by surprise. Resting upon her bottom, she kicked off her boots and pulled down her stockings, feeling the burn of his gaze upon her bare calves.

"The water will be cold," he warned, still refusing to join in the fun.

"I don't mind." With a grin she reached up, latching on to his hand and pulling him down upon the blanket. Reluctantly he settled beside her, but she didn't miss the way his eyes traveled her face, to her neck, down to the swell of her breasts, completely visible through the fine linen of her shift.

Alex swallowed hard, and his gaze jumped back to her face. She knew that look well, that heated desire. Grace felt oddly bold and powerful under his attention.

"What are you doing to me, Gracie?" Was it her imagination, or had his breath grown harsh?

"We're free, Alex. *Free.* You have a home, this wonderful spot of land, and there is a treasure just waiting to be found. There is nothing you can't do."

He leaned closer to her, his arm brushing hers. "Nothing *we* can't do," he said softly.

Her heart swelled with a tenderness that brought a sudden sting of tears to her eyes. Grace jumped to her feet, hiding the emotions she knew were written across her face. "Come swim with me, Alex. There are so many things we've yet to experience together." And she wanted to experience *everything* with him.

"You *do* know how to swim?"

At his question she turned. Alex was working the buttons down his shirt, his muscled chest bare. Had it grown suddenly warm? Grace's toes curled into the gritty, wet sand.

"Not at all," she managed in a strangled whisper.

He quirked a brow as he pulled the shirt from his body. Her gaze traveled the thin line of dark hair that trailed into his waistband. How she wanted to run her fingers over those dips and valleys of muscle that traced his abdomen.

"That, we will have to remedy." He kicked off his boots, watching her, always watching her in a way that left her heated and trembling and so confused by her body's reaction.

Suddenly nervous, she walked backward, keeping an even pace until her feet touched the bitterly cold, wet sand near the water's edge. Although Alex was a good stone's throw away, she felt his nearness all the same.

He surged to his feet, his hands resting at the waistband of his trousers. Temptation trailed a sweet path to that area at the junction of her thighs. Need erupted deep within her core, an aching desire to touch, to be touched. Grace's fingers curled into the skirt of her shift, her pulse pounding madly under her skin. How many nights had she spent imagining this moment?

With deft fingers Alex undid the buttons at his trousers and let the material travel down his hard thighs. His erection sprang forward, the tip of that thickened bulb glistening with moisture. The sheer size of him should have frightened her. At the least made her nervous. Instead, she only felt the intense need to finally have him completely.

Utterly naked, he started toward her. Alex had nothing to be ashamed of; Alex was honorable, he was beautiful, he was completely comfortable with his own body. She, on the other hand, had the sudden urge to dig a hole in the sand and hide. The muscles under his skin stretched and flexed as he stalked toward her, a complete work of art. She could merely wait for him, refusing to give in to the desire to hide.

"You will live here with me forever; say you will, Gracie."

The vulnerable emotion within his gaze was almost her undoing.

"I will," she replied immediately.

He didn't pause until he was a breath away, so close his body's heat whispered seductively around her. So close she felt his hard erection pulse against her lower belly. The evening breeze caressed his hair, the setting sun sending warm, golden rays across his face. Grace couldn't look away. She wanted to touch him, everywhere. To hold him close. To tell him she cared.

Alex reached out, sliding his fingers under the ribbon-thin straps of her shift. Without pause he slowly trailed the material down her arms. Embarrassment and desire mixed in a heated flush that spread throughout her body. When she'd set out to seduce him, she'd thought to have him in the cottage. Even though the hills were overgrown, anyone could happen upon them. Dare she allow him to undress her completely?

The shift moved lower, past her breasts, brushing over her hardened nipples. The ache between her thighs tightened. Lower still the shift traveled, only to pause at her hips. He left the material there and settled his hands into the curve at her waist. His touch branded her, burned her flesh, until she felt him all the way to her bones. She couldn't stop him. Didn't want to stop him.

His warm hands traveled up her body, over her rib cage to the area underneath her breasts. His movements were unhurried, his hands trembling with what could only be desire. Grace held her breath, willing him to move higher. As if knowing her need, he traced his fingers up over the soft mounds to cup her breasts. But he wasn't done with his torture. No. Softly his thumbs flicked over the hardened nipples. Grace shivered.

"You are rather perfect, you know," he whispered.

She knew it wasn't true, but she believed him in that moment. And she believed that he meant the words. Waves licked at her feet, the water cold, yet her body so bloody hot. She must touch him, felt as if she would die if she didn't.

Eagerly Grace lifted up on tiptoes and pressed her body to his, her breasts cushioned to his hard chest, his erection pressed to her lower belly. Her only barrier was the thin linen shift that prevented them from touching completely. "I...I love you, Alex."

He stiffened, apparently stunned by her admittance. But the surprised look in his gaze fled and the emotion there brought tears to her eyes. Vulnerability. Need. Affection. Grace leaned forward, her mouth just hovering against his. "I need you, Alex. I want you."

Alex growled low in his throat and lifted her into his arms. Grace instinctively curled against him, resting her head on his shoulder. Her body practically hummed with pleasure...with a knowing of what was to come.

Grace pressed her lips to his neck, breathing in his scent. "Do you want me?"

"Of course I do," he whispered, his voice catching with an emotion that made her weak.

He dropped to his knees, laying her gently upon the blanket. How beautiful he was, with the backdrop of blue skies that matched his eyes. His hands found her shift, pulling it down, over her hips, the material erotic against her skin. Lower still, until he pulled the shift free from her body. She was naked. Utterly naked.

His hand moved over the curve of her hip. "How perfectly lovely you are."

As if she was a work of art, Alex lovingly smoothed his hands up her long legs, over the curve of her hips. There he paused, slipping his hands underneath her so he cupped her lush bottom.

"I had no idea," she whispered, "how incredibly wonderful a simple touch could feel."

He grinned. "Only a touch from the right person."

So very true. How could she ever have thought about marrying Rodrick? Alex's hands tightened on her bottom, bringing her closer to his body, and Grace forgot all about Rodrick and her former life.

She bit her lower lip as aching need pooled low in her belly. Nudging his knee between her thighs, Alex finally stretched his lean body atop hers, warm and heavy. His cock pulsed against the curls hiding her femininity. Grace moaned, lifting her hips, urging him closer.

"How I dream about you at night, think of nothing other than you during the day."

Her body instantly responded to his words of love. Responded to the friction. No barrier, only skin upon skin. Although she should have felt trapped by the weight of him, his heat and nearness soaked into her muscles and relaxed her very being.

"I was dead inside before I met you, Gracie."

His velvet tongue slipped between her lips, delving into her mouth with a punishing kiss that left her breathless and wanting more. More of Alex. All of him. When he pulled away, trailing kisses across her jawline, lower to her neck, she could take it no longer.

"Now, Alex, please."

Instead of taking her completely, he pressed his mouth to hers, his tongue slipping between her lips once more. How she wanted to touch him! Her hands moved over his broad shoulders, down his arms where her fingers curled into his bulging biceps. He was so damn strong, yet so gentle with her.

Alex's hand moved to her right thigh, sliding over the silky smooth skin. Grace moaned, shifting her legs farther apart. As his hand moved to those soft curls at the junction of her thighs, her need flared with a desire so intense she thought she might die.

"Please, Alex," she said.

Ever so gently, his finger moved through the curls, lower, between her wet folds.

"I'm trying, Grace, so very hard to go slow."

"Don't. I've waited too long." She lifted her head, drawing her tongue up his neck and tasting his salty skin. Alex sucked in a sharp breath, his body trembling. Just when she thought she held all the power, he touched the sensitive bud between her folds. Grace gasped, arching her back as pleasure rippled through her very being.

"Are you sure?" he asked, his breath warm against her ear. "Are you sure you want this?"

How could he ask her now, when she was swimming in a sea of such pleasure she thought she might drown? "Yes, oh yes."

His fingers parted her folds, and the rest of her response got lost. Although he had never whispered words of love, it didn't matter. He showed her that he cared with his gentle touch.

Alex nuzzled the side of his face against her neck, the scruff on his cheek erotic against her sensitive skin. "Do you want me, Gracie?"

"So very much," she managed.

His finger entered her, slipping into her tight passage. Grace gasped, arching her back and lifting her hips to take him deeper. But it wasn't enough, never enough. Alex wasn't done tormenting her. He lowered his head to her neck, pressing gentle kisses to the skin. Lower still he traveled, his warm lips at her collarbone.

Grace squirmed, restless. Just when she thought she'd die from want, she felt his warm breath on her nipple. Grace's fingernails pierced the skin of his back, a desperate moan of pleasure and need slipping from her lips. She hadn't known, never could have guessed how wonderful he would feel. His tongue wrapped around the hard bud, drawing the peak into his mouth until pleasure shot from her breasts and down to her womb. The cool ocean breeze provided stark contrast to the heat raging within.

"Alex, please. No more! I need you now."

He shifted, positioning his erection between her legs. That smooth cock, as velvety as that rose petal she'd touched earlier, slid seductively between her folds. A shiver of desire shook her very soul. She felt the damp tip of his erection nudging inside of her and let her thighs fall open, wanting all of him.

"How long I've wanted this." Sweat dampened his brow; his jaw clenched with a fierce determination that should have frightened her, yet only made her want him all the more. "How I've needed you, Grace. How I've wanted you forever." Alex lifted his hips and thrust into her.

Pleasure mixed with pain…a stinging sensation that gave her pause and made her toes curl. She was no longer a virgin. An odd mixture of feelings swept through her body: shock and awe, need, desire, yet no regret. Never. His body was heavy, so heavy. He surrounded her, inside and out, completely fully.

"It will fade," he whispered, kissing her gently. "The pain."

But already the stinging sensation was lessening, and when he shifted ever so slightly, that deep, aching need swept through her body once more, there, always there, lurking, waiting.

Alex brushed his lips across her brow, his hands offering only comfort as he stroked her hair. "I don't want to hurt you." Braced on his elbows, he stared down at her as if attempting to read her soul.

"Then take me, all of me," she urged.

He lifted his hips slower, more gently this time. As he pulled from her, his cock receding, that aching need flared to life. Grace tightened her arms around him, squeezing her thighs to hold him close. "Don't leave me."

"Never." He thrust into her again. This time when he moved, she lifted her hips, meeting him, taking him as deeply as she could. Alex closed his eyes, groaning. His reaction emboldened her. "Blast, but you'll be the death of me."

"A wonderful death it will be," she said with a cheeky grin.

He found no amusement in her jest. His eyes had grown dark, full of a desire so intense that a shudder swept through her body. Grace's smile wavered, her breath catching. He looked at her as if he owned her, and perhaps he did. She belonged to him, body, heart, and soul. But did he belong to her as well?

"I adore you," he whispered as he lifted his hips and thrust into her again.

He rocked against her, and with each thrust he sent her spiraling higher…higher, toward that ultimate reward. Grace wrapped her legs around his calves, clinging to the man as if her life depended upon it. As her body grew desperate, her emotions got the better of her.

"Show me you care," she whispered.

Alex, as if sensing the desperation of her feelings, paused, those beautiful blue eyes softening. He slipped his finger under her chin, tilting her head back, and pressed his mouth to hers in a devastating kiss. Grace moaned, meeting his tongue thrust for thrust.

Desire shot to her core, swirling down between her legs once more. She wanted to get closer, wanted to move, wanted the ache to ease, wanted to crawl completely inside of him. She shifted her hips, taking him deeper.

"Come for me, Gracie."

The ache inside her intensified, coiling tightly. Stars were there, just out of reach. Brilliant, achingly beautiful stars.

"Alex," she whispered his name.

He lifted his hips, surging into her again, and again. His hard body rocked against her, pushing her into the sand, sending her toward those stars.

Just when she thought she could take it no longer, Grace burst forward upon a wave of pleasure so intense her entire world faded. White stars danced behind her eyelids as she floated, floated in a world she never wanted to leave. It wasn't what she'd expected. It was more, so much more.

Vaguely she heard Alex groan, felt his body shudder as his wet seed burst into her womb, and Grace trembled all over again. He collapsed atop her, his hard body sleek with sweat and bringing her back into reality.

But Grace was happy to be back on earth, if it meant she could touch him, kiss him, taste him. She swept her hands down his back, pausing near his bottom and cupping the tight mounds. When she pulled him closer, Alex sucked in a sharp breath.

"You'll kill me," he rasped.

She couldn't quite help herself. Giddy with a happiness that could barely be contained, she moved her hands up his muscled back. His scent was on her skin, branding her. He was hers finally, completely.

"We shouldn't have done that here." He lifted just enough to rest upon his elbows and kiss her forehead. "What would the neighbors think should they happen upon us?"

There was no seriousness to his tone. Grace giggled. "'Tis the perfect place. Our own spot of heaven."

She felt as if she had just experienced perfection. Perhaps this was heaven. She slid her fingers through the soft curls at his temple, shaking loose the bits of sand that had found their way into the shiny locks.

He grinned down at her, those dimples flashing. "Do you know how lovely you look with the glow of the setting sun kissing your skin?" His hand trailed down the side of her face, his fingers outlining every feature as if trying to memorize the details. "You've exhausted me. You've brought me back to life only to kill me here. But oh, what a way to die."

"Tomorrow we shall search for the treasure, but tonight," she whispered, "we shall bring you back to life once more, this time in your new home."

"*Our* new home," he said, kissing her gently.

Grace grinned and wrapped her arms around his neck, clinging to him much like the tiny pieces of sand clung to her arms and legs. The gritty texture didn't bother her in the least. Not even the thought of being seen in such a compromising position by the neighbors made her stir.

She was content here with Alex…her life…her love.

Nothing could be more perfect.

Chapter 21

Nothing could be worse.

For three days it rained. Dreary, cold weather that left them huddled in the house, wishing for coal and a hearth that was clean. Alex supposed some would have found their banishment romantic, and there was nothing more Alex would have liked than to be ensconced in a cottage with Grace...if he hadn't been so bloody worried about the treasure.

Truth was the more time he spent with Grace, the more his feelings grew, spreading through his body, seeping into his heart... his soul. The first night Alex had made love to Grace in a sweet and slow manner that left them both trembling and vulnerable. She'd snuck into his heart and he knew he never wanted her to leave. Much to his relief and dismay, she'd told him she loved him once more and then had promptly fallen asleep, curled like a kitten against the side of his body. He'd gone to bed with dreams of a future, hope for a new life, and fear that it would be taken away.

But by morning, when they'd awoken to rain dripping from a hole in the ceiling and soaking their pathetic bed, his hope had faded, swept away on the cool breeze that seeped through the cracks in the walls. First he worried the cottage would fall down upon their very heads. Then he worried that between the cool air and rain, Grace would get sick.

She'd insisted she was quite hardy and had gone about the day helping him search the house as if they were on a grand adventure. And for a while…he'd managed to forget his despair and worry. For a while, she'd managed to make him believe.

But after three days of searching the house for a mythical treasure, the situation was growing rather dire.

Grace, the wonderful, blasted woman, didn't know when to give up. She knew as well as he that he couldn't support her, her mother, and her sister without that treasure, but he sure as hell would die trying.

Even now she was trudging through the weed-ridden front garden, studying the house and searching for something odd that might indicate a secret hiding place. At least the rain had cleared, leaving behind a garden of brilliant green.

His shirtsleeves rolled to his elbows, trousers covered in dust, Alex leaned against the doorjamb, content merely watching her. The way her hips swayed when she paced. Her brows drawn together in concentration. Locks of hair had come loose and floated on the late afternoon breeze. She was so devoted to finding that bloody treasure she didn't notice he stood there. Grace wouldn't give up, ever. He admired her for that. Respected her, even. Yet there was a time when one needed to accept reality.

Impatiently she brushed back a lock of hair and nibbled on her lower lip. The brown dress she wore had a smudge of dirt on the skirt and the hem had torn when they'd searched the gardens. Beautiful, always beautiful, but damn it all, she didn't deserve this life. Alex's heart clenched painfully, the emotions so intense he was forced to look away. He wanted to build her a bloody castle. Dress her in silks. Drape her in jewels.

"Perhaps I shall go to town to look for work tomorrow." His voice came out unnaturally gruff.

Grace paused between a red rosebush and a patch of wild daisies. Her horrified gaze flashed toward him, her every emotion in her hazel eyes. "No, Alex! You will not work in the mines! It's too dangerous."

He stepped off the stoop and started toward her, cursing every weed that wrapped around his boots, preventing him from reaching her more quickly. "Gracie." He cupped the sides of her face, breathing in her warm vanilla scent and taking comfort in her presence. "Just until we can save enough money." But they both knew that wasn't true. He'd never have enough.

She stepped back, away from his touch, shaking her head so furiously another lock came loose, falling charmingly against her right cheek. "Not yet. I feel it. Today we'll find the treasure."

But what if they didn't? Surely it was better to be realistic instead of clinging to some ridiculous fantasy. "Grace—"

"We will find it," Grace assured him, her voice coming out a little harder than normal. There was a frantic gleam in her eyes. A gleam that saddened him, that touched his heart, his soul. He didn't dare destroy her hope.

"Right." He gave her a tight smile as a low rumble of thunder shook the skies. Another storm was coming and their clothing had barely had time to dry from the last. "Of course we will."

But obviously he'd never make a career on the stage. Sighing, she turned away from him and moved toward the path that led to the beach where they'd first made love. "We will find it, Alex. We will."

The setting sun pierced the dark clouds and outlined her body with a heavenly glow. Her hair practically sparkled with flames of red and gold. A goddess so deserving of more than he could offer.

Whether he accepted it now or later, he knew deep down he had failed her.

"Grace."

"No, we can't stop, Alex, we can't," she called out over the roar of ocean waves.

They'd eaten the last of their food today. Tomorrow their bellies would be empty. He would not see Grace hungry. He would not see her in pain as he'd had to see his mother and brother those few days before he'd left with Ophelia.

"Fish!" Grace called out, her face flushed with excitement as she turned toward him. "And...and oysters." She raced up the beach toward Alex, her skirts hiked to her knees. "We have plenty of food here! Along the shore!"

As she danced in excitement around him, Alex glanced toward the beach where the waves were great, gray, and tumbling from the approaching storm. Years ago he and Dem had fished. He could still remember jumping and skipping along the boulders, looking for hidden treats. Perhaps she was right. The memory of his grandfather searching for oysters was fresh in his mind. They did have food here, all around them. In summer the berries up on the hill would be ripe. Wasn't there an apple orchard not far down the lane?

"Stop worrying, Alex!" She spun around, twirling so her skirts flared wide. Her laughter warmed his very being; how he always wanted her this happy. She was a perfect portrait of a fairy, one at ease and in love with life and nature. "We are free! We have everything we need here!"

A burst of sunlight pierced the clouds, making the dew on the grass sparkle like diamonds, as if the very heavens were applauding her effort. And for a moment, a brief moment, he thought perhaps she was right. Perhaps Grace was a fey person, full of magic and hope. Mayhap she knew more than he did about life.

"We have each other, Alex." She paused, smiling up at him. In her smile was love, acceptance. "Alex." She stepped closer to him and wrapped her arms around his neck. "I do love you."

The emotion in her gaze almost brought him to his knees. She loved him. She trusted him. She believed in him. Just like that, any hope vanished. How he wanted to beg her to forgive him for bringing her here. Yet at the same time he wanted to beg her to stay. When she uncovered the truth, that he hadn't a bloody clue how to support her and the treasure was most likely family lore, what would she think of him? And she would uncover the truth eventually. Then what?

As she leaned into him, her eyes closing, her head tilted to kiss him, he thought of their children. They would have children. Children who would need clothing, toys, and food other than fish and oysters. What about winter when the food was scarce? Startled, horrified, Alex stepped back, away from her touch, away from her comfort. Christ, even now she could be with child. *His* child. And what would his son or daughter think if the truth of his past was ever uncovered?

"Don't, Alex," Grace demanded, her lower lip quivering. She knew where his thoughts led. Anger and frustration flashed in her hazel eyes. "Don't push me away. Don't look at me with that haunted gaze." She marched by him, headed toward the house once more. "I will not let you destroy what we have, what we *can* have."

"Grace, I'm merely being realistic."

But she didn't pause, didn't even slow her pace. "I will not give in. We can uncover a way to make this work, we *must*."

He sighed and started after her, exasperated. "Life is not a fairy tale."

"Life is whatever you want it to be," she snapped back, pausing in the doorway. She spun around to face him, her eyes flashing with a furiousness he'd never seen before. An anger that gave him pause. "She controls you still, Alex. Even now. You may not be at her estate, but she is still here." She shoved her finger into his chest for emphasis.

His insides grew stiff and chill. "What do you mean?"

"Lady Lavender." Grace gripped the sides of the door frame. "Don't you see? She stole your childhood, but you are no longer a child! You're an adult! Don't let her steal your future as well."

"You're talking nonsense." Avoiding her gaze, he brushed by her and entered the foyer. Her words made him nervous, anxious, and he knew why…perhaps she was right. But how could he move forward when his past haunted him so? When he constantly feared the future and what lurked behind the shadowed corners of time?

"Am I talking nonsense?" Frustrated, Grace followed. "When will you stop giving her power over you—"

"We aren't all like you, Grace." Alex paused in the foyer, his back to her, for he wouldn't dare look her in the eyes for fear she'd read the truth. He was afraid. Afraid of life and what it could do to a person. "We don't all believe in fairy tales and magic and…"

Something shifted in the darkness of the parlor, a shadow that didn't belong. Alex held his breath, not daring to look directly. He didn't need to turn to know who stood, unwelcome, in his cottage. The very air was tainted with the scent of lavender. Instinctively he searched for Grace, knowing she stood behind him, having seen the shadow as well. Neither of them made a sound, neither moved. Alex felt that chain tightening around his neck once more. He'd been right all along; he would never escape the woman.

"Do let her go on, Alex," Ophelia said, her voice like a snake hissing from the darkness. "I truly do wish to hear what she has to say. Quite intriguing."

Grace flattened her hands on his back, her fingers curling into the material of his shirt, her grip tight. He could practically feel her fear. The fact that Grace was afraid angered him more than anything. This was their cottage. *Their* home. How dare Ophelia enter!

Alex trembled deep within, resisting the urge to shout, to hit something. His anger would only amuse Ophelia, and Grace was right, he'd given her enough power. He wasn't surprised when the two hulking forms of Wavers and Jensen appeared beside their mistress, always there to protect.

"What are you doing here?" he demanded.

Lady Lavender tsked. "Not exactly the greeting I expected." Slowly she moved from the empty hearth, smoothing down the skirts of her light lavender gown. "And she is not exactly what I was expecting." She moved closer, pausing in the splash of afternoon light coming from the windows. "Who knew Alex liked them so pure and virginal? I remember quite well you saying you were tired of virgins."

Anger simmered inside his blood so that he thought he might explode. Damn it all, he should have known she would come after him. He'd hoped, prayed that she had too many other things to occupy her time. But Gideon had been right all along: Ophelia wanted them for an entirely different reason. She must, to have traveled all this way. Why was he so important to her?

"Why are you here?"

"To collect what I own, of course."

Grace's fingers bit into his shirt, tightening in the material. He could practically feel the anger vibrating from her body. But she wouldn't react; she was too smart for that. Grace was waiting for his cue. Alex gritted his teeth, forcing himself to remain calm. Inside, he seethed. How he wanted to kill the woman. How he wished he had tightened his fingers around her throat when he'd had the chance. But killing her would have made him no better than she.

"You do not own me. You do not own anyone."

Lady Lavender sighed and sashayed forward, that satiny velvet skirt swooshing over her polished slippers. The woman's cloying French perfume permeated the room, leaving him nauseated.

"Alex," she said in the same tone a mother would use to speak to a wayward child. "Dear, dear Alex. Grace here is correct. Perhaps I don't own you on paper, but I own your soul, don't I? The truth is you can't go to sleep at night without thinking about me.

You don't spend your day without wondering when I will appear. I will forever be in your thoughts, your soul."

Bitterness tasted sour upon his tongue. Alex saw red as his fingers curled into claws, the monster within released. With a growl, he surged forward. Jensen moved fast, stepping directly in front of Lady Lavender.

At the same time Grace called out, "No, Alex! She's baiting you."

Alex stopped short, coming to his senses. Grace's warm hands flattened against his body, her very life and essence seeping into his skin, his soul. Calming him.

"Why," he seethed through gritted teeth, "are you here?"

Ophelia moved around Jensen, trailing her fingers down the slope of the man's broad shoulders, her glittering gaze locked on Alex. She knew exactly what she was doing: torturing Alex with information she didn't mean to share. "An eye for an eye."

He didn't understand her words, but he knew it was a clue as to why she hated him so. His heart pumped madly, his hands curling as he resisted the urge to beg for more. She was playing with him, yet she was practically admitting there was more to their chance meeting those many years back.

An eye for an eye.

Ophelia tilted her head to the side in a thoughtful manner, studying Grace. "I've been thinking of expanding my empire to include women. I know your family is in desperate need of money. If you'd like the work…"

Alex's entire body stiffened as he resisted the urge to surge forward once more.

"Go back to hell where you belong," Grace whispered.

"A fiery temper." Lady Ophelia laughed. "There are plenty of men who love a woman with a temper. Makes it more…" She lifted her shoulders high as if delighted. "Exciting. I certainly can't sell you as a virgin any longer, though, can I? Shame, they do go for so much more."

Alex clenched his jaw, squeezing his teeth so tightly together surely they would crack. Her vile words and accusations would not taint what he had with Grace. How could she, a monster with no soul, possibly understand their feelings toward one another? "I will ask you one last time, what do you want? Why will you not leave me in peace?"

She was silent for a moment, a silence laced with condemnation. A silence so heavy that he knew her next words would change their lives forever. "Do you truly wish to know, Alex? If she hears the truth," she slid Grace a glance, "she may never wish to see you again."

Even though he didn't understand her in the least, Ophelia's words sent a cold chill down his body. Surely he'd done nothing so ill toward her. He was a mere child when she'd recruited him.

"Tell me," he demanded.

"Rape, my dear." The harsh word hung suspended in the air. Lady Lavender stepped closer. Although she still smiled, her gaze had grown hard, void of feelings, void of soul. "At least that's what most would call it. Of course, when it's done by a man who is titled, it isn't called rape. It's the woman's fault, you know, and swept under the carpet." She paced slowly in front of them. "Fifteen years ago in France it happened quite often. And with his best friend helping him cover his crime, a friend related to Russian royalty, who would believe the poor woman's accusations? The victim was left to rot, and with her innocence a vague memory, her value was gone as well."

She paused in front of him, so close the scent of her lavender perfume made him nauseous, but her gaze was on Grace. He felt off-balance, his emotions at war, unsure which would win.

"If a man was dishonored so, he would kill the person responsible, and not one soul would blame him." Her gaze went to Alex. She was smirking once more. "But women, we're much, much more clever, aren't we? I destroyed the men involved in another way, by destroying their pride and joy."

Bile rose to Alex's throat. The pieces fell together in soft whispers of denial. His stomach churned with the revolting image she spread before them. A memory too horrible for anyone, even her.

And with his best friend helping him cover his crime, a friend related to Russian royalty…

Russian royalty. Related to *royalty*. Alex felt dizzy. He knew his father was a bastard, but surely he couldn't have been that horrible. So why did his heart feel as if it had been crushed? Why did he feel as if he could not possibly have a soul because he was his father's offspring?

It made sense…the reason why Ophelia acted as she did. The reason why she was intent on destroying Alex. It all made sense now. Desperately Alex found Grace. But she merely stood to the side, refusing to meet his gaze, focused on Lady Lavender. Had he lost her? Alex wanted to reach for her, wanted to swear he was not his father and beg her to believe him.

Instead, he swallowed hard and focused on Ophelia. "Your problem," Alex stated, attempting to keep his tone even, "was in thinking I was my father's pride and joy."

Lady Ophelia laughed a joyous sound. "I'm a patient woman, Alex. Very patient. Perhaps your father wasn't destroyed by your sudden disappearance, but your family has reestablished themselves, haven't they? What would happen to them if they found out what you are? If the world found out what you've been doing for the past twelve years?"

Alex didn't even flinch, although he felt her words like a knife to the gut. Grace's face had gone pale and he knew she understood what his father had done.

"You will return with me," Lady Lavender proclaimed, "or I will see your family humiliated. But worse, I will see that your dear Grace is destroyed as well."

Chapter 22

To the untrained eye, Alex would seem at ease. But Grace knew him well enough by now. She noticed the slight flaring of his pupils, the way that pulse in the side of his neck jumped to life. The way his hands curled ever so slightly.

"And so," he said, "what will you do? Force me to leave? Shoot me if I don't?"

Lady Lavender released a rich chuckle. "No, of course not." Her gaze slid to Grace. "I'll shoot her."

Grace hadn't time to think upon the woman's dire words before a steel arm wrapped around her waist and she was jerked back into a chest that smelled of pipe tobacco. Wavers moved faster than she'd thought possible.

The cool point of a pistol pressed into her temple.

She didn't move, didn't even flinch. Flinching would show her fear, and she would be damned if she would allow Lady Lavender to witness her vulnerability.

But Alex, sweet, noble, and self-sacrificing Alex, was falling for the woman's threats. She could see it in his eyes. "Alex," Grace whispered. "Don't believe her."

"No one will miss her, Alex." Lady Lavender stood before them, a petite specimen of a woman. In reality she could so easily be destroyed. But here, in this world where nothing was normal, she reigned supreme.

"You think I didn't know you were sneaking visits with her?" She turned and smiled at Alex. "When you left to see her, I knew. When she came to see you, I was completely aware. I allowed your visits. I allowed you to fall in love, knowing in the end that your love would destroy you. No one will miss her but you. It would be so easy to hide her death. Or perhaps...the world would blame you. After all, you've been seen together, haven't you?"

"You wouldn't kill an innocent," Grace tried, hoping that deep down the woman must have some sense of right and wrong. "I've had nothing to do with your world. Alex had nothing to do with what happened to you. You've used him, destroyed his childhood. Let him go."

When the woman turned her cold eyes toward her, Grace understood the truth. Lady Lavender no longer had a soul. "You'd be surprised by what I can do, my dear."

"It doesn't have to be this way," Grace said, refusing to give in. "You can forget the pain. You can have a life as well."

Ophelia sighed. "I do have a life, now that I've taken control. I know the secrets of so many powerful men and women. I own half this country."

No words or begging would influence Ophelia. The woman was too far gone into madness. Vendetta had kept her going all these years, and she would see all destroyed, even if it meant destroying herself in the process. Grace almost felt sorry for the woman.

"Gracie." The tone of Alex's voice tore through her body. A yearning. A sadness. An acceptance. Grace could barely stand to meet his gaze. "You'll always be my Grace. You'll do well enough on your own. You'll find your way home to your mother and sister. Perhaps one day you'll find a man who will give you the life you deserve."

His words were so final, so heart wrenching. He'd made up his mind; he'd given up on hope. "No, Alex," Grace said, surging toward him. Wavers jerked her back, his arms so tight around her Grace could barely breathe.

Alex looked away, refusing to meet her gaze. "I'll go with you."

Misery and horror wrapped around Grace's heart and squeezed. "No!" She sank into Wavers, her knees too weak to hold her. "No!"

Alex's fingers curled into his thighs, his entire body trembling. So lost, so far removed from her already. "Gracie, I must. You'll find your way back…"

Her lower lip quivered, but Grace swallowed her sob. She would not beg him to stay; she would not beg Ophelia to leave them in peace. Neither would listen to her. The world around her grew blurry as tears swam in her eyes. Alex, always out to save another lost soul, even if that soul didn't need saving.

Ophelia left the cottage and started through the garden.

Wavers released Grace and moved forward, following Lady Lavender like a little lapdog. Grace stumbled outside, tripping down the stoop as they moved through the front garden. He was leaving…leaving her here alone. The future was gone. Raw pain surged through her being. Grace crossed her arms around her waist, wanting to sink to the ground.

Lady Ophelia glanced over her shoulder, her gaze hard as ice. "Kill her."

Confused, it took Grace a moment to realize the woman was speaking of her. The world seemed to pause as the blood roared to her ears in denial. Alex jerked away from Wavers, his gaze frantic and haunted, and that's when Grace realized she was to be murdered, shot in the very garden they'd hoped to make a home.

Jensen lifted his pistol, the barrel pointed directly at her chest. Everything slowed, yet she couldn't move, knew she couldn't protect herself in time. Knew she was going to die.

A shot rang out. Gasping, Grace stumbled back, tripping on her own feet.

"No!" she thought she heard Alex scream.

Off-balance, she fell to the ground with a thud, half-hidden behind a rosebush. The entire world seemed to disappear as Grace waited to feel the pain. But nothing came. For a moment she merely lay there on the ground, staring up at the gray clouds, vaguely aware of shouts and thundering feet. Suddenly Alex hovered over her, his gaze so soft, so warm, that she thought he might be preparing to cry.

"Are you well?" Alex demanded, his voice gruff.

"Y...yes. I believe so." She blinked, confused. "Was I shot?"

"No, thank God, no." His voice caught in a show of emotion. Alex collapsed atop her, pressing his lips to hers, the warmth of his breath comforting. "Thank God, no." His trembling hands traveled her body as if he didn't quite believe his own words and was looking for a wound. "Thank God," he murmured once more, his voice catching.

"I don't understand," she whispered. Alex slipped his arm around her back and helped her sit upright. "What happened?"

"My...father."

Shocked, she peeked over his shoulder, attempting to make sense of the situation. Alex's father stood some ten feet from them, dressed in the finest of suits, looking for all the world like a gentleman but for the smoking pistol in his hand. Behind him stood three other men, all holding pistols of their own. He had brought his own little army.

Lady Lavender had gone pale, standing as still as a statue in the middle of the garden, her well-kept composure gone. Frozen in time. She looked as if she'd seen a ghost. Perhaps she had.

Alex's father swallowed hard, emotion playing across the weathered lines of his face. He looked old, downtrodden, so unlike the brusque man she'd met in London. "You vill take your men and leave my son alone."

Grace's heart swelled with hope. She reached for Alex's hand, needing to feel the warmth of his touch. Slowly Alex wrapped his arm around her waist and helped her to her feet. Jensen was sprawled out on the grass not ten feet from her. A horrible image indeed. A pool of blood soaked his jacket, his face shiny with perspiration as he attempted to contain his grunts of pain.

Ophelia laughed, a manic laugh, barely acknowledging her injured man. "You think you have any control over me? You lost control twenty years ago. I can destroy you, and you know it."

Alex's father's jaw clenched. "I stood by vhile you vere harmed, and for that I vill forever be guilty. But you have ruined my life. The lives of my family. Ve are even." His father lowered the gun. "You shall keep my son's former life to yourself and I shall not tell the world who you truly are."

Startled, Grace studied the woman's pale face. She no longer laughed. The words had stung Lady Lavender, made her quiver with what could only be fear. Had she been right all along; was Lady Lavender from a titled family?

"You've already done vhat you came here to do," his father added. "You've destroyed my son's life. You've destroyed us. It's over."

Ophelia slid Alex a glance. An odd smile played upon her lips...almost a smirk, as if she suddenly realized something he didn't. A shudder whispered over Grace's skin. She slid her arm around Alex's waist and rested her head on his chest as if she could protect him with her touch.

"You'll be a happy family now?" Ophelia's voice sounded odd, almost childlike. The woman was mad, completely and utterly mad. "No. You know as vell as I that can never happen," his father replied. "Be proud of yourself, for you've ruined our lives. You've done vhat you vanted to accomplish. You've done everything you can to me," his father added. "Let my son be."

Wavers, as quiet as ever, leaned down, helping Jensen to his feet. Even if Lady Lavender didn't know when to quit, her men did. It seemed wrong, so incredibly wrong that they would get away with what they had done with no true punishment.

"Take them to the carriage," his father demanded. "See that they don't return."

The small army escorted Lady Lavender, Jensen, and Wavers through the trees. Not once did Ophelia look back.

"I understand why you did what you did, Alex." His father's gaze was on him. "I understand, and I hope you understand why it is that ve can never see you again."

"No!" Grace cried out.

"Shhh," Alex whispered, holding her close. "It's all right."

She pressed her lips into a firm line and glared at the hateful man before them. How could he treat his son so? The man had the decency to flush and look away.

"Any association vould ruin your brother," his father explained.

Alex nodded. "I understand."

But Grace didn't understand at all. Unable to look the man in his dark eyes, she focused on Alex's lovely face. Alex, so damn honorable, always thinking of others.

"I've done horrible things in this life, Alex. I don't expect you to forgive me." His father made no move to come closer. "But I hope this vill help." He pulled a missive from his pocket and set it on the top of their crumbling rock wall. "Please, take it, 'tis your mother's vish."

The man turned and slowly made his way through the trees, following the others.

"Will they be back, do you think?" Grace asked.

"No. When my father makes a promise, he always sees it through. Ophelia will not return…neither will my father."

The garden grew silent, so empty, so odd. Only the scent of gunpowder remained, but that too would soon be gone, and once again their roses would overpower the air. Perhaps Ophelia would return, but Grace had a feeling she wouldn't. Whatever her past might be, it was obvious she wanted no one to uncover her secrets. The emotions that had pumped through her blood receded, leaving her vulnerable and shaking.

"And you," she whispered. "Can you let her go; can you believe in us? In a future? Will you stay, Alex?"

He pulled her close, hugging her tightly. "I will never leave you again, Gracie."

For one long moment, as the birds chirped in the trees and the waves roared in the distance, Alex merely held her. She was content to stand there in his embrace, but she knew Alex needed to see what was in that envelope, know what his father had left him.

"Go on," she said, pushing away from him.

Pausing only for a moment, Alex finally reached for the envelope. With trembling fingers he opened the missive. His face was blank, his eyes unreadable. "An inheritance. From my grandfather."

Slowly he moved to the door and sank down on the front stoop, the paper in hand. Grace hadn't a clue how much it was, nor did she care. She only worried about Alex and his pale face. Slowly she settled next to him. He lifted his stunned gaze to her. "We won't be rich, but we won't starve either. I can support you, your family."

"That's wonderful, but oh, Alex. I never cared about money!" Grace threw her arms around his neck and held him close, so close she felt his heart slam wildly against her own. "I'm here, Alex. I'll always be here no matter what."

He cupped the back of her head. "You were right all along," he whispered into her hair. "I was letting Ophelia control me. I didn't believe we could have a future. It won't happen again."

She pulled back, smiling at him through her tears. "It's all right. I believed enough for both of us."

He took her hands in his, his face serious. So serious. "I want you, Grace. I want a life with you, a future."

The tears she'd been trying desperately to hold back trailed down her cheeks. "I thought I'd lose you."

He cupped the sides of her face. "Never again." There, on the front stoop of their little cottage, with a soft storm breeze whispering through the roses, he leaned down and kissed her. A gentle kiss. A kiss she'd never experienced from him before, a kiss of dreams, of hope, of a future.

"There's something else." He pulled back, leaving her bewildered and wishing for more.

Tilting the envelope, a golden ring fell onto his palm. Blue sapphire petals formed a flower around a small yellow stone. "My grandmother's."

The ring sparkled and shone in what little light managed to pierce the thick clouds. "It's not much, but they never seemed to need much. Yet…they were happy. So very happy."

"A forget-me-not flower." Grace's lower lip quivered. She couldn't quite help herself and reached up, slipping her fingers through the windswept locks at his temple. "'Tis lovely."

He looked up at her and the vulnerability in his eyes was almost her undoing. "I have no position in society."

"I never fit in anyway," she countered.

Alex took her hand in his. "I have no family."

"We'll start our own."

"I—"

Grace cupped the sides of his face, the day's growth of whiskers erotic against her sensitive palms. "Do you love me?"

"Yes," he whispered; the sincerity in his gaze warmed her inside and out. "I do love you."

She smiled as longing and happiness burst through her chest. "Ask me, Alex."

He slid the ring upon her finger. "Will you marry me?"

"Yes," she whispered against his mouth.

"Then that's all I need."

Epilogue

Afternoon was his favorite time of day. That moment right before evening. The sun low upon the horizon, spreading brilliant rays of orange and pink through the sky. Waves glistened and sparkled while gulls cried overhead. A time when the household began to settle. Scents of dinner simmering, laughter in the garden, a time of quiet evenings and passionate nights.

Alex leaned against the door frame, his shirtsleeves rolled to his elbows, Julian in his arms. The boy chewed upon his fist, drool trailing from his chin and soaking Alex's shoulder. His dark curls waved in the warm summer breeze.

"And how does your fist taste today, my dear lad?" he whispered, nuzzling his face against the child's soft cheek.

Julian giggled, his hazel eyes sparkling.

"Papa!" Hope cried out, skipping toward him through the open gate, her auburn curls bouncing. The excitement in her eyes thrilled him as much as it had when she was a babe. Always happy to see him, his first child had slipped into his heart even before she was born.

He leaned down, lifting her into his arms; with a child on either side, he had never felt more content. Hope leaned over and pressed a kiss to Julian's head and then rested her palm on Alex's face. With a giggle she leaned closer and brushed the tip of her nose against his.

"Where is your mother?" he asked, stepping into the garden and searching for Grace.

"She's visiting Grandmama."

Alex smiled, ignoring the twinge of sadness that pierced his chest. "I see."

Every evening Grace laid flowers upon her mother's grave. The woman had had three years of peace in their cottage, until one evening, while taking a nap, she hadn't awakened. Grace had been grateful that she'd had those three years with her mother. Alex had been devastated, wishing that he could have given more time to the soft-spoken woman he'd come to care for as a mother. It had been a year now since Grace's mama had died, and the pain was still there, a deep ache they all felt.

I can leave now, knowing my children are cared for. Knowing my Grace is so happy."

The last words her mother had spoken to Alex. And although they mourned her, Grace swore she could feel her spirit in the caress of the wind, smell her scent in the flowers that bloomed in the front garden.

He was trying. Trying not to focus on the negative. And he was happier than he'd ever been, ever imagined he could be. When Grace told him to look at the beauty of a flower, he looked. *Truly* looked. She'd changed his life for the better, and he wouldn't give up anything, not for his royal title, not for jewels and riches unimaginable.

Grace and Patience came strolling over the hill, smiling and chatting the way only sisters could. Four years later, he still couldn't look at Grace without wanting to drop to his knees and thank God. The soft roar of the ocean waves in the distance and gulls crying overhead called out their approval.

Grace lifted her head and met his gaze. A shiver of awareness went through his body. The cottage had changed. The thatched roof had long ago been repaired. The floorboards had been replaced. Furniture had been purchased. The gardens trimmed. Even he had changed, taking a more optimistic view of life. How could he not when he had Grace, a family, a life?

He had a family now. A charmingly delightful daughter who was perfect in every way and as intelligent as her mama. A son who was the most good-natured babe he'd ever seen, always smiling, never cross. He even thought of Patience as his family and worried about her as he would his own sister.

An adult now, she deserved a season in London, but proclaimed she hadn't the slightest desire to wear ball gowns and act the ninny. She was quite content to stay here, and why wouldn't she be? But Grace wanted Patience to find love, and so far her only prospect was the local butcher's son, who was a good head shorter than she and liked to talk in grotesque detail about butchering techniques. Somehow he'd find a way to send Patience to London, at least for one season.

But one thing hadn't changed…Grace. She was still so lovely that when she looked at him, his breath caught in his chest. Still so beautiful that she rarely saw the negative side of life. And he was still completely and madly in love with her.

Daisies brushed against her blue skirts as she spun her forget-me-not ring round and round her finger. Alex had wanted to buy her something new, something larger and more expensive. Grace had wanted to keep her ring…a piece of jewelry that she said represented more than anything else ever could…love.

As she moved through the open gate, the sunlight glinted off her dark hair, highlighting the auburn. His heart swelled with love.

"Mama!" Hope called out, scrambling from his arms.

Grace knelt in the garden, the wind tugging at the loose tendrils framing her face. Laughing, she caught Hope in her arms and held her close. Alex couldn't help but smile over the picture they made. He could stand there all day, watching them.

"Has the mail arrived?" Patience asked.

"Yes, inside."

She rushed into the cottage.

As she stood, Grace's gaze shifted from Alex to Julian. "Why are you awake? You're supposed to be taking a nap."

Alex tried to look serious. "He was crying; I couldn't resist."

Grace quirked a brow. "Our son never cries."

"There is a first time for everything, and he looked decidedly as if he *might* cry."

Grace moved toward them, Hope skipping after her. "Well then, you had to pick him up!" She brushed her hand over Julian's downy head, then leaned into Alex, pressing her lips to his.

"I can't believe the *ton* have started wearing our jewelry," Patience declared, brushing by them and hopping with glee down the front steps. "Look! A new order from a jeweler in London!" She held out a letter for the briefest of moments and then clutched it to her chest.

"That reminds me," Alex said. "There is a new basket of shells by the gate."

"There is!" Patience spun around and rushed toward the stone wall to study her treasure.

It had been Grace's brilliant idea to take the shells they'd found and make jewelry from the polished insides. Alex had swallowed his pride and sent a piece to his mother. She'd worn it to a ball, and the business had taken off quite well. Alex hunted for the shells. Grace and Patience made them. Patience provided the face for the business. The girl was surprisingly persuasive.

Between the money they were making with their jewelry and Alex's inheritance, they were better off than ever before. Yet they wouldn't move on to greener pastures. No, he and Grace were quite content in their little cottage by the sea. If they needed more room, which they would very soon indeed, they'd add on.

This was home. This was the place where Julian, Hope, and Patience thrived. Where Grace's mama had spent her last years in peace. Where he and Grace had started to live, truly *live*.

"Gracie," Patience called out. "Do you mind if I dig up a patch of forget-me-nots? I'd like to take some inside to study the blooms for a new necklace design."

"No," Grace said, smoothing a finger over her own ring and smiling in a dreamy way that delighted Alex. "Of course not."

"Can I help?" Hope raced after Patience. She adored her aunt and constantly followed at her heels, giving Alex and Grace much desired time alone.

"He's sleeping," Grace whispered.

Sure enough, Julian's eyes were closed. Alex moved into the parlor and settled him in the cradle. At almost a year old, he was getting rather large for the cradle.

Grace followed, gazing down at their son with pure adoration. "He's so beautiful, so perfect. So like his father."

Alex stood, taking her into his arms, grateful for any moment alone with his wife. "I think it's time to add a room or two onto the cottage. I thought perhaps we could build a bedchamber and sitting area downstairs for Patience. She should have her own space."

Grace lifted a brow. "You're sure you wish to spend the money?"

He grinned. "I think we'll need the space."

She laughed. "How long have you known?"

"Three weeks."

"I've only known for two weeks!"

He pulled her up flush to his body and kissed her quickly. "You think I don't know you?" He leaned down, pressing his lips to her ear. "The fullness of your breasts. The way you cringed when I made eggs this morn. Going to bed early, sleeping late."

"Are you saying you know me better than I know myself?"

"Perhaps." He grinned.

She parted her lips to respond with something biting and wry, no doubt, but fortunately for him, Patience interrupted.

"Gracie! Alex!"

Reluctantly Grace turned away. "What is she screeching about?"

They moved to the open door. Patience knelt by the large elm tree, a carpet of tiny blue flowers at her feet, Hope at her side.

"What is it?" Grace asked.

Patience glanced over her shoulder, her brows pinched together in confusion, a small shovel in her hand. "I've found something."

Alex slid Grace a glance, and she laughed. It wasn't the first time Patience had "found something." It was always, of course, a great treasure, until the object was completely uncovered. An old shoe. A rusty pail. Alex took her hand and they strolled unconcerned toward the two girls.

"What is it?" Grace asked again.

"A...box of some sort." Patience brushed the dirt from her hands and shifted as Alex knelt beside her.

"Treasure," Hope squealed, hopping up and down so her blue dress flared like flower petals on the wind.

Grace sighed, and he knew what she was thinking. Hope's first word hadn't been *Mama* or even *Papa*. No, Patience had taught Hope how to say *treasure*, and the word had stuck. Alex pulled the box from the ground and brushed off the loose dirt. It wasn't particularly decorative, merely a wooden box slightly longer than his forearm.

"Shall I open it?" Patience asked.

Alex stood and wrapped his arm around Grace's waist. "Sure, why not." He leaned toward Grace and nuzzled her hair. "Are you feeling well?" Julian wasn't quite a year old and already Grace was carrying another. Perhaps it was too soon.

She grinned up at him, completely unconcerned. "Of course."

"Oh my," Hope whispered.

At the odd tone of her voice, Grace and Alex turned. "What is it?"

"Grace…" Patience looked up, her eyes wide. "Remember how you wanted to make improvements to the cottage?"

"Yes." Grace moved around Hope, settling on the grass next to Patience.

"I think you can now."

There, in the box, lay golden coins…pearls…jewels. Their brilliance was not dulled with age, but caught the light and sparkled to life.

Grace gasped, resting her hand on her chest. "It can't be." She looked up at Alex, who stood frozen, too shocked to move. "Alex, it was here all along! The treasure is real!"

For days they'd searched for that bloody treasure. And now… now he was sadly lacking in enthusiasm. Certainly money was a welcome gift, yet he wasn't as excited as he should have been. Those many years ago the treasure had consumed his thoughts, had been of upmost importance. Now…now he had everything he needed.

"Pretty," Hope cooed and knelt, grabbing a fistful of jewelry.

"So I'm not imagining it," Patience whispered.

"No," Alex replied. "It's real. The treasure is real."

"We can search for more!" Patience jumped to her feet. "Just think, it could be anywhere." She raced around the tree, under and over branches until her skirts got caught.

Grace stood. "No."

Patience froze. "But…"

Grace shook her head. "No. You may search, Patience, if you wish. The treasure is wonderful and we can certainly use the money." She looked up at Alex, her gaze soft and loving. "But I won't waste my time searching when I already have my treasure."

Alex's heart constricted.

Patience sighed and started through the trees. "Very well." She didn't understand, but how could she? She was young. She'd never been this content. She'd never been in love.

"Do you mean it?" Alex asked, drawing her close while Hope played with the pretty jewels, tossing them about as if they were rose petals at a wedding.

"I do mean it. We have everything we need, Alex. Everything." She wrapped her arms around his neck and stood on her tiptoes, kissing him. It was a soft and gentle kiss. All too soon she was stepping back.

"You could wear satins…velvets—"

"I'd rather wear nothing and spend time with you."

Alex grinned. "Nothing?"

"Indeed."

"Patience," Alex called. "Do you mind taking Hope along on your treasure hunt?"

Patience sighed long and loud through the trees. "Oh fine, but really, you two should wait until you're inside for that."

"Very well." Alex scooped Grace up into his arms and started toward the cottage door.

The End

Acknowledgments

Thanks to Harris Channing, Leigh LaValle, and Beverley Kendall for all of your support. A special thanks to Eleni for believing in *To Seduce an Earl*.

About the Author

One Six Studios, Oct. 2009

As a child, Lori Brighton relished the thought of a life filled with adventure in far-off places. Determined to become an archaeologist, she earned a degree in anthropology—only to discover that digging in the dirt beneath the punishing sun wasn't much fun. She packed up her love of history and took a job in an air-conditioned museum, yet still her thirst for adventure wasn't satisfied. And so she began to write, bringing the people in her imagination to life on the printed page. With her debut novel *Wild Heart*, she finally married her loves of history and adventure. Today she is the author of more than a half-dozen historical romance, paranormal romance, and young-adult novels.

Made in the USA
Charleston, SC
13 November 2012